ALSO BY HAROLD SCHECHTER

NONFICTION

The A to Z Encyclopedia of Serial Killers (with David Everitt)

BESTIAL: *The Savage Trail of a True American Monster*

DERANGED: *The Shocking True Story of America's Most Fiendish Killer*

DEPRAVED: *The Shocking True Story of America's First Serial Killer*

DEVIANT: *The Shocking True Story of Ed Gein, the Original "Psycho"*

FATAL: *The Poisonous Life of a Female Serial Killer*

FIEND: *The Shocking True Story of America's Youngest Serial Killer*

THE SERIAL KILLER FILES: *The Who, What, Where, How,
and Why of the World's Most Terrifying Murderers*

FICTION

Nevermore

Outcry

The Hum Bug

The Mask *of* Red Death

The Mask
~ of ~
Red Death

An Edgar Allan Poe Mystery

HAROLD SCHECHTER

BALLANTINE BOOKS • NEW YORK

A Ballantine Book
Published by The Random House Publishing Group

Copyright © 2004 by Harold Schechter

www.ballantinebooks.com

Library of Congress Cataloging-in-Publication Data
Schechter, Harold.
The mask of red death / Harold Schechter.— 1st ed.
p.   cm.
ISBN 0-345-44841-3
1. Poe, Edgar Allan, 1809–1849—Fiction.   2. Indians of North America—Crimes against—Fiction.
3. Johnston, John, ca. 1822–1900—Fiction.   4. Cannibalism—Fiction.   5. Trappers—Fiction.
6. Authors—Fiction.   I. Title.
PS3569.C4776M37 2004
813'.54—dc22
2003070908

Manufactured in the United States of America

Book design by Susan Turner

First Edition: August 2004

1 3 5 7 9 10 8 6 4 2

For my sister
SANDY

AUTHOR'S NOTE

⌒

THIS IS A WORK OF FICTION. It was inspired, however, by historical fact. Among the most colorful of the nineteenth-century mountain men—those lone and fearless adventurers who braved the rigors of the great Western wilderness to trap beaver, trade fur, and live free of civilization—was a red-bearded giant named John Johnson. His gravestone and a single daguerreotype portrait are the only physical traces of his existence that still remain. But we know a fair amount about him, thanks to a historian named Raymond Thorpe who interviewed a number of old-timers who had crossed paths with Johnson years before. Johnson himself was long dead by the time these interviews were conducted. But he continued to loom large in the imaginations of his former acquaintances.

A sullen, surly brute of a man, Johnson was as skilled at taking scalps as he was at skinning beaver. Throughout his career, he collected hundreds of these grisly trophies from his Native American victims. Though he sold most of them for bounties, he never parted with the dried scalp of the first Arapaho he killed, sporting it on his belt as an ornament.

What really made his reputation, however, was his taste for human flesh. Embarking on a one-man vendetta against the Crow nation, he slaughtered warriors by the dozen, carving up their corpses and eating their livers raw. Before long, he had acquired the nickname by which he would forever be known among his contemporaries: "Liver-Eating" Johnson (or sometimes just "The Liver-Eater").

Johnson's depredations were not limited to the Crows. In one notorious incident, he and a bunch of cohorts massacred a band of thirty-two Sioux camped by a river. Then—after commemorating the occasion by devouring his favorite body part—Johnson superintended as his companions decapitated the corpses, boiled down the skulls, mounted them on poles, and planted them along the riverbank for the benefit of gawking steamboat passengers. Escapades like this made Johnson a figure of awe and admiration among his fellow mountain men—a living legend.

The life and deeds of "The Liver-Eater" are an example of something we tend to overlook in our own violence-obsessed times. Bloodshed and mayhem were no less endemic to American society a hundred years ago than they are today. On the contrary. The history of the American frontier—with its appalling record of lynchings, massacres, shootings, and other everyday barbarities—makes our own time seem like a Golden Age. One big difference between the past and the present is that, back in the days of John Johnson, people with particularly savage tendencies could find various socially approved outlets for their behavior. They might even be rewarded for it. A man with a taste for human blood could travel out West and satisfy his cravings to his heart's content—as long as he vented his sadism on "redskins."

Nowadays, a man who slaughters a succession of strangers, butchers their bodies, and dines on their flesh is called a serial killer. But a hundred years ago—because his victims weren't white—a man like "Liver-Eating" Johnson was called something else.

He was called a hero.

PART ONE

The Virginian

CHAPTER ONE

T HERE ARE CERTAIN SUBJECTS in which the interest is all-absorbing. In our own country, stories of frontier captivity—of Western pioneers taken prisoner by the Indians—have always exerted a singular fascination. From the days of the earliest settlers, firsthand accounts by survivors of this harrowing ordeal have invariably been among the most popular of all our literary productions, as even a cursory glance at the shelves of any bookseller on Broadway will readily confirm.

Not long ago (I am composing this in the summer of 1846), no fewer than five of these volumes were sent to me for review. In accordance with convention, each of these books featured an exceedingly sensational title, promising a tale of Extraordinary Hardship!—Unprecedented Adventure!—Uncommon Suffering!—and Remarkable Deliverance! Unsurprisingly, all five proved, upon perusal, to be entirely devoid of aesthetic value. And yet, in spite of their many egregious flaws, each became an immediate commercial success—a circumstance bound to be a source of the keenest vexation to any true literary artist whose own infinitely superior works have failed to receive the recognition (and remuneration) they deserve.

What was it about these books—I was left to ponder—what was it that accounted for their inordinate appeal? The answer, I concluded, resides in a peculiarity of our nature that—however shameful to confess—is unquestionably as old as our species itself. I refer, of course, to the innate human appetite for stories involving bloodshed and cruelty. Whatever other thrilling or suspenseful incidents may be found in narratives of Indian captivity, such books depend for the greatest impact on their graphic portrayal of the ghastly horrors of frontier combat—and, in particular, on the unspeakable tortures to which helpless prisoners are routinely subjected by their savage foes!

Even today, there are images I retain from these books that are impossible to banish from my mind. How shall I ever forget the dreadful scene in the memoirs of John Roger Tanner when his young comrade, Toby Squires, is strung up by his wrists and flayed alive by a gloating Iroquois chieftain? Or the equally gruesome moment in the narrative of the French fur-trader Jean Laframboise, when he is forced to consume a bleeding collop of his own flesh, sliced from his leg by an Apache tormentor? Or—most horrific of all—the episode recounted by Captain John Salter, in which a Comanche brave tortures a captive by making a small incision in the poor man's abdomen, removing one end of the small intestine, nailing it to a wooden post, and forcing the victim to run in a circle until his entrails are completely unwound! The mere recitation of these atrocities is enough to suffuse my bosom with a tumultuous mix of emotions, compounded equally of dread—revulsion—and rapt fascination.

It is, of course, horrors such as these that have fixed in the popular mind a lasting impression of the Western wilderness as a realm, not merely of sublime natural beauty, but of ever-present mortal peril, and of its aboriginal inhabitants as creatures of unsurpassed savagery, whose ingenuity in devising diabolical methods of torture outdoes even the infernal cruelties of the Inquisitors of Toledo. And yet it may be argued that, in committing even the most hideous outrages, the Indian is engaging in behavior wholly consistent with the primordial harshness of his natural surroundings—indeed, that his rituals of torture and bloodshed are perfectly in keeping with the ethical and even religious conceptions of his kind. In short, judged by the standards of his own tribal beliefs, such acts are not merely acceptable but positively honorable.

The same claim can hardly be made for those members of the white race who engage in similar atrocities; for it can scarcely be doubted (as the reader of these pages will quickly discover) that such creatures do in fact exist. Indeed, if there was any lesson to be gleaned from the grim—the ghastly—the appalling—events that took place in Manhattan slightly more than one year ago, it was this: that, of all savage beings, the most deplorable is not the untamed Indian but the civilized man who reverts to outright barbarism; and that, for all the violence and brutality endemic to life on the frontier, no place on earth can match the ugliness—the evil—the sheer unspeakable depravity—to be found in the *city*!

In attempting to reconstruct an extraordinary occurrence from the past, the historian is often struck by the disparity between the ultimate magnitude of the event and its mundane beginnings. So it was with the singularly shocking affair that held the great metropolis in thrall during the spring of 1845. It began on a Wednesday afternoon in the latter part of May. I was seated at my desk in the office of Mr. Charles Frederick Briggs's recently established magazine, the *Broadway Journal*. Even for that time of year, the weather was inordinately warm, if not positively sultry. Apart from the unseasonable heat, however, there was nothing else remarkable about the day—certainly nothing to suggest that it would mark the beginning of one of the most unique and startling episodes in the annals of New York City crime!

I had arrived at the office, as was my habit, at precisely ten o'clock that morning, and had spent the day composing various items for inclusion in the forthcoming number of the magazine: a lengthy review of Mr. Joseph Holt Ingraham's mildly entertaining (if woefully improbable and poorly written) novel, *Lafitte: The Pirate of the Gulf*—a short article on Professor Henry Horncastle's recent, remarkably misinformed lecture on mesmerism at the Society Library—a devastating exposé of Mr. Longfellow's numerous, flagrant plagiarisms from my own poetical works—and an amusing *vignette* on the picturesque shanties of the poor Irish squatters who reside on the periphery of the city. For nearly five successive hours, I applied myself assiduously to my work, taking only a short respite to refresh myself with the simple but exceedingly nutritious lunch of cheese, brown bread, and strawberries, prepared for me by my ever-devoted Muddy (the affectionate cognomen by which I referred to my Aunt Maria Clemm, whose angelic daughter, Virginia, I was blessed to call my wife).

Under ordinary circumstances, I would have continued at my labors until the daylight had begun to wane. So oppressive was the heat, however, that, by midafternoon, I felt myself lapsing into a kind of stupor. As I was completely alone in the office—my employer, Mr. Briggs, having gone off for the day on a business errand—I was under no obligation to maintain a strictly punctilious appearance. Even with my jacket removed, my cravat loosened, and my collar undone, however, I found myself perspiring so freely that rivulets of moisture were continuously trickling down my forehead and stinging my eyes. Throwing open the window beside my desk did little to alleviate my discomfort. If anything, the cacophony thus admitted—the clatter of the wagons—the rattle of the omnibuses—the shouts and oaths of the teamsters and hackmen—the cries of the street-vendors—only rendered sustained concentration even more difficult, if not impossible.

At length—unable to carry on productively under such intolerable circumstances—I decided to quit the office for the day and return home. After putting my desk in order, I rose from my chair, threw on my jacket, and departed, taking along a handsomely bound volume that had arrived earlier that day by post. This was a work entitled *Journal of an Exploring Tour Beyond the Rocky Mountains*, composed by a personage heretofore unknown to me by the name of Samuel Parker. My intention was to peruse this book after dinner in the comfort of my home in preparation for reviewing it on the morrow.

Emerging onto Broadway, I was struck anew by the stifling closeness of the atmosphere, which felt like nothing so much as the airless heat of the tropical Brazilian jungles as vividly described by the infamous Lope de Aguirre in his colorful (if often prolix) letters to King Philip of Spain. Indeed, I noted little discernible difference between the temperature outside on the street and that of the cramped and suffocating office I had just fled.

It might be supposed that the enervating effects of the weather had induced a general torpor in the population of the metropolis. Nothing, however, could have been further from the truth. The oppressive heat had in no way slowed or even seriously moderated the frenzied bustle of both the vehicular and pedestrian traffic on the great thoroughfare. Throwing myself into the dense and continuous tide of humanity rushing along the sidewalk, I bent my steps toward home.

My route led me past the corner of Broadway and Ann Street, the site—as every New Yorker knows—of the city's most celebrated place of public amusement. I refer, of course, to Mr. P. T. Barnum's American Museum, home to one of the world's largest collections of natural marvels—scientific wonders—historical relics—zoological specimens (both living and stuffed)—and human curiosities. Several months had elapsed since I had last set eyes on the self-styled "King of Showmen," who had recently arrived back on these shores following a triumphant tour of the European capitals. I had been pleased to find that my old comrade (who—whatever his other defects of character—had always displayed the greatest consideration to my family) had not forgotten us in his absence; for, shortly after his return, we had received a large wicker basket from the showman containing a delicious assortment of mouthwatering delicacies: Belgian chocolates, English tea-biscuits, French preserves, and more. I had replied with a gracious letter of thanks, promising to pay him a personal visit as soon as opportunity allowed.*

Now, as I approached the corner occupied by Barnum's garish showplace, I perceived a group of perhaps a dozen people congregated just outside the entranceway. In itself there was nothing odd about such a gathering. As one of the city's leading attractions, the American Museum drew large numbers of visitors at all hours of the day. This particular assemblage, however, seemed unusual in several respects.

Normally, the crowds to be seen outside Barnum's establishment comprised a wide assortment of types: dignified gentlemen and humble laborers—dandified bachelors and sedate, long-married couples—cheerful sweethearts enjoying a day on the town—and weary-looking parents with a flock of children in tow. By contrast, the present group was composed entirely of males, several so young as to be barely past boyhood, though the preponderance were adult men. From their exceedingly shabby dress and disreputable appearance I inferred that they were denizens of one of the city's more degraded quarters, no doubt the Bowery.

Most striking of all, however, was the aura of sullen discontent emanating from the group. Unlike the festive crowds normally gathered before the museum, they wore ugly scowls on their faces, and muttered angrily among themselves as they nodded and gestured toward the building. As I hurried past this unsavory bunch, I could overhear exclamations of the most offensive variety issuing from their midst—"bastard"—"son of a bitch"—and others too profane to repeat.

Casting a dark look at these ill-bred wretches—whose foul speech and coarse demeanor seemed to epitomize all that was most vulgar and debased about the city—I crossed Broadway and (insofar as the congestion of the streets would allow) accelerated my pace toward home.

By this point, my mood had become one of extreme irritability. The suffocating atmosphere—the nerve-wracking tumult of the streets—the shocking incivility of the populace—all conspired to plunge me into the most disgruntled of humors. For the hundredth—nay, the thousandth!—time since we had moved back into the city, I inwardly cursed the unhappy circumstances that had necessitated our return.

For the better part of the preceding year, Muddy, Sissy, and I had been residing on a charming farmstead in the northern suburbs, above Eighty-sixth

---

* A full account of my adventures with Barnum can be found in my earlier chronicle *The Hum Bug.*

Street, where we had enjoyed the many incalculable benefits of pastoral life. Not the least of these was the exceedingly fresh country air, which had served as a veritable elixir for my poor, afflicted Sissy, whose physical condition—never strong to begin with—had been undergoing a gradual, but seemingly inexorable, process of deterioration.

For all its many delights, however—its verdant meadows—its perfumed atmosphere—its sweeping views of the magnificent Hudson River—our rural locale had one grave disadvantage. My isolation from the city had made it difficult for me to find sustained employment, rendering our always shaky financial circumstances even more precarious. Even the phenomenal success of my poem "The Raven"—which had proved an immediate and widespread sensation upon its initial publication—had brought me little by way of material reward. Thus, when Mr. Briggs had proposed to hire me as editor of the *Broadway Journal,* I could hardly refuse—particularly since, in lieu of a salary, he had offered me a one-third pecuniary interest in the magazine!

It was with particularly divided emotions, therefore—regret over abandoning our idyllic country home, mixed with excited optimism over my future prospects—that I had accepted Mr. Briggs's offer and returned, with my loved ones, to the heart of the city.

Unfortunately the profits I had hoped to realize had not, thus far, materialized. Of course, the magazine was still new. I had no doubt that it would eventually prove a great success and earn a substantial income for its owner and myself. In the meantime, however, my circumstances remained as financially straitened as ever. Were it not for the domestic genius of my blessed Muddy—who somehow managed to maintain our household on the pittance I was able to provide each week—our situation would have been intolerably bleak.

The dire state of my finances was brought home to me at that very moment. Making my way along Canal Street, I saw, directly ahead of me, one of the many Chinese street-vendors who peddled cheap cigars and candies around the city. He was stationed behind a little wooden stand that consisted of a shallow tray supported by four rickety legs. Unlike the majority of his race, he had discarded his traditional garb and was attired like an ordinary American—in trousers, vest, and a somewhat threadbare frock coat that hung loosely upon his slender frame. Beneath his battered felt hat, his thick black hair was cut to a respectable Christian length and shorn of its heathenish, dangling *queue.* A trio of ragged urchins hovered nearby, gazing at his merchandise with expressions of intense, if hopeless, longing.

As I drew nearer, I saw that the tray held an assortment of sweets: peanut brittle, sugar almonds, licorice, gumdrops, jujube pastes, peppermints. All at once, I was seized with the urge to purchase a selection of these dainties for Muddy and Sissy (each of whom possessed an avid, if not insatiable, "sweet tooth"). When I searched my pockets for money, however, I was dismayed to discover that my entire store of cash amounted to a few pennies.

For several moments, I remained standing on the curb, debating the wisdom of spending my all-too-meager funds on such inessential trifles. It occurred to me at that moment that—despite my great prominence in the world of letters—my situation, in monetary terms, was hardly better than that of the penniless waifs beside me. A more devastating commentary on America's deplorable treatment of her artists could scarcely be imagined. A bitter laugh escaped my lips, somewhat startling the children and causing the Asiatic fellow to look at me in alarm.

Still, I refused to succumb to despair. Stepping boldly forward, I made my wishes known to the vendor, who filled a cone-shaped paper bag with candies and—after accepting my payment—handed it to me with a polite bow. I then turned and continued on my way—though not before offering a morsel of peppermint to each of the three hungry-eyed children, who snatched them from my hand and went skipping down the street without bothering with the nicety of a thank you.

Our residence consisted of five rented rooms on the second floor of a respectable, if somewhat dilapidated, building on Amity Street. Arrived at length at this destination, I ascended the narrow staircase, opened the apartment door, and stepped into the little foyer.

From the parlor drifted the wonderfully melodious sound of my Sissy's voice: "Muddy?"

"No," I called out in reply. "It is I—your own dear Eddie."

A little Dutch table was situated beside the door. Setting down the volume I had brought home with me, I removed the confectionery bag from my pocket—extracted one of the red-swirled pieces of peppermint—concealed this in my right hand—and crossed into the parlor.

The former tenant of our apartment (as our landlady, Mrs. Whitaker, had informed us) was—like myself—a Southern gentleman, apparently of French extraction. He had come to New York City with the great hope—so he told Mrs. Whitaker—of making a fortune as an importer of porcelain ware from Limoges. Less than three months after his arrival, however, he had absconded in the dead of night. The reason for his abrupt departure was a matter of conjecture, though the likeliest explanation—and the one to which our landlady subscribed—was that he had suffered sudden, catastrophic reversals and had fled the city in a desperate bid to elude his creditors.

Whatever the truth of this hypothesis, it could scarcely be doubted that he had decamped in enormous haste, for he had left behind most, if not all, of his furnishings. The parlor, like the rest of the flat, reflected his genteel, if uninspired, sense of decor. Its walls were hung with hand-tinted lithographs of biblical subjects—its windows curtained in red silk damask—its floor covered with a brightly colored "Aubusson" carpet. A rosewood bookcase stood against one wall, beside a matching *étagère*. The remaining articles of furniture in the room consisted of a pair of armchairs—a tall clock in an inlaid mahogany case—an oval-topped tripod table—and a sofa upholstered in well-worn brocade which supported, at that moment, the divine—the *ethereal*—form of my darling Sissy.

She was seated at one end of the couch, a drawing pad resting on her lap and a charcoal pencil gripped in one delicate hand. As I entered the room, she looked up at me with an expression of happy surprise. As always, I was struck by the ineffable loveliness of her countenance, which—if anything—had been rendered even more sublime by the steady progress of her illness. Apart from the faint, febrile rouge that tinged her cheeks, her always-flawless complexion now possessed an unearthly pallor that surpassed even the snowy whiteness of her simple cambric dress. Her large, dark eyes blazed with a glorious effulgence, and her heavenly mouth was formed into a smile such as can be seen only on the visage of da Vinci's justly renowned masterwork, *La Gioconda*.

"Eddie," she exclaimed. "What are you doing home so early?"

"The excessive heat forced me to lay aside my work and abandon the insufferable confines of the office," I replied. I then stepped to the sofa and—making my hands into fists—extended them outward.

"I have a treat for you, Sissy," I said in a playful tone. "In order to receive it, however, you must tell me which of my hands it is concealed within."

"This one," she replied without hesitation, pointing at the left.

Emitting a cry of amazement—for she had, indeed, guessed the truth with unerring accuracy—I exclaimed: "Ah, Sissy. How foolish of me to believe that I could deceive you with so simple a ruse. So profound—so *complete*—is the affinity that exists between our two intermingled souls that no secret of mine, however small, could ever remain hidden from your knowledge. Here, then, is your reward," I continued, inverting my hand and disclosing the inordinately sticky lump of candy.

"Actually," she replied, "I could see it between your fingers. You weren't making a very tight fist, Eddie." And so saying, she plucked the sweet from my palm and inserted it into her mouth. "Mmmmm," she said. "Yummy. Thank you so much, Eddie."

The sheer disarming candor of her admission brought a burst of hilarity from my lips. Seating myself on the sofa beside her, I bestowed an affectionate kiss upon her alabaster brow.

"How are you feeling, Sissy dearest?" I gently inquired.

"Fine," she answered. "I haven't had a coughing fit all day."

"No news could be more welcome to my ears," I said.

Gazing down at the pad on her lap, I saw that she had been working on a sketch of our beloved feline, Cattarina, who was sprawled upon the sill of the wide-flung window directly across the room. The oppressive heat had reduced the poor beast to a state of utter torpor. She lay inertly on her side, eyes shut, head pillowed upon one outstretched front leg.

"Your skills as a draftsman grow more impressive by the day," I remarked. "You have captured our Cattarina to perfection."

"Think so?" said Sissy, regarding the drawing with a decidedly skeptical expression. "Don't you think the right leg looks funny?"

In truth, there was something distinctly awkward—if not positively unnatural—about the way in which Sissy had depicted the limb, as though it had healed improperly after being fractured in several places. Still, I saw no point in criticizing her handiwork.

"Not at all," I said. "It is exceedingly lifelike."

"Muddy seemed to think so, too. She said the picture looked so real she could almost hear it purr."

"And where is our dear Muddy?" I inquired.

"She went out to buy salad greens for dinner. She'll be back in a jiffy."

No sooner had she spoken these words than I heard the apartment door open. An instant later—as though she had been waiting offstage to make her entrance on Sissy's cue—Muddy stood framed in the doorway of the parlor, her right arm looped through the handle of her wicker marketing basket.

She was garbed, as always, in her black widow's weeds, with a white lace bonnet-cap atop her head. Her broad, benevolent countenance—flushed from the heat and damp with perspiration—wore a look of the greatest surprise.

"Why, Eddie," she cried as I rose to greet her. "I did not expect you home until later. Is something the matter?"

"Nothing at all," I replied with a smile. Briefly, I explained the circumstances that had occasioned my early departure from my workplace.

"And you, Muddy," I continued, regarding her closely. "Is anything amiss?" Acutely sensitive to every nuance of the dear woman's moods, I perceived by the look in her eyes that something was troubling her.

"Why, haven't you heard?" she said. "Everyone in the marketplace was talking about it."

"I have heard nothing," I replied. "Since leaving home this morning, I have communicated with no one. I worked alone in the office, then hurried directly back here, pausing only briefly to purchase some sweets for you and Sissy from a Chinese vendor."

"What is it, Muddy?" asked Sissy from the couch. "What has happened?"

"Murder—dreadful murder," the good woman replied, reaching into her basket and removing a newspaper, which she handed to me. "A little girl butchered by a savage—just like the last time. Oh, Eddie," she exclaimed in a tremulous voice. "I fear there is a monster on the loose!"

CHAPTER TWO

T HE NEWSPAPER PURCHASED by Muddy was the *New York Herald*, whose publisher, James Gordon Bennett, had grown rich by catering to the exceedingly crass taste of the masses. Utterly shameless in his exploitation of the scandalous—the sordid—and the sensational—Bennett possessed a keen appreciation of the public's perennial fascination with crimes of violence. No one understood better than he that few occurrences have the power to generate as much excitement as a particularly heinous and gruesome murder.

Now, as I glanced at the front page of the paper that Muddy had brought home, I saw at once that the crime which had been discovered that morning was precisely of this sort—i.e., one whose sheer overwhelming horror was certain to arouse the morbid passions of the entire populace.

DREADFUL MURDER! the headline stated. ANOTHER CHILD KILLED! GIRL'S BODY FOUND HORRIBLY BUTCHERED IN PARK!

Before I could proceed with the article, I was interrupted by the sound of Sissy's voice. "What does it say?" she asked from the sofa. "Read it out loud, Eddie."

"Of course," I replied.

"Wait," said Muddy. "I want to hear it, too. Just let me put down my groceries."

While Muddy bustled off to the kitchen, I settled myself in one of the armchairs. A moment later, she returned and lowered herself onto the cushion beside Sissy, who reached out and took her mother by the hand.

Then, after clearing my throat, I commenced to read the story aloud, while my two darling auditors listened intently, emitting an occasional startled gasp of pity or dismay:

"A dreadful crime came to light in the early hours of this morning when the fearfully mutilated corpse of a young girl was discovered by Mr. Frank Pelham of Wooster Street. Mr. Pelham was on his way to work at Ochmann's Livery Stable when, passing through the little park at Hudson Square, he stumbled upon the horribly ravaged figure which lay on the grass. He immediately ran to notify the police.

"Although the name of the little victim remains unknown, it is believed that she may well be Rosalie Edmonds, the ten-year-old daughter of Mr. and Mrs. Hugh Edmonds of Number 25 Walker Street. As reported in yesterday's edition of the *Herald*, little Rosalie departed from home on Tuesday afternoon to purchase a new writing tablet for school. When she failed to return after several hours, her parents made a thorough search of the neighborhood. Finding no trace of their daughter, they notified the police, whose indefatigable efforts to locate the missing child proved unavailing. While no official confirmation of the victim's identity has been forthcoming, the *Herald*'s reporter has learned that the badly torn dress found on the corpse precisely matches the garment that little Rosalie was reported to have been wearing when she left home that fateful afternoon. A piece of stout rope was tightly lashed around the child's ankles, evidently to prevent any possibility of escape from her fiendish captor.

"A full description of the outrages suffered by the little victim has not been made public by the police, though rumor has it that these were of the most vile and revolting nature imaginable. It appears almost certain, however, that, among other atrocities, the little girl had been *scalped*—and with such ferocity that her ears had been ripped from her skull along with her entire headful of curly blond tresses!

"Should this prove the case, it would appear to confirm the worst apprehensions of both the public and the police—to wit, that a creature of inhuman depravity is at large in our city, preying on its youngest and most innocent inhabitants. As every reader no doubt recalls, it was only two weeks ago that another little girl, Miss Annie Dobbs, the seven-year-old daughter of Mr. and Mrs. Alexander Dobbs of Franklin Street, was discovered slain in a similarly gruesome manner. Despite the unstinting efforts of the police, her killer has been neither identified nor apprehended.

"There has been some speculation—which the latest atrocity is certain to encourage—that butchery of the sort committed on young Annie Dobbs (and now, evidently, on little Rosalie Edmonds as well) could only be perpetrated by a member of one of the savage tribes indigenous to America. As the Indians have long been banished from this region, however, it is natural to wonder where such a creature might be found in the great metropolis of New York City.

"Without wishing to cast unwarranted blame on any party, we feel duty-bound to point out that there is one place in our city where savage 'redskins' can still be found. We refer, of course, to Mr. P. T. Barnum's American Museum, whose countless curiosities include several full-blooded male members of the Crow Indian tribe. Mr. Barnum, as every New Yorker is no doubt aware, has been tireless in his promotion of these aborigines, who—according to his advertisements—are among the most fearsome warriors of their kind, and who can be viewed at his establishment bedecked in their full barbaric splendor and equipped with knives, tomahawks, and war-lances adorned with the scalps of their defeated foes!

"We do not mean to say that one of these savages is necessarily guilty. We are, however, obliged to express our concern over Mr. Barnum's ill-advised habit of importing the most dangerous and unpredictable creatures into our midst. This practice has already produced disastrous results, as the recent affair involving his unfortunate lion-tamer, the Great Mazeppa, attests. The wild beast responsible for that tragedy was promptly put to death. Should one of the wild Indians currently on display at the American Museum prove to be the inhuman fiend now being sought by the police, he will certainly be deserving of the same swift and terrible penalty—and his employer, Mr. Barnum, of the most severe condemnation from a justly outraged citizenry!"

"Oh, it's too awful for words," Sissy exclaimed when I had concluded the article. "That poor child."

"And her parents," added Muddy in a voice laden with sorrow.

"What do you think, Eddie?" asked Sissy. "Could the killer really be an Indian from Mr. Barnum's museum?"

Folding the newspaper in half, I set it down upon the little table beside my chair before responding thusly:

"It must not be supposed that every mystery is an elaborate and convoluted puzzle leading to an unexpected solution. Sometimes, the most obvious conclusion proves to be the correct one. Certainly, the perpetrator of these enormities *might* be one of Barnum's Indians.

"Nevertheless," I continued, "the logic by which Mr. Bennett has arrived at his conclusion rests on several seriously flawed assumptions. His accusation—or, more properly, insinuation—is based on the following implied syllogism:

The little victims of these hideous crimes were both scalped. Scalping is a barbarity practiced by the native Indian tribes of North America. Ergo, the killer must be an Indian.

"Now, it can scarcely be denied that many, though by no means all, of the various Indian tribes engage in this savage custom. Contrary to what is commonly believed, however, scalping did not originate with the aboriginal people of North America. History records many earlier instances of this practice both in Europe and in Asia. Both the Visigoths and the Franks commonly scalped their enemies, as did the ancient Persians and—according to no less an authority than Herodotus—the Scythians.

"In light of these facts, there are some who believe that—far from being indigenous to America—scalping was imported to these shores by the white man. Whatever the truth of this theory, there can be little doubt that a great many supposedly civilized Europeans have not only encouraged the practice among their Indian allies but engaged in it themselves. During the Colonial era, bounties were routinely placed on Indian scalps by both the French and the English. Moreover, it is a well-established fact that, among the untamed pioneers of the Far West, there are white men who engage in this barbaric practice with an avidity surpassing even that of the most bloodthirsty native.

"In short, the fact that the two little girls were scalped cannot, in itself, be taken as definitive proof that the perpetrator was one of Mr. Barnum's Indians.

"There is another consideration that must be borne in mind as well. According to the newspaper accounts, both girls were scalped in a singularly vicious manner, their skulls being completely denuded of hair. Indeed, in the case of the most recent victim, this act was committed with such barbaric force that both ears were torn away from the poor victim's head.

"Now, while this particular method of scalping—in which the entire head of hair is taken—is certainly not unheard of among certain Indian tribes, it is by no means characteristic of the Crow. Without entering into each grisly detail—for I perceive by your expressions that this exceedingly distasteful subject has already begun to cause you a certain degree of uneasiness—I will merely state that when an Indian performs this savage operation upon a fallen foe, he does so in the following manner:

"After turning his enemy face down, the victor stands upon the latter's back, pressing one foot into the space between the shoulder blades. Next, he seizes the victim's hair in one hand and—with a scalping knife clutched in the other—makes a swift incision around the head. With a violent pull, he then tears off the hair with the scalp still attached. Once he is at leisure to do so, he will preserve his trophy by scraping the skin free of blood and fibre, stretching it upon a hoop of green wood, drying it in the sun or over a fire, and daubing the underside with red paint.

"This mode of removing and preparing a scalp is universal. However, the *size* of the trophy thus taken varies considerably among different tribes. Among the Indians of the Great Plains—including the Crow—it is customary to remove only a relatively small portion of an enemy's scalp, often measuring no more than three or four inches in diameter. To be scalped in this way, though inordinately painful, is not necessarily fatal. As a result, it is not at all uncommon for the victim to survive his ordeal. Indeed, the Plains Indian— rather than slay an enemy outright—prefers to inflict this milder form of mutilation upon a vanquished but still-living foe, thus condemning him to spend the remainder of his life with a deeply unsightly and humiliating disfigurement.

"We are therefore entitled to conclude," I said by way of summation, "that— even if these crimes *were* committed by an Indian—it is doubtful that the perpetrator was a member of the Crow tribe."

My remarks were followed by a protracted period of silence, during which Muddy and Sissy regarded me with somewhat stricken expressions. At length, speaking in a slightly tremulous voice, Sissy addressed me thusly:

"Well, Eddie, that was certainly informative. But if you're right, then it is terribly unfair of the papers to suggest that Mr. Barnum is in any way responsible for these awful crimes."

"Very true," I answered. "Nevertheless, Sissy dearest, there is little need to feel incensed on behalf of our friend. Unless I am very much mistaken, he will not be at all displeased at finding himself attacked in this fashion. Far from shunning notoriety, Barnum actively courts it. To be embroiled in a controversy is merely a way of generating publicity for himself and his establishment. Moreover, as has been proved on numerous occasions, Nature has endowed the showman with a remarkable gift for transforming professional adversity into personal profit. Indeed, the incident alluded to in the newspaper, involving the unfortunate Mazeppa, is a case in point."

Mazeppa Vivaldi—Barnum's world-renowned lion-tamer—had, for several years, been one of the museum's leading attractions. A short but exceedingly muscular man of perhaps thirty years of age, he possessed a remarkably handsome countenance and a head of wavy black hair that, for sheer luxuriance, might have rivaled the fabled locks of Samson. His striking physical appearance, combined with the inordinately daring nature of his act, rendered him a particular favorite of young females, who constituted a disproportionately high percentage of the audience at each of his shows.

In truth, his act was thrilling in the extreme. I myself had attended one of his performances and watched it in a veritable agony of suspense. Armed only with a whip and a three-legged stool that he wielded as a kind of shield, he would enter a small, circular cage filled with snarling jungle cats and—through sheer, fearless audacity—subdue them until they behaved as docilely as a bunch of purring kittens. Most exciting of all was the climax of the show. Setting down his whip and stool, he would slowly approach an enormous black-maned lion named Ajax. Kneeling at the creature's feet, he would take its muzzle into his hands—pry open its powerful jaws—insert his entire head into its mouth—and remain in that posture for a full minute before extracting himself from the gaping maw of the man-eating beast!

In the course of his career, he had performed this feat innumerable times without incident. During the last week of March, however, an inexplicable tragedy had occurred. Mazeppa had just thrust his head into the mouth of the great cat, when suddenly—and with tremendous force—its jaws snapped shut!

Among the spectators, pandemonium erupted. Women shrieked and fainted—little children burst into tears—grown men cried out in horror. Several male audience members—displaying that reckless disregard for their own safety which, when exercised on behalf of a fellow human being, is synonymous with the highest heroism—immediately leapt from their seats and dashed into the cage. By then, Ajax had already reopened his mouth, releasing the lion-tamer. He lay face down in the sawdust, blood pouring from the ghastly, mortal wound in his frightfully mutilated head. Long before a physician arrived on the scene, Mazeppa had expired.

The incident provoked a vociferous outcry in the "penny press." The *Herald*, in particular, lost no time in condemning Barnum for having permitted such a dangerous act to be performed on his premises. A demand quickly arose for the immediate execution of the deadly beast. Barnum had no choice but to comply. In the end, however, the entire disastrous episode proved in no way harmful to his business. On the contrary. With his genius (if I may employ the term so loosely) for exploiting the morbid interests of his public, Barnum had the dead lion stuffed and mounted in a seated posture with its jaws agape. He then had his artisans produce a life-sized wax figure of a kneeling Mazeppa, which was garbed in the latter's actual—and still heavily blood-stained!—costume. The two lifeless figures were then arranged in a manner simulating the awful moment when Ajax had clamped his mouth shut on the lion-tamer's head. This gruesome *tableau*—which immediately became one of the most popular attractions at the museum—was supplemented by a display case containing a number of artifacts belonging to Mazeppa, including his whip, his stool, and the jar of pomade with which he had treated his famously beautiful hair.

"I suppose you're right, Eddie," Sissy now remarked. "Mr. Barnum *does* have a knack for turning bad things to his advantage."

"Well," interposed Muddy, "if you want to know *my* opinion, I think it's disgraceful of Mr. Bennett to cast blame on dear Mr. Barnum. Shame on him! Still, the *Herald* is right about one thing. The fiend who butchered those innocent children deserves to be treated no better than a wild animal when he's caught. Why, I have more sympathy for the dumb beast that killed poor Mr. Mazeppa. After all, the creature was simply acting according to its nature. But this foul, inhuman monster—why, hanging is too good for him!"

The sheer vehemence of this outburst took me by surprise. Rarely, if ever, had I heard Muddy—a woman of such surpassingly tender feelings that it pained her to extinguish the life of a housefly—express herself so forcefully.

"Your point is well taken, Muddy dear," I said. "The execution of Ajax the lion was carried out less to punish the beast for his sanguinary deed—which, as you say, was consistent with his nature—than to prevent any possibility of its recurrence. Once having tasted the blood of man, no wild creature—not even the most seemingly docile—can ever again be trusted. In this regard, the perpetrator of these hideous crimes has, indeed, descended to the level of the most vicious brute; for the motive that drives him is nothing less than a depraved and ever-growing appetite for human prey."

For several moments, a heavy silence settled over the room. At length, it was broken by Sissy. "Well," she remarked with a sigh, "I must say that all this gruesome talk hasn't done much for my own appetite. I *was* looking forward to dinner, but now—"

"Come, come, Virginia," Muddy said, patting her daughter on the knee. "You must eat something. Your health depends upon it.

"And you, dear boy," she continued, turning to address me. "May I bring you something to drink—a nice glass of lemonade, perhaps? From the look of it, you could do with a little refreshment."

"The beverage you propose would be very welcome," I replied. "For in truth, the heat has left me feeling exceedingly enervated."

"Oh my," Muddy exclaimed, getting hurriedly to her feet and making for the kitchen. "I will go fix you some at once!"

No sooner had she gone than I gazed at my darling wife and said: "You were not, I hope, too greatly distressed by our discussion."

"I'm fine, Eddie," she answered. "I just pray that the police can find the killer quickly. It's terrible to think that he is out there right now, probably planning his next dreadful crime even as we speak!"

"Fear not. I am certain that he will be apprehended in short order," I said, expressing a degree of confidence in the professional competence of the New York City constabulary that, in truth, I did not entirely feel.

"And now, if you will excuse me, Sissy dear," I continued, "I shall go divest myself of my jacket and wash up a bit while Muddy is preparing her *elixir vitae*."

"Of course, Eddie," she said. "By the way, a letter arrived for you earlier. I put it on your writing table."

"Thank you for doing so," I replied. "I will see you shortly, then."

Rising from the armchair, I crossed the carpeted floor to the parlor door-way. All at once, a thought came to me. Pausing at the threshold, I turned back toward the sofa, reached into my jacket pocket, and—extracting the little bag of sweets—said: "I had almost forgotten these. I trust your appetite is not so severely diminished that you will be unable to eat another peppermint candy."

"You needn't worry about that, Eddie," she replied.

"I shall leave it in the hallway, on the Dutch stand," I said.

"I'll come get it in a moment," declared Sissy, then added with an endearing little smile: "Just as soon as I finish my masterpiece."

Then, raising her pencil, she turned back to her drawing of Cattarina, who continued to repose upon the windowsill in a state of such complete immo-bility that she might have been one of Barnum's taxidermical specimens.

In addition to the kitchen and parlor, our apartment consisted of three bed-rooms, two of modest dimensions, the third extremely spacious. The latter was occupied by my loved ones, an arrangement that allowed Muddy to re-main in close proximity to her daughter on those all-too-frequent nights when poor Sissy lay awake with an excess of coughing and required the tender ministrations of her mother. As my wife and I had never actually shared a room, much less a bed—our relationship existing on an infinitely higher plane than the merely carnal—this setup proved highly suitable to our vari-ous needs.

Of the two remaining, much smaller rooms, one served as my study, the other as my sleeping quarters. It was to the latter that I now repaired after taking leave of Sissy.

Once inside, I swiftly doffed my coat and refreshed myself at the washstand. I had just finished drying my face with a towel when Muddy appeared at the doorway with the promised potation. So extreme was my thirst by this point that I imbibed the entire drink in one long, grateful swallow. Thanking Muddy—who took the empty glass from my hand and returned to the kitchen—I then stepped across the hallway and into my study.

As Sissy had indicated, there was a piece of mail lying on the desktop. Settling myself into the chair, I picked up the envelope and examined the return address. At my first glimpse of the sender's name, my upper lip curled into a disdainful sneer. Snatching up the implement I employed for the purpose—a slender-bladed knife with a bone handle—I slit open the envelope, extracted the letter, and cast my eyes over its contents, a hot flush of anger suffusing my countenance as I perused the infuriating missive.

Its author was a personage named Cartwright, who had recently published a novel entitled *The Night-Watch* that I had reviewed in the previous number of the *Broadway Journal*. For reasons that can only be attributed to the prevailing imbecility of the American public, this singularly inept work of fiction had proved tremendously popular, selling in excess of forty thousand copies within months of its appearance! While Cartwright's inordinate good fortune could hardly fail to *rankle*—the success of the unworthy being, to the worthy, the bitterest of all wrongs—I had in no way allowed mere personal sentiment to color my opinion of his production. My review had been characterized by that rigorously analytical and unbiased judgment which is the absolute *sine qua non* of all effective criticism. Nevertheless, it was clear from the singularly offensive tone of Cartwright's letter that its sender had taken extreme umbrage at my remarks.

The letter read as follows:

Sir—

I have recently been made aware of your scandalous attack upon my work—my character—and my good name. I am not a thin-skinned man. Criticism I welcome. Condemnation I can endure. What I cannot, nor will not, tolerate is gratuitous insult.

Under the pretense of offering an impartial review, you dare to deride my novel as "the most arrant piece of stupidity ever produced on these shores"—to ridicule my style as "the inept scribbling of a nincompoop"— and to attack me personally as a "literary laughingstock whose grasp of English is no better than a baboon's." Even these outrageous aspersions, however, pale beside your repeated references to me as "Mr. Cant-write"— a puerile but unforgivable mockery of a family name that, to me, is nothing less than sacred.

Though I have never (thankfully!) met you, I am fully familiar with your reputation for intemperance in regard to both your language and personal habits. Perhaps—to put the most charitable construction on the matter—you composed your odious tirade while your better judgment was clouded by the effects of alcohol. Even if that were the case, however, I should find your behavior no less inexcusable.

Friends have urged me to respond in kind by publishing—perhaps in one of our city's newspapers—an unbridled attack on your own highly dubious character. I refuse, however, to descend to your level. Nor do I wish to afford you any additional notoriety by engaging in a public dispute.

I will content myself, then, with this warning. Should you ever again write about me in such an offensive manner, you will live to regret it. I am prepared to take action in this matter. Heed my words, Mr. Poe. You ignore them at your peril!

C. A. Cartwright

My reaction to this letter can hardly be described in words. My hands shook—my heart pounded—my bosom seethed—with barely controlled rage. The sheer effrontery of Cartwright's accusations was infuriating in the extreme. While accurately quoting several of my comments, he had utterly distorted their overall *tenor* by removing them from their original context. My intention, after all, had not been to insult him, but rather to alert potential readers to the deficiencies in his work. As this constituted one of my primary responsibilities as a reviewer, I did not see anything wrong with what I had written—certainly nothing to have provoked such an insolent response.

For several minutes, I sat at my desk, reflecting on how best to reply to Cartwright's intolerable missive. Should I seek him out at home and administer a well-deserved thrashing? Horsewhip him in the street? Challenge him to a pistol duel at some remote location outside the city?

All at once, I was seized with an inspiration. Taking up my pen, I removed a sheaf of blank writing paper from the center of my desk and inscribed, on the topmost sheet, the following heading: THE NIT-WIT BY MR. Y. I. CANT-WRITE. I then commenced to write at a furious pace, not pausing until I had filled a half-dozen pages with a savagely amusing satire of Cartwright's execrable novel. At length, having reached the conclusion, I leaned back in my chair and read over my composition, chuckling heartily at its many brilliantly mordant touches—and deriving no end of delight from imagining Cartwright's re-action when he saw it in *print*.

No sooner had I finished reading over my hilariously scathing lampoon than I heard Muddy's voice, summoning me to supper. Setting my manuscript down on the desktop, I rose and quit the study.

Entering the dining room, I was surprised to see that Sissy was not present. When I inquired as to her whereabouts, Muddy replied, in a tone of mild ex-asperation, "I told that girl to come in five minutes ago." Stepping to the door-way, she raised her voice and called: "Virginia! Stop whatever you're doing, and come to the table right now. Eddie and I are waiting for you."

An instant later, my darling wife appeared in the dining room and took her seat at the table.

"Sorry," she said. "I was looking at that book you brought home, Eddie. I noticed it when I went to fetch the candies."

It took me a moment to recall the volume in question. "Ah, yes," I said at length, lowering myself into the chair beside her. "Mr. Parker's journal."

"What is it a journal *of*?" Muddy inquired, setting down a platter of cold chicken and taking her place across the table.

"His journey across the Rocky Mountains to Oregon," said Sissy. "It's won-derfully engrossing—I couldn't put it down. Do you know that he actually met Kit Carson?"

"No!" exclaimed Muddy. "How thrilling!"

"Oh, you can't imagine," Sissy declared excitedly. "Mr. Parker was there when Kit fought a duel with a French trapper named Shunar. A terrible bully, enormously strong. Everyone in camp was absolutely terrified of him. Well, this Shunar made the mistake of saying that Americans were all weaklings and cowards. When Kit heard about it, he went straight up to the Frenchman and warned him to keep his mouth shut. Without a word, Shunar turned right around, got his rifle, mounted his horse, and came charging at Kit. Kit just had time to leap onto his own steed, draw his pistol, and take aim. The two men fired at the same time. Shunar's bullet went whizzing so close to Kit's head that it cut through his hair. Kit's bullet hit Shunar in the arm, causing the

Frenchman to drop his weapon and fall from the saddle. He immediately scrambled to his knees and begged Kit to spare his life. Kit agreed, but made him promise never to speak another insulting word about Americans again, and from that day on, Shunar was as meek as a baby."

"Oh my," Muddy said. "I've never heard anything so amazing. Why, it's like something out of one of Mr. Scott's romances—*Ivanhoe* or *Quentin Durwood*."

"Except that it's all true," Sissy exclaimed. "That's what's so wonderful about it. Don't you agree, Eddie?"

Throughout Sissy's breathless recitation, I had sat listening in silence while devouring a slice of Muddy's succulent fowl. Now, washing down the contents of my mouth with a swallow of lemonade, I said, with an indulgent smile:

"It is conceivable, I suppose, that Mr. Carson is just such a paragon of nobility as Mr. Parker describes. Certainly, in the numerous books that have already celebrated his exploits, he is consistently portrayed as a nearly legendary figure on the order of Hector or Achilles. It must be borne in mind, however, that even Hector and Achilles were, in all likelihood, little more than bloodthirsty barbarians, exalted to the level of demigods by the transfiguring powers of poetry. In short, I suspect that, in person, Mr. Carson would prove to be a far less heroic figure than he is made out to be by Mr. Parker and his ilk, who seek to sell books by appealing to the credulity of an all-too-gullible public."

"Oh, Eddie, you can't possibly be serious!" Sissy exclaimed. "Why, everyone who has ever known Kit Carson has described him as the finest, bravest, most admirable man in the world."

"That fact in itself is cause for skepticism," I replied. "I ask you, Sissy—have you ever known *anyone* who has inspired absolute, universal acclaim? Indeed, were Carson truly a man of such remarkable endowments, he would undoubtedly be the subject of countless dark whispers and pernicious rumors. In view of the place that sheer, gnawing envy occupies in the heart of man, no truly exceptional individual can ever escape the vicious backbiting of smallminded detractors. Take myself, for example. The letter I received today—the one which you so kindly placed upon my desk—was sent by a writer who, clearly mortified by my own, infinitely superior talents, has gone so far as to threaten me with personal violence."

"Threaten you?" gasped Muddy, frozen in the act of raising a forkful of boiled peas to her mouth. "Why, what on earth do you mean, Eddie?"

Immediately, I regretted my indiscretion in having mentioned Cartwright's letter. So intense—so all-consuming—was Muddy's solicitude for my wellbeing that the slightest provocation could easily send her into a paroxysm of alarm. Seeking to reassure her, I waved my hand dismissively and said, in an offhanded tone:

"There is not the slightest need to worry, Muddy dear. The fellow is not to be taken seriously. He is simply—to employ a colorful colloquialism—'full of hot air.' Besides, I have devised a response that will inflict such a blow to his vanity as to utterly demolish his morale. He will have no recourse but to slink back into that total obscurity he so richly deserves."

This reply appeared to have the desired effect. Muddy—who had grown instantly agitated at my ill-considered remark—now became visibly relaxed and returned to her eating. For the next twenty or thirty minutes, the three of us chatted lightly about various inconsequential subjects. Once we had completed the main part of our repast, Muddy rose from the table, cleared off the dishes, carried them into the kitchen, and returned a few minutes later, bearing three bowls heaped with her deservedly famed batter pudding.

We had just commenced to devour this delectable treat when we were interrupted by a startling sound. Someone was knocking on the apartment door! So unexpected was this occurrence—particularly at the dinner hour—that, for a moment, none of us made a move to respond.

"Who on earth could that be?" Muddy inquired at length.

"There is but one way to find out," I said, pushing back my chair.

"No, no," Muddy said. "You stay here and finish your pudding. I'll go see who it is." And so saying, she quickly rose from the table and hurried from the dining room.

Straining my auditory faculties, I heard her walk to the foyer, open the door, and engage in a muffled exchange with the mysterious caller. A moment later, she reappeared.

There are some timeworn phrases which, however debased by overuse, retain a certain expressive power. Now, as I gazed at Muddy's countenance as she stood in the doorway of the dining room, one of these came immediately to my mind. As events would quickly prove, it was an expression that was singularly apt, not only in terms of Muddy's appearance, but in regard to that of the unknown stranger with whom I was about to come face-to-face.

She looked—to employ the cliché—as if she had just seen a ghost.

CHAPTER THREE

"WHO IS AT THE DOOR, Muddy?" I inquired in a voice tinged with concern. From the unsettled look on her face, I could only assume that there was something exceedingly peculiar, if not positively disturbing, about the caller.

"A gentleman to see you," she replied. "I told him to wait in the parlor." Then—lowering her voice until it was barely louder than a whisper—she added: "He's a very strange-looking man, Eddie!"

My curiosity piqued, I turned to Sissy and—excusing myself—immediately rose from the table and directed my steps to the parlor.

Had I not been forewarned by Muddy, I might well have emitted an astonished gasp at the sight that greeted me. Seated in the armchair, gazing curiously about the room, was one of the most remarkable specimens of human *albinism* that I had ever set eyes upon.

I had, of course, seen such anomalous beings before. An entire family of them, by the name of Blazek, were featured attractions at Barnum's museum. In respect to sheer uncanniness of appearance, however, even those world-renowned prodigies fell short of the personage before me.

At a mere glance, his age was impossible to determine, though I judged him to be a man in his late middle years. Even in his present posture, he appeared to be singularly tall, and thin to the point of emaciation. His skin was of such an absolute, almost translucent, whiteness that I easily understood why Muddy, upon glimpsing him, had reacted with a kind of awe. His utterly hueless complexion, combined with his attenuated frame, endowed him with an appearance that was positively otherworldly.

This impression was heightened by his facial characteristics, which were remarkable in the extreme. A finely moulded chin—lips of surpassingly beautiful curve—a nose whose delicate shape was to be found only in the graceful medallions of the Hebrews—a broad and lofty forehead that bespoke both vigor of mind and nobility of character—made up a countenance not easily to be forgotten. The irises of his eyes were of an exceedingly light roseate hue, so pale as to seem nearly transparent, and his long, wavy, snow-white hair descended to the level of his shoulders. He wore an expression in which acuity and benevolence seemed equally commingled. Altogether he resembled nothing so much as one of the radiant seraphs depicted by Murillo in his mature, so-called "vaporous" style.

His garb was almost as remarkable as his appearance, consisting of clothing—trousers, jacket, vest, shirt, and cravat—made of a supple, ivory-colored fabric. Even the hat resting on his lap was of the identical hue. Only his highly polished black boots deviated from the prevailing whiteness of his outfit.

As I crossed the threshold into the parlor, this altogether extraordinary-looking stranger unfolded himself from the chair, rose to his feet, and extended his long, slender right hand in the time-honored gesture of greeting. Grasping it in my own, I was almost surprised to find that it consisted of solid flesh and bone, and not of some airy substance. His voice, when he spoke, was consistent with the ethereal quality of his appearance. Rarely, if ever, had I heard a sound so lilting—so sheerly mellifluous—issue from a human throat.

"It is a pleasure to meet you, sir," he said. "My name is Wyatt. William Wyatt."

Gazing up into his eyes—for he was even taller than I had judged—I bade him welcome, then motioned for him to resume his place in the armchair, while I seated myself on the sofa.

"Forgive me for coming by at such an inconvenient hour," he said. "But I was most eager to see you. I trust that my arrival has not caused too great a disturbance in your household."

"Not at all," I graciously replied. "My family and I have just completed our dinner."

"I'm very glad to hear it. The lady who opened the door seemed quite startled to see me. Of course," he continued with a gentle laugh, "I'm accustomed to that sort of thing, as you can imagine. Strange, isn't it, how something as superficial, by its very nature, as the pigmentation of our skin—or, in my case, the lack of it—can elicit such powerful reactions in others. Shock. Horror. Fear. Even out-and-out hatred."

"If by *strange*," I answered, "you intend to denote something *unusual*, then I cannot entirely concur with your statement; for—however deplorable such a trait may be—an instinctive distrust of those who appear different from ourselves is not merely common but universal, being deeply rooted in human nature."

"Maybe so," he said in a voice tinged with sadness. "Or perhaps it is merely a form of bigotry, transmitted through the generations. In any case," he continued after a momentary pause, "I will tell you something that even you, I'm sure, *will* find strange."

"Yes?"

"First, permit me to ask you a question. Do you believe, Mr. Poe, that those events we call *coincidental* are the product of pure accident? Or that something else lurks behind them—a mysterious purpose, an unseen design?"

Somewhat taken aback by this unexpected query, I hesitated a moment before replying thusly: "Certainly, there are some coincidences of so startling— so marvelous—a character that, even to the calmest mind, they appear to have an element of the supernatural about them."

"Exactly so. And that is why," he said, turning his pale eyes away from me and casting his gaze about the room, "I now believe that you and I were fated to meet."

So surprising was this remark that, for a moment, I merely stared at my visitor in mute astonishment.

"It was only today," he continued, fixing me again with his uncanny look, "that I decided to seek you out, for reasons that I will explain in a moment. Imagine my amazement when I discovered that you were occupying this very apartment. You see, I have already visited it on a number of occasions. I was acquainted with its former tenant, Mr. Devereaux. Indeed, he was involved in the very matter that brings me here tonight!"

By this point, my surprise had turned into utter bewilderment. "I fear, Mr. Wyatt, that your remarks have left me very much at a loss," I said.

"Forgive me," he replied. "Allow me to explain. I am a man of independent means. My father became rich in the fur trade and left the bulk of his estate to me. Most people regard inherited wealth as a tremendous stroke of good fortune—and as a general rule, they're right. In spite of all scriptural admonishments, money can be a wonderful thing, Mr. Poe. Especially in my case, since it relieved me of the need to work. I say this not because I am lazy, but because my condition would have unfitted me for so many of the professions I might have wished to pursue. Can you imagine me, Mr. Poe, defending a client before a jury? Or comforting the sick? Or delivering a university lecture before an audience of young people? I suppose," he added dryly, "that I might have displayed myself in Barnum's sideshow. But somehow, I don't think that would have been a very rewarding career.

"At all events," he continued, "with so much time and money at my disposal, I have been at liberty to pursue my interests wherever they have led me. Recently, they led me to the acquisition of a very rare, if not invaluable, document. This is where the former tenant of your apartment, Mr. Devereaux, comes into the picture. I met him quite by accident while enjoying a most invigorating julep at the Metropolitan Hotel. As you can imagine, I am used to being stared at by strangers. Most of them, however, keep a wary distance. Not Mr. Devereaux. He came right up to me and began to chat. You may think that he was presumptuous to do so, but, in fact, I found it quite refreshing to be treated as just another fellow at the bar, having a perfect stranger strike up a casual conversation with me.

"In the course of our talk, I told him of my interests. It was then that he mentioned the document. He claimed to be acquainted with its owner in the South. Needless to say, I was very excited to learn of its existence. Mr. Devereaux offered to serve as my agent and negotiate its purchase. He proved as good as his word. Soon after the transaction was completed and the document was in my possession, he departed for Europe, evidently on some urgent business."

"I was under a different impression as to the reason for his sudden disappearance," I remarked. "From certain statements made by our landlady, I assumed that he had fallen hopelessly in debt and had fled the country barely one step ahead of his creditors."

"Really?" said my visitor with a frown. "I must say that surprises me. He never seemed hard up for money. And he certainly earned a generous fee for serving as my go-between. Still," he added with a shrug, "I didn't know the gentleman very well. It's possible, I suppose, that his financial circumstances were more desperate than he let on. In any case, I haven't seen or heard from him since he put the document in my hands."

"But what," I exclaimed, "is the precise nature of this document? I must confess that your story has greatly whetted my curiosity."

"I certainly don't mean to tantalize you, Mr. Poe, but I'm afraid that I cannot say more about it, at least for now. The document is of a quite—how shall

I put it?—*sensitive* nature. So much so that, until the appropriate time arrives, its contents must be kept in strictest secrecy. I *can* tell you this, however: it was written by a figure of great renown and is of potentially far-reaching significance. One condition, however, attaches to its importance. It must be proved, beyond a reasonable doubt, to be authentic."

Then, leaning forward in his chair, he added: "That is why I have come to see you."

Once again, my visitor had managed to astonish me. "But how can *I* be of assistance?" I exclaimed.

Resuming his former position, Wyatt crossed one long, inordinately slender leg over the other. As he did, I was struck by a peculiarity in the construction of his footwear. The underside of his right boot now being revealed to me, I perceived that the heel was of more-than-ordinary thickness. I knew, of course, that gentlemen of diminutive stature sometimes resorted to this expedient to endow themselves with an illusion of height. Even barefooted, though, Wyatt must have stood at least six feet.

I did not, however, have time to dwell on this conundrum, my attention being absorbed by my visitor's speech.

"It will come as no surprise to you to learn," he declared, "that—like others with my condition—I suffer from lamentably poor vision. Reading for more than a few minutes at a time places a tremendous strain on my eyes. Fortunately, I've found at least a partial solution to this problem. For the past several years, I have paid a young man named Harrison—a bright and enterprising lad who works by day as a junior clerk in a law office—to come to my residence several evenings a week and read to me. Sometimes, he regales me with a work of fiction; at others, with essays or reviews from various periodicals. Not long ago, he arrived with a copy of the *Broadway Journal*. Among its contents was a fascinating piece on the subject of handwriting analysis. You, Mr. Poe, were its author."

"Ah," I remarked. "Your intent is at last becoming clear to me."

The article to which he referred had been occasioned by the recent vogue among certain members of the city's wealthiest—and most frivolous—class for consulting so-called "graphologists," who claimed that—merely by examining a sample of someone's penmanship—they could ascertain all sorts of hidden truths about the individual's life, character, and even future destiny. With cool, unassailable logic, I had exposed these self-professed "experts" as nothing more than rank charlatans, hardly different from the most cunning and deceitful Gypsy fortune-tellers.

I had gone on to contrast their fraudulent activities with the legitimate practices of those genuine handwriting specialists who—through the rigorous application of scientific principles—were able to determine with absolute precision the particular tell-tale traits that differentiate one person's penmanship from another's. I had then illustrated my point by reproducing two seemingly identical specimens of longhand and demonstrating how—by comparing the subtle dissimilarities in the formation of the individual characters—the skilled analyst could easily discriminate between an original piece of writing and a mere forgery.

"Do I understand you to say," I now inquired of my visitor, "that you wish me to examine this mysterious document in order to judge its authenticity?"

"That's exactly what I mean, yes. Of course, I can't show you the entire document. As I've said, its contents must be closely guarded for now. But as you so ably proved in your article, a clever man like yourself can make such a judgment by examining only a sentence or two. Isn't that right?"

"Indeed, you are correct. One thing, however, is absolutely necessary in order for such an analysis to be undertaken—i.e., a second, undeniably genuine sample of the person's handwriting with which the document may be compared."

"You can rest easy on that score, Mr. Poe. I already have in my possession a letter written by the same illustrious individual, absolutely guaranteed to be the real thing."

"Then I see no reason why I could not perform such a service," I said. "Assuming, of course, that the demands on my time—which are already of an inordinately strenuous nature—permitted me to undertake such an assignment."

"Of course. I fully appreciate your situation. And I'm prepared to reimburse you accordingly. How does one hundred dollars sound?"

To say that I was taken aback by the sheer magnitude of this sum would constitute a significant understatement. Indeed, it required every bit of self-control at my disposal to conceal the astonishment provoked by Wyatt's offer. Arranging my features into what I *hoped* was a convincing display of indifference, I nonchalantly replied:

"The amount you propose is by no means unreasonable. To the man who pursues a high intellectual calling, however, money, in and of itself, can never be more than a secondary consideration. Of far greater importance is the intrinsic merit of the undertaking, the extent to which it promises to engage—stimulate—and challenge the mind. As it happens, your case clearly meets this criterion. Therefore—I accept."

"Excellent," Wyatt exclaimed with a satisfied smile. Even his teeth, I now noticed for the first time, were of a preternaturally bright and unblemished whiteness.

"And now," he continued, rising from the armchair and settling his hat upon his head, "I will take up no more of your time." Reaching a hand inside his jacket, he withdrew a small leather case, from which he extracted a calling card. "Here's the address of my residence. Shall we say tomorrow evening at seven o'clock?"

Taking the card from his long, exceedingly tapered fingers, I quickly perused it before nodding in assent. "I will come directly from work," I said. I then ushered him to the front door, where we shook hands.

In the vast range of social conduct, few forms of behavior are more peculiar than the tendency of a departing guest to pause on the very brink of his leave-taking and engage his host in a new, previously unbroached subject. This is precisely what now occurred with Wyatt. No sooner had the two of us exchanged a cordial farewell than he looked at me narrowly and said: "I've been meaning to ask, Mr. Poe. From the inflections of your speech, I assume you hail from the South. Am I right?"

Though the sheer abruptness of this query caught me by surprise, I saw no reason not to respond.

"I am a Southerner by upbringing, though not by birth," said I. "My place of nativity was Boston. Following the untimely demise of my sainted mother, the renowned actress Eliza Poe, I was taken, at an exceedingly early age, into the household of a prominent family of Richmond, Virginia."

"How peculiar," my visitor remarked in a musing tone. "My own life history is a mirror of yours—the same, but in reverse. I was born in Virginia but raised in Boston. It seems that you and I share a number of strange connections, Mr. Poe. And how long did you live in Richmond?"

"Apart from an *interregnum* of several years during which we resided in England," I replied, "my entire youth was passed in that city. I then briefly attended the University of Virginia before leaving the South for good. Why do you ask?"

"Idle curiosity, nothing more," said Wyatt with a casual shrug. "The University of Virginia, eh? Were you there when its great founder was still alive?"

This query—as the reader is no doubt aware—was in reference to Thomas Jefferson, who had not only been the *primum mobile* behind the creation of the university but had served as its first rector. Though Jefferson had died during my brief tenure at the school, I had glimpsed him on more than one occasion—a frail but still-imposing octogenarian who continued to pay regular visits to the library until the very last days of his life. I now related this fact to Wyatt, who—clearly impressed—raised his eyebrows and exclaimed:

"Still visiting the library in his eighties, eh? Wonderful! What an amazing intellect that man possessed. Nothing was beyond the scope of his interests. Do you know that he even wrote about albinos?"

I was forced to concede my ignorance of this fact.

"It's true," said Wyatt. "In his *Notes on Virginia*. Surely, Mr. Poe, you are familiar with that marvelous work."

"Indeed, it was a favorite book of my youth," I replied. "On the occasion of my twelfth birthday, my foster mother, Mrs. Allan, presented me with a copy that is still among my cherished possessions. Many years have elapsed, however, since I last perused it."

"Permit me to refresh your memory, then. Mr. Jefferson describes in great detail a number of albinos personally known to him—all of them Negro slaves owned by planters of his acquaintance. As I'm sure you know, albinism is far from unknown among blacks. Imagine—being whiter than the whitest plantation owner and yet condemned to the hell of Negro servitude!"

Here, Wyatt paused and gave his head a rueful shake before continuing thusly:

"Forgive me, Mr. Poe. I'm sure you have better things to do than stand here and listen to me ramble on about albino slaves. Until tomorrow evening, then." Raising a hand to the brim of his hat, he dipped his head in farewell, then turned and descended the gloomy stairwell—his luminous form disappearing from view like a spectral apparition returning to its subterranean haunts after a midnight visitation.

Eager as I was to tell Muddy and Sissy everything that had just transpired, Wyatt's parting words had so aroused my curiosity that—before returning to the dining room—I quickly repaired to my study, where I removed my copy of *Notes on Virginia* from its place on my bookshelf, carried it to my desk, and began to search through its pages. It took me no time at all to locate the passage to which my visitor had referred. In it, Jefferson describes at some length no fewer than seven albino Negroes known to him either from direct observation or from "faithful accounts."

"The circumstances in which all the individuals agree are these," he writes:

> They are of a pallid cadaverous white, untinged with red, without any colored spots or seams; their hair of the same kind of white, short, coarse, and

curled as is that of the negro; all of them well formed, strong, and healthy, perfect in their senses, except that of sight, and born of parents who had no mixture of white blood.

Three of these individuals were sisters, "the property of Colonel Skipworth, of Cumberland." Two others were an adult female and her infant child, "the property of Colonel Carter, of Albemarle." The sixth was a woman belonging to "Mr. Butler, near Petersburg"; while the seventh—"the only male of the albinos which have come within my information"—was a man owned by "Mr. Lee of Cumberland."

To these, Jefferson adds a description of "a negro man, born black and of black parents, on whose chin, when a boy, a white spot appeared. This continued to increase till he became a man, by which time it had extended over his chin, lips, one cheek, the under jaw, and neck on that side. It is of the albino white, without any mixture of red, and has for several years been stationary."

As I perused Jefferson's account, I was filled with a sudden sense of recognition, for I now vividly remembered having read—and been deeply impressed by—this passage as a boy. Never having seen or heard of such anomalous beings until that time, I had been astonished to learn of their existence. The description of the Negro man whose condition had initially manifested itself as a small white spot on his chin had also occasioned me a great deal of uneasiness; for—in the hypochondriacal way common to acutely sensitive children—I had worried that I, too, might awaken one day with the identical affliction. For weeks afterward, I had nervously examined myself in the mirror each morning, dreading that I would discover a mysterious discoloration that would eventually overspread my entire countenance, transforming me into something hideously unsightly.

There was one aspect of Jefferson's work, however, that I had never noticed as a boy—or, having noticed, had not in any way deemed peculiar. Now, however, I was struck by its incongruity. It was the particular *context* in which the author—the great champion of liberty, democracy, and equality—had chosen to place his description of the albino Negroes.

Rather than include it in his section on the makeup of Virginia's human population, he had relegated it to his discussion of the state's *fauna*—inserting it between his catalogue of the region's native birds and his account of its indigenous insects.

CHAPTER FOUR

UDDY AND SISSY were as eager to hear my account of Wyatt's visit as I was to share it with them. Unbeknownst to me, Sissy had taken a covert look at the albino, stealing to the entrance of the parlor while he and I were absorbed in our talk, and peeking around the doorway to observe him. Like me, she had been struck by the strange, otherworldly aura that he seemed to emanate. Indeed, to an even greater extent than I, she had felt, upon first glimpsing him, that there was something decidedly portentous about the white-hued caller—as though he were less a fellow human creature than, as she put it, a supernatural "harbinger." Whether his arrival prefigured good or ill fortune, however, she was not able to say.

"The answer to that mystery is readily supplied," I remarked with a smile. "For—in regard to the financial circumstances of our household—Mr. Wyatt's unexpected appearance this evening can only be seen as auspicious." I then proceeded to inform them of the exceedingly generous proposal he had made me.

"One hundred dollars!" Muddy gasped, clasping her hands to her bosom.

"Can it be true?" exclaimed Sissy.

I assured them that it was. Immediately, they began chattering gaily about the various items that they would now be able to afford—a new dress and bonnet for Sissy, a much-needed pair of shoes for Muddy. It was a source of the deepest satisfaction for me to sit back and observe their reaction. In all our years of struggle and privation, we had never enjoyed such a windfall, and their excitement was palpable; so much so that when Sissy's bedtime arrived a short while later, Muddy—fearful that her daughter would be unable to sleep—insisted on preparing her a soothing glass of hot milk. After imbibing this beverage, Sissy bid us good-night—bestowed an affectionate kiss upon each of us—and retired to her chamber.

Soon afterward, I repaired to my study, where I spent the remainder of the evening perusing—and making marginal notes in—Mr. Parker's volume in preparation for reviewing it on the morrow. By the time I had completed this task, the hour was approaching midnight. Changing into my nightclothes, I performed my ablutions and threw myself into bed, where I instantly subsided into sleep.

Sometime during the night, I had a most peculiar dream. In it, I found myself wandering through an Eastern-looking city, such as we read of in the Arabian tales, but of a character even more singular than any there described. Its long, serpentine streets swarmed with a countless multitude of people, normal in every regard except for the grotesque coloration of their skin. Some were green—others bright orange—still others of a wildly variegated hue. Among all this vast assemblage, however, one form stood out with a special prominence—a shrouded human figure, very far larger in its proportions than any dweller among men.

And the hue of the skin of this figure was the perfect whiteness of snow.

The following morning after breakfast, I set out for work, carrying with me Mr. Parkman's volume, along with the manuscript I had composed the previous afternoon—my hilariously scathing lampoon of C. A. Cartwright's egregious novel. In my eagerness to subject Cartwright to the ridicule he so richly deserved, I had made up my mind to publish my satire, not in the *Broadway Journal*—the next issue of which would not appear for several months—but rather in the *Daily Mirror*, a newspaper that had run a number of my writings in the past, and whose editor, a Mr. Morris, had made it clear that my contributions were always welcome. My intention was to deliver the piece to the offices of the newspaper on my way to my own workplace.

As determined as I was to have my revenge on Cartwright, however, he was no longer foremost among my concerns. From the moment I had awakened, I had been preoccupied with thoughts of my strange albino caller and his mysterious document. Indeed, so deeply engrossed was I with my ruminations on the subject that I had entirely forgotten about the hideous murder that had lately occurred, and the hunt for the fiend who had perpetrated that unspeakable atrocity.

This state of affairs was not destined to last. I had proceeded only a short distance from my home when I was roused from my musings by the shrill cry of a newsboy, peddling his wares on the corner of Amity Street.

"Extra! Extra! Read all about it!" he cried. "Child killer still at large! Police question Barnum's Indian! Angry crowd attacks museum!"

In view of my friendship with the showman, I could hardly fail to be dismayed by this intelligence—particularly by the news that his establishment had been made the target of a violent mob. Immediately, I recalled the sullen group of shabbily attired men and boys I had passed the previous day, who had so repelled me with their profane speech and vulgar demeanor. I now wondered if these had been the very wretches responsible for the reported assault. As the museum lay on the route between my residence and office, I resolved to pay my long-deferred visit to Barnum that very morning and inquire after my friend's well-being.

Ten minutes later, I came in sight of his establishment. Even from the distance of several city blocks, the building was conspicuous in the extreme. Exercising his considerable talent for brazen self-promotion, the showman had transformed his property into a species of architectural *fanfare*, trumpeting itself to the world. Atop its roof floated scores of brightly colored flags; while the entire façade was adorned with countless garishly painted signs, banners, and placards, advertising the myriad wonders within. Barnum's own name was spelled out in enormous cherry-red letters strung across the upper portion of the building. Altogether, the edifice stood out from its sober, commercial surroundings like a harlequin at a Puritan meetinghouse.

Added to these flagrant embellishments was a four-piece brass band that played continuously from a third-floor balcony. At the moment, they were engaged in a characteristically off-key rendition of the popular favorite "Make Me No Gaudy Chaplet," from Donizetti's *Lucrezia Borgia*. Audible even above the general din of the downtown traffic, the ear-splitting cacophony produced by these deplorable musicians was designed—I suspected—not to attract customers but rather to drive them inside the museum in the hope of escaping the infernal noise.

Drawing near my destination, I saw that—despite the earliness of the hour—a sizable crowd had already congregated outside the museum. As they were gathered at some little distance from the entrance, I deduced that they were not customers awaiting admission.

Could this, I wondered, be the same gang of ruffians I observed the previous afternoon—now assembled once again to vent their outrage on the showman for harboring the suspected killer?

But no. The closer I came to the museum, the more clearly I saw that the individuals assembled on the sidewalk were (apart from a handful of juvenile ragamuffins) perfectly respectable citizens of both sexes. They were staring intently at something that—from my present vantage point—I could not discern, the object of their scrutiny being located on the side of the building facing Ann Street.

No sooner had I made my way—with the greatest possible caution—across the chaotic thoroughfare of Broadway than I perceived what had so riveted their attention. Standing beside the building was a figure I recognized at a single glance. I could hardly fail to do so. Even with his back turned in my direction, it was impossible to mistake his identity.

To begin with, he stood more than eight feet in height, towering by a considerable margin over the tallest man among the assembled onlookers. His garb, moreover, was of a fashion absolutely unique to himself. He wore a flowing red coat adorned with gold epaulets, and secured about his waist by a thick leather belt from which depended a scabbard holding a military sabre. In relation to his enormous stature, however, this weapon seemed no larger than a sheath knife. His head was crowned with a distinctive Ottoman cap, or fez, purple in hue and topped with a silver tassel.

This remarkable figure, I knew, was the "Arabian Giant," Colonel Routh Goshen, one of the most popular of the many human anomalies featured at the museum. He appeared to be engaged in a conversation with someone. Though I could not see his interlocutor—who was obstructed from my view by the titanic torso of the giant—I wondered if it might not be Barnum himself.

Upon working my way through the mass of spectators and arriving at the front of the crowd, I was able to verify this conjecture. There stood the showman, looking little different from when I had last seen him. If anything, his most conspicuous features seemed even more pronounced than I remembered: his double chin more pendulous—his cheeks more florid—his unusually large and bulbous nose more noticeably mottled with red.

Handsomely attired in a costly black frock coat with gray-striped trousers—

his massive head topped by a beaver hat—he was pointing upward at a gaudily painted sign that hung from the wall of the building at a height of approximately twelve feet above the sidewalk. This picture, daubed in lurid colors on a sheet of canvas, consisted of the crudely rendered figure of an Indian chief, bedecked in an elaborate feathered headdress. In one raised hand, he clutched a bloody tomahawk; in the other, a sinuous yellow mass that was clearly meant to suggest the golden tresses of some unfortunate female victim. Head thrown back, mouth agape—as though he were emitting a triumphant *whoop*—he stood with one foot raised in a capering posture. SEE THE SAVAGE SCALP DANCE OF CHIEF WOLF BEAR! read the crimson lettering on the bottom of the sign.

Unlike the numerous other banners that adorned the museum, however, this one had been badly defaced, as though it had been subjected to a heavy bombardment of garbage, rotten vegetable matter, offal, mud, and worse. The areas of the wall immediately surrounding the sign were similarly spattered. From the nature of his gestures—as well as from the few scattered words that I could make out amidst the clatter of the traffic and the discord of the band—I deduced that Barnum was instructing the giant to take down the defiled painting, then scrub the wall clean with a long-handled mop that, I now perceived, was resting nearby beside a bucket brimming with soapsuds.

Why Barnum would employ one of his premier attractions to perform this menial chore is a question that will only be asked by those unfamiliar with the showman's guiding philosophy. In brief, he believed—with a fervor bordering on the religious—that no opportunity to draw attention to himself and his enterprise should ever go unexploited. To be sure, a custodian armed with a stepladder could easily have accomplished the job. But then, such a prosaic solution would not have aroused the excitement produced by the sight of an eight-foot-tall giant—garbed in a purple fez and crimson military coat— engaged in the same task.

And, indeed, Barnum's strategy had more than achieved its goal. Not only had Goshen's presence attracted a rapidly growing crowd of sidewalk spectators (all of them potential paying customers), it also elicited a continuous barrage of remarks from the drivers of passing carriages, buggies, and wagons, who called: "Hello, Tiny!" "How's the weather up there?" "Fee fi fo fum!" and other such feeble witticisms.

Ignoring these shouts, Goshen proceeded to reach up with both enormous hands and remove the badly soiled picture, which he let fall on the sidewalk, where Barnum gazed down upon it with a scowl of disgust. The giant then grabbed the mop (which seemed no larger than a toothbrush in his hands) and scrubbed clean the bespattered bricks. When this job was completed, he stooped and replaced the mop in the bucket; whereupon Barnum turned to the onlookers and, in his usual orotund style, addressed them thusly:

"Friends, it is with a heavy heart that I greet you here this morning. The sun may be shining—the sky may be blue. But don't let appearances fool you. It's a dark day in this city—dark as they come! You've just been witness to an event so chilling it makes my blood run cold just thinking about it! Something whose dire implications threaten the very fabric—the very warp and woof—of our American way of life!

"Now, I know what you're thinking. You're thinking: 'What in heaven's name is Barnum talking about? Why, I haven't witnessed anything very particular this morning. True, there was that eight-foot-tall giant removing a spattered old painting from the side of the building! But I wouldn't call that *chilling.*'

"Friends, let me take a minute of your time to explain what I mean.

"Now, I may say, in all humility and without the slightest fear of contradiction, that—from the start of my long and storied career as the world's greatest showman—I have been driven by one overriding motive. And that is to bring you, the great American public, the most extraordinary—the most stupendous—the most morally elevating entertainment in human history! And I've done so without giving a single thought to the immense cost and incalculable effort required to obtain the greatest wonders from around the globe! 'Spare no trouble or expense'—that's P. T. Barnum's motto!

"Oh, I don't say I haven't profited somewhat. Of course, I've earned a few shekels! After all, a man has to keep body and soul together! A man has to feed and clothe his family! But for the most part, all my time and income have been devoted to one purpose and one purpose only—to create a place of entertainment and edification worthy of the greatest city on earth! Have I succeeded? Well, I'll let you be the judge of that. Just open your eyes and see what's in front of you. The most spectacular emporium of wonder in all of Christendom! The grandest museum ever conceived by man! Containing more than a hundred thousand prodigies and curiosities, including the fabled dwarf elephant of Pakistan!—Dr. Hall's harmonizing Newfoundland dog choir!—the largest collection of rare and exotic seashells in existence!—the monster living alligator, over twelve feet in length!—and other phenomena of art, science, and nature too various to enumerate!

"And what, you may ask, is my reward? What thanks do I receive for my unremitting labors and self-sacrifice on behalf of others? It pains—no, it *grieves*—me to say that the answer to that question is lying right here at my feet—in this defaced, defiled, utterly desecrated piece of rare and costly art-work I have just been compelled to take down with the help of my assistant, Colonel Goshen—the tallest man alive, one of the countless human marvels on display in my world-renowned Hall of Oddities!

"Friends, if I told you what it cost me to have this painting made, you wouldn't believe me. You'd say I was exaggerating. You'd say I was embellish-ing the truth. Let me only remark, then, that—like all the pictures adorn-ing my museum—it was executed in Florence, Italy, by a master craftsman trained in the traditional method of Renaissance fresco painting! The same technique employed by the immortal Giotto in the Arena Chapel at Padua! And just look at it now! Great Scot, it's nothing but rubbish, pure rubbish! Ut-terly vandalized by a mob of vicious ruffians, their brutish passions inflamed by the libelous accusations of an irresponsible press!

"But it's not just this splendid example of Italianate art that lies in ruins at my feet. No! Something even more precious—even more invaluable—has been attacked here! And what could that possibly be? Why, nothing less than the very basis of our democratic system of government! Just think of it, ladies and gentlemen! Is *this* what the brave patriots of the Revolution gave their lives for? To see the cherished principles of free expression overthrown by mob rule—spat on, pelted by garbage, and trampled in the dust? Is *this* what the Founding Fathers had in mind when they established our glorious Repub-lic? And, incidentally, for those of you with a particular interest in these mat-ters, permit me to point out that—among the hundreds of other unique and astounding attractions to be found in my museum—I have recently acquired the actual flintlock rifle that fired the fabled 'shot heard round the world' at the Battle of Lexington, on view at all times in my newly renovated Hall of American History!

"In conclusion, my dear friends, allow me to make this heartfelt appeal to your sense of patriotic duty. I ask—no, *urge!*—that you demonstrate your scorn, your detestation, of this outrageous act of mob tyranny. How? Why, by judging for yourself whether there is anything within the walls of the Barnum Museum that isn't of the purest, most uplifting nature—good, clean, whole-some entertainment, suitable for the whole family! Only in that way—by exercising your own fair and impartial judgment—can you assert your God-given rights and freedoms as American citizens.

"So step right up, ladies and gentlemen! The museum is open for business, sunrise till ten P.M., twenty-five cents admission, children and servants half price, peanuts and all other luxuries of the season to be purchased in all parts of the house!"

Having concluded this remarkable speech, Barnum gestured to the giant, who—stooping—snatched the crumpled sheet of canvas from the sidewalk with one colossal hand; while, with the other, he took hold of the bucket and mop. He then swiveled on his heels and trudged away toward the side entrance of the museum, trailing in his wake a procession of gamboling children.

For several moments, Barnum lingered at the scene, watching with evident satisfaction as a sizable portion of the dispersing crowd proceeded directly to the ticket booth and began lining up for admission. He then turned in the direction that the giant had taken.

Up until that point, the showman had been unaware of my presence; for—though situated near the front of his audience—I had been standing some-what off to one side, on the periphery of his vision. Now, as he made ready to leave, he suddenly caught sight of me and—grinning broadly—came striding in my direction.

"Poe!" he exclaimed, grabbing my right hand in both of his own and pump-ing it so furiously that I felt as if my entire arm were in danger of being dis-lodged from its socket. "By George, I'm glad to see you, m'boy—perfectly delighted to see you! Here, let me take a gander at you. Lord bless me, you're looking well! Not a day older since I last set eyes on you."

I returned his greeting with commensurate warmth, complimenting him on his own appearance, which, if anything, had grown even more robust since his departure for Europe.

" 'Robust,' eh?" he replied with a chuckle. "I suppose that's a polite way of saying *fat*. No, no, m'boy—no need to deny it. I know I've put on a little *avoir-dupois*, as our French cousins say. Bless my life, I could hardly avoid it, the way they feed you over there. I tell you, m'boy, there's nothing in the world that compares to French cuisine, nothing even remotely like it. All those cream sauces and buttered meats and chocolate pastries! Great Scot, it's a wonder the whole population isn't bursting at the seams! Why, if I'd remained in Paris an-other month, I would've been big enough to appear in my own sideshow. 'See P. T. Barnum—the Human Colossus! The World's Fattest Living Showman!'

"But tell me, Poe, what brings you here this morning?" he continued, ges-turing at the area of the wall from which the defaced banner had just been removed. "Come to see this sorry spectacle?"

"Indeed," I replied, "though I have been intending, for some weeks, to welcome you back to these shores, it was partly my concern over this unfortunate incident—reports of which are on the lips of every newsboy—that induced me to visit at this time."

"Well, I appreciate your worries, m'boy, appreciate them with all my heart," he said with a sigh. "Yes, it's a nasty business, all right. I won't deny it. But come," he continued, "let's head down to my office and have a little chat. Lord, it does my heart good to look at you, Poe!"

Taking me by the arm, he led me to the side door of the building—ushered me inside—and preceded me down the stairwell to the basement.

As I knew from my numerous previous visits to the museum, the corridors of this subterranean region were inordinately difficult to negotiate. Dimly lit and mazelike in construction, they were also exceedingly narrow, their walls being lined by barrels, crates, and a wildly promiscuous assortment of bizarre and exotic *objets*. So vast and ever-expanding was Barnum's collection that—despite the extensive size of his establishment (which comprised five entire floors, each containing several spacious galleries)—he was compelled to employ the basement as a storage area for his surplus curiosities.

Now, guided by the showman, I made my way through the cramped and dismal labyrinth, while the flickering gas jets—mounted at irregular intervals high on the walls—cast their lurid glow on the many strange and dusty artifacts around me: a stuffed African ostrich—an enormous dried starfish, measuring at least three feet in diameter—an iron punishment cage housing a human skeleton—a waxworks manikin of Anne Boleyn, cradling her decapitated head under one arm—a ship's figurehead in the shape of a voluptuous woman, her bosom shamelessly exposed—the mummified remains of an Egyptian ibex—an Esquimaux dogsled—the partial lower jaw of a sperm whale—a matched pair of medieval halberds—and countless other, equally unusual artifacts.

At length we arrived at our destination. Unlocking the door, Barnum stepped into his office, turned up the illumination, then motioned me inside, gesturing for me to take one of the chairs arranged in the center of the room.

"Take a load off your feet, m'boy," he said, seating himself behind his massive, claw-footed desk. "Make yourself comfortable. Cigar? No? Well, I take it you won't mind if I indulge."

Extracting an enormous Havana from a carved mahogany box on his desktop, he clipped one end with a small silver implement and ignited the other with a phosphorus match.

"Ah, that's better—that's just what the doctor ordered. Nothing like a good smoke for settling the nerves. I don't mind telling you, Poe, I'm not at all happy about the loss of that banner. Why, it was Oswald's greatest creation! His masterpiece! Took him a whole afternoon to paint it!"

"Oswald?"

"My new handyman. Does all the artwork for my museum now—posters, signs, advertising placards. Man's a natural-born talent—an absolute whiz! Now, don't misunderstand me. I'm not saying he's necessarily as good as some of your old masters. His paintings may lack a certain element of technical finesse. But, by God, they have something even more important—they're *alive!*"

Barnum's earlier claim concerning the banner's Italianate origins having been such a flagrant piece of "humbug," this information hardly came as a surprise. The painting of the rampant Indian warrior had been rendered in a style of surpassing crudeness. Even I was forced to concede, however, that—in spite (or perhaps because) of its exceedingly primitive quality—it had possessed an oddly expressive power.

"But what," I inquired, "were the precise circumstances surrounding the destruction of this prized banner?"

"Circumstances?" the showman exclaimed, plucking the cigar from his mouth. "Why, it was made the target of a vicious and cowardly attack by a gang of young vandals! Started congregating outside my museum yesterday afternoon. You should have seen them, Poe. As nasty a pack of brutes as you'd ever hope to meet! Made the band of man-eating Australian bushmen in my Gallery of Ethnological Wonders look positively *genteel!*"

"As a matter of fact," I interposed, "I *did* see them. Returning home from work early yesterday afternoon, I passed by your establishment and observed a group of male loiterers, perhaps a dozen in number, whose deplorable dress and odious manners rendered them exceedingly conspicuous."

"Yes, those were the rascals, all right," said Barnum. "The lowest order of Bowery riffraff! Nothing better to do than loaf around street corners, looking for ways to cause mischief. At first, I tried reasoning with them. Asked them nice as you please to move along. 'It's a free country!' they sneered. Insolent pups! I tell you, Poe, I'm as much in favor of freedom as the next man. I'm a patriot—a patriot down to my bones! Heavens, you've attended my famous Fourth of July pageant! Grandest spectacle ever staged in the history of the world! More than one hundred performers, each garbed in authentic period costume, re-creating the highlights of the American Revolution, from the Boston Tea Party to the Battle of Saratoga! Dazzling fireworks! Scenes of unparalleled splendor! Last thing in the world I need is some damned Bowery ruffians lecturing me on the principles of democracy!"

By this point, Barnum—whose burning cigar was still clamped between the first and second fingers of his right hand—had begun to gesticulate wildly, causing a shower of ashes to sprinkle down upon his desktop.

"I take it, then," I said, "that you were unsuccessful in your efforts to persuade them to disperse."

"Well, I couldn't stand there forever, arguing with the trash. Some of us have better things to do than hang around street corners all day. What I didn't know, of course, was that they'd come hell-bent on trouble. As soon as I was back inside the museum, they started gathering up whatever garbage they could find—pig swill, putrid vegetables. Even horse apples, if you can believe it! Then they let loose a barrage. As soon as I heard about it, I came dashing outside with a few reinforcements—my strongman, my giant, a couple of my Zulu warriors. But the wretches had already fled—scattered like chickens."

Leaning back in his chair, the showman took a long, meditative draw on his cigar before continuing thusly: "I'll tell you the truth, Poe. Strange as it sounds, I don't hold those scoundrels entirely to blame. After all, you don't blame a hog for wallowing in muck, nor a sewer rat for dining on garbage. They're just acting according to their God-given nature. No sir! As far as I'm concerned, the real culprit is that blackguard Bennett. He's the true instigator of the whole affair. Inciting the rabble with his outrageous accusations! Why, if he doesn't let up, he's likely to set off a bona fide riot! Believe me, I've seen it happen before. Angry mobs, swarming out of the slums like the Visigoths descending on Rome! It wouldn't take much, not much at all—especially in weather like this, when everyone's temper is already at the boiling point. That damned Bennett is playing with fire, I tell you."

"But what motive could he possibly have for pursuing such an irresponsible course?" I asked.

"Why, Poe, you surprise me. I don't mind saying that I am positively astonished by such a question! A man of your brilliance—of your immense perspicacity! Why, the answer's obvious—plain as the nose on my face! Envy, m'boy! Envy, pure and simple! He can't tolerate my stupendous success! It rankles. Eats away at his soul like a canker. Keeps him awake all night concocting ways of hurting my business. Imagine! Accusing Chief Wolf Bear of perpetrating those unspeakable barbarities! Butchering and scalping young girls! Why, it's preposterous! Most outrageous thing I've ever heard—and believe me, Poe, I've heard my share of dillies!"

By this point, the complexion of the showman had achieved such a vivid coloration that I feared he might, at any moment, succumb to a fit of apoplexy.

"Indeed," I said, "from what I read in the papers, it seemed exceedingly unlikely that these dreadful crimes were committed by a member of the tribe to which Chief Wolf Bear belongs—to wit, the Crow."

"Right you are, m'boy, right you are! Not that old Wolf Bear is an angel. Far from it! Why, back in his prime, he was as bloodthirsty a savage as ever brandished a tomahawk. But those days are long over for him. Lord bless me, the fellow's older than I am—sixty, if he's a day. Joints so creaky with the rheumatiz that he can barely shuffle through his war dance. And lazy? Why, if he had his way, he'd do nothing but sit around all day, eating beefsteak and playing cards with John Hanson Craig, my Carolina Fat Boy."

"But what countermeasures do you propose to employ in response to Bennett's actions?" I inquired.

"Why, I intend to wage war using Bennett's own chosen weapon," Barnum replied. "The daily newspapers! 'Fight fire with fire'—that's P. T. Barnum's motto. Here, feast your eyes on this, m'boy."

Sliding open the center drawer of his desk, he extracted a single piece of paper and handed it to me.

"Just finished composing it this morning," Barnum explained as I perused the handwritten sheet.

Though clearly intended as an advertisement, the item was written in the form of a newspaper article. The headline, inscribed in bold block letters, read: BARNUM WINS COVETED "BENEFACTOR OF HUMANITY" PRIZE! AMERICAN MUSEUM HAILED AS MOST WHOLESOME INSTITUTION OF ITS KIND IN CHRISTENDOM! According to the text, Barnum had recently been honored as "Man of the Year" by an organization composed of the country's leading clergymen and educators, who had awarded him a "solid gold medallion" for his "unstinting efforts to promote the ideals of decency, purity, and morality." Accompanying the story were a slew of glowing testimonials, typical of which was a statement by one Reverend Micah Billingsworth, who was quoted as saying: "Besides the Christian church itself, there has never been an establishment so wholesome and uplifting as the American Museum. Next to weekly attendance at a house of God, regular visits to Mr. Barnum's establishment ought to be made by every man, woman, and child in this country!"

"Permit me to offer my congratulation on this high honor," I said upon reaching the conclusion of the piece. "I am embarrassed to say that I have never heard of this organization, the Committee to Encourage Decency in Public Entertainment."

"No need for embarrassment, m'boy," said Barnum, stubbing out his cigar in a ceramic ashtray. "It doesn't actually exist—not in any literal sense. But it's all perfectly true in *essence*. The *essence* is the key! Why, everyone knows that my museum offers nothing but the finest in family entertainment! And most of those testimonials are the genuine article! Well, all right, perhaps 'most' is a slight exaggeration. But any number of them are absolutely, one hundred percent authentic!"

Through my long acquaintance with the showman, I had become so accustomed to his cheerfully fraudulent ways that I could hardly work up even a modicum of indignation at this latest piece of chicanery. Setting the paper back down on the desk, I merely said: "And what use do you propose to make of this item?"

"Why, I mean to have it published on the front page of tomorrow's *Mirror*! The editor, Henry Morris, is a dear friend of mine. Plus, he hates Bennett's guts almost as much as I do!"

"As it happens," I said, "I intend to pay Mr. Morris a visit this very morning. I, too, have a piece of writing that I plan to leave with him."

"Really?" said Barnum. "Well then, you can do me a favor." Removing a blank sheet of paper from his desk, he quickly scribbled a note—folded it in half—and inserted it into an envelope, along with his spurious "article."

"Give this to Morris, will you? Save me the trouble of dispatching a messenger," he said, holding out the envelope.

"I shall be happy to do so," I said, taking it from his hand and placing it in the side pocket of my jacket, beside my own folded manuscript.

"And now," I continued, glancing at the handsome mantel clock that stood atop a nearby cabinet, "I am afraid I must be going."

"So soon?" Barnum exclaimed. "Why, I haven't even asked you about those two dear ladies of yours."

"At present, they are both doing well," I replied, "though my darling wife's all-too-fragile health continues to be a source of concern. Both of them were exceedingly grateful—as was I—for the basket of delicacies that you so generously sent to us."

"Think nothing of it, m'boy, think nothing of it! Please send my warmest regards to the dear ladies. And tell them they're welcome guests at Barnum's Museum at all times, weekends and holidays included!"

"I will be sure to do so," I said, rising from my seat. "And now I had better be off. I am already expected at work, and I must first stop off at the offices of the *Daily Mirror* to deliver our respective documents."

"Yes, of course, m'boy, won't keep you a moment longer," said Barnum, springing to his feet and striding around his desk. "Besides, I've got an errand of my own to run. Have to hunt up Oswald. Ask him to whip up another painting to replace that tragically ruined banner."

Though I had already begun moving toward the doorway, this statement brought me to a sudden halt. Turning back to face the showman, I said: "Surely, in view of the present exceedingly volatile situation, you do not intend to hang another picture of Chief Wolf Bear on the exterior of your museum. Such an act would almost certainly be perceived as a deliberate provocation by the lawless gang of rowdies who have already been the cause of so much mischief."

"You're right about that, m'boy—no point in fanning the flames. Still, it wouldn't do to leave that big empty spot on the front of my museum. Why, it's prime advertising space! I suppose I'll ask Oswald to depict one of my newer attractions. My giant living anaconda, perhaps. Or maybe Mother Cary's astounding trained chickens. No, wait—I have it! I'll have him do a painting of Monsieur Vox! Yes, by Jove—that's just the ticket!"

"I am afraid I am unfamiliar with the gentleman to whom you refer," I said.

"Well, he's new to the museum—just signed on board a few months ago," said Barnum. "Still, I'm a tad surprised that you've never heard of him. Why, he's one of the most celebrated performers in existence—renowned throughout the civilized world! Most extraordinary ventriloquist ever to practice the venerable art of biloquism! Bless my soul, the man's act is miraculous— absolutely staggering. Not just your usual low comedic banter with a bunch of clownish dummies. Oh, yes, there's *some* of that, of course. Have to please the groundlings, you know. But that's just a small part of his show. Why, he enacts entire scenes from classical drama, employing the most astonishingly lifelike manikins ever fashioned by the hand of man! Does all the vocal parts himself, of course. You should see his rendition of Desdemona's death scene! Lord bless me, it has the audience in tears every time!"

The notion of performing a ventriloquial version of Shakespeare's shattering (if somewhat improbably motivated) tragedy *Othello* was too absurd for words. Managing, with the greatest difficulty, to keep from bursting into a gale of derisive laughter, I said: "It sounds quite remarkable."

"Oh, it is, m'boy, it is!" said Barnum. "You *must* come see his act sometime— you owe it to yourself! Bring the little ladies, too!"

Promising that I would most certainly return in the near future to view this singular performer, I bid the showman farewell and took my leave.

CHAPTER FIVE

UPON DEPARTING FROM THE MUSEUM, I directed my steps toward the offices of the *Daily Mirror*, situated on Nassau Street. As I strode down Broadway, my mind was entirely occupied with thoughts of my meeting with Barnum.

However deplorable, the reported attack on his museum had amounted to little more than a comparatively trivial act of vandalism. Even so, it could hardly be doubted that the situation remained highly combustible. The Bowery ruffians responsible for the deed were of that low and shiftless species who—disdaining all honest labor—vent their natural energies in acts of wild and random destruction. Very little would be required to transform such creatures into a rampaging mob, bent on wholesale destruction. Riots involving the denizens of Manhattan's worst slum districts had occurred with alarming frequency in the history of New York City. Indeed, one of the most infamous of these incidents was memorialized in an exhibition in Barnum's own establishment.

I refer, of course, to the notorious "Doctors Riot" that had convulsed Manhattan some fifty years earlier. Underlying this deplorable episode was the public's bitter resentment against the ghoulish—and, at the time, by no means uncommon—practice of grave-robbing.

Owing to the legal restrictions of the day—which permitted anatomical dissections to be performed solely on the dead bodies of paupers and executed murderers—it was exceedingly difficult for medical schools to obtain a sufficient number of human specimens for research. As a result, professors of surgery, as well as their students, were compelled to resort to expedients of an extreme—and often extra-legal—nature.

In his determination to unlock the secrets of the human circulatory system, for example, the great William Harvey—whose classic volume, *De moto cordis et sanguinis*, stands as one of the landmarks in the advancement of human knowledge—found it necessary to employ the corpses of his own relations as the raw material for his studies, dissecting the bodies of both his father and sister following their deaths from natural causes. Even more remarkable was the case of the French surgeon Rondelet, a professor of the medical school of Montpellier, who—lacking any other subject for use in his anatomy class—dissected the body of his own dead child in front of his students!

Perhaps unsurprisingly, the solution arrived at by Harvey and Rondelet—i.e., exploiting one's own family as a convenient source of anatomical material—failed to achieve widespread acceptance. Instead, anatomists began to look to a place where cadavers were always readily available and in abundant supply: the cemetery. The earliest grave-robbers appear to have been medical men themselves, bent on acquiring fresh subjects for their studies. Eventually, however, grave-robbing became a profession practiced by so-called "resurrectionists" who made their odious living by exhuming newly buried corpses and supplying them to medical schools.

Needless to say, the notion that a recently deceased loved one might be removed from the grave and end up on a surgical table, subjected to the gross indignity of public dissection, was a cause of profound consternation to the general populace, and particularly to members of the poorer classes, who were the most likely to suffer this fate (the bodies of the wealthy being interred within more-or-less impregnable vaults or caskets). Fear, distrust, and even outright hatred of anatomical professors and their students became the order of the day.

It was within this highly fraught context that the infamous "Doctors Riot" occurred toward the close of the previous century in New York City.

This violent civic eruption began when a young boy—whose name has gone unrecorded by history—climbed a ladder propped against the side of New York Hospital (which was undergoing some minor repairs) and, prompted by a morbid curiosity, peered into the window of the dissecting room. There, he observed a medical student who was in the process of examining a human arm that had recently been removed from a female cadaver.

On perceiving the boy, the student—motivated by a misguided and malicious sense of humor—picked up the severed limb, brandished it in the air, and announced that it belonged to the boy's mother!

By an unfortunate happenstance, the child's mother had, in fact, died not long before and was buried in Trinity churchyard. Taking the student at his word, the horrified lad immediately ran off to inform his father, who was employed as a mason at Macomb's building on Broadway. This man immediately shared the appalling intelligence with his comrades, who—seizing such of their tools as might best serve as weapons—marched in a body to the hospital, where they proceeded to ransack the building and attack several medical students, who were spared from severe, perhaps even fatal, injury only by the timely intervention of several magistrates.

In the course of their rampage through the hospital, the men had discovered the partially dissected remains of several human bodies. None of the subjects, however, could be identified. It was then proposed by one member of the party that they repair to the churchyard and examine the grave in which the mason's wife had been laid to rest. This was immediately done, the original group gathering additional reinforcements as they marched toward Trinity Church.

Arrived at their destination, they set about their grim task. A shovel was procured—the grave excavated—the coffin exposed and brought to the surface. The men crowded about the plain pine box as the lid was removed.

What was their shock—their astonishment—their unutterable horror—at finding the coffin to be empty!

This discovery sent the mob into a frenzy. During the course of the next twenty-four hours, the rioters—who had grown to a force of five thousand strong—stormed the buildings of Columbia College, ransacked the dwellings of the city doctors, and laid siege to the municipal jail, where a number of physicians and medical students had taken refuge.

Matters assumed so dire an aspect as to create a general alarm in the city and call forth the exertions of the principal citizens to aid in restoring the peace. Among those who intervened were Governor George Clinton, Mayor James Duane, Chancellor Robert Livingston, and Mr. John Jay (then Secretary of Foreign Affairs to Congress). Their efforts, however, proved unavailing. When the mob responded to their pleas by showering them with brick-bats (one of which knocked Mr. Jay unconscious), the militia was summoned and ordered to fire on the crowd. It was only after suffering several fatalities from the first volley of the militiamen's rifles that the mob dispersed for good.

In spite of having occurred a half-century earlier, this disconcerting episode remained very much alive in the awareness of New Yorkers, owing partly to P. T. Barnum himself. Among the most popular exhibits at his museum was a large display case containing assorted items related to the incident, including a preserved female arm purported to be the actual limb responsible for igniting the riot. Of course—as with so many of Barnum's rarities—the absolute authenticity of this ghastly relic was open to doubt. Certainly, there was no definitive way of establishing its provenance.

What could *not* be doubted, however, was that Barnum now occupied much the same position as the city surgeons and anatomists of fifty years earlier. That is to say, he was at the center of an exceedingly explosive situation that threatened, at any moment, to erupt into full-blown civic disorder.

True, there was little outward sign of a potential crisis. As I proceeded toward the offices of the *Daily Mirror*, the throngs hurrying past me on Broadway appeared to be going about their ordinary business, oblivious of anything beyond their own, urgent affairs. Nevertheless, it could scarcely be doubted that—like a seemingly indestructible building beneath whose foundations the first, barely perceptible tremors of an earthquake have begun to occur—the city could, at any moment, be plunged into chaos.

The situation was rendered even more ominous by another consideration. Barnum's revelations concerning Chief Wolf Bear's age—physical condition—and indolent propensities—had only confirmed my own assumptions regarding the latter's probable innocence. With the Indian discounted as a suspect, however, any hope of a prompt resolution of the case was certain to go unrealized. Though the New York City police possessed a certain dogged determination, they were notoriously lacking in those investigatory skills necessary for tracking down a criminal of more-than-usual cunning. It seemed inevitable, then, that, before very long, the city would be subjected to further enormities at the hands of the unknown killer, whose crimes—as I was about to discover— were even ghastlier than had thus far been reported by the press.

Arrived at the building in which the offices of the *Daily Mirror* were housed, I ascended to the second floor, where—as I knew from my previous visits—the editorial rooms were located. No sooner had I reached the landing than I spied the personage I was seeking.

Short and stockily built, Mr. Morris was a man of perhaps sixty years of age, with a massive head—thick, gray hair—bushy eyebrows of the same grizzled hue—and red full lips. He was standing at the far end of the hall beside a slender young gentleman whose identity was unknown to me.

In contrast to his counterparts at the other city newspapers—who were almost universally known for their gruff, dictatorial manners—Morris possessed an unusually genial disposition. At the moment, however, his normal good cheer appeared to have abandoned him. Even from the distance at which I now viewed him, I could see that his expression was exceedingly grim. Clutched in one of his hands was a single sheet of paper that he was examining intently. As he read, he shook his head slowly from side to side, while making soft, tongue-clucking noises of dismay.

So absorbed was he in scrutinizing the page that he failed to take note of my presence even when I crossed the hall and came to a halt directly in front of him. His companion—a sallow-complexioned fellow in his middle or late twenties with black, close-curling hair, angular features, and a disproportionately large and jutting chin—offered me a curt nod of greeting, while regarding me curiously from beneath his dark, inordinately arched eyebrows.

At length—muttering an uncharacteristically bitter imprecation—Morris glanced up from the sheet of paper, his countenance assuming a look of intense surprise as he saw me.

"Poe!" he exclaimed. "Where did *you* come from?"

"I arrived several moments ago," I said, "but did not wish to interrupt you."

"By Jupiter, you startled me half to death," said Morris. "Thought you'd sprung out of thin air, like one of Barnum's conjurers."

"I am afraid," I replied, "that my arrival was effectuated by means that were, in both a literal and figurative sense, far more *pedestrian*. It is partly on behalf of our friend Mr. Barnum, however, that I have come."

I then reached into my pocket and extracted the envelope from the showman, which I handed to Morris. Removing the contents, he quickly perused them before emitting a snort of amusement.

"Up to his usual tricks," he said. "Well, I'm always happy to oblige an old friend like Phineas. But Poe," he continued, giving me a quizzical look, "surely, you didn't come all the way here just to deliver *this*?"

Assuring him that he was correct in his assumption, I proceeded to explain the principal reason for my visit. I described the impossibly insolent letter I had received from C. A. Cartwright, and summarized—in terms that could hardly fail to whet my listener's interest—the bitingly humorous satire I had composed in response. Removing the latter from my pocket and handing it to

Morris, I expressed my hope that he might find a place for it in his newspaper, stressing that he would be under no obligation to pay me for the piece, my personal satisfaction being recompense enough.

"Another of your literary quarrels, eh Poe?" Morris remarked with a soft chuckle. "Well, they're always good for selling a few papers. You might think twice, though, before starting a feud with this Cartwright fellow. Never met him myself, but from what I hear, he's not a man to be trifled with."

"Nor," I said in a tone of grim resolve, "am I."

"True enough," said Morris, inserting my still-folded manuscript into the side pocket of his double-breasted frock coat. "Well, I'll be happy to read it over as soon as I have a minute. If it's as amusing as you say, it'll offer a welcome relief from *this* unpleasantness."

This latter remark was made in reference to the sheet of paper that he had been perusing when I arrived and that remained clutched in his left hand.

"And what, may I ask, is the precise nature of that document?" I said.

"Autopsy report on little Rosalie Edmonds," said Morris. "That poor butchered child who was found the other day." Raising his chin toward the young man beside him, he continued thusly: "Townsend here managed to get hold of a copy just this morning. You two know each other? Poe, this is George Townsend, finest news reporter in the city. Townsend, Mr. Edgar A. Poe."

"Sure," said the sharp-featured young man. "Author of 'The Raven.' Hell of a poem. Creepiest damned thing I've ever read."

"Except for this," said Morris grimly, holding up the autopsy report. "Even *you* couldn't have dreamed it up, Poe. Care to have a look?"

Taking the proffered page from his hand, I began to peruse it. Almost at once, my soul sickened, and I was seized with the dizziness of one who gazes downward into some hideous and unfathomable abyss. It was true—as Morris had implied—that, in appealing to the public's unslakable desire for sensationalism, my own fiction was often replete with incidents of a singularly lurid nature. Nothing in my work, however, could compare to the sheer gruesome horror of the butchery described in the coroner's document.

The extent and severity of the mutilations inflicted on the innocent young victim were far greater than I had imagined. In addition to having been scalped—with a ferocity that had ripped the very ears from her head—her eyes had been gouged out and the corners of her mouth slit upward, as though her killer had deliberately set about to carve her visage into the ghastly semblance of a Hallowe'en jack-o'-lantern. Several fingers had also been sliced from her hands. The apparent cause of death was a terrible wound to her throat which had been gashed with such inhuman savagery that the vertebrae of her neck were laid bare. All of these atrocities were detailed by the medical examiner in a tone of cold, scientific detachment that only added to the indescribably awful effect of the report. Even the descriptions of the lesser injuries—such as the rope burns on the poor child's tightly bound ankles—were dismaying in the extreme.

One detail in particular arrested my attention. The killer had made an incision on the right side of the little girl's abdominal region, just beneath the rib cage. In probing this wound, the medical examiner had discovered that the liver was missing! As this organ had not been found near the body, it was assumed that the fiend had carried it off for his own unspeakable reasons, along with the scalp and severed fingers.

I was just completing my perusal of the document when I became aware that Morris was addressing me.

"You all right, Poe?" he asked.

I inferred from this query that the intense feelings of shock—horror—and revulsion occasioned in me by the autopsy report were reflected in my countenance. And indeed, my brow felt somewhat clammy, as though coated with a film of sickly perspiration. Passing the paper back to Morris, I said:

"Yes, I am fine, though somewhat unsettled by the appalling contents of this report. You were correct in suggesting that nothing in the realm of mere fiction could surpass—or even equal—its sheer, overwhelming horror. The published accounts of the crime barely hinted at the awful nature of the atrocities."

"Well, of course, you can't print all the grisly details in a newspaper," said Morris. "They're far too shocking for the public. Even *I* could hardly bear to read the part about the poor child's mutilated face."

Here, he shook his head and grimaced in disgust before adding: "What kind of monster could do such a thing to another human being—let alone a little girl?"

By this point, the vertiginous feelings induced in me by the autopsy report had somewhat subsided, and I was able to think with greater clarity about the facts contained therein.

"In seeking to answer that all-important question," I remarked, "we must attempt to subdue our natural revulsion and regard the report with the same quality of professional detachment that a coroner's physician brings to his examination of a victim's corpse. Only in that way can the document serve as a source not merely of morbid interest, but of useful knowledge, offering clues as to the psychology, if not the identity, of the criminal. One fact, in particular, struck me as significant—the detail regarding the removal of the child's liver."

"I was wondering about that myself," interposed the young reporter, George Townsend. "The same thing happened to the first victim, the Dobbs girl."

"What do you make of it, Poe?" asked Morris, regarding me narrowly.

"Though somewhat hesitant to propose such an alarming hypothesis," I replied, "one possibility immediately suggests itself. It is conceivable that, among his other hideous propensities, the being who committed these atrocities possesses a taste for anthropophagy."

"For *what*?" the two men simultaneously exclaimed.

"Cannibalism," I declared, employing the more common terminology.

The effect of this utterance on Morris and Townsend was pronounced. Their jaws fell open and they gaped at me in thunderstruck silence.

"Though the mere thought of cannibalism is deeply offensive to civilized sensibilities," I continued, "an appetite for human flesh appears to be deeply ingrained in our common nature. The very ubiquity of the prohibitions against this activity suggests that there is a universal tendency to indulge in it. Among its practitioners, the liver is regarded as a particular delicacy. That the monster who butchered the two little girls took deliberate care in excising—and absconding with—this specific organ is indisputable. Indeed, to judge from the autopsy report, his removal of the liver was conducted with a precision that stood in marked contrast to the frenzied butchery of the other mutilations."

"Why, that's the most horrendous thing I've ever heard," exclaimed Morris. "I hope to hell you're wrong, Poe. For one thing, if you *aren't*, then that scoundrel Bennett must be right. The killer's got to be some damned Indian—more likely than not, that Big Chief What's-his-name at Barnum's museum."

"On the contrary," I said. "Should my theory prove correct, it would only confirm what I have already come to believe—to wit, that the killer cannot possibly be Chief Wolf Bear. While cannibalism is by no means unknown among the American Indians, it is abjured by the tribe to which Wolf Bear belongs—the Crow."

"Well, then," said Morris, "it must be some other redskinned savage."

"That the perpetrator of these hideous crimes is a savage cannot be disputed," I said. "By their very nature, they could only have been committed by a being lost to all sense of civilized humanity. As to the color of the killer's skin, however, the barbaric nature of his crimes allows for no definitive conclusions. As the history of the world makes all too abundantly clear, the primitive races of man have no monopoly on savage behavior. Atrocities of the most unspeakable sort are as likely to be committed by white men as by any of the other multifariously hued peoples who populate the globe, and who have soaked its soil with the blood of their fellow man from time immemorial."

"Yes, we're a murderous species, all right, there's no denying that," said Morris. "Still, this takes the cake. Worst case of butchery I've run across in forty years as a newspaper man. I tell you, boys, the longer I'm in this business, the more I despair of the whole damned human race."

A brief interval of silence ensued, during which Morris merely shook his head pensively, his countenance wrought into an intensely somber expression. At length—as though rousing himself from his ruminations—he rolled the autopsy report into a long, slender tube and tapped one end briskly against the open palm of his right hand.

"Well," he declared with a sigh, "as long as I *am* in this business, I'd better be getting back to work. You, too, Townsend."

At this remark, the latter turned to me with a wry half-smile on his countenance and, extending his right hand, said: " 'Be that word our sign of parting.' "

This line—as the reader is undoubtedly aware—was a verbatim quote from "The Raven." That Townsend had not merely admired my poem but had evidently committed it to memory was, of course, a source of intense gratification to me.

Shaking his proffered hand warmly, I expressed my pleasure at having made his acquaintance.

"Pleasure's all mine," said the exceptional young man. "Hope to see you again."

"Nothing would afford me greater happiness," I replied, little guessing at how soon—or under what appalling circumstances—we two would meet again.

CHAPTER SIX

ESS THAN TWENTY MINUTES LATER, I was seated at my desk in the offices of the *Broadway Journal*, Mr. Samuel Parker's narrative of his Western adventures open in front of me.

Since the arrival of my strange albino caller the previous evening, my mind had been largely preoccupied by matters bearing no direct relation to my professional activities. Now—as Morris had put it—it was time to get back to business. Putting aside all thoughts of the recent dreadful murder—as well as of the still-tantalizing question of Mr. Wyatt's mysterious document—I focused my attention entirely on the task at hand: to wit, critiquing Parker's book.

As always, my review—the composition of which occupied the remainder of the morning—was a model of critical objectivity and evenhandedness. I was at pains to point out the indisputable merits of the volume—primarily, the exceptionally fine paper on which it was printed, as well as the richness of its handsome Morocco binding—while carefully delineating its various deficiencies, which included its wooden style, incompetent organization, and overall amateurishness of both conception and execution.

Of its multitudinous flaws, perhaps the most flagrant was the author's wildly unconvincing treatment of Christopher "Kit" Carson, the celebrated scout and Indian fighter whom Parker allegedly encountered in the course of his journey. I emphasize the word "allegedly"; for his portrait of Carson was so idealized—so reverential—so extravagant in its claims—as to strain credulity, and make the reader wonder if their meeting had not been invented out of whole cloth.

In Parker's telling, Carson was a figure of nothing less than epic dimensions— a hero out of Homeric myth or Arthurian legend—a shining exemplar of manly virtue who combined the highest ideals of chivalric comportment with the lethal powers of the savage frontier. Sensitive, soft-spoken—a natural-born *gentilhomme* of inordinate physical grace and delicate, almost feminine, beauty— he was also possessed of extraordinary martial skills and a cool, indomitable courage: qualities that had earned him a universal reputation as one of the most fearsome warriors ever to roam the trackless forests of the West.

The deeds attributed to this paragon were of a sort to put the combined exploits of Herakles and Lancelot to shame. According to Parker, he had once seen Carson single-handedly dispatch a dozen Blackfoot Indians in a skirmish on the Shoshone River. On another occasion, though wounded in the shoulder by a Comanche arrow, Carson had supposedly stopped a runaway wagon by galloping alongside it on horseback, leaping from his saddle onto the driver's seat of the vehicle, and grabbing hold of the reins.

The most incredible of all the incidents recounted by Parker ostensibly occurred late one October afternoon, when the author and his traveling companions were camped on the bank of the Colorado River. All at once, they were approached by an enormous band of Apache braves, numbering—according to Parker's estimate—in the hundreds, and led by a chief whose face bore a long, jagged scar that ran from hairline to jaw. Though the Indians put on a show of friendship, it soon became clear that their intentions were anything but peaceful. As Parker and his companions stood by uncertainly, their anxiety growing more intense by the moment, Carson—who was acting as their guide—strode up to the fierce-looking chief and, in a soft, commanding voice, announced that he would give the Indians five minutes to depart from the camp.

"And if we do not?" said the chief.

Speaking in a perfectly matter-of-fact tone, as though he were merely stating the obvious, Carson replied: "Then I will kill you, and the rest of your braves, being deprived of their leader, will scatter."

For several exceedingly tense moments, the Indian merely glared at Carson, with a look that would have frozen the blood of a lesser man. At length, however—as though perceiving that Carson was not a man to issue idle threats—the chief leapt onto his pony, waved to his men, and led them in a gallop over the distant hills.

In my review, I cited this episode as a particularly flagrant example of the author's propensity for extreme exaggeration, if not outright fabrication. Its inclusion, so I argued, displayed not merely Parker's cavalier attitude toward the truth, but his utter contempt for the reader's intelligence. Who, after all, would be so gullible as to believe that a single man—even one as reportedly fearless as Carson—could "face down" an entire army of Apache warriors and cause them to retreat? For all his undoubted prowess and courage, even my erstwhile companion Colonel David Crockett would not have been capable of such a feat!

That Parker's narrative contained many thrilling passages I granted. In a work that purported to be strictly autobiographical, however, it was not merely excitement that the reader demanded but rigorous adherence to the truth. I concluded my review by stating that—as a highly colorful work of wilderness adventure on the order of Mr. Cooper's entertaining (if hopelessly juvenile) "Leatherstocking" saga—Parker's volume might serve as a suitable diversion for the undiscriminating reader. As a serious narrative of unembellished personal experience, however, it could only be regarded as a lamentable failure, if not a deliberate and cynical fraud.

Having completed my piece, I spent the remainder of the day seeing to the many tasks attendant upon the production of a literary journal. By the time I was finished, the dinner hour had arrived. As there was no point in my returning home before proceeding to my appointment with Wyatt, I decided to indulge myself in a meal at Sweeney's, a nearby restaurant where—according to a sign prominently displayed in the window—a complete supper could be obtained for fifteen cents. Following a surprisingly palatable repast of fricasseed chicken with dumplings, I then left the restaurant and directed my steps toward Wyatt's residence, which—as I knew from the card he had given me—was located on the north side of Washington Square Park.

The evening was one of singular tranquility and loveliness. The temperature had moderated, and the atmosphere was suffused with that faint, bluish tinge that heralds the onset of twilight. As I made my way through the park—which, owing to the lateness of the hour, was largely deserted—I was seized with an unexpectedly pleasurable sensation.

Partly, this derived from the picturesque charm of the setting. Though its history was steeped in suffering and horror—the grounds of the park having served, many years earlier, as a burial place for the many victims of the terrible yellow fever epidemic of 1798—Washington Square was now among the most gracious and fashionable neighborhoods in the city. My feelings on this occasion were such as to put me in mind of the transcendental rhapsodies of Mr. Emerson, who has written with such poetic (if overwrought) emotion of the sheer exhilaration inspired within him by the simple act of crossing a bare common at dusk.

Adding to my sense of pleasure, of course, was a circumstance of a far less rarefied nature—to wit, my awareness that I was soon to be in possession of a handsome sum of money that would go far toward relieving the straitened conditions of myself and my loved ones.

Having reached the northern border of the park, I crossed the cobblestoned street and paused for a moment in front of Wyatt's dwelling. It was an elegant, wide-fronted house, ornamented in the Greek Revival style that had been regarded as the height of architectural fashion during the preceding decade. Like its immediate neighbors—which it exactly resembled—it featured a handsome brick façade adorned with Grecian trim. A high stoop of white marble led up to a deeply recessed doorway framed by Ionic columns that supported a simple emblature.

Dusk was now gathering, and the warm light issuing from the two tall windows on either side of the doorway cast a welcoming glow onto the sidewalk. These windows, I was somewhat surprised to notice, were tightly closed, unlike those of the upper stories, which—as one would expect in midsummer— were open to their fullest extent.

Mounting the stoop, I paused before the imposing portal—took hold of the heavy brass knocker—and announced my presence with a succession of vigorous raps. In the hushed and tranquil atmosphere of the crepuscular street, the sound echoed loudly. In spite of this fact, however, my knocking brought no response from inside the house. I therefore tried again—but with equally futile results.

Puzzled—and more than a little vexed—by this unexpected development, I wondered if Wyatt had forgotten our appointment. In view of the extreme sense of urgency he had displayed the previous evening, however, I dismissed this thought as exceedingly unlikely. Besides, the light burning through the two front windows offered sufficient proof that someone was at home.

All at once, as I stood there in a state of irresolution, I became cognizant of a noise emanating from somewhere within the house—a noise so faint that, at first, I thought I might have imagined it. Placing one ear close to the door, I strained my auditory faculty to the utmost. After the lapse of several seconds, I heard it again—a ragged, tortured gurgle that caused the hairs of my nape to bristle.

It was the sound of a person in the throes of extreme, perhaps mortal, distress!

Reflexively, I grabbed hold of the doorknob and twisted it violently—but to no avail. The door was bolted from inside. As for the two front windows, they were set at too great a distance from the stoop for me to reach.

Perhaps, I thought, I could find some means of ingress from the rear. Dashing down onto the street, I rounded the corner of the building and immediately spied a narrow mews lane leading to Wyatt's backyard, which was surrounded by a waist-high wooden fence. Clambering over this enclosure, I hurried to the rear door of the house and tried the knob, only to find that it, too, was locked.

For an instant, I was filled with an acute sense of helplessness and frustration. All at once, as I cast my gaze about, I saw something that brought a grunt of satisfaction to my lips. There were two first-story windows. One of these—like its counterparts at the front of the house—was shut tight. The lower sash of the other, however, had been partially raised.

Here, at last, was a possible point of entry. The problem now facing me was the relative inaccessibility of this window, whose ledge was set at a distance of approximately eight feet from the ground. Fortunately, while this obstacle might have proved insuperable to a lesser man, I was in possession of the requisite physical resources to overcome it. Nature had endowed me with exceptional athletic abilities. In my boyhood, my prodigious skills as a runner—leaper—and swimmer—had won the admiration of all who knew me. Though my adult occupations were, by and large, of a sedentary character, I still retained a considerable share of my youthful strength and agility.

Now, positioning myself beneath the open window, I bent my legs and sprang upward with arms outstretched. Grabbing hold of the ledge, I hoisted myself up and, in another moment, was standing inside Wyatt's house.

The chamber in which I found myself was shrouded in darkness, though it appeared to be a small study. Through the open doorway, I could see the glow of lamplight emanating from a farther room. At that instant, from the same direction as the light, there came drifting through the silent house the unnerving, liquid moan I had detected while standing outside.

With the intensest anxiety, I hurried from the study and made my way down a long, shadowy corridor that terminated at the entrance of a brightly lit room. For a moment, I feared to cross the threshold, so filled was I with a sense of overpowering premonitory dread. At length, subduing the extreme agitation of spirit that threatened to unman me, I drew a deep breath and stepped inside.

My immediate reaction to the sight that greeted me was one of stunned incomprehension. The room was a large, comfortably furnished parlor. In the center of the floor stood a handsome Chippendale armchair. A figure was seated—or rather, sprawled—in the chair, his head thrown back, his arms resting on the curved wooden supports, his legs fully outstretched on the carpet.

At first—before my initial stupefaction was replaced by a horrified realization of the truth—I was struck with the wildly fanciful notion that I was looking at the person of Mr. Joe Pentland, the celebrated clown who performed at Barnum's museum and whose distinctive appearance consisted of a white costume mottled with bright patches of red—a powder-white face with a leering red grin painted over his lips—a fiery red headpiece worn atop his skull—and oversized red gloves.

When, after the lapse of several seconds, the reality of what I was seeing finally smote me, it required the greatest possible effort on my part to prevent myself from swooning. The personage in the armchair was not Joe Pentland, decked out in his gaudy red-and-white costume. It was none other than William Wyatt, and the crimson substance that splattered his clothing—coated his head—smeared his countenance—and imbrued his hands—was his own copious blood. It was clear at a glance that the poor man had not only sustained the gravest possible injuries, but had been subjected to tortures of the most hideous variety.

As the reader will recall, the mere perusal of Rosalie Edmonds's autopsy report had elicited feelings of intense dismay within my bosom. The violence of my reaction to the ghastly spectacle now confronting me may therefore be easily imagined. My brain reeled, and I grew deadly sick. I did not, however, lapse into insensibility. At the very instant that my vision began to dim, the fearfully mutilated victim emitted another of his feeble, bubbling groans. The heart-rending—indescribably piteous—sound roused me to action. I hurried to his side, determined to offer him whatever succor I could, while his poor, savaged body clung to the last vestiges of life.

That Wyatt was poised on the very brink of death there could be no doubt. Indeed—in view of the nature and extent of his injuries—it seemed miraculous that he was still alive at all. He had, to begin with, been scalped. In place of his long, flowing mane of silky white hair, there was now a raw and pulsating dome of ragged tissue—oozing blood—and quivering veins. His arms—which, from a distance, had appeared to be resting comfortably on their supports—were, I now perceived, tightly secured to the chair with leather thongs. All five fingers of his right hand, along with the thumb of the left, had been sliced off.

Blood bubbled from his partially open mouth—the result, so I initially assumed, of the internal hemorrhaging caused by the two gaping punctures in his chest. The sheer volume of blood streaming from these savage stab wounds made it sufficiently clear that he was beyond any hope of salvation.

Given the extremity of his condition, I was at a loss as to how to assist him. All at once, as I stared helplessly down at him, his eyelids fluttered open and he fixed his gaze on me. He appeared to recognize me at once. He began to move his lips, producing a thick, gurgling sound that I could not comprehend. Thinking I might better understand him if I held my ear directly to his mouth, I took a step closer to the chair. As I did so, the sole of my shoe descended on something that felt like a lump of raw meat. Reflexively, I pulled my foot back and glanced downward. An instinctive cry of revulsion burst from my lips, and I saw in a flash the reason for Wyatt's copious oral hemorrhaging and garbled speech.

The poor man's tongue had been severed and was lying on the carpet!

A wave of nausea rose from the pit of my stomach. Struggling to suppress it, I bent my ear close to his still-working lips.

"He—" he was saying. "He—"

It seemed clear to me that, with his dying breath, he was attempting to convey some crucial intelligence about his murderer—perhaps even the fiend's identity.

"He?" I said. "Who is *he?*"

So rapidly was life draining from him, however, that he could not complete his intended communication. At that instant, his right foot began to bang spasmodically on the floor, signaling the onset of his death throes.

A moment later, a ghastly rattle issued from deep inside his throat, his eyes rolled back in their sockets, a violent paroxysm convulsed his body, and William Wyatt subsided—mercifully, I could not help but feel—into death.

PART TWO

Man of the West

Chapter Seven

I T WAS TRUE THAT I barely knew William Wyatt. I had seen and spoken to him only once, for the duration of an hour, in the parlor of my home on the evening previous to his murder. Even from that brief encounter, however, I had derived a fair conception of his personality.

He had impressed me as a man of singular dignity and high moral character. His anomalous condition had clearly acquainted him firsthand with the deplorable realities of human ignorance and bigotry. And yet, his experiences had not, to all appearances, embittered him. That so estimable a being had been subjected to tortures of such extreme—such surpassing—cruelty struck me as an injustice almost too grotesque for words. That his death would serve—within hours of its occurrence—to foment even further acts of violence and barbarity only rendered the situation even more inexpressibly tragic.

No sooner had Wyatt exhaled his last, agonized breath than I dashed to the front of the house—unbolted and threw open the door—and, cupping my hands to my mouth, shouted for help.

Several months prior to this time, the state legislature had abolished the city's antiquated police system, which consisted largely of a citizens' security force made up of poorly paid laborers who pursued their ordinary vocations during the day and patrolled the streets after dark in distinctive leather helmets.

In place of this obsolete army of amateur watchmen (or "leatherheads," as they were derisively called by the populace), a professional force was established, known popularly as the "Star Police" for the official, stelliform badges worn on their outer coats.

As chance would have it, one of these officers was perambulating the park at that very moment and, hearing my cry, came rushing to my aid. He was a squat, compactly built young man with small, rather porcine eyes that widened to an almost comical extent when—in reply to his query as to what was the matter—I gasped out the word: "murder!"

Grabbing him by the arm, I then hurried him inside. At his first glimpse of the horribly mutilated figure sprawled lifelessly in the chair, his mouth fell open and the color drained from his face. Ordering me to "stay put" while he went to summon help, he then spun on his heels and raced from the house. The instant he was gone, I staggered toward a richly upholstered armchair that stood in a far corner of the room and, with a tremulous groan, collapsed onto the cushioned seat, the terrible strains of the evening having at last depleted me of my final reserves of strength.

An hour later, I was still occupying the chair. By then, Wyatt's parlor was crowded with people, who had arrived on the scene in response to the young officer's summons. Including the latter—whose cognomen, I had learned, was Boyle—there were a half-dozen policemen in all. The highest-ranking of these was a captain named Dunnegan, a tall, powerfully constructed, coarse-complexioned man whose visage was wrought into a perpetual scowl and whose every utterance was a harsh, commanding bark.

The coroner, an appropriately cadaverous-looking fellow named Coates, was also present, along with a portly physician, Dr. Lyle Honeycutt, who served in the capacity of medical examiner. These two had just completed their inspection of poor Wyatt's body, which—having been removed from the chair and laid out on the carpet—was now mercifully covered with a white bedsheet upon whose blood-spotted surface a half-dozen iridescent-green flies were in the process of exploring.

To relieve the stifling closeness of the room—whose oppressive atmosphere was rendered even more insufferable by the faint but unmistakable foetor beginning to reek from the corpse—Captain Dunnegan had ordered that all the windows be thrown open. Seated not far from one of these casements, I was cognizant of a steadily increasing hubbub directly outside Wyatt's dwelling, where a crowd of people—composed largely, I surmised, of that intensely morbid species who descend, vulturelike, upon the scene of every horrendous crime—had been growing in magnitude since the arrival of the police.

On several different occasions, fingers would clutch at the outer ledge of the window, and one or another particularly brazen young curiosity-seeker—evidently supported on the shoulders of a comrade—would raise his head above the sill and peer into the parlor. When Captain Dunnegan noticed this, he would roar at the fellow, denouncing him as a "damned Peeping Tom" and ordering him to get down from the window at once. One young scamp, ignoring this command, had his fingers smartly rapped with Dunnegan's "billy club," causing him to release his hold on the window ledge and go tumbling back into the crowd.

Shortly after Captain Dunnegan's arrival, he had questioned me extensively about my discovery of the body. I had detailed for him the sequence of events leading up to that awful moment, beginning with Wyatt's appearance at my dwelling the previous evening and continuing with my trip to his residence at the preappointed hour following my workday. In a succinct yet thorough manner, I described my futile knockings at the front door—the unnerving noise I had detected from within—my entrance through the open rear window—and the hideous spectacle I had encountered in the parlor.

When, at length, I had concluded my recitation, the captain—who had been regarding me intently through narrowed eyes—demanded to know the precise nature of the document that I had been asked to inspect. I informed him that I could shed very little light on the matter, Wyatt having been exceedingly evasive as to its contents. I only knew that its author had ostensibly been a man of great repute and that, consequently, the document possessed a substantial, if indeterminate, value—potentially making it, I added, an irresistible lure to any felon who knew of its existence.

This reply had caused Dunnegan's habitual scowl to grow even more pronounced.

"Well, this wasn't no burglary, that's for damned sure," he had said. "Why, just look at this room. Not a thing out of place. Same with the rest of the house."

It was indeed the case that the parlor showed not the slightest sign of having been ransacked. On the contrary. The sheer fury of the violence inflicted on the victim was in marked contrast to the perfect orderliness of the surroundings, which had not, to the visible eye, been disturbed in the least degree. The luxurious furnishings and elegant appointments seemed as harmoniously arranged as if a housemaid had just finished tidying up the premises. Were it not for the fearfully mutilated corpse itself—and the ugly bloodstains darkening the carpet and defiling the chair to which the victim had been bound—it would have been impossible to tell that a crime of any sort had occurred within the room.

"Plain butchery, that's what it is," continued Captain Dunnegan. "And I know who done it, too. That damned scalping fiend, that's who. He's struck again—and not more than two days after his last inhuman murder!"

"So it would seem," I stated in a noncommittal tone.

Before returning to the investigation, Dunnegan had made it clear that—as he might have further questions to put to me—I was not, under any circumstances, to leave the premises without first receiving his express permission to do so. I assured him that I would remain precisely where I was until I was no longer needed.

The reader will hardly be surprised to learn that the exceedingly trying events of the preceding few hours had exacted an enormous toll on my sensitively organized constitution. My nerves were thoroughly unstrung, and I was suffering from a sense of the deepest mental and emotional fatigue. In view of this fact, the prospect of prolonging my repose in the comfort of the luxuriously upholstered armchair was far from displeasing. Partly from exhaustion—but mostly to avoid the sight of poor Wyatt's ghastly remains—I had shut my eyes and leaned my head backward. Almost at once—in spite of the growing tumult of voices outside the window and of the bustle of police activity within the room—I had sunk into a species of half-conscious lethargy.

How long I remained in this stuporous condition, I cannot say with precision. Gradually, however, I became dimly aware that someone was speaking my name in a low, urgent tone and shaking me gently by the arm. Sitting bolt upright, I looked around in confusion, momentarily uncertain as to my whereabouts. In another instant, my head cleared, and I found myself gazing up into the countenance of Mr. George Townsend, the young reporter I had met early in the day during my visit to the offices of the *Daily Mirror*.

The distressing events of the evening had so wrought upon my nerves that the mere sight of an acquaintance—even one as barely familiar to me as young Townsend—filled me with an inordinate sense of gratitude. Shaking him by the hand, I asked how he came to be there, no other representative of the press having as yet arrived on the scene.

In reply, he explained that he had been working late in the office—as was his wont—when news of the latest calamity reached his ear. He had immediately dropped what he was doing and, securing a hansom cab, had offered the driver a bonus of fifty cents above his normal fare to speed him uptown.

"They'll be swarming all over this place soon enough, don't you worry," he said, referring to his professional rivals. "Word is spreading though the city like a brushfire. But tell me, Mr. Poe, what on earth are *you* doing here?"

I informed him that it was I who had first come upon the victim's body. Hearing this, he grew very excited and—removing a notepad and a stubby lead pencil from the side pocket of his coat—perched himself on the edge of a nearby sofa and began to ask me questions. For the second time that evening, I found myself providing a detailed account of my dealings with Wyatt and my *rôle* in the discovery of his murder. As I spoke, Townsend scribbled furiously in his pad, taking down every word I uttered.

I had nearly arrived at the conclusion of my narrative when I grew cognizant of a stir in the room, as if some new and disruptive element had been suddenly introduced onto the scene. Townsend also became aware of it, and—suspending our interview—we turned simultaneously toward the source of the disturbance.

Something—or rather, some*one*—had indeed entered the room: a tall, unusually narrow-shouldered gentleman, very respectably dressed, who had stridden directly up to Captain Dunnegan and was now addressing him in the most indignant tones. His back being toward us, we could not perceive the countenance of the stranger; but his heavy Scottish accent, no less than the vehemence of his harangue, served to render his identity sufficiently plain.

"Bennett," muttered Townsend with a frown.

James Gordon Bennett, publisher of the *New York Herald*, was one of the city's most prominent citizens, enjoying a degree of celebrity equal to that of such luminaries as John Jacob Astor—Cornelius Vanderbilt—and P. T. Barnum himself. Though I had never encountered him in person, I—like all but the most benighted denizens of the metropolis—was familiar with the substance of his remarkable life story: how, as a young boy in Scotland, he had trained for the priesthood, until, chancing upon a copy of Benjamin Franklin's *Autobiography*, he had abandoned all thought of a clerical life and had emigrated to America to seek his fortune—how he had arrived in the New World as a friendless and penniless lad of nineteen—how, after more than a decade of bitter struggle, he had revolutionized the practice of journalism by establishing the *Herald*, the first of the so-called "penny papers" that catered to the common man by emphasizing stories of a spicy, not to say sensational, nature.

Apart from the typesetting and printing of his gazette, Bennett had initially performed every task necessary to its publication entirely by himself: collecting the news, writing the contents, selling the papers, and soliciting the advertisements. For years, he had devoted a minimum of eighteen hours each working day to his enterprise. Through his extraordinary diligence and almost superhuman capacity for hard work, he had at length achieved a level of financial success surpassing even that of his great model, Dr. Franklin.

Even now, though free of any mere pecuniary necessity for such unremitting labor, he maintained an active hand not merely in the supervision of his paper, but in its day-to-day production. Indeed, he personally continued to investigate and report on those stories that he deemed of particular significance or interest—a circumstance that undoubtedly accounted for his presence at this very moment.

From all that I had heard of Bennett, he was a person of unimpeachable honesty in his business dealings. Perhaps unsurprisingly, however—given the ferocious determination that was a hallmark of his character—he was reputed to be an exceedingly difficult personality: a man who possessed a notoriously short temper—who brooked no disagreement with his wishes—and who did not scruple to express himself in the most blunt, if not arrogant, terms. This overbearing aspect of his character was now very much in evidence as he spoke to Captain Dunnegan.

"Why, it's an outrage, man! The people won't stand for it! How many more have to die before you do your job and arrest the culprit?"

"We're doing our best," replied the police captain, straining—to judge from the distinct note of tension in his voice—to control his own fractious temper. "We can't make an arrest without a suspect."

"What of that bloodthirsty savage at Barnum's museum?" demanded Bennett.

"We talked to Barnum yesterday," said Dunnegan. "He swears the redskin didn't have nothing to do with it."

"And you believed him?" cried Bennett in an incredulous tone. "The world's greatest charlatan? The man who proudly calls himself the Prince of Humbugs?"

"He sounded truthful enough to me," Dunnegan replied somewhat defensively.

"Well, it seems Barnum was right about one thing," said Bennett with a derisive snort. "There really *is* a sucker born every minute. I tell you, Dunnegan, this city's ready to explode. There are plenty of angry citizens out there, and they'll take matters into their own hands if something isn't done soon."

"Hard to get anything done while I'm standing here gabbing with you," said Dunnegan. "So if you'll excuse me, Mr. Bennett."

This conversation had occurred while Dunnegan stood in a corner of the room, his back to the wall. Bennett, who had positioned himself directly in front of the police captain, was now forced to move aside in order to allow the latter to go about his business. As Bennett did so, his head turned in my direction, and he noticed me for the first time.

"Who is that fellow?" he asked Dunnegan.

"Name's Poe. He's the one who found the body."

"Poe, eh?" said Bennett. "Well, well."

Turning on his heel, he strode across the room and halted before the arm-chair in which I remained seated. For the first time, I found myself face-to-face with the celebrated newspaperman.

The countenance of Mr. Bennett was one of the least prepossessing I had ever beheld. His head was of immense size—his complexion absolutely bloodless—his nose excessively crooked and disproportionately large in relation to his other features. His thin-lipped mouth wore a habitually pinched expression, and his teeth, which revealed themselves when he spoke, were wildly uneven.

Most disconcerting of all, however, were his dark brown eyes. As much as I had heard of Bennett, I had never been aware, until that moment, that he suffered from an acute case of that ocular defect known as *strabismus*. In short, he was badly cross-eyed. Such was the sheer, imposing force of his personality, however, that even this affliction (which often endows its sufferers with an unfortunately comical appearance) did nothing to detract from the dominating aura that he emanated as he loomed over me.

Reaching into his inside breast pocket, Bennett withdrew a cigar, took a moment to ignite it, then positioned it in a corner of his mouth.

"So you're Poe, eh?" he said, his irregular teeth clamped on the cigar.

I acknowledged the accuracy of this observation with a small nod of the head.

"Same fellow who helped Barnum solve those red rose murders last year?"

This remark—as the reader is no doubt aware—referred to the ghastly string of killings which had held the city in the grip of terror the preceding spring, and which had been characterized by a particularly grotesque *modus operandi*, the mutilated victims being left with their hands removed and a long-stemmed red rose inserted between their teeth. That I had merely assisted Barnum in the solution of these crimes—as Bennett's comment had implied—was a misconception enthusiastically promoted by the showman himself, who, in his cheerfully shameless manner, had contrived to take the lion's share of the credit for our joint achievement in his interviews with the press.

"I was, indeed, the man, who—in partnership with Mr. Barnum—was responsible for uncovering the perpetrator of those atrocities," I now said to Bennett, stating the matter in a far more accurate way.

"How convenient," said Bennett in a voice laden with irony. "How very convenient."

"Why, whatever do you mean?" I exclaimed, bristling at the insinuating tenor of his remark.

"Oh, nothing really. Only it seems a wee coincidental to me that the first person on the scene is one of Barnum's cronies. Why, if I were a suspicious man, I might think he dispatched you here himself, to cover up the evidence before the police arrived."

So dumbfounding—so sheerly outrageous—was this statement that, for a moment, I was rendered absolutely mute. Even when, after the lapse of several seconds, I recovered my powers of speech, my sense of indignation was so extreme that I could not reply without sputtering badly.

"I do not hesitate to say, Mr. Bennett," I declared, "that I take the greatest possible exception to your comment. To intimate that I was here on a mission such as you describe—one which involves the deliberate obstruction of justice—is not merely insulting, but slanderous. Your position of power and prominence in the city does not entitle you to level wild and baseless charges against whomever you wish. On the contrary, it imposes a particular obligation on you to maintain the highest standards of fairness in your dealings with others—standards which, sadly, you have violated in a most egregious manner by falsely accusing me of such unethical, if not criminal, behavior."

The sheer rhetorical force of this rebuke produced a marked effect on Bennett. His eyes appeared to grow even more crossed than before, and he raised both hands, palms outward, in a gesture of surrender, as if urging me to desist from any further remonstrations.

"All right, all right," he said. "Perhaps I've done you a disservice. Tell you what." Reaching inside his coat, he extracted a notepad and pencil and made ready to write. "Why don't you give me the whole story just as it happened, and I'll see that your version gets printed word for word in tomorrow's *Herald*."

Throughout my exchange with Bennett, young Townsend had remained perched on the sofa, observing us in silence. Now it was his turn to spring to his feet. Interposing himself between Bennett and me, he exclaimed to the former: "I'm afraid he can't do that, Mr. Bennett. He's already promised to give me an exclusive interview."

Cocking an eyebrow at Townsend, Bennett said: "And who the devil are you?"

"George Townsend of the *Mirror.*"

"Ah," Bennett sneered. "One of Morris's flunkies." Then, turning his skewed gaze on me, he demanded: "Is this true, Poe?"

In point of fact, I had not made any such explicit promise to Townsend. At the same time—and in spite of the potential advantages to be derived from cultivating the goodwill of a figure like Bennett—I had no wish to accommodate the latter in any way whatsoever. Aside from his scurrilous imputations regarding my presence at the crime scene, he bore an unmitigated animosity toward my good friend P. T. Barnum. Moreover, I felt a strong bond of allegiance both to Townsend—who had displayed such warm admiration for my poetry—and to his employer, Mr. Morris, who had so generously agreed to take my satirical attack on C. A. Cartwright.

"Mr. Townsend is correct," I therefore replied to Bennett. "He is the sole representative of the press with whom I intend to share the full particulars of my story."

"I see," said Bennett, plucking the cigar from his mouth. "All right, then, gentlemen. Have it your way. I'll manage just fine without your help. Believe me, I was covering murders in this town while you laddies were still suckling at your mothers' teats."

The vulgarity of this remark—especially coming from the lips of a man who had once pursued a religious calling—was nothing less than stupefying. Turning on his heels, Bennett stalked across the room to where the coroner and his examining physician were conferring beside the still-draped body of Wyatt. Up until that moment, Bennett had not viewed the victim's remains. Now—after exchanging a few words with Coroner Coates and Dr. Honeycutt—Bennett suddenly knelt down, grabbed the blood-stained sheet by a corner, and swiftly drew it away from the butchered cadaver.

The spectacle presented by Wyatt's hideously savaged corpse had lost none of its power to shock. If anything, the condition of the body—the denuded skull with its coating of clotted gore; the gaping, blood-choked mouth; the fearfully mangled hands—had assumed an even more loathsome aspect in the hours since I had first come upon the dying man.

Far from having become in any way inured to the dreadful sight, I was immediately overcome with a sensation of vertigo even more intense than that which had initially seized me. The room swam, and I felt the blood drain from my countenance.

"Mr. Poe, are you all right?" asked Townsend.

"I confess," I replied in a tremulous voice, "that I am feeling somewhat shaky from the cumulative strains of this evening."

"Maybe it's time for you to leave," said Townsend. "I'll be happy to walk you home. We can finish our talk on the way."

Acceding to his suggestion, I immediately sought out Captain Dunnegan. I found him in Wyatt's study, where he was issuing orders to several of his underlings, including Officer Boyle, the young patrolman who had first responded to my frantic cries for help. Begging his pardon for the interruption, I told him that—if my presence was no longer required—I was eager to return to my abode.

My extreme state of bodily and emotional debility must have been palpable; for, upon hearing my request, Dunnegan consented without hesitation, stipulating only that I make myself available to him in the days to come should the need arise for further questioning. To this demand I readily agreed. Then, with Townsend at my side, I proceeded to the front of the house and made my exit.

Upon emerging, I was astonished to discover that the number of people gathered outside Wyatt's dwelling was far greater than I had supposed. In the fitful and garish lustre of the gas lamps, the milling crowd appeared to consist of perhaps two hundred people, at the very least. They occupied the steps leading up to the doorway—filled the sidewalk—packed the street—and spilled into the park itself. At their first glimpse of Townsend and me—the only people to have so far emerged from the interior of the house—a chorus of shouted remarks arose from the throng.

"Look! Someone's coming out!"

"Tell us what happened!"

"Was the victim scalped?"

"Did he really have his tongue cut out?"

"Do the police know who did it?"

"Was it Barnum's redskin?"

From the nature of these and other comments, it was clear that a host of rumors—some consistent with the facts, others of a wildly fanciful nature—had rapidly spread through the assemblage. Keeping our heads low and ignoring the many strident queries directed at us, Townsend and I worked our way down the front steps, pushed through the jostling crowd, and bent our steps in the direction of my residence.

The night was clear, and a pleasant breeze stirred the air. Freed from the grim—the charnel-house—confines of Wyatt's parlor, I felt immeasurably improved. As Townsend and I proceeded downtown, however, I became aware of a phenomenon that produced a tremor of anxiety within my bosom. At sporadic intervals, small parties of men came hurrying past us, all headed in the same direction as we. Many of them had objects clutched in their hands. On one or two occasions, in the glow of the street lamps, I caught fleeting glimpses of some of these items. They seemed to be weapons of various kinds—clubs, wooden boards, even (so it appeared) firearms!

My apprehensions intensified as we continued down Broadway. Townsend and I were only a block or two away from Ann Street when we drew to a sudden halt. In the near distance, we could hear a riotous commotion. A lurid glow illuminated the night, as from a multitude of torches.

The terrible realization smote us at the same moment, causing us to turn to each other and simultaneously exclaim the identical words:

"They are attacking Barnum's museum!"

CHAPTER EIGHT

THE REALIZATION THAT MY FRIEND'S establishment was under assault struck me with the shock of a galvanic battery. The debilitating effects of that long and intensely trying night vanished in an instant. A sense of overpowering urgency infused every fibre of my being. Without another word, I darted off in the direction of the nearby disturbance, leaving Townsend to catch up as best he could.

A moment later, I came within view of Barnum's building. The spectacle that greeted me caused my heart to quail with dismay. Drawing to a halt in front of a darkened barbershop located catercorner to the museum, I took refuge in the doorway and surveyed the scene.

Few things in this world are more deeply appalling than the sight of an immense—infuriated—and implacable mob. Viewed from a certain perspective, even the most sheerly destructive forces of nature—the great whirlpool of the Maelström—the mighty avalanche of the Himalayas—the raging typhoon of the South Seas—have about them a distinct element of the awesomely sublime. The same cannot be said for a mob. On the contrary, it is hard to conceive of a more debased and repellent phenomenon than a throng of human beings who—relinquishing every trace of their God-given individuality—have merged into a brutish and mindless entity for the sole purpose of wreaking hatred and havoc.

The horde now gathered before Barnum's museum was even more unnerving than most. To begin with, it was of uncommon magnitude, comprising—

according to my estimate—no fewer than five hundred people. I had, of course, seen whole droves of people assembled there before. Even the largest of these, however—such as the crowds that had turned out the previous year to view Barnum's highly touted Giant Sacred Beetle of Lost Atlantis—could not compare in size to the present throng.

The prevailing character of the assemblage was also in marked contrast to the gay and generally prosperous crowds that normally flocked to Barnum's museum. So far as I could see, the mob was composed entirely of grown men, whose ragged dress and uncouth demeanor identified them as members of the same unsavory species I had observed outside the building on the previous afternoon. Their upturned countenances were grimy and coarse-featured—their mouths twisted into grimaces of sheer malice—their eyes aflame with a rabid intensity. Many appeared to be in an advanced stage of inebriation. Dozens were brandishing weapons—cudgels, pitchforks, mallets, axe handles. From their hate-contorted lips there issued a hellish cacophony of ugly catcalls—angry shouts—and shocking obscenities.

Adding to the demonic quality of the scene was the multitude of torches that bathed the mob in a ghastly—an infernal—light. Observing the red-lit sea of humanity from my refuge in the barbershop doorway, I was put in mind of certain of the grotesque conceptions of the medieval visionary Hieronymus Bosch, whose paintings of the teeming armies of hell stand among the most startling *phantasmagoria* ever to spring from a human brain.

From my vantage point near the outer perimeter of the crowd, I could easily overhear the excited chatter of various individuals. I was amazed not merely at the speed with which news of the latest atrocity had spread, but at the wild distortions it had undergone in transmission. One fellow swore that the victim was a two-year-old child, so horribly butchered as to scarcely retain any semblance of humanity. Another claimed it was a nubile maiden who had not only been scalped but defiled in the most unspeakable manner. Still a third insisted that the killer had annihilated an entire household of people!

As I stood there listening to these rumors, Townsend came panting up beside me. "Good Lord," he gasped. "This looks mighty serious!"

Before I could reply, my attention was riveted by a movement on the museum's second-floor balcony, from which—during the day—Barnum's egregious brass band sent its ear-rending discord cascading onto Broadway. In the light of the torches, I saw a figure emerge from the shadows of the building and step onto the balcony.

It was Barnum.

From my long acquaintance with the showman, I knew him to be a man of unparalleled audacity, with a nearly unbounded faith in his own powers of persuasion. And indeed, that faith was not wholly unjustified. In the course of his singular career, he had managed to convince vast numbers of otherwise rational human beings of the most palpable absurdities: that an elderly Negro woman, for example, was the 161-year-old former nurse of George Washington—that a mummified monkey with a fish tail attached to its bottom was the authentic remains of a mermaid—and so on.

The challenge now facing Barnum, however, promised to test his oratorical skills to the utmost. It was one thing, after all, to impose even such a colossal hoax as "Joice Heth" or the "Feejee Mermaid" on an all-too-credulous public. It was quite another to persuade a mob of armed and hate-inflamed ruffians to disband peacefully—as the showman now evidently intended to do.

Stepping to the wrought-iron railing that surrounded the balcony, he raised both arms like a sovereign enjoining his subjects to silence. As, by slow degrees, the rabble grew aware of his presence, the wild clamor of their voices began to subside. In the unwonted hush that descended on the great thoroughfare, Barnum began to speak.

"Look here, you men!" he declared at a resounding volume. "Stop this nonsense at once and get back to your homes! Why, this is outrageous, perfectly outrageous! Most disgraceful behavior I've ever witnessed! Never heard of anything like it! Oh yes, I suppose they do it in Europe from time to time—storm the Bastille, lay siege to a castle, that sort of thing. But this is America, God bless her, in case you haven't noticed. We don't go around attacking other folks' property in the middle of the night!"

"We want that murdering redskin!" interrupted a strident voice from the crowd. "He's done his last killing!"

"Yeah," shouted another. "Hand the son of a bitch over, Barnum!"

"So you fine gentlemen are here for Chief Wolf Bear, eh?" the showman replied with a distinct note of disdain in his voice. "Well, you're more than welcome to attend his performances during regular business hours. Come back tomorrow, doors open to the public from sunrise to ten P.M., admission to all the attractions of the house a mere twenty-five cents! Just make sure to leave your weapons at home! The American Museum is a place of wholesome family entertainment. No lewd behavior, alcoholic beverages, or implements of destruction allowed on the premises. And now, gentlemen, if you'll be so kind as to—"

He did not have the opportunity to complete this remarkable peroration.

All at once, a rotten tomato flew up from the crowd and struck him with a *splat* on the chest. As though awaiting this signal, a dozen more of the cowardly ruffians let fly with various small projectiles, viciously pelting the showman.

Retreating a few steps, Barnum raised both forearms crossways to shield his face from the barrage. His self-protective gesture, however, proved futile. Just then, a rock as large as a grown man's fist came hurtling upward and struck him on the head, knocking off his hat and sending him tumbling backward.

The showman's collapse sent the rabble into a frenzy. With a savage roar, they surged forward, those in the foremost ranks of the mob vanishing into the building.

"He is hurt!" I cried, standing on tiptoe in a vain attempt to gain a view of the fallen showman. "We must go to his assistance at once!"

"We'll never make it inside," replied my companion, grimly regarding the howling swarm now forcing its way into the main entrance of the museum.

My principal sensation at that instant was of an overpowering helplessness. To be within such close proximity to my injured friend and yet unable to help him filled me with a torturous sense of frustration. For some moments, I felt paralyzed beyond the possibility of making any exertion.

All at once, I was seized with an idea. Grabbing Townsend by the arm, I drew him from the protective shelter of the doorway and cried: "Come! I know another way in!"

Unseen by any members of the rampaging mob—whose attention was entirely focused on the front of the building—I led Townsend across Broadway, then guided him down the north end of the museum, toward the inconspicuous side doorway that Barnum and I had utilized that morning. It was hidden in shadow, being situated beyond the range of the flickering street lamps that cast small pools of light on the otherwise night-shrouded sidewalk. Recalling its approximate location, I was able to find it with little difficulty.

Pausing before the door, I grabbed hold of the knob, uttering a silent prayer that I would find it unlatched. Alas, my supplications proved unavailing. Emitting a bitter oath of disappointment, I turned to Townsend and said: "It is no use. The door is locked."

"Not to worry," my companion whispered in reply. An instant later, I heard the unmistakable sound of a phosphorous match being struck. A light flared in the darkness, illuminating the person of the young reporter. "Here," he said, holding out the flaming match.

Taking it from his hand, I held it aloft while he dug one hand into his trouser pocket and withdrew a penknife. He then opened the blade—lowered himself to one knee before the door—and commenced to operate on the lock. The match-flame was just beginning to singe the tips of my thumb and forefinger when I heard a sharp metallic click, followed by a self-satisfied grunt from the redoubtable young man. Springing to his feet, he gave the knob a decisive twist, and the door swung in upon its hinges.

"Little trick I learned from an old 'crib-cracker' named Coleman," he said, closing his knife and returning it to his pocket.

"You do your felonious mentor proud," I said, extinguishing the match with a vigorous shake of my hand. "Your dexterity would be the envy of the most seasoned housebreaker."

We then slipped inside the building and hurriedly made our way down the narrow flight of steps leading to the basement.

My plan, insofar as I had formulated one, was to traverse the length of the basement to the opposite end, where the main stairwell leading up into the museum lobby was situated. Once we were upstairs, we would make our way to the second-floor balcony. The pandemonium of the scene would serve to camouflage our presence; for even if we were noticed by any members of the mob, they would simply assume that we were fellow participants in the riot.

As I proceeded along the cramped and mazelike hallway, however, it occurred to me that we might do well to furnish ourselves with weapons, partly for the purpose of self-protection, partly so that we would better blend in with the horde of heavily armed ruffians into whose midst we now proposed to insinuate ourselves. Pausing, I shared my idea with Townsend, who readily concurred. As we continued our progress down the dimly lit hallway, we therefore scanned the stored piles of exotic artifacts lining the walls. In short order, we had equipped ourselves with suitable weapons—Townsend with a three-pronged trident of the sort employed by Roman gladiators; myself with an exact facsimile of the savage-looking Polynesian war-club used to slay Captain Cook.

Moments later, we arrived at the foot of the main stairwell and rapidly ascended to the first floor. The scene that greeted us was, if anything, even more chaotic than I had anticipated. Rioters by the score continued to pour into the museum entranceway and swarm up the grand central staircase, evidently in search of Chief Wolf Bear, who—like the great majority of Barnum's human attractions—resided in a kind of dormitory on the topmost floor of the building.

Many other members of the mob, however, had broken away from the main body and were running wildly through the museum, seemingly bent on wreaking as much havoc as possible. Shouting at the top of their voices and swinging their weapons about their heads, they were engaged in the most random and gratuitous acts of vandalism: demolishing the grand cosmoramic display of the Conflagration of Moscow—beheading the waxworks figures in the Assassination of Julius Caesar tableau—shattering the working, scale-model replica of Niagara Falls. Their cries of savage exultation as they conducted their rampage caused the blood to run cold in my veins.

Still—apart from offering a silent, fervent prayer for the prompt intervention of the police—there was nothing that either Townsend or I could do to prevent the destruction of Barnum's property. In any case, our first concern was for the well-being of the showman himself. Hurrying toward the main staircase, we raised our weapons above our heads and—with a wild shout—plunged into the torrential mass of bodies rushing upward.

Within moments we had been swept along to the second-floor landing. Extricating ourselves from the swarming rabble, we took momentary refuge behind a display case containing the mummified remains of an Egyptian alligator.

"Listen, Mr. Poe," said Townsend, whose clothing had become badly disheveled from the crush of the mob, "I ought to keep on going—see what's happening upstairs. That's where the story is. Can you take care of Barnum yourself?"

I assured him that I could manage on my own. Then—bidding him to be careful—I watched as he hurried back to the staircase and threw himself into the turbulent stream of the ascending mob.

No sooner had he vanished amid the jostling bodies and bobbing heads than I stole from behind the display case and made my way down the hallway in the direction of the balcony. I had only gone a few steps, however, when my right shoulder was seized from behind in a crushing grip. Emitting a startled cry, I swiveled about and found myself face-to-face with a figure so unnerving as to cause an instantaneous shiver of dread to course through my frame.

He was a man of enormous stature. His height could not have been less than six feet three inches. His arms and chest were massive. His large, singularly square-shaped head appeared to rest upon his shoulders without the intervening support of a neck. His clothing was filthy—ragged—and so excessively ill-fitting that the frayed cuffs of his jacket barely extended to his wrists. From his person there emanated a powerful—an overwhelming—reek of stale perspiration and cheap rum.

It was not his size—his shabbiness—nor even his individual lineaments (which, however unprepossessing, were free of any marked abnormalities) that rendered his appearance so disquieting. Rather, it was the absolute idiosyncrasy of his expression. Anything even remotely resembling it I had never seen before. My first thought, upon beholding it, was that Retsch, had he viewed it, would have greatly preferred it to his own pictorial incarnations of the Fiend.

As I endeavored, during the brief minute of my original survey, to form some analysis of the meaning conveyed, there arose within my mind the impression of greed, cunning, brutality, malice—of a base, animal intelligence unregulated by decency or morality. In its overall cast, his physiognomy might have served as a perfect illustration for the qualities of extreme depravity and hopeless dissipation in one of Dr. Fowler's manuals of phrenology.

Now, surveying my person with narrowed, rheumy eyes, he addressed me thusly: "Where you off to, friend?"

In keeping with my pose as a fellow member of the lawless rabble, I arranged my features into a sly, conspiratorial expression. "Why, I am merely exploring the various portions of Barnum's museum," I replied, "to see what costly and aimless damage I might wreak upon the showman's property."

"You sure don't look like no tough," he said in a voice heavy with suspicion. "Don't talk like none, either." All at once, he thrust out one large, grimy hand—took hold of the front of my jacket—and began fingering the fabric in a most presumptuous manner. "Awful fancy duds," he sneered.

Owing to my perennially straitened finances, my garments were, in truth, in a fairly deplorable condition. Indeed, were it not for the surpassing sartorial skills of my beloved Aunt Maria—who devoted much of her energies to mending my increasingly threadbare wardrobe—my jacket would have long since reached the point of hopeless dilapidation. In comparison to the execrable garb of my interlocutor, however, I must have appeared as elegantly dressed as a member of the Court of St. James's.

"Yes," I cleverly replied, taking a step backward and freeing my jacket from his impudent grasp. "They belonged to a gentleman of the upper classes whose home I ransacked during an earlier episode of civic disorder."

For a moment, the fiercesome-looking fellow—whose slurred speech, no less than his redolent breath, gave clear indication of his inebriated state—merely stared at me in befuddlement.

"And what," I said quickly, "is *your* purpose, my good man?"

Here, he gave a malevolent smile, revealing a set of badly discolored teeth from which several of the front incisors were missing. Reaching under his coat, he extracted an old, double-barreled pistol whose battered appearance rendered it no less formidable-looking.

"Hunting for Barnum," he said. "Son of a bitch won't be causing no more trouble once I'm done with him."

The sheer cold-blooded villainy of this remark caused my heart to palpitate with alarm. "What a splendid notion," I exclaimed, feigning enthusiastic support for his murderous design. "I shall accompany you and watch the showman receive his just desserts."

"All right, then, little man," said the loathsome ruffian, clapping me on the shoulder with a force that caused me to stagger slightly. "Follow me." He then turned on his heels and lumbered off in the direction of the balcony.

As those who know me will attest, I am a man who, though abjuring violence for its own sake, will not hesitate to employ the most desperate measures—not excluding extreme physical force—to protect my friends and loved ones from harm. Now, coming up behind the hulking brute who was evidently bent on assassinating Barnum, I took my war-club in both hands—raised it high in the air—and brought it crashing down upon his head.

Sadly, this action proved less efficacious than I had hoped. Owing partly to the disparity in our heights, which caused the brunt of my blow to fall on his upper shoulders, and partly to the awkward angle from which I was forced to deliver it, I did not render him immediately unconscious. Emitting a startled grunt, he stumbled to his knees.

Before he could recover himself sufficiently to take any defensive action, I struck him again, this time on the very top of his skull. With a fluttering groan, he crashed face down onto the floor, his arms extended outward, the pistol slipping from his grasp and sliding several feet away from where he sprawled.

Without a moment's hesitation, I leapt over his fallen bulk—stooped to snatch up the weapon—shoved it into the waistband of my trousers—and dashed toward the balcony.

I arrived just in time to find Barnum returning to sensibility. He had drawn himself up to his knees and, with the fingertips of one hand, was gingerly exploring the lump on his temple.

As I crouched beside him, he gazed at me with somewhat unfocused eyes and said: "Poe, m'boy, how in the world did you—ouch! Bless my soul, what a goose-egg! Why, it's massive! Immense! Feels like I'm sprouting a second head—like Harwell Phelps, my Astounding Hydra Boy! What the devil happened?"

Helping him to his feet, I led him inside the building, where he leaned against an enormous cabinet holding his vast collection of conchilogical specimens gathered from every quarter of the globe.

"Have you no memory at all of what transpired?" I asked with concern, as he continued to lightly palpate his injury.

"Yes, yes, it's all coming back to me now, clear as day," he said. "I was beaned with a rock. Felt like a whopper, too—big as the giant Icelandic meteorite in my Hall of Astronomical Marvels. Good heavens, I can hardly believe it. Pelted by a mob! *Me*—P. T. Barnum! The Napoleon of Showmen! The Sun of the Entertainment World! Why, nothing of the kind has ever happened to me in the course of my long, storied career! Well, all right, once or twice, perhaps, back in the old days, when I was traveling down South with my Grand Touring Circus of Science and Amusement. Bunch of yokels took exception to Professor Parelli's lantern-slide lecture on the Miracle of Birth. Claimed it was indecent. But that was many years ago, when—wait! What's that racket? Sounds like someone's smashing up the place!"

"The noise to which you refer is indeed that of wanton destruction," I grimly replied. "I fear, my friend, that your museum is under siege. No sooner were you struck down in that cowardly fashion than the mob, inflamed by the sight of your fall, broke into your establishment. While the majority of the rioters rushed upstairs in search of Chief Wolf Bear, a smaller—though by no means insignificant—number embarked on a rampage of unbridled vandalism."

"What!" cried Barnum, his visage flushing with outrage. "Pillaging my museum, are they? Why, the scoundrels—the dastardly miscreants! I'll show 'em! Come, Poe! We must go muster my troops! My Italian strong man! My Arabian giant! My Hungarian knife-thrower! My Turkish harem guards! We'll teach the villains a lesson!"

Grabbing me by the arm, he attempted to pull me from the shelter of the towering cabinet at the rear of which we had been standing. I would not, however, allow myself to be budged.

"While I sympathize with your impulse," I said, speaking in low, urgent tones, "I must beseech you to refrain from exposing yourself to unnecessary peril. Even now, there are ruffians at large who are intent on inflicting the most severe, if not lethal, harm upon your person. Indeed, I encountered one of these brutes only moments ago. It was only by dint of my superior martial skills that I was able to render him unconscious and relieve him of this." Here

I withdrew the double-barreled pistol from my waistband and displayed it to Barnum.

My appeal, however, had little apparent effect on the showman. "Damn the risk!" he cried. "Lord bless me, do I look like the sort of man who would stand helplessly by while the greatest outrage since the sacking of Rome takes place right under his nose?"

"But you do not comprehend the danger to which you are—" I began to say. Before I could complete the statement, however, I was interrupted by a noise that caused an icy chill to course through my veins.

It was the sound of rapid footsteps, growing louder by the instant. Someone was hurrying in our direction!

Assuming that the brute I had felled had now regained consciousness and was in search of both Barnum and myself, I gestured for silence by placing my forefinger on my lips. I then carefully peered around the side of the cabinet, my pistol at the ready. Though I had not wielded a firearm in the nearly twenty years since my discharge from the U.S. Military Academy at West Point—where I had distinguished myself as a marksman of singular proficiency—I was fully prepared to employ the weapon should the need arise.

Narrowing my eyes, I squinted into the darkness. All at once, a figure emerged from the shadows. Immediately, I breathed a sigh of relief; for I saw at a glance that it was not my recently vanquished foe.

It was George Townsend.

Lowering the pistol, I stepped out from behind the cabinet, bringing the young man to a startled halt.

"Mr. Poe!" he cried. "I was just looking for you and Barnum."

"Your quest is at an end, young man," said the showman as he emerged from his place of concealment. "Here we are, big as life. And who the blazes are you?"

Hastily introducing himself, Townsend—who appeared to be in an even greater state of dishevelment than when I had last seen him—proceeded to inform us of the dire events he had witnessed since our parting.

"At first, no one knew where to look," he said. "Then they ran into your custodian."

"Oswald," said Barnum. "He stayed late tonight. Helping to set up the auditorium for tomorrow's Fat Baby contest."

"They stuck a pistol to his head," Townsend went on. "Forced him to reveal the chief's whereabouts. Then the whole mob ran howling upstairs. Broke into the fifth-floor sleeping quarters. Grabbed hold of the chief. The other performers tried to protect him. Even General Tom Thumb."

"He's all heart, the general," said Barnum. "Twenty-five inches of pure spunk."

"It was no use, though," said Townsend. "How do you fend off a whole mob of blood-crazed hyenas? The Indian did his damnedest, I'll say that for him—fought like the very devil. Took six men to subdue him. Of course, that just made them even angrier. They're bringing him down now. Swear they'll string him up from a lamppost on Broadway."

"Poe," Barnum said, "we've got to get out now and bring reinforcements! Alert the police! Rouse the militia!"

"Indeed," I replied, "that appears to be our only hope of preventing the cowards from carrying out their damnable act of vigilantism."

"Now's the time to do it," said Townsend. "We can slip out easily. The mob hasn't made its way downstairs yet. And everyone else is too busy breaking up the place."

This latter remark caused the color to drain from the showman's countenance. Without another word, he hurried off in the direction of the staircase, Townsend and I following close behind. As we reached the spot where I had rendered Barnum's would-be assassin *hors de combat*, I saw that the brute remained face down on the floor, precisely as I had left him. For an instant, I experienced a sharp twinge of anxiety, fearing that my blow had proved fatal. As we made our way past his inert form, however, he stirred slightly and emitted a muffled moan.

As Townsend had indicated, the grand marble staircase was vacant, allowing the three of us to make our descent unmolested. No sooner had we reached the ground floor, however, than we heard a wild commotion behind us—a mighty, intensifying roar, like the sound of an approaching tidal wave. Turning back to the stairs, I saw a sight that filled me with dismay.

The mob was pouring down from the upper stories. At their head was Chief Wolf Bear. Arms bound behind him, a noose encircling his neck, he was flanked by a crew of singularly vicious-looking ruffians, several of whom held pistols and rifles to his head.

He was, like most men of his tribe, very striking in appearance. Garbed in a buffalo-skin shirt and leggings that extended to his hips, he had a tall, muscular physique—long, somewhat graying hair braided at the sides—and fine, chiseled features, betokening a steady soul. Even under the present circumstances of extraordinary duress, he radiated an air of unshakable strength and dignity.

A moment later, the vanguard of the mob arrived at the foot of the descent. All at once, Barnum—who, along with Townsend and myself, had moved to one side of the staircase—stepped forward and planted himself directly in the path of the oncoming horde. Rarely, if ever, had I witnessed so bold—so courageous—an act. Even as my heart filled with anxiety for my friend's personal safety, my bosom was infused with a new appreciation of his character.

"Stop!" he cried. "I forbid you to remove that man from my premises."

"Out of the way, Barnum, or we'll string you up, too," said the apparent leader of the mob, a hatchet-faced fellow whose most prominent feature was a large, angry carbuncle—resembling a blood-engorged member of the tick family—that protruded from the center of his brow. In one hand, he clutched the coiled rope whose elaborately knotted end was looped around Chief Wolf Bear's neck; while in his other, he held a cocked pistol.

"Why, the nerve—the pure unmitigated gall!" the showman exclaimed. "That Indian belongs to *me*! Signed him to a full one-year contract! Brought him all the way out from the farthest reaches of the West! Paid a fortune, an absolute fortune, just on transportation fees! Now, I'll thank you to stop this nonsense, free that man at once, and remove yourselves from my premises!"

The hatchet-faced churl opened his mouth to reply. Before he could speak, however, his eyes narrowed, and a strange, somewhat uncertain expression came over his altogether repulsive countenance.

Studying the fellow, I saw that his gaze had shifted slightly and was directed at a spot behind Barnum's shoulder. Several of the men beside him were also looking curiously in the same direction. Even the attention of Chief Wolf Bear was now focused on this spot.

Exactly what they were staring at I could scarcely imagine. Nor—when I turned to follow their gaze—was I at all prepared for what I saw.

Chapter Nine

I T WAS A LONE MALE FIGURE. He was standing by the ticket booth near the entrance of the grand foyer, silently observing the chaotic scene on the staircase. In asserting that the person of the stranger was altogether *remarkable*, I do not mean to suggest that he in any way resembled the freakishly deformed human anomalies to whom that adjective was customarily applied at the American Museum: the giants and dwarves, fat men and living skeletons, armless wonders, dog-faced boys, Siamese twins, and other grotesque "curiosities." On the contrary. He was, in regard to his physiology, a perfectly normal—indeed quite well-made—specimen of young manhood. In stature, he was of medium height, with a compact, symmetrical frame, tending toward the slender. His countenance, insofar as I could observe it from the distance that currently separated us, was lean, sun-creased, and unobtrusively handsome, with a tapering chin—high, sharply defined cheekbones—and clean, regular features.

There were, however, several elements of his appearance that accounted for the striking impression he created.

The first was his attire. His shirt was of dressed deerskin, fringed across the bosom and along the seams of the arms. His trousers, fashioned from the same material, were tucked into tall leather boots. Girdling his waist was a black leather belt, tooled in an intricate design. A matching holster—encasing a walnut-handled pistol of a type I had never before seen—lay against his right hip. He wore a black neckerchief, loosely knotted at the throat, and, upon his head, a wide-brimmed black hat, the crown of which was adorned with a band of braided rawhide. While this style of dress would doubtlessly have excited little curiosity, or even notice, in the rugged domains of the Far West, here—within the confines of civilization—it was conspicuous in the extreme.

The second, more intangible (if no less salient) trait that rendered him noteworthy was his overall *comportment*, particularly at that moment of high drama—acute tension—and unfolding crisis. He stood posed in that relaxed, supremely self-confident attitude that is seen in Michelangelo's magnificent (if somewhat oddly proportioned) statue of David, and that is denominated by the Italians as the *contrapposto*. His right leg bore the brunt of his body weight—his corresponding arm hung loosely at his side—while his opposing foot was extended slightly to the front. In spite of the apparent ease of his posture, however, he radiated a palpable aura of coiled power—latent energy— and habitual alertness: a sense that, if provoked, he would spring into swift, instantaneous, and deadly activity.

Now, as though he had finished taking stock of the situation and resolved upon a course of action, he straightened up and strode unhurriedly forward. His gait was slightly bowlegged, in a manner suggesting that he had passed a substantial portion of his life upon horseback. In the absolute silence that prevailed, the sound of his boot heels on the marble floor echoed loudly in the cavernous foyer.

As this singular personage approached the staircase, I suddenly became cognizant of a second figure, crouching in the shadows by the ticket booth. This appeared to be a young boy, dressed in a manner almost identical to that of the older man (albeit bareheaded). One of his arms was draped across the shoulders of a mongrel yellow dog, who stood at full alert, intently watching the progress of the buckskin-clad individual.

In another instant, the latter came to a halt directly before the staircase, and gazed up from beneath the downswept brim of his hat. His steel-gray eyes briefly scanned the brutish faces of the ruffians at the head of the mob, before coming to rest on that of the carbuncular individual who stood beside Chief Wolf Bear, holding the rope that was looped around the Indian's neck.

Though the stranger had yet to speak a word, there was something so imposing about his demeanor that even Barnum—who had instinctively taken a step backward to make way for him—was rendered speechless. He merely studied the stranger wordlessly, his countenance registering both perplexity and wonder.

An instant later, the silence in the great hall was broken by the repulsive-looking leader of the rabble, who, in a tone of false *bonhomie*, addressed the stranger thusly: "Welcome, friend. Come to join our little necktie party?"

When the latter answered, he spoke in a voice whose very softness carried a hint of indescribable menace. "Sorry, boys," he said. "Party's over."

So unexpected was this reply that, for an instant, the ringleader appeared dumbstruck. At length, he emitted a derisive snort. "That so?" he said, looking the stranger up and down. "Say, what the hell kind of getup is that? Looks like you just crawled out of some goddamned forest."

"Sorry it ain't to your liking," the stranger replied. "Left my Sunday church-going duds at home. Didn't know I'd be mingling with such high-toned folks as yourself."

At that instant, another member of the mob spoke up. This was an exceed-ingly coarse-looking fellow, with a massively protuberant underjaw—a low, receding forehead—and a badly flattened nose. He stood on the opposite side of Chief Wolf Bear, pointing a rifle at the Indian's chest. "C'mon, Pete," he growled, addressing the ringleader. "Stop yapping with this damned asshole. Let's get on with it."

Ignoring this wholly unsavory being, the stranger tilted his chin toward Chief Wolf Bear and said: "What's he done?"

"Guess you really *was* living in the woods," sneered the ringleader, who had just been denominated as "Pete." "What'd he do? Oh, nothing much. Just butchered and scalped a bunch of people, is all. Including a whole family tonight."

Turning his gaze upon the captive, the stranger began to converse with him in a harsh, guttural vocabulary that was, I inferred, the variety of Siouan lan-guage employed by the Crow. Having devoted my linguistic studies to the mastery of Latin, Greek, Hebrew, German, and Sanskrit—as well as to the full range of Romance languages (not excluding Rumanian and Provençal)—I was entirely ignorant of this (or indeed any other) tribal speech, and thus could not interpret what was being said. At several points, however, the stranger uttered a phrase that sounded much like *Dapiek Absaroka.*

The effect of these words upon Chief Wolf Bear was pronounced. As I have already stated, even the desperate circumstances under which he now found himself had failed to shake his stoic demeanor. At the mere mention of the aforesaid phrase, however, a startled—even (so I fancied) somewhat alarmed—expression passed over his countenance.

A moment later—his brief exchange with the captive being concluded—the stranger gazed coolly back at the ruffian named Pete and said: "You got the wrong man. Now, let him go."

"And what if we don't?" came the scornful reply.

By way of answer, the stranger rested the heel of his right hand upon the protruding butt of his holstered gun.

This gesture caused the ringleader's sneer to vanish from his unsightly countenance. For a moment, he gazed uncertainly at the formidable-looking weapon in its tooled black-leather holster. At length—mustering an air of bravado that was belied by the slight, yet audible, quiver of nervousness in his voice—he curled his upper lip and said: "You figure on killing all of us?"

The stranger stared back at him with unblinking eyes. "Nope," he said pointedly. "Not all."

The ensuing moments were among the most tense I have ever experienced. The entire assemblage appeared to be holding its breath. No one dared to move a muscle. Time seemed suspended. The silence was so complete that the noise made by a falling pin would have resounded like the clatter of a dropped crowbar.

All at once, there was a blur of motion, occurring with such blinding speed that the actions themselves occupied far less time than is required to describe them.

As though at some prearranged signal, the two men flanking Chief Wolf Bear—the ringleader, Pete, and the coarse-looking brute with the flattened nose and prognathous jaw—turned their weapons away from the Indian and directed them at the stranger. Before either could discharge his gun, however, the stranger—moving with the fluid swiftness of a striking Egyptian cobra—whipped the pistol from his holster. Two shots—fired in such rapid succession that they blended into a single deafening roar—exploded from the barrel of his gun. At the first, the ringleader emitted a sharp cry—dropped his pistol—and sank to his knees, cradling his bleeding right hand. The second shot struck the flat-nosed brute in his left shoulder. Letting go of his rifle, he clutched at his wound, and fell backward into the arms of the person behind him.

For an instant, the rest of the assemblage remained absolutely frozen in place. The buckskin-clad stranger maintained his half-crouching posture, his smoking gun trained on the mob before him. All at once, as I stood there gaping at him—my nostrils filled with the odor of gunpowder, my ears ringing from the dual blast of his weapon—I became aware of a movement to his rear. Casting my gaze in that direction, I saw that a piratical-looking ruffian with a hawklike nose and a black eye-patch had emerged from the shadowy depths of the Grand Cosmorama Salon and was sneaking up on the stranger from behind. Raised high above his head was a wooden bludgeon, the surface of which was studded with small, metal spikes.

I opened my mouth to shout a warning. Before I could emit a sound, however, I heard a deep, ferocious growl, followed by a frantic scrabbling. An instant later, the mongrel dog I had observed earlier came bounding across the foyer. Throwing itself at the would-be assailant, it clamped its jaws around his arm. With a scream of agony, the man let go of his weapon and dropped to his knees, vainly attempting to dislodge the snarling canine, who was tearing so furiously at the limb as to seem intent on ripping it to pieces.

It was only the timely intervention of the dog's master that saved the fellow's arm from being mangled beyond any hope of recovery. Without so much as turning his head to assess the nature of the disturbance behind him, the stranger merely called out: "Dog!"

Instantly, the canine released his hold on his victim and trotted back to the ticket booth to rejoin the young boy, who remained crouching in the shadows.

Only a minute or two had elapsed since the ringleader and his cohort had leveled their weapons at the stranger. Now—along with the one-eyed scoundrel, who lay moaning on the ground—they had been rendered utterly helpless. The speed, no less than the sheer ruthless efficiency, with which these bloody-minded ruffians had been disabled had left their comrades in a state of stunned irresolution. It seemed only a matter of time, however, before the rest of the mob rallied themselves and set upon the stranger. However formidable a warrior he might be—and however deadly his weapon—he was, after all, only a single individual. How, I wondered, would he react, should the rabble attack him *en masse*?

Happily, the question proved moot. No sooner had the dog returned to his place by the ticket booth than a great commotion—emanating from the main entrance of the museum and rapidly swelling in volume—could be heard. A moment later, an army of police officers, led by Captain Dunnegan, came pouring into the building. Shouted commands echoed through the grand foyer: "Stay where you are!" "Lay down your weapons!" "Release that man!"

As the lawmen swarmed about, disarming the rabble (who put up little or no resistance to the legion of officers), Barnum strode up to the stranger, arms thrown wide as though to envelop him in a bear hug. The latter, looking as unfazed as though he had just completed the most mundane task imaginable, reholstered his gun and gazed at the showman with a somewhat puzzled expression.

"My boy, I want to congratulate you!" exclaimed Barnum. "I want to shake you by the hand! Lord bless me, I've never witnessed anything so stupendous! Greatest display of martial prowess since Achilles got his dander up and laid low the soldiers of Troy! Why, the conquests of Alexander the Great were nothing by comparison—mere child's play! Who in heaven's name are you? Tell me your name, dear boy, so that I might commemorate it for all eternity within the walls of my museum! Mount a bronze plaque in your honor! Erect a waxworks tableau of your deeds! Recount your life story in a lavishly illustrated souvenir booklet!"

At this effusion, the stranger merely continued to stare wordlessly at the showman. At length, he made reply. The day had already been so fraught with the most startling developments that I believed myself impervious to any further shocks. His words, however, proved me wrong.

"Name's Carson," he said. "My friends call me Kit."

Chapter Ten

⌒

ORTY-FIVE MINUTES LATER, I was seated in Barnum's commodious office, along with a half-dozen other individuals who had gathered there in the aftermath of the siege.

Occupying the chair directly beside my own was George Townsend, his writing implement poised above the open page of his ever-present notepad. On his other side sat Captain Dunnegan. Upon hearing that a riot was in progress, Dunnegan had assembled a large force of men and marched to the museum. Now—having succeeded in dispersing the mob and placing its main participants under arrest (including the two wretches wounded by Carson)—he had repaired to Barnum's office to garner additional details about the incident, leaving a subordinate in charge upstairs.

Chief Wolf Bear was standing erect in a far corner of the office. From the absolute impassivity of his expression, it was impossible to tell that, only a short time earlier, he had been in imminent peril of suffering a harrowing death. His arms were folded loosely over his chest, his dark eyes fixed on the person of Carson, who half sat, half leaned—in an attitude of perfect nonchalance—against the edge of Barnum's desk.

The young boy—Carson's five-year-old son, whose name, I had discovered, was Jeremiah—lay stretched out, fast asleep, on a divan that stood against one wall of the office. Even in repose, his features greatly resembled those of his famous father. His skin, however, was of an even darker hue than the latter's sun-browned complexion, and his hair—unlike Carson's (which was of a blond tint and gossamer texture)—was thick, glossy, and raven-black. Curled at the foot of the divan on which the lad slumbered was the intrepid canine that had leapt so ferociously to his master's defense and that evidently bore no other denomination than "Dog."

The showman himself was seated behind his massive desk, staring at Carson with all the avidity of a gourmand contemplating a particularly delectable slice of *filet de boeuf*. Indeed, from the instant he had learned the true identity of the stranger, Barnum had appeared to be in a state of barely suppressed excitement. Even the damage wrought upon his museum by the rampaging mob had left him relatively unfazed. Partly, no doubt, this was due to his innate resilience. He had, after all, rebounded from many prior catastrophes—from the scandals attending the exposure of his more flagrant hoaxes—to the unexpected deaths of several of his most popular (and lucrative) performers—to a devastating fire that had destroyed a sizable portion of his collection several years earlier. I assumed, moreover, that he would automatically recoup most of his losses, his property, no doubt, being heavily insured.

Largely, however, it was the unforeseen advent of the legendary scout that accounted for the glint of excitement I could discern in Barnum's eyes. Watching him, I could almost see the gears and cams of commercial calculation whirring in his mind. To the showman, Carson was nothing more nor less than a potentially lucrative windfall, dropped into his lap by a beneficent fate. Unless I was very much mistaken, the biggest problem now vexing my old friend was how best to exploit Carson to the fullest, most profitable extent.

The final person in the room was seated in a chair at the side of Barnum's desk. He was a short, stout, middle-aged fellow, entirely bald apart from two unruly tufts of wiry brown hair sprouting from his temples. He had large blue eyes—a wide mouth with inordinately red lips—a "pug" nose—and a pendulous underchin resembling the wattle of a turkey. This was Oswald, Barnum's custodian—jack-of-all-trades—and sign-painter *extraordinaire*, who had been coerced at gunpoint into divulging the chief's whereabouts to the lynch mob. The experiences of the evening had evidently left him badly shaken. To help calm his nerves, the showman had offered him a cigar. As the custodian sat puffing it nervously, his hands trembled so violently that a small quantity of ash showered down upon his lap every time he removed it from his lips.

As for myself, my nerves had been subjected to such an unparalleled series of shocks in the course of that long, seemingly endless day that I felt largely benumbed. The strongest of my emotions was a sort of stunned disbelief—a sensation that had first taken hold of me when Carson had announced his identity an hour before, and which had hardly abated in the interim.

This is not to say that I suspected the handsome Westerner of being an impostor. I did not doubt for an instant that he was who he claimed to be. Not only did his appearance correspond in every respect to the description given in Mr. Parker's volume, but his almost inconceivably heroic conduct in single-handedly facing down the lynch mob was consistent with the extraordinary feats of valor ascribed to him by that author—feats which I had once dismissed as hopelessly far-fetched but which (I was now forced to concede) were well within the bounds of possibility, at least for such a prodigy as Carson.

No. My feelings of incredulity did not proceed from any doubts as to the latter's identity. On the contrary. It was my awareness that the actual person of Kit Carson was now present in Barnum's office that filled me with amazement—the realization that, only hours after I had finished writing about him in my review of Parker's book, the living, flesh-and-blood figure of the legendary scout had materialized before my very eyes!

How could I account for so startling—so extraordinary—a circumstance? In the end, I could only conclude that it was a striking illustration of a universally recognized truism: that life is replete with coincidences of so wild and improbable a nature that—were they to appear in a work of mere fiction—no reader would be inclined to believe them.

To be sure, there was a reason for Carson's arrival in New York City at this specific time. As he was now in the process of explaining to Captain Dunnegan, he had traveled all the way from his normal haunts in the Rocky Mountains on a very particular mission.

He was there to track down a man. When he found him—so Carson matter-of-factly declared—he intended to kill him.

"You don't say?" remarked Dunnegan with a scowl. "Tell us more."

The object of his hunt, Carson explained, was a renegade mountain man named Johnson. "Leastways, that's what he calls himself," said the scout. To the assorted inhabitants of the Western frontier, he was known by a variety of sobriquets. Among Chief Wolf Bear's people, he was called *Dapiek Absaroka*—the "Crow Killer"—as a result of the sheer number of victims he had claimed from that tribe. His depredations, however, were by no means limited to the Crow. Other Indians—the Blackfoot, the Flatheads, the Arapaho—had also suffered greatly at his hands. They referred to him as "Red Death," an epithet stemming from his distinctive coloration, his shoulder-length hair and luxuriant beard being of a startling crimson hue.

To his fellow mountain men—as well as to the white settlers of the region—he was known by yet another appellation: "Liver-Eating" Johnson, or simply "The Liver-Eater." This name, Carson explained, derived from a practice that—even within the context of frontier warfare, whose combatants commonly resorted to the most barbarous acts imaginable—was looked upon with unique horror and revulsion by white men and Indians alike.

Johnson was a cannibal.

At this pronouncement, Oswald—in the act of taking a long draw on his cigar—was so startled that he inadvertently inhaled the smoke into his lungs and began coughing spasmodically. Carson paused for a moment until the custodian's hacking had subsided, before proceeding with his account of Johnson's grisly predilection.

Not content with despoiling the corpses of his foes in the usual manner—i.e., by taking their scalps and other gruesome trophies (such as fingers and ears)—Johnson would routinely batten on the flesh of his victims. Specifically, he would make an incision with his hunting knife just below the rib cage on the right side of the abdominal area—tear out the liver—and devour the warm and reeking organ in its entirety!

"Why the hell would he do something like that?" Dunnegan growled.

Carson shrugged. "Likes the taste, I reckon."

Townsend, who had been scribbling furiously in his notepad, now glanced up at me with a meaningful look. It was evident that—upon hearing Carson's description of Johnson's gruesome *modus operandi*—he and I had immediately been struck with the same realization.

Before either of us could interject a word, however, Barnum spoke up.

"Raw liver!" he exclaimed. "Bless my soul, it's the ghastliest thing I ever heard—worse than the most barbarous practices of the man-eating savages of the jungle! Why, no self-respecting cannibal would ever stoop so low! Believe me, I've known a few. Take my Polynesian Wild Man, Prince Kokovoko. Wouldn't *dream* of eating someone who wasn't roasted to a tee! But tell me, Kit, what makes you think this Johnson creature is here in Manhattan?"

"Heard it from a fellow named Del Gue," replied the scout. "Him and Johnson used to be pards. Spent the summers trapping beaver together."

"I see, I see," said Barnum, stroking his chin. "And this—what's his name?—Del Gue person volunteered the information to you?"

"Wouldn't say 'volunteered,' " Carson replied. "He was a mite reluctant to tell me where Johnson took off to." Here the scout paused for an instant before adding: "But I persuaded him."

As I knew from my readings, the mountain men of the Far West possessed a degree of physical fortitude that bordered on the superhuman. Their ability to survive the most grueling hardships conceivable—from months of snow-bound solitude to the ferocious attacks of that most terrifying of all members of the ursine family, the North American grizzly—was legendary. That Carson had managed to "persuade" one of these surpassingly hard-bitten men to betray the whereabouts of a friend would have struck me as highly implausible, had I not already glimpsed the fierce—the *deadly*—determination that lurked within the person of the soft-spoken, slenderly built scout.

Now—clearing my throat to attract his attention—I said: "There can be no doubt, Mr. Carson, that the man you are seeking is not only here in New York City, but is the fiend responsible for the recent rash of barbarities that have been perpetrated on a string of innocent victims."

Though this statement was addressed to the scout, it was the police captain who responded. From the moment he had become aware of my presence, Dunnegan—who had last seen me as I was leaving the site of Wyatt's murder, presumably to return home—had regarded me with unconcealed suspicion. Though I had explained the circumstances that had led me to the museum, his attitude toward me remained excessively wary, if not actively hostile.

"What the hell are you talking about, Poe?" he now demanded harshly.

Before I could respond to this inordinately ill-mannered remark, Townsend spoke up. "Haven't you read the autopsy report on the Edmonds girl?" he asked Dunnegan.

This query brought a flush of annoyance to the latter's countenance. "Reading ain't what I was hired to do, Townsend," he said. The sneering tone of this remark made it sufficiently plain that—so far as Dunnegan was concerned—any man of literate habits must be of questionable virility. "I'll leave that to the likes of you and your friend."

Ignoring the insulting implications of this comment, I turned to Carson and declared: "The document to which my friend Mr. Townsend is referring describes the nature of the injuries inflicted upon young Rosalie Edmonds, the ten-year-old girl who, until this evening, was the most recent victim of the killer. According to this report, the unfortunate child was subjected to a variety of grisly mutilations—among which was the removal of her liver. As it happens, this same atrocity was also committed upon his earlier victim, a seven-year-old child named Annie Dobbs. That the perpetrator of these hideous crimes possesses a depraved appetite for human flesh may be reasonably assumed. Indeed—as Mr. Townsend will attest—my own perusal of the autopsy report led me to that very deduction. Taken together, these facts point to only one possible conclusion—i.e., that the quarry you are hunting is indeed at large somewhere in the city."

Carson studied me closely for several moments before asking: "You a lawman, Mr. Poe?"

"Hardly," I replied. "By profession, I am a man of letters, one of the leading *literati* of New York: poet—critic—creator of tales of the grotesque and arabesque. I have, however, been involved in the investigation of several notorious murders, both here and in the city of Baltimore, and have—by dint of a certain aptitude for ratiocinative analysis—been instrumental in bringing those cases to a swift and satisfactory resolution."

"*Certain aptitude?*" Barnum cried. "Why, the man's too modest by half! He's a marvel, I tell you—an absolute mental colossus! *Dazzling* doesn't begin to describe the workings of that mind! And observant? Got the eyes of a hunting falcon! Nothing escapes him! Notices things you and I couldn't see without the aid of a magnifying lens!"

This extravagant—if not entirely unwarranted—*accolade* was interrupted by Dunnegan. "I got a question," he gruffly remarked. "If this Johnson character is the killer we're looking for, how come he didn't cut out Wyatt's liver?" Then, turning to fix me with a scornful look, he added: "Or didn't those falcon eyes of yours notice *that*?"

"Who's Wyatt?" asked Carson.

"Mr. William Wyatt was the maniac's latest victim," I replied. "His unspeakably savage murder—which occurred earlier this very evening—was the precipitating cause of that violent uprising whose defeat owed so much to your own timely intervention. As it happened, it was I myself who—arriving at Wyatt's home for a prearranged meeting—discovered his dreadfully mutilated body, to which life was still clinging by the merest thread. Unfortunately—beyond uttering the barely intelligible word 'he'—the poor man could offer no clue as to the identity of his killer, his tongue having been excised at the root.

"As for your needlessly taunting observation, Captain Dunnegan," I continued, turning to face the latter, "surely you must be aware that my examination of the dying victim was cursory in the extreme, and conducted under the most difficult circumstances imaginable. Even so, I did not fail to perceive that he had not, to all outward appearances, suffered any lacerations to his abdominal region. By no means, however, does the absence of such a wound eliminate Johnson as a suspect. It is entirely possible, for example, that something—perhaps my own arrival at that particular moment—caused the murderer to flee the premises before he could complete his intended butchery. Do not forget that he had much more time to indulge his cannibalistic proclivities with his two juvenile victims, both of whom were abducted several days prior to the discovery of their remains."

To this statement, Dunnegan merely responded with a grunt.

"That seems about right," observed Carson, who had been listening attentively to my remarks. "Anyways, Johnson killed plenty of folks he didn't eat. Always enjoyed butchering them up, though—even when he wasn't in the mood for a taste of their innards."

"Why, it's incredible!" cried Barnum. "Absolutely staggers belief! Don't get me wrong, Kit—I harbor few illusions about my fellow man. You can call P. T. Barnum many things, but naive isn't one of them. I've seen a good deal of this world—enough to know a bit about human wickedness and corruption. But this Johnson creature is beyond the bounds of anything I've ever heard. To think that such a monster could exist! And among the trappers of the great Rocky Mountains—those hardy trailblazers risking life and limb to advance the westward march of civilization! Why, if I hadn't heard it from your own lips, I'd have trouble believing it!"

Gazing at the showman, Carson cocked one eyebrow slightly, a motion that—in light of the scout's extreme economy of expression—was eloquent of the keenest surprise.

"Men go into the mountains for all kinds of reasons, Mr. Barnum," he said. "But trailblazing for civilization don't rank high on the list. Some do it for the money, though I ain't never yet been acquainted with a wealthy trapper. Others are running away from something."

"Like what?" interposed Townsend, who was busily engaged in transcribing every word uttered by Carson.

"The past, mostly," replied the latter. "Then there's the ones who are partial to the way of life. The mountains can kill you in a hundred different ways, but it's God's country up there."

"And to which of these several categories does Johnson belong?" I inquired.

"None of them," said Carson. "There's another breed out there. Men who head for the mountains because there ain't no law. Nothing to stop them from doing whatever they damn well please. Hell, nobody cared about Johnson's butchery. No white folks, anyways. Never yet run across a mountain man who didn't admire the Liver-Eater. He'd still be out there today, murdering all the Indians he could, if he hadn't killed the wrong one."

"The wrong one?" exclaimed Barnum. "Why, who do you mean?"

For a moment, Carson made no reply. He merely looked at his slumbering son, who remained curled on his side on the divan.

At length—in a tone so grim as to cause my nape-hairs to prickle—he said: "The one I was married to."

Though Carson's renown rested, to a large extent, on his exploits as an Indian fighter, his hostilities were restricted to those tribes who—fearing the constant encroachments of white civilization—bore a fierce and implacable hatred toward every individual of European descent. With other tribes—who viewed the white man with greater tolerance—he maintained the most cordial relations.

In this respect, he was no different from many other mountain men, whose attitude toward the native inhabitants of the Far West was a peculiar admixture of brutal prejudice and fraternal admiration. In adapting to life in the wilderness, these rugged pioneers—even while guilty of the most horrific acts of savagery against the red man—embraced many aspects of the latter's way of life, from his diet and dress to his woodcraft and manners. Indeed, after enough time spent in the mountains, the typical trapper seemed more than half Indian himself.

Partly for this reason (though also because of the scarcity of marriageable white females within the wild domains of the Western frontier), it was common for a mountain man to wed an Indian woman. This had been the case with Kit Carson.

She was an Arapaho maiden named Waa-nibe, an appellation that, in the language of her tribe, meant "Singing Grass." Carson had taken her for his bride in the spring of 1839, an act that—lacking every trace of that higher sentimentality which attaches to the matrimonial practices of our own culture—more closely resembled the purchase of a mule, horse, or other beast of burden. Following a period of intense negotiations with her father, Carson had agreed to pay the sum of one Hawken rifle, two Bowie knives, and a supply of sugar and salt in exchange for the maiden. The two were then joined in the traditional tribal ceremonies, whereupon Carson and his new wife took their leave of the village and rode off together into the mountains. Their son, Jeremiah, was born less than a year later.

Carson being a man not given to verbosity, his comments regarding his wife were exceedingly sparse—so much so that at no point during our acquaintance was I able to form a clear conception of either her physical appearance or her character. From the manner in which he spoke of her, however, I gathered that his feelings for Waa-nibe had been of a most affectionate nature, a circumstance that distinguished Carson from the common run of trappers, who tended to regard their Indian spouses as nothing more than domestic drudges and convenient bedmates.

For several years, Carson and his family had lived contentedly in a small log cabin that he had constructed on the banks of the Musselshell River. Tragedy had struck in the fall of 1844—approximately nine months prior to his arrival in New York City. He had gone off hunting, to acquire provisions for the coming winter, and was absent from his home for a period of nearly a week. He had returned to find a scene of indescribable devastation and horror—his cabin burned to the ground, his wife hideously murdered, mutilated, and defiled.

Fortunately, his son had escaped destruction by taking flight into the surrounding woods and insinuating himself into the hollow trunk of a fallen tree, where he had remained hidden until the monster departed. Though physically unscathed, the boy had suffered an emotional shock so severe as to render him mute; indeed, he had barely uttered a word since. By means of various gestures, however, he had managed to convey that the killer was a red-bearded man of gigantic stature. There could be no doubt that this description referred to the infamous person of "Liver-Eating" Johnson—particularly since an examination of poor Waa-nibe's corpse revealed a ghastly, tell-tale incision on the right side of her upper abdomen, slightly beneath the rib cage.

Shortly thereafter, it was rumored that Johnson had fled the mountains after discovering that the squaw he had slain was the wife of the celebrated scout and hunter, who was now single-mindedly bent on avenging her murder. After learning Johnson's intended destination from the trapper named Del Gue, Carson—accompanied by his still-silent son and his trusty canine—had made his way east.

It was during the final leg of his journey, while crossing the ferry to Manhattan Island, that he had overheard a conversation between two gentlemen, who were discussing the many astounding sights to be witnessed at Barnum's establishment. One of these speakers happened to mention the bloodcurdling "scalp dance" performed by Chief Wolf Bear. Carson immediately resolved to seek out the latter on the chance, however remote, that the Indian might have some knowledge of Johnson. Upon disembarking, the scout had therefore proceeded uptown with the intention of finding suitable lodgings near the museum. Instead, he had found himself in the midst of a riot.

A short interval of silence followed the conclusion of the scout's remarkable narrative. At length, Captain Dunnegan declared: "This Johnson sounds like a bad one, all right. Wonder why he headed for New York."

"Reckon he might've been here before," said Carson. "Knows the lay of the land. And there ain't no shortage of easy prey, just waiting to be plucked off the streets. Besides, it's a good place to hide out in. Even a man like Johnson ain't likely to draw much notice. Not amongst so many different folks."

"What exactly does he look like?" Dunnegan inquired.

"Saw him once at a rendezvous," said Carson.

Perceiving the puzzled expression on the captain's visage, the scout briefly explained the nature of these annual gatherings, during which hundreds of trappers journeyed from their remote mountain haunts to sell their furs—to stock up on provisions—but chiefly to mingle and carouse with their brethren. It was while attending one of these boisterous events in the summer of 1842 that Carson had caught his only glimpse of the Liver-Eater, whose singular appearance, until that time, he had known about only through hearsay.

"He's a big man," said the scout. "Bigger than you, Captain. Must stand six foot two, maybe three, in his moccasins. Got real thick, red hair, and a beard that hangs down to his chest. Wild, bushy eyebrows, same color. And he's strong as three ordinary men. Saw him get into a scrape with a couple of brothers named Beidler. They weren't no pip-squeaks, neither. The Liver-Eater picked 'em both up by the scruff of their necks and slammed their heads together. They was dead before he dropped them to the ground."

At that moment, Barnum emitted a startling "Hah!" in the triumphant tone undoubtedly employed by Archimedes upon his discovery of the principle of volumetric displacement.

"What is it?" I cried, turning to the showman.

"Why, I've been struck with a brainstorm!" he exclaimed. "A perfectly amazing notion—absolutely stupendous! Let's have Oswald here knock off a sketch of this Johnson creature, based on Kit's description. You can do that easily enough, can't you, Oswald m'boy?"

"I suppose so, Mr. B," said the latter, sounding less than fully confident.

"Suppose so? Why, there's no question about it! You've seen his work, Poe. Bless my soul, the man's a virtuoso of the graphic arts! A second Leonardo! He'll dash off a perfect likeness of the fellow in no time! Then we'll give it to Morris to print in the *Mirror*. He'll leap at the chance, don't you agree, Mr. Townsend?"

"Why, yes, I imagine he will," replied the latter.

"Of course he will! No doubt about it! Johnson's mug will be all over page one! Why, every citizen in the whole metropolis will be on the lookout for him! We'll flush him out of hiding in no time! Lord bless me, how's *that* for an idea?"

"Reckon it wouldn't hurt none," said Carson. " 'Course, it might not help much, neither. Johnson's a mighty slippery character. Catching him won't be no Sunday picnic. But I mean to do it."

"And when you find him?" asked Dunnegan.

Carson made no reply. From the look of grim determination on his face, however, it was not difficult to infer that he intended to exact a full and fatal retribution for the murder of his wife.

For several moments, Dunnegan said nothing. At length, indicating Carson's gun with a tilt of his heavy chin, he asked: "Mind if I have a look at that sidearm?"

Carson—whose thumbs had been lazily hooked through the front of his belt on either side of the buckle—hesitated for a moment before sliding his right hand toward the holster and removing the pistol. With a deft motion, he flipped it about, so that its butt was facing the police captain.

"I've heard about these," said Dunnegan, taking the proffered weapon from Carson's hand and closely scrutinizing it. "Never seen one before, though."

"Colt revolver," said Carson. "Paterson model."

"Five shots without reloading, eh?" Dunnegan said. "That's something."

"Yes, it's come in right handy a time or two," said Carson.

Getting to his feet, the captain then did something so unexpected as to elicit a soft gasp of surprise from George Townsend, who was closely observing the two men. With a determined shove, Dunnegan thrust the gun—barrel first—through his broad leather belt and said: "Afraid I'll have to hold on to this, Mr. Carson."

For a moment, the scout merely glared at Dunnegan. "That don't sit right with me, Captain," he said at length.

"Sorry, Carson. I can't have you running around the city taking potshots at suspects. This ain't the Wild West. I appreciate the help you've given, but I'll handle it from here."

Though somewhat loath to empathize with the surly, overbearing police captain, I was forced to concede that there was a certain validity to his position. However morally justified Carson's mission might be, he was, strictly speaking, a lone vigilante, operating outside the legitimate channels of the law. Moreover, as a high-ranking member of the newly established Metropolitan Police Force, it behooved Dunnegan to demonstrate—both to the public at large and to his superiors in the municipal government—that he and his men were capable of tracking down and apprehending the fiend who had been terrorizing the city.

Carson, however, was evidently a man unused to bending to authority. For several moments, he continued to glare at the captain with an intensity so unsettling that Dunnegan could be observed swallowing nervously as he attempted to return Carson's baleful stare.

This period of tension was broken in a most unexpected way. Chief Wolf Bear, who had been standing mutely at the rear of the office, suddenly began to address Carson in the harsh, guttural language of the Crow. Carson then answered in the same tongue, whereupon the chief offered a final response. This latter remark was accompanied by a single eloquent gesture, the chief extending his open right hand, palm downward, then abruptly inverting it, as though to suggest a creature rolling over onto its back.

"What the hell are you two talking about?" Dunnegan demanded.

"Why, that's just what the chief was asking," said Carson. "I told him you was set on hunting the Liver-Eater on your own."

"And what did he say to that?" asked Dunnegan.

For an instant, Carson said nothing. Then, with the merest hint of a smile, he replied: "He said you're a brave man."

At this, Dunnegan gave a little grunt of satisfaction. He had been standing with his back toward the Indian, and so had failed to see the latter's gesture. I, however, had clearly observed it. Though ignorant of the Crow tongue (as I have already indicated), I possessed some little knowledge of the sign language employed by those unfortunates deprived of the faculties of hearing and speech, having reviewed a volume on the subject by Thomas Hopkins Galluadet. I was therefore able to recognize a striking similarity between the Indian's hand motion and the deaf-mute sign for the verb "to perish or expire."

Carson, I perceived, had not been entirely candid in reporting the contents of Chief Wolf Bear's remarks. The Indian had evidently said not that the captain was a brave man, but that—in attempting to hunt down the Liver-Eater on his own—Dunnegan would most probably end up a dead one.

CHAPTER ELEVEN

⟨~⟩

THE HOUR WAS NEARING two o'clock in the morning when I finally arrived back at my dwelling. By then, my loved ones had long since betaken themselves to bed. Entering my room, I saw—with a sense of the deepest gratitude—that my ever-solicitous Muddy had made sure not merely to leave a lamp burning on my side table but to turn down my bedclothes and fluff my pillow. Resting upon the latter I found a brief note written in her firm, somewhat childlike hand, explaining that she had awaited my return until nearly midnight, at which point she retired for the evening, assuming that I had been detained for an indefinite period by my meeting with Mr. Wyatt.

Though my fondest wish at the moment was to fling myself onto the mattress and quaff the sweet nepenthe of sleep, I took a moment to compose a short reply, informing Muddy that my evening had been replete with events of a most startling and disconcerting nature. Though exceedingly eager to recount these incidents to Sissy and herself, I hoped to refresh my severely depleted energies with a protracted slumber, and requested that she refrain from knocking on the door to awaken me for breakfast, as was her custom. I then folded this message in half and placed it on the floor of the hallway, just outside my room, where Muddy would be certain to see it in the morning.

Closing the door, I staggered to my bedside and began to divest myself of my clothing. As I did, I made two unexpected discoveries. First, I found that I was still in possession of the ugly, double-barreled pistol that I had taken from the murderous brute whom I had encountered—and rendered unconscious—in the halls of Barnum's museum. Despite the weight and unwieldiness of the gun—which was thrust inside the waistband of my trousers—I had become completely oblivious of its presence: a circumstance perhaps not as surprising as it might seem, in view of the state of near-stupefaction to which the extraordinary turns of the evening had reduced me.

Removing the weapon from my pants, I placed it atop my bureau with the intention of deciding on the morrow how best to dispose of it.

The second discovery was, in effect, the opposite of the first. Instead of finding something unexpected on my person, I became aware that I was *missing* one of my possessions; for—as I emptied my pockets preparatory to stripping off my garments and donning my nightshirt—I realized that my wallet was gone from my frock coat! After confirming the loss of this object by conducting a rapid search of my person, I concluded that it had undoubtedly fallen from my pocket at some point during the evening, perhaps while I was climbing through the window of Wyatt's dwelling, perhaps in the confusion of the violent uprising in which I had become embroiled. There was, however, little to be gained at present from speculating on the question of where or how the wallet might have slipped from my possession. The foremost—the incontrovertible—fact was that it was *gone.*

It might be supposed that I was deeply dismayed by this discovery. The fact is, however, that I was so benumbed with exhaustion that I was capable of feeling nothing beyond a desperate craving for sleep. Besides, there was little to bemoan in the loss of my wallet; for the sad truth was that it held nothing of any real value, its entire contents comprising the calling card that Wyatt had given me—several similar cards imprinted with my own name and address— and a newspaper clipping from the *Times* of London, sent to me by an English admirer, in which it was reported that Queen Victoria had expressed her personal admiration for my poem "The Raven."

As for money, my pecuniary circumstances were such that the wallet had been entirely devoid of currency, my entire fund of cash consisting of less than one dollar in small coins carried loosely in the hip pocket of my trousers. In short, my most significant material loss was of the wallet itself—and even this object was of no very great value, being nearly ten years old and in excessively timeworn condition.

In short, after assuring myself that the wallet was gone, I gave a small shrug of acceptance—quickly completed my bedtime preparations—and threw myself onto the mattress. No sooner did my head touch the pillow than I plunged into oblivion and slept like the dead.

My first sensation upon awakening was of the greatest confusion. For several moments, I lay with my eyes still closed, recalling what seemed to be the details of a remarkable dream, involving a horribly butchered man with the glowing white skin of a seraph—a fearfully destructive riot in a great hall of wonder—the sudden appearance of a heroic, larger-than-life figure who managed to quell the disturbance by an extraordinary display of his power—and other incidents of an equally improbable nature. It was only when I opened my eyes and observed the clumsy-looking firearm resting atop my bureau that I sat up with a start, struck with the realization that these fantastic events were all true!

From the intensity of the daylight streaming through my bedroom window—as well as from my extreme sensations of hunger—I deduced that the day must already be well advanced. Evidently, Muddy had discovered my directive and permitted me to sleep until whatever hour I naturally awoke. Rising with a groan—for my muscles and joints felt inordinately stiff after the singular exertions of the previous night—I made my way to the bureau and consulted my pocket watch. What was my surprise to discover that the time was already several minutes past eleven o'clock!

Rapidly performing my ablutions, I donned my clothes and threw open the door to my room. As I stepped into the hallway, I could discern the low murmuring of my loved ones' voices emanating from the parlor—music more divine to my ears than the lulling melody of the harp of Aeolus. Eager to share with them the tale of my recent, remarkable adventures, I hurried toward the ineffably sweet—the *enthralling*—sound.

I found them seated across from each other, Muddy in an armchair, Sissy on the sofa with Cattarina curled serenely on her lap. At their first glimpse of me, both of my dear ones sprang to their feet—Sissy thereby displacing the slumbering feline, who dropped to the floor with a soft mewl of protest—and came hurrying toward me. Flinging wide my arms, I caught them in a fond embrace.

"Oh, Eddie," cried Muddy, taking my countenance in both her hands and scrutinizing it narrowly. "Let me have a look at you! I've been worried sick all morning!"

"Thank God you were able to get some sleep," Sissy said, her exquisitely delicate eyebrows knitted in concern as she gazed up at me. "You must have been an absolute *wreck* by the time you got home."

"Your description is exceedingly apt, Sissy dearest," I replied. "For the tempestuous events of the evening did indeed leave me feeling not unlike a vessel that—having embarked on an easy voyage during fair, perfectly tranquil weather—is overtaken by a violent storm and subjected to a buffeting so severe as to cause it to founder."

"Poor boy!" said Muddy. "I know *just* what you need to make you feel better. Now, go sit down with Sissy, and I'll be back in a jiffy."

As the dear woman bustled off in the direction of the kitchen, Sissy took me by the hand and led me to the sofa. By this time, I had begun to suspect—from their expressions of intense concern—that my loved ones had already heard something about my grueling experiences of the previous night. Now my supposition was confirmed; for as my darling wife and I settled ourselves on the cushion, I observed a copy of the *Daily Mirror* lying atop the little side table next to the sofa.

"Is that this morning's paper?" I inquired.

"Yes," Sissy answered. "Muddy bought it. She went out early to buy some fresh eggs for breakfast. She was in an absolute *tizzy* by the time she got home. Apparently, the whole city is talking about what happened last night."

Reaching for the paper, I began to peruse it with the most intense curiosity. Apart from a single column devoted to President Polk's decision to order the blockade of all Mexican ports on the Pacific Ocean, the entire front page consisted of stories about Wyatt's murder, the riot at Barnum's museum, and other related matters.

My own *rôle* in the affair was described in a separate piece under the headline: BODY DISCOVERED BY FAMOUS AUTHOR OF HORROR STORIES! MR. E. A. POE IN REAL-LIFE MURDER MYSTERY! Written by George Townsend, this article not only offered a most flattering assessment of my place in the pantheon of contemporary American writers but concluded by printing—as an "extra bonus, exclusive to the *Mirror*"—what the paper described as a "biting satire, typical of Mr. Poe's famously caustic critical style." This, of course, was the lampoon I had submitted to the editor of the *Mirror*, Mr. Morris.

Under normal circumstances, I would have been highly gratified to see my work given such prominence in the paper. So momentous, however, were the events of the preceding twenty-four hours that my feud with C. A. Cartwright now appeared—even to myself—somewhat trivial by comparison.

As I continued my reading, Sissy—who was seated close beside me with her eyes on the paper—suddenly exclaimed: "Oh, Eddie, do you really think that any man could possibly look so hideous?"

This latter comment was in reference to the illustration that occupied the center of the front page—a crude, if vigorously rendered, portrait of a ferocious-looking individual, beneath a heading that read, HAVE YOU SEEN THIS MAN? A caption below the picture informed the reader that the drawing—attributed to "P. T. Barnum's celebrated artist, Mr. Horace J. Oswald"—depicted the visage of "Liver-Eating" Johnson, the savage mountain man who was thought to be responsible for the recent rash of atrocities committed in the city, and who was being sought by the "legendary scout and Indian fighter, Christopher 'Kit' Carson."

As Sissy's comment had indicated, the countenance sketched by Oswald was so grim—so grotesque—so sheerly ferocious—as to seem scarcely human. Indeed, it bore a closer resemblance to the grimacing, masklike faces of certain of the more terrifying demons to be found in the sacred artwork of the Hindoos.

The head was massive and topped with a thatch of thick, exceedingly unruly hair (black in the picture, though the accompanying text made it clear that its true color was bright red). The eyebrows were equally overgrown, forming a single continuous band above two bulging orbs that seemed to glow with a deranged intensity. The nose was jutting and somewhat misshapen—the nostrils flared like those of an enraged stallion. The mouth—which was surrounded by a heavy mustache and luxuriant beard—was contorted into an expression of overwhelming malice. To what degree this singularly unsettling countenance resembled the actual person of Johnson I could not say. There was little doubt, however, that—poorly executed though it was—the drawing created a vivid impression of extreme—of implacable—evil.

"Having never laid eyes on the fellow," I said in reply to Sissy's comment, "I cannot verify the strict accuracy of this portrait. In its general outlines, however, it appears to conform to the description provided by Mr. Carson."

"So it's true, then?" Sissy said in a somewhat awestruck tone. "The man who helped break up the riot really *was* Kit Carson?"

"The note of amazement in your voice is perfectly apt," I replied, continuing to scan the front page of the paper as I spoke. "For the events of last night were of so wild and unprecedented a character as to strain credulity. Nevertheless, I am able to vouch for their truth."

"No wonder you collapsed after getting home, Eddie dearest," said Sissy, giving my arm an affectionate squeeze. "What an awful night. And poor Mr. Wyatt! I can't even bear to think about it. It must have been such a dreadful shock when you found him."

"Indeed, the unfortunate man's savaged body presented a most ghastly spectacle—one which, I fear, shall continue to haunt my thoughts for months, if not years, to come." Even as I spoke these words, an exceedingly vivid image of the butchered albino arose before my mind's eye.

At that moment, Muddy reentered the parlor, bearing a tray laden with a delicious assortment of foodstuffs: toasted bread, several varieties of cheese, hard-boiled eggs, strawberry jam, and tea. So acute was my hunger that even the recollection of the fearful mutilations suffered by Mr. Wyatt could not succeed in dampening it. The instant Muddy placed the meal on the side table, I set upon it with all the voracity of a ravenous member of the species *Panthera leo* pouncing upon its helpless prey.

Resuming her place in the armchair, Muddy folded her hands—rested them on her capacious lap—and watched approvingly while I devoured the food. Seated beside me, Sissy also remained silent, not wishing to interrupt my feast with conversation. For a moment, the loudest sound to be heard in the room was the scraping of the toast as I spread a large dollop of strawberry jam across its surface.

All at once, I became aware of a strange commotion emanating from the street, as if from the noise of many chattering voices. Cattarina—who had jumped onto the window ledge and was staring intently outside—had also begun to act in a somewhat peculiar manner, switching her tail violently from side to side and emitting a low, ominous growl.

"What on earth is the matter with that cat?" Muddy asked, rising from her seat and stepping to the open window. As she peered outside, she raised a hand to her bosom and let out a soft cry of surprise.

"What is it, Muddy?" Sissy asked, getting up and joining her mother. I, too—after bolting down the final morsel of egg—rose to my feet and went to stand beside them at the window.

"Eddie," gasped Sissy as she stared outside. "Is that who I think it is?"

"Yes," I replied. "Though what he is doing here I am at a loss to say."

These remarks pertained to none other than Kit Carson, who was standing on the sidewalk in front of our dwelling, studying the house number painted on the lintel of the door frame. He was accompanied by his son, Jeremiah, as well as their mongrel dog (the evident cause of Cattarina's agitation). Exceedingly conspicuous in his fringed buckskin clothing, Carson had attracted the notice of a sizable crowd of neighborhood residents, who seemed giddy with excitement at finding the celebrated scout in their midst.

Among the assemblage was our plump, gray-haired landlady, Mrs. Whitaker. Perceiving that Carson was in search of our address, she stepped forward and engaged him in a brief conversation. An instant later, she pointed upward in the direction of our window. Following her gesture, Carson met my gaze.

"Morning, Mr. Poe," he called up to me. "I'd appreciate a few minutes of your time."

"Of course," I replied. "Please come upstairs."

"Much obliged," said the scout. Placing his hand on his son's shoulder, he then led the boy to the front door, closely followed by the ever-present dog.

"Oh dear," cried Muddy as the threesome disappeared into the building. Stepping back from the window, she gazed around the parlor in distress, as though the household were in a state of the greatest disorder. Without another word, she hurried to the side table—snatched up the breakfast tray—and went bustling from the room. Sissy, in the meantime, made for the nearest mirror and began to scrutinize her appearance, making small, self-critical, tongue-clucking noises while patting her stray hairs into place and pinching her cheeks to heighten their color.

Somewhat amused by these reactions, I strode to our little foyer and threw open the door to the apartment. I could hear the echo of Carson's boot heels on the wooden steps as he and his small companions mounted the stairwell. An instant later, they arrived at the head of the landing.

"Sorry to come barging in on you like this, Mr. Poe," said the scout.

"There is no need to apologize, Mr. Carson," I graciously replied. "You are welcome here anytime. And you, too, Master Jeremiah," I added, smiling down at the boy, who quickly lowered his eyes and gazed shyly down at his moccasined feet. "Please come in."

With his son and the dog in the lead, Carson entered the apartment. He was dressed, as I have already indicated, in the same wilderness garb he had been wearing the previous night, albeit with one notable exception. The leather belt that encircled his waist was no longer equipped with its holster, Carson having evidently removed this now-superfluous article following the confiscation of his gun by Captain Dunnegan.

Entering the parlor, we found Muddy and Sissy standing side by side in the center of the room, wearing identical expressions of barely suppressed excitement.

"Mr. Carson," I said, "allow me to introduce my aunt, Mrs. Maria Clemm."

"Nice to meet you, ma'am," said Carson, removing his hat.

"And this," I said, indicating Sissy, "is her daughter, Virginia, whom I am blessed to call my own dearest wife."

"Pleasure," said Carson with a nod.

Curtsying daintily, Sissy favored him with a radiant smile. "I can't tell you how thrilling it is to meet you in person, Mr. Carson," she said. "I don't know if Eddie mentioned it, but I was just reading all about you in a book by a gentleman named Parker, who met you while traveling through the Rocky Mountains."

"Don't recollect the man," said the scout.

"Well, he certainly remembered you!" Sissy exclaimed. "He says the most wonderful things about you."

Carson seemed slightly abashed. "Don't go believing everything you read in books, Mrs. Poe. Some of them writers have mighty lively imaginations."

"Oh, I'm well aware of that," laughed Sissy, gazing fondly in my direction.

"And who is this handsome young man?" Muddy said, smiling down at Carson's son.

"My boy, Jeremiah," Carson said. "He don't talk much."

"I am very pleased to make your acquaintance, Jeremiah," said Muddy. "My, what an unusual necklace that is." This remark was in reference to a polished white disk (fashioned, as Carson would later inform me, from the bleached shoulder blade of a buffalo) that depended from a leather thong worn about the boy's throat.

"Belonged to his mother," said Carson.

"I'm so sorry about your loss, Mr. Carson," said Sissy, who had learned the entire story of the murder of Carson's wife from the newspaper. "It must have been so horrible for you. And for your boy."

"Appreciate your sympathies, Mrs. Poe," said the scout.

"And this must be the marvelous creature I was reading about," said Sissy, bending to pat the head of the yellow dog. Standing beside the boy, the mongrel was glancing alertly about the room, as though having sensed the presence of Cattarina. The latter, however, was nowhere in sight, having vanished upon the entrance of the canine.

"Don't know about marvelous," said the scout. "He's a good old pup, though."

"May I offer you something to drink, Mr. Carson?" inquired Muddy. "A nice cup of tea, perhaps?"

"Thank you, ma'am, no. Afraid I ain't got time for socializing."

"What about Jeremiah?" said Muddy. "Wait! I have something right here that I'm sure he'll enjoy." Digging into the pocket of her apron, she extracted one of the peppermint candies I had brought home two days earlier, and extended it to the boy in her open palm.

Jeremiah regarded it eagerly for a moment before glancing up at his father, who gave a nod of assent. Plucking it from Muddy's hand, the boy then popped the sweet into his mouth and began sucking it avidly.

"Thank you, ma'am," said Carson. "He appears to like it."

"He's a beautiful child," said Sissy. Indeed, the blending of white and Indian blood in the boy had produced an individual of most striking appearance, one who combined his father's classically regular features with his mother's raven hair—prominent cheekbones—and bronzed coloring.

"Yes," said Carson with a gentle smile as he reached down and tousled the boy's hair. "Favors his mother. He's the reason I'm here."

"Why, what do you mean?" I asked in surprise.

"I was hoping to leave the boy here," replied the scout. "Just till tonight, mind. While I tend to business."

"I take it, then," I said, "that you have decided to ignore Captain Dunnegan's wishes and proceed with your search for Johnson?"

"Didn't come all this way for nothing," Carson said gravely.

"Why, of course," Muddy replied. "We'll be happy to watch Jeremiah. It's no trouble at all."

"We bunked at the museum last night," the scout explained. "Mr. Barnum was right eager to have us. Offered to let us stay as long as we cared to. Didn't feel just right, though, leaving the boy there. Not that the folks ain't friendly. You should've seen the way they fussed over him. Especially that bearded fat lady."

"Willie Schnitzler," said Sissy. "She's a dear-hearted woman."

"Seemed nice enough, for a fact," said Carson. "All of 'em did—that little Tom Thumb feller, them two Chinamen stuck together at the ribs, that gal with no arms nor legs. Made the boy feel a mite uneasy, though. When I told Mr. Barnum I was leaving, he seemed awful put out at first. He's shut down the place for a spell, you know, so's he can fix it up after last night's ruckus. Anyways, he suggested I come see you folks. Said you two ladies was real accommodating and wouldn't mind watching Jeremiah until I found us a place to stay."

"Why, we'd be delighted to," Muddy repeated, smiling down at the boy, who was gazing slowly about the room. To judge from his marveling expression, the lad was evidently much impressed with our furnishings and *decora*, which—

though hardly resplendent—were undoubtedly of a far more luxurious order than the rough-hewn frontier dwellings to which he was accustomed.

"But where," continued Muddy, "do you intend to find lodgings?"

"Ain't figured that out just yet, ma'am," said the scout.

"Why not speak to our landlady?" Sissy interposed. "She has plenty of space downstairs."

This suggestion struck me as exceedingly sensible, and I hastened to endorse it. "Living alone as a widow whose grown children have long since departed from home," I said, "Mrs. Whitaker inhabits quarters that are far too spacious for her needs. Indeed—from what I gather—there are several rooms that she rarely, if ever, so much as enters.

"Moreover," I added, knowing that pets were not always welcome in the boardinghouses of the city, "she is particularly fond of dogs, having herself owned a succession of canines until age and increasing disability rendered the care of these animals impracticable."

"If you wish," Muddy volunteered, "I will have a word with her about it."

"Thank you, ma'am," said Carson. "That would suit me just fine. Now, if you folks don't mind, I'd best get started."

"May I inquire, Mr. Carson," I said, "as to the precise nature of your plans?"

"To do what I come for," he replied. "Track down Johnson."

"And where, may I inquire, do you propose to begin?"

"Where the trail's least cold," he said.

"In other words," I said, "those places where Johnson has most recently made his baleful presence known?"

"Reckon so," said the scout.

Drawing myself up to my full height, I addressed the scout thusly: "Mr. Carson, I wish to volunteer my services. I am ready—nay, eager!—to assist in your hunt for the murderous wretch who has brought such suffering upon yourself, your son, and so many others."

This pronouncement elicited soft gasps of astonishment from both Muddy and Sissy. Indeed—insofar as my offer was wholly unpremeditated—it came as a surprise even to myself.

Still, there was no real mystery as to my motivation. The courageous resolve of the scout had produced a sympathetic vibration deep within my bosom. In contemplating both his quietly commanding person and his heroic undertaking, I felt my heart stir with an ardent desire to join him on his quest. Every true man will immediately recognize this sensation as being one of the highest and most noble attributes of our sex. That I had directly witnessed the killer's dreadful handiwork—in the form of William Wyatt's unspeakably savaged person—also contributed to my wish to assist in Johnson's capture before he could perpetrate other such enormities.

For a moment, Carson merely regarded me in silence. "I am obliged for your offer. But I wasn't counting on having company."

"That is understandable," I replied. "In the remote and untamed precincts of the Western frontier—where a man must survive on his own, far from the sustaining props of civilization—no virtue is more highly prized than that of self-sufficiency. It is important to remember, however, that you are now venturing into territory whose features are wholly new and unfamiliar to you. You, if anyone, should appreciate the value of having a knowledgeable guide in such circumstances. Indeed, were it not for your own great skills in that capacity, Mr. Frémont might never have reached California."

This latter remark, of course, alluded to the celebrated explorer, John C. Frémont, whose various expeditions had relied heavily on Carson's intimate knowledge of the rugged terrain west of the Mississippi.

"Oh, I reckon he would've stumbled on it by now," replied the scout with the faintest hint of a smile on his handsome countenance. For a moment, he studied me appraisingly. "Feels mighty peculiar, having someone guide *me*," he said at length. "I suppose it makes good sense, though."

"But, Eddie," Muddy exclaimed, her brow knit with anxiety. "Won't it be dangerous?"

"Your concern for my welfare, Muddy dearest, warms my heart to the very core," I replied. "I cannot, however, allow considerations of mere personal safety to deflect me from my duties as both a citizen and a man."

"Don't worry, ma'am," said Carson. "I'll see to it that he don't come to no harm."

"Fair enough," Muddy said with a smile. "I'll take care of your boy, while you take care of mine."

Reaching down a hand, Carson gave his son an affectionate squeeze on the shoulder. "You be good, son," said Carson. "Mind what the ladies say."

"Oh, we'll be just fine, won't we, Jeremiah?" said Muddy. "Do you like lemonade? Well, I know just where to find some."

Urging us to be careful, Muddy bid us farewell, then took the boy by the hand and led him toward the kitchen, the dog trotting close behind.

"Time to go," said Carson, settling his black, wide-brimmed hat on his head.

"May I offer a suggestion, Mr. Carson?" I said.

"Might as well call me Kit," said the scout, "seeing as how you and me are now pards."

"Very well, then, Kit. I could not fail to notice the intense public excitement that attended your arrival at our abode this morning. Your distinctive appearance—and more particularly your picturesque mode of dress—ensures that you will be recognized wherever you go. Crowds are certain to gather around you, drawn by that strange, magnetic power that inheres in the person of every true celebrity. I fear, however, that such attention will only serve to impede our investigation. I therefore propose that you exchange your frontier habiliments for the less colorful garb of the typical city dweller."

"I ain't saying you're wrong, Mr. Poe—" he began to say.

"Eddie," I interjected.

"—but these here are the only duds I got, Eddie. Reckon I could buy me some. But I'm plumb eager to get started. The day ain't getting younger."

"I have an idea," I said. Without another word, I hurried to my bedroom. Though my wardrobe was pitifully meager, I did possess an extra set of somewhat threadbare black trousers and a matching frock coat. Gathering up these garments—along with a white shirt, gray-striped vest, and gray cravat—I quickly returned to the parlor and handed them to the scout.

"You can change in my study," I said. "You'll find it just to the right of the front door."

He regarded the clothing dubiously for a moment, then nodded and strode off in the direction I had indicated.

The moment he was gone, Sissy looked at me and said: "Do you really think your clothing will fit him, Eddie?"

"Why, of course," I replied in surprise. "We are nearly identical in stature."

"Really?" she said. "He seems—I don't know—so *big*."

Indeed, so imposing was the presence of the scout that he did create an impression of inordinate height and strength. In reality, however, he was almost precisely my own size—a fact demonstrated when he returned to the parlor several moments later.

"Ain't quite used to store-bought clothes," he said, gazing down at himself with some bemusement.

"You were right, Eddie," Sissy exclaimed. "Why, the two of you might be twins."

This observation was, of course, hyperbolic in the extreme. If anything, the scout's appearance was the very obverse of my own: blond-haired, gray-eyed, sun-browned, and clean-shaven; whereas my own hair was jet black, my eyes nearly as dark, my complexion pallid to the point of cadaverousness, and my upper lip adorned with a neatly trimmed mustache. Nevertheless, dressed as we were in nearly identical suits, there did appear to be a strange kinship between us.

The sartorial transformation of the scout having been completed, we made our farewells to Sissy and proceeded to the front door, where I removed my beaver hat from its wall-hook and placed it atop my head prior to departing. Though I possessed only one such item of haberdashery, there was no need for another in the present circumstances, Carson having insisted on retaining his own broad-brimmed Western hat—the only item of apparel he refused to relinquish for a more fashionable model.

I had just thrown open the apartment door and was on the brink of stepping over the threshold when Carson let out a sigh.

"Feel a mite naked, going hunting this way," he said, gazing down at the area of his hips.

I understood immediately that he was referring to the absence of his gun belt and revolver. All at once, I was struck with another inspiration. Instructing the scout to wait for me in the corridor, I hurried to my bedroom and removed the double-barreled pistol from atop my bureau. An instant later, I returned to Carson and handed him the weapon, explaining how it had come to be in my possession.

For several moments, he studied it closely, hefting it in his hand—peering along the barrels—scrutinizing its firing mechanism. All at once, with the first digit of his right hand inserted through the trigger guard, he twirled the gun several times around his finger and thrust it into the waistband of his trousers.

Then—buttoning his coat so that the weapon was invisible—he said in a tone of grim satisfaction: "She ain't much. But she'll do."

PART THREE

The Searchers

Chapter Twelve

S T. John's Park at Hudson Square—where the fearfully butchered remains of ten-year-old Rosalie Edmonds had been discovered early Wednesday morning—had, at one time, been the hub of one of the most fashionable neighborhoods in Manhattan. Gracefully landscaped and planted with a splendid variety of trees—catalpas, cottonwoods, horse chestnuts, silver birches, and others—it served as a private oasis for the wealthy inhabitants of the handsome dwellings that engirdled it.

In recent years, however, the neighborhood had undergone a dramatic decline, owing to the northward migration of the city's wealthier classes, who—in response to the growing number of immigrants flooding into the southernmost districts of Manhattan—had abandoned their former enclaves and fled uptown to the relatively unpopulated area above Fourteenth Street. As a result, the charming little park had suffered a severe deterioration. Its manicured lawns were now rank with vegetation—its carefully tended flower beds choked with weeds—its pristine grounds littered with refuse. In place of the elegant couples strolling arm-in-arm along its gently winding gravel paths, there could be found indigent wretches of both sexes who, lacking any proper home, made the park their squatting place in all but the most severely inclement weather.

In spite of his eagerness to embark on his manhunt, Carson had rejected my proposal that we travel to the park by omnibus. He preferred to go on foot, he declared. Though he offered no reason, I gathered—from the manner in which his narrowed eyes moved restlessly from side to side, taking in all the sights around him—that he wished to familiarize himself with both the specific details and overall character of his new environment: to get, in his own words, "the lay of the land."

Owing to my suggestion that he exchange his frontier costume for more suitable garb, Carson drew little, if any, notice from our fellow pedestrians. Apart from his Western-style hat and tell-tale, bowlegged gait, he appeared no different from any other city-dweller. We were thus able to pass freely along the streets, unmolested by those who might otherwise have recognized—and been inclined to accost—the famous scout.

Partly because of the intensity with which he was studying his surroundings—and partly because of his inherently taciturn nature—he spoke very little as we proceeded toward our destination. Occasionally, to be sure, he would ask me a question. Never having visited a town larger than Santa Fe, he was naturally curious about many aspects of city life—its unique architecture, exotic inhabitants, and peculiar customs. What, he wanted to know, was that lofty edifice on Broadway through whose ornate entrance a parade of fashionably attired men and women were steadily trooping? Who were those olive-skinned musicians playing hand-cranked organs on street corners, while costumed monkeys capered at their feet? Why was that pitifully thin, raggedly dressed little girl selling flowers made of paper? What language were those dark-clothed men with unkempt beards and peculiar headwear speaking?

In addition to answering these queries, I was able—by dint of much prodding—to coax a certain amount of new information from him about the individual we were seeking. According to the scout, Johnson was renowned among his fellow mountain men not merely for his superhuman strength and unparalleled ferocity but also for his reputedly preternatural skills as a tracker and woodsman.

"They say he can sniff the ashes of a burned-out Indian campfire and tell how many men was gathered there and what tribe they belong to," said Carson.

"Oh, come now!" I exclaimed. "I cannot believe that any human being—even one with the most highly developed sense of olfaction—could be capable of such a feat."

"I admit it ain't common," replied the scout. "But I've known more than one trapper with a mighty keen nose."

Carson also related an anecdote that graphically illustrated the sheer inhuman savagery that had made the Liver-Eater a figure of awe even among the hardened frontiersmen of the Far West. Some years earlier, Johnson—along with several companions (including his sometime partner, Del Gue)—had managed to ambush and exterminate a party of two-dozen unsuspecting Sioux warriors who had camped for the night on the banks of the Milk River. After scalping the victims, he had then performed his trademark atrocity, consuming the uncooked liver of the leader of the slain band of Sioux.

This barbarous deed, however, was by no means the end of his enormities. With clots of gore still clinging to his beard, he ordered his companions to decapitate all twenty-four of the corpses. Next, he placed the heads in a large iron pot and boiled them until the flesh had fallen away from the bone. The gleaming skulls were then impaled on two-dozen sharpened stakes placed at intervals along the riverbank, where they could be viewed by horrified steamboat passengers who were making their way to a nearby outpost.

"Why, I have never heard of anything so dreadful!" I gasped at the conclusion of this grim—this appalling—tale. "What sort of man would conceive of, let alone carry out, such an outrage?"

"A bad one," said Carson simply.

Shaking my head, I continued thusly: "Though I am not a man who is given to vengeful desires, it is hard not to wish for the swift and utter destruction of this loathsome monster."

"Got to find him first," said Carson.

I inquired of Carson if he had seen the portrait of Johnson that had appeared in that morning's edition of the *Mirror*.

The scout nodded. "Mr. Barnum showed me."

"And what did you think of the likeness? Did it bear any resemblance at all to his actual visage?"

"Not hardly. Looked more like one of them carved masks I seen worn by some Assiniboin medicine men."

"I, too, felt that Mr. Oswald's rendering possessed a distinctly masklike quality. Moreover, it is difficult to believe that—with the entire city alerted to his presence—Johnson will not attempt to disguise himself by altering his most conspicuous features. At the very least, I would expect him to shave off his distinctive red beard, and quite possibly to change the color of his hair by means of boot polish or some other blacking agent."

"Likely you're right," Carson concurred.

Less than ten minutes later, the little park came into view. As we began to make our way across Laight Street, Carson's attention was suddenly attracted by a disturbing sight. The driver of a coal-wagon—a squat, barrel-chested fellow, whose enormous forearms were so heavily matted with hair as to appear to be covered with animal fur—had leapt down from his seat, strode up to his horse, and was mercilessly lashing the beast. The poor creature—a painfully underfed, swaybacked nag—had come to a halt in the middle of the street, evidently unable to pull the overloaded wagon another step. Shouting grievous execrations, the red-faced man continued to apply his whip in a most savage manner, while the helpless beast whinnied in pain and fear under the relentless torrent of blows.

At his first glimpse of this deplorable spectacle, Carson stopped dead in his tracks. Though his expression remained impassive, I could see by the rippling muscles of his tightly clenched jaw that his anger was rapidly building to a dangerous, if not deadly, pitch.

"I perceive, Kit, that you are exceedingly incensed by this sickening display of brutality," I remarked. "Your humane feelings do you credit. Unfortunately, the mistreatment of animals is an all-too-common feature of our city. The lower classes in particular show little, if any, tenderness toward members of the four-legged kingdom. Though you may be tempted to intercede in this matter, I would urge you to refrain from doing so. To become embroiled at this moment in a public altercation would run counter to our immediate purpose, which is to proceed with our investigation in a manner that calls the least possible attention to yourself."

"I'll just have a word with him," Carson replied, his voice taut.

Less than one minute later, the brawny coal-hauler—though wielding a whip and weighing at least twice as much as the slender scout—was lying unconscious in the gutter, blood issuing copiously from his broken nose.

Turning away from the prostrate fellow, Carson unclenched his fists and walked back to my side. "Let's go," he said.

"Your definition of the phrase 'to have a word with someone' is most unusual, Kit," I remarked as we crossed into the park. "So far as I can tell, you said nothing at all to the fellow before beating him into a state of insensibility."

"Oh, I believe he got the point," he replied.

Six or seven months had elapsed since I last had occasion to visit the neighborhood of Hudson Square. Even at that time, there was ample evidence of its sad decline. Now I was positively shocked by the appalling condition into which the once-delightful park had deteriorated. Littered with refuse, infested with weeds, overgrown to the point of rankness, it possessed a palpable aura of neglect and even *seediness*.

Few people could be seen inside the park, and those who were present appeared to be of the lowest and most degraded order of society. Two male juveniles, dressed in badly tattered garments, stood face-to-face on a patch of lawn, alternately hurling a jackknife into the turf in a game of mumblety-peg. Nearby, a young girl sat cross-legged in the grass, plucking up dandelions by their stems and sending their delicate, tufted seeds floating through the air by means of repeated exhalations. Using a gnarled stick as a cane, a white-haired crone in a threadbare shawl made her way slowly along one of the garbage-strewn paths, occasionally stooping to pick up and examine a scrap of refuse. On a slatted bench lay a filthy heap of rags that, upon closer inspection, turned out to be a slumbering vagrant. Apart from these wretches—and, of course, ourselves—the park appeared to be entirely devoid of humanity.

For a moment, Carson stood just inside the entrance, gazing about the grounds with a look of intense concentration. Beyond reporting that the child's corpse had been discovered within the park, the newspapers had given no indication of its precise location. All at once, the scout strode away decisively, while I hurried close behind. Crossing the lawn on which the three urchins were engrossed in their respective pastimes, he came to a halt before the shoulder-high wall of hedges that formed the northernmost boundary of the park, separating it from Vestry Street.

Still not speaking a word, Carson dropped to one knee and began to scrutinize the ground. All around him, the grass had been badly crushed. In some places, small patches of bare soil were visible. I saw at once that he had unerringly discovered the spot where the victim's body had lain; for the trampled ground bore unmistakable witness to the large number of people who had recently visited the site—not only police officers and newspapermen but those morbid curiosity-seekers who immediately descend upon the scene of every sensational crime. That Carson had been able to discern the location from his vantage point at the opposite end of the park was, of course, a source of much wonderment to me.

I began to compliment him on his remarkable powers of observation, but he quickly held up one hand and uttered an emphatic, "Shhh!"—plainly indicating he required unbroken concentration.

For several moments, he maintained his kneeling position, running his hand over the grass—lifting up small amounts of the exposed soil and sifting them between his fingers—and even, at one point, bending his face to the ground and sniffing the earth!

At length, he rose to his feet and turned his attention to the hedges beside him. At one time, these had been so carefully tended that their tops might have been trimmed with the aid of a carpenter's level. Now—like all the vegetation in the sadly neglected park—they had been allowed to become wildly overgrown.

Carson was inspecting an area of the hedge that—at a glance—was indistinguishable from the surrounding growth. As I scrutinized this spot more narrowly, however, I perceived what appeared to be a barely discernible breach in the densely interwoven foliage—as though the branches, stalks, and leaves had undergone a recent disturbance. Reaching both hands into the hedge, Carson forced it apart and peered into its midst. Standing close beside him in a thick clump of grass that reached to the level of my shins, I followed his gaze, attempting to interpret the signs that had riveted his attention.

A moment later, Carson straightened up—stepped back from the hedge— and turned to face me.

"It was him, all right," he said in a measured voice.

"I assumed as much," I replied. "But on what basis can you make such an unequivocal assertion? Did you find concrete evidence of his presence—footprints, perhaps, that you were able to identify as those of Johnson?"

Carson shook his head. "Too many folks been tromping around. Ground's all tore up."

"Then how are you able to state with such assurance that Johnson was here?"

"Smelled him," said the scout.

So unexpected was this statement that, for a moment, I was rendered mute with astonishment. At length, having recovered myself sufficiently to speak, I addressed my companion thusly:

"I do not hesitate to say, Kit, that, while in no way questioning your veracity, I cannot conceive of any mortal performing the act you have just described— i.e., detecting, after the lapse of several days, the aromatic residue of a specific individual. Why, such a thing borders on the miraculous, outdoing even the extraordinary olfactory feat you attributed earlier to Johnson."

"It don't hardly qualify as a miracle, Eddie," said the scout. "Johnson spent nigh on ten years trapping beaver. Ain't no mistaking his scent."

From my perusal of Mr. Parker's journal—as well as from other volumes that treated the subject—I knew something about the method by which the mountain man of the Far West practiced his singular craft. After locating a stream where his quarry was to be found in abundant numbers, he would set his traps in the shallows and secure them to the banks by means of wooden stakes. He would then apply the bait. The most common substance used for this purpose was the oil derived from the castor gland of a male beaver. The exudation from this oil would deceive another beaver into thinking that an intruder had encroached upon his territory. Coming to investigate, the unwary rodent would step upon the submerged trap and find himself hopelessly ensnared.

From Carson's remark regarding Johnson's long years as a trapper, I inferred that constant exposure to the odoriferous bait had imbued the latter with a distinctive scent. While this emanation might be undetectable to an ordinary man, it was evidently palpable to the scout, who—like others of his remarkable breed—relied for his very survival on a seemingly uncanny ability to interpret, through his exquisitely attuned sensory organs, every nuance of his surroundings.

"And have you arrived at any further conclusions regarding Johnson?" I proceeded to inquire.

"He come in through here, toting the body," answered the scout, gesturing toward the area of the hedge he had just been examining. "Left the same way."

"I presume," I said, "that he chose this particular place of ingress in order to minimize any possibility of detection. It cannot have escaped your notice that the entrance to the park is flanked by a pair of street lamps; whereas this area is relatively unilluminated. However depraved a man Johnson may be, he is not, evidently, a reckless one; for—besides disposing of the body in the dead of night, when no witnesses were likely to observe him—he took the added precaution of entering the park at a spot shrouded in darkness."

"Reckon he's holed up somewheres around here?" asked the scout.

"That seems exceedingly unlikely, partly for the reason I have just adduced," I said. "To abduct a victim from the very neighborhood in which he himself resides would be a supremely incautious act, wholly inconsistent with the diabolical cunning that is clearly one of the hallmarks of his character. Moreover, his other recent atrocities were committed in widely different areas of the city. As a result, we can infer nothing about his whereabouts from the mere *locations* of his crimes."

"So you figure he carried her off somewheres else to kill her, then troubled himself to haul the body back here?" the scout said.

"That is indeed my conjecture. I would even go so far as to suggest that, in returning the girl's remains to this location, he traveled a considerable distance—far enough, in any case, to require the use of a horse. Permit me," I continued, pointing over the top of the hedge, "to direct your attention to the house across the way."

Craning his neck, Carson peered at the dwelling in question—a three-story, high-stoop brick dwelling whose original elegance had not been entirely effaced by its current state of disrepair.

"You will observe," I remarked, "that there is a rather elaborately wrought hitching post on the curb in front of the house. This post stands *directly opposite* the spot at which, according to your own conclusions, Johnson entered the park. Is it unreasonable to assume that he chose this point of ingress precisely because of its proximity to the hitching post—in other words, because it offered a convenient place to tie up his horse while he disposed of his grisly burden?"

"That seems a pretty fair guess," the scout concurred.

"The question, of course, still remains," I went on. "Why—after satisfying his monstrous appetites by performing his dreadful butchery on the abducted child—did Johnson assume even the smallest risk of discovery by transporting the body all the way back here? The answer, no doubt, lies in his singularly malevolent nature—his desire to cause the greatest possible consternation by ensuring that the hideously mutilated remains of little Rosalie Edmonds would be discovered in her own backyard, as it were, possibly by a neighbor, friend, or even relation."

"Yes, he's a mean son of a bitch, for a fact," said the scout. "You say the child was butchered something dreadful?"

"So much so," I replied, "that the mere perusal of her autopsy report elicited sensations of almost unendurable horror within my bosom. Why do you ask?"

Stepping back to the badly trampled spot where the victim's corpse had evidently lain, Carson squatted on his haunches, his forearms resting on his thighs. I came up beside him and lowered myself into an identical position.

"Notice anything?" he asked, pointing a finger at the exposed patch of earth.

Peering narrowly at the area, I studied it briefly before answering in the negative.

"That's just the point," said Carson. "You'd think there'd be some sign of blood if she was cut up that bad—even allowing for most of it to have got soaked up. But there ain't. Not a pebble, nor a blade of grass, nor even a speck of dirt with a trace of blood anywheres."

For a moment, I contemplated this startling fact in silence. All at once, I was seized with a violent tremor as the hideous implication flashed upon me.

"There can be only one explanation for the phenomenon you have noted," I said in a quivering voice. "The poor child's body must have been thoroughly exsanguinated prior to its disposal. In short—she was bled dry!"

"That's how I figure it," the scout replied solemnly.

"I now understand a detail of the crime that has occasioned me a certain degree of perplexity," I said with a gasp. "The child's ankles were tightly secured with a length of rope. According to both the newspaper accounts and the autopsy reports, this was done to prevent her escape. Most captives, however, are bound *hand* and foot—that is to say, about the wrists as well. That Johnson lashed only her ankles together suggests that he did so for another, inconceivably horrible purpose."

For a moment, Carson merely regarded me narrowly. "I see what you're getting at," he said at length. "You figure he strung her up by the feet, slit her throat, and bled her out. Like butchering a hog."

"I fear that may well be the case," I replied, "though the mere thought of it is too ghastly to dwell on."

"Yes, it is," said the scout, standing up. "But he's bound to do it again, unless we stop him right quick."

As I rose to my feet, I was suddenly overcome with a sensation of vertigo—occasioned, no doubt, by the shocking mental image of the mutilated little girl, dangling upside down in the manner of a slaughtered farm animal. Shutting my eyes, I remained absolutely motionless for several moments.

The dizziness had just begun to subside when I heard a strange, high-pitched voice directly behind me. Opening my eyes, I turned and found myself facing an exceedingly shriveled old woman whom I recognized at once as the crone I had observed upon first entering the park. With her grizzled hair—rheumy eyes—wizened complexion—and long, crooked nose—she resembled nothing so much as one of the malefic Weird Sisters encountered by the titular hero in the opening scene of *Macbeth*.

"I beg your pardon?" I said to the elderly female, who was draped in a shawl so excessively tattered that it hung from her haggard frame in shreds. "Were you addressing my friend and myself?"

"Have you seen her?" she asked in an urgent tone.

"*Her?*" I said. "Do you mean the little Edmonds girl, Rosalie?"

A look of intense bewilderment passed over her countenance. "Is that her name? Rosalie? I seem to remember it different." She shook her head slowly from side to side and mournfully added: "It's been so long—so long."

"Did you know the child, ma'am?" Carson inquired.

"Know her?" cried the old woman. Lifting her chin, she raised the bony index finger of her right hand to the base of her withered throat. "Look!"

Though reluctant to come any closer to the bedraggled crone than was absolutely necessary, I bent slightly forward and peered at the spot to which she was pointing. Encircling her neck was a narrow strip of fabric. So execrable was its condition—so soiled and frayed—that, at first, I could not tell what it was. Gradually, however, I was able to identify it as a length of once-pink ribbon, of the sort that a young girl might wear as an ornament in her hair.

"Surely you do not mean to suggest," I said, "that this mouldering band of silk—which appears to be nearly as ancient as yourself—belonged to the little victim?"

"Oh yes. It was her favorite," replied the old woman in a tremulous voice. "I'm saving it for her. You gentlemen will tell me when you find her, won't you?"

Turning to my companion, I whispered: "I fear, Kit, that this wretched creature is one of the vast horde of penniless outcasts adrift in the city. Advanced age and unremitting adversity have reduced her to a state of extreme physical and mental debility. Indeed, she appears to be hopelessly *non compos mentis*. We cannot expect to learn anything from her that will aid in our investigation."

Nodding in agreement, Carson then did something unexpected. He reached into his pocket and extracted a small leather pouch, from which he proceeded to remove a new silver dollar. He then pressed this coin into the hand of the old woman, who raised it to her eyes and stared at it for several moments, her expression slowly changing from one of deep perplexity to equally profound amazement.

Then—without saying a word—she turned hurriedly away and went shuffling along the curving path, her gnarled walking stick making soft, crunching sounds in the gravel.

CHAPTER THIRTEEN

T HE AFTERNOON BEING well advanced by this point, Carson was eager to proceed with our investigation. Accordingly, we took leave of St. John's Park and bent our steps toward the site of Johnson's most recent atrocity: William Wyatt's residence in Washington Square.

As we made our way along the clamorous streets, my companion maintained an even more steadfast silence than before, allowing me abundant opportunity to reflect upon his singular character. That the scout possessed an unusually kind and sympathetic heart there could be no doubt. Twice that afternoon I had seen him offer unhesitating assistance to a weak and needy being—first, the savagely mistreated dray-horse, then the piteous and sadly deluded old woman.

There was, however, an entirely different—if not diametrically opposite—side of the Westerner. Along with his more benevolent instincts, he possessed, to a remarkable degree, the attributes of a skilled and deadly warrior. I had personally witnessed this latter aspect of his character in the swift and summary way that he had dealt both with the rioters at the Barnum museum and with the brutal teamster outside the little park. This peculiar combination of gentleness and ferocity—of altruism and violence—was also fully documented in Mr. Parker's journal. One of the anecdotes in that volume had made a particularly forcible impression on me.

In the winter of 1833, an acquaintance of Carson's—a French trapper named Antoine Robidoux—discovered that a fellow in his employ had stolen a half-dozen of his finest horses. Knowing Carson's extraordinary skills as a tracker, Robidoux had prevailed upon him to pursue the thief. Two days later, Carson came riding back into camp, leading all six of the recovered animals.

When Robidoux eagerly questioned Carson as to precisely what had transpired between himself and the renegade, the scout, with a shrug, had merely replied:

"I was under the necessity of killing him."

In recounting this episode in his book, Parker had laid special emphasis on this exceedingly laconic statement, for it seemed to him to epitomize all that was most contradictory about the self-effacing—soft-spoken—yet coolly implacable scout. Now, as Carson and I strode toward our destination, I, too, found myself marveling at the paradoxical nature of my new acquaintance: a man who, when the occasion demanded it, was equally ready to dispense either Christian charity or savage retribution—kindness or destruction—mercy or death.

Arrived at length at the northern end of Washington Square Park, Carson and I stood for a moment on the side of the street across from Wyatt's residence and surveyed the scene. A small number of people—most of them, to judge by their attire, residents of the fashionable neighborhood—were congregated on the sidewalk directly in front of the two-story building, seemingly transfixed by the sight of its handsome façade, behind which so much suffering and horror had recently occurred. Though I had anticipated finding one or more police officers posted at the site, none was visible anywhere.

As I had yet to impart to Carson the full details of my experiences of the previous evening, I now took the opportunity to do so. I succinctly described the entire sequence of events, beginning with my arrival for my preappointed meeting with Wyatt—continuing with my efforts to enter the house—and concluding with my shocking discovery of the victim, and the police activity that followed. As I spoke, Carson listened in silence, every sense on the alert as he absorbed the many impressions of his surroundings.

At length, my recitation having been concluded, he turned to me and said: "Let's have us a look inside." He then began to cross the street, evidently intent upon entering through the front door.

Coming up beside him, I said: "It is exceedingly unlikely that the interior of the house will be so readily accessible."

"Ain't no harm in trying," was his reply.

Assuming an air of authority, we marched boldly up to the gathered spectators, who—at our command—parted to make way for us. We then strode directly up the marble stoop—halted before the door—and tried the knob. As I had anticipated, this proved to be locked, the police undoubtedly having taken this precaution to protect the contents of Wyatt's dwelling from the depredations of both professional thieves and morbid souvenir-hunters.

"Wouldn't take much to break that lock," Carson mused.

"In view of the number of people presently observing us," I said, "such a measure seems highly imprudent."

Nodding, Carson said: "Let's head on around back." We then turned and descended the steps. No sooner had we reached the sidewalk than a well-dressed gentleman—perhaps sixty years of age, with a white "goatee" beard and a complexion strongly pitted by the small-pox—stepped away from the crowd and approached us.

"Are you two fellows officers of the law?" he inquired.

"Nope," said the scout.

Inferring from the old man's expression that he was eager to convey some piece of information, I hastily interjected: "What my friend means to say is that, while not *officially* affiliated with the police, we are assisting them in the pursuit of the killer responsible for the heinous murder that took place on these premises. And who, my good sir, are you?"

Raising one gloved hand to the brim of his tall beaver hat, the old man introduced himself thusly: "Haswell. Charles Haswell. Live just a few doors down—Number 26."

"I take it, then," I said, "that you were closely acquainted with the victim."

"Not really, no. Just in a neighborly sort of way—exchanging hellos when we passed on the street, pausing to converse every now and again." Shaking his head, he dolefully added: "Can't imagine why anyone would do such a dreadful thing. Just heard about it a little while ago. I still can't believe it."

"A little while ago?" I exclaimed. "But how is that possible? The events of last evening produced an immediate uproar in your neighborhood. The square was thronged—the tumult excessive. By early this morning, news of the atrocity was on the lips of every newsboy in the city."

"That's just it," said Haswell. "I wasn't *in* the city. Left last evening for Rahway. Business trip—won't bore you with the details. Didn't get back into town until an hour ago. That's why I haven't told the police yet."

"Told them what?" inquired Carson, who had been eyeing the old man narrowly.

"Had an odd experience with Wyatt yesterday," Haswell answered. "Mighty odd."

"Pray go on," I said.

"Bumped into him on the street around lunchtime. Hadn't seen him for a week or two. We chatted a while. I was telling him about a splendid history of the Punic Wars I'd just finished. He loved books, you know, though his vision wasn't worth a damn. Trouble was, I couldn't recall the author's name. Memory's not what it used to be, I'm afraid. It came to me later, though—just as I was about to set off on my trip. Figured I'd let him know before I forgot it again. So as soon as I left the house, I stepped over to his place. Banged on the door. A few moments later, I hear footsteps on the other side. 'Who's there?' says a man's voice. 'It's Charlie Haswell,' I say. 'I remembered the name of that historian— Artunius.' 'Thank you,' he says. Then I hear him walk away."

"I assume," I said, "that in describing this episode as *odd*, you are referring to the fact that your neighbor never opened the door."

"Not so much as a crack," Haswell affirmed.

"And you are certain that the voice you heard was that of Mr. Wyatt?"

"Why, of course," he exclaimed. "No mistaking it. Had a perfectly unique quality—like a flute."

"Are you able to state with any degree of precision the time at which this incident occurred?" I inquired.

Nodding emphatically, the old man replied: "Walked out my front door at 7:32 on the dot."

"You are quite sure of the time?"

"Positively. Had a steamboat to catch at Battery Place. Kept checking my watch."

"I see," I replied. "Well, Mr. Haswell, I thank you for this information. It may indeed prove highly useful in our attempts to identify and apprehend the perpetrator of this outrage. Now, if you will excuse us, my companion and I must proceed with our investigation."

Gesturing for Carson to follow, I made for the narrow mews lane that led to the rear of Wyatt's residence.

"What do you make of that old-timer?" Carson asked.

"I find his story most intriguing," I replied. "I confess, however, to being somewhat puzzled by one aspect of his account. I refer to the question of *chronology*. Haswell asserts that he departed from his home at precisely 7:32 P.M. Let us assume that his gait has been somewhat slowed by age. Even so, it cannot possibly have taken him more than half-a-minute, at the most, to traverse the distance between his own residence and Wyatt's. He then ascended Wyatt's stoop, knocked on the door, and waited, as he says, 'several moments' before receiving a reply. Let us therefore add, at a generous estimate, an additional one or two minutes. The time at which he held his brief exchange with Mr. Wyatt would therefore have been no later than, let us say, twenty-five or -six minutes before eight o'clock.

"Now, at that very moment, I had just paid the bill for my dinner at Sweeney's restaurant, where I had gone to partake of a light supper before proceeding to Wyatt's. I know the time for a certainty, as I made sure to consult my own watch prior to leaving the restaurant. The distance from Sweeney's to Wyatt's front door is no more than a half-mile. I was walking at a rapid pace, partly because of my eagerness to proceed with the business at hand, and partly to enjoy the salutary pleasures of a brisk postprandial stroll. Though I did not check my watch again upon reaching my destination, the time cannot possibly have been later than, let us say, 7:45—approximately ten minutes after the period at which, according to his account, Haswell spoke through the closed door with his neighbor. Here, then, is the source of my perplexity. Is it possible that Wyatt could sound perfectly normal at one moment and, a mere ten minutes later, be discovered in the appalling condition in which I found him? That Johnson could have committed such extensive—such horrific— atrocities in so brief a span?"

"I've knowed men who could butcher a whole buffalo in near as little time," said Carson.

A shudder coursed through my frame as I recalled the ghastly mutilations to which poor Wyatt had been subjected—and which were indeed not unlike the butcheries a Western hunter might perform upon the carcass of a slain member of the species *Bison bison*.

By this point, my companion and I had reached Wyatt's backyard. To surmount the waist-high wooden fence that partitioned it from its neighbors was the work of a moment. Carson spent several minutes examining the premises with the same degree of intensity he had displayed earlier in St. John's Park. He then asked how I had effected my entrance on the previous night.

"Through that window," I replied, pointing upward. "Its lower sash was partially raised. As you can see, however, it has since been shut tight, no doubt by the police in their efforts to ensure that no unauthorized persons enter the crime scene."

"How's about that door?" said Carson with a tilt of his chin.

Trying the knob, I said: "Locked, as it was last evening." All at once, I was struck with an idea. Extracting my penknife from my pocket, I unfolded the little blade and said: "Yesterday, I was with Mr. Townsend—the young reporter for the *Mirror*—when he undid a door lock with the aid of his penknife. Having closely witnessed this trick, I believe I may be able to duplicate it."

Dropping to one knee, I inserted the little blade into the hole in the doorplate and began to manipulate the inner workings of the lock, employing—so far as I could tell—the same technique used by Townsend. After the lapse of several fruitless minutes, however, I was gripped with a keen sense of frustration.

"Let me have a whack at it," said Carson.

Lifting up the right leg of his trousers, he exposed the top of his high black-leather boot, from which there protruded a stag knife-handle. Grasping this, he slid out an exceedingly formidable-looking blade, approximately eight inches in length.

As I stepped aside to make room for him, Carson took my place and wedged the point of his hunting knife into the crack between the door and the frame. Then, gripping the stag handle as though it were a chisel, he clenched his opposite hand into a fist and delivered a hammerlike blow to the pommel. The door gave slightly. At a second blow, the lock broke with a snap and the door flew in upon its hinges.

Replacing his knife inside his boot and lowering his pants leg, Carson crossed into the house, while I followed closely behind. Moments later, after ascending a narrow flight of stairs, we found ourselves inside the parlor.

At my first glimpse of the surroundings, I emitted a gasp of surprise. On the previous evening, as the reader will no doubt recall, I had been struck by the fact that—despite the extreme savagery with which Wyatt had been attacked—the room itself had been relatively undisturbed. Now, as I glanced about me, I was startled to see that it had been reduced to a state of the wildest—the most chaotic—disorder. The ornamental objects arranged with such fastidious care on the rosewood *étagère* had been violently displaced. Chairs lay on their sides. The drawers of the Hepplewhite secretary had been pulled open and rifled. Even the sofa cushions had been torn from their place and lay scattered on the floor.

As he moved about the room—stepping over a porcelain vase here—stooping to examine the broken crystals of an argand lamp there—raising his head to sniff the air—Carson said: "Looks like the Liver-Eater went plumb loco in here."

"No one who witnessed, as I did, the unspeakable savageries inflicted on poor Mr. Wyatt would dispute your assessment of Johnson's sanity," I replied. "If, however, you are referring to the excessive disarray of the room itself, the blame must fall not on the fiend we are hunting, but on the police."

"You mean Dunnegan's men done this?"

"I am afraid so. Certainly the parlor showed no signs of having been ransacked before their arrival."

"Why'd they go and wreck the place?" Carson asked.

"The investigatory method favored by the New York City police is notoriously heavy-handed," I said. "Essentially, it consists of tearing apart a crime scene in their search for clues. It is possible, moreover, that Dunnegan commanded his men to scour the premises for the missing document of which I had informed him, with the chaotic results that we see."

"Document?" asked Carson, who, in his slow circumambulation of the parlor, had paused at the fireplace—an Italianate mantel with caryatid supports in the shape of two classically draped maidens.

"My reason for coming here last evening," I said, "involved a mysterious document, the authenticity of which Mr. Wyatt wished me to verify. Unfortunately, I know nothing at all about this item, apart from the fact that it was evidently of great value."

Carson, who had been studying the inner portion of the hearth, now lowered himself onto his haunches. I came up beside him and—looking down—saw what he was staring at.

It was a small pile of ash.

"What do you reckon this might be?" said Carson, touching the tip of his right forefinger to the pile.

"Perhaps it is merely the residue of a winter hearth-fire," I remarked, squatting beside him. Even as I offered this suggestion, however, it struck me as unlikely. From my observations of the previous evening, it was clear that Wyatt's domicile was normally kept in impeccable condition. Surely, the fireplace would have been thoroughly swept out and scrubbed by his housekeeper in the months since it had last been used.

My thoughts on this score were confirmed an instant later when—after rubbing the ash gently between the pads of his thumb and index finger—Carson announced: "Ain't more than a day old."

"Can you tell what it is?"

"Paper, most likely," said Carson. "Wonder if it ain't your document."

He reached again into the little mound of ash and, this time, plucked out something so small that, at first, I could not tell what it was. Gripping it as lightly as a lepidopterist might clutch the infinitely fragile wings of a member of the family *Papilionidae*, he held this item out for my inspection. I saw at once that it was a bit of badly charred paper—roughly circular in shape and no more than a half-inch in diameter—that had escaped obliteration by the flames.

Taking it from Carson's fingers, I raised it to my eyes and scrutinized it closely. Two letters—originally written in a bold script but now badly faded—were visible on the singed little scrap: *Lo.*

"Little, if anything, can be gleaned from this fragment," I remarked. "Nevertheless, it will behoove us to preserve it."

Rising to my feet, I glanced about the room. Immediately, my eyes fell upon the mahogany secretary-bookcase that stood against the opposite wall. That the police—perhaps in their hunt for the missing document—had paid particular attention to this piece of furniture was evident from the thoroughness with which it had been ransacked. Its drawers—which hung open to their fullest extent—had been subjected to a violent rummaging, as had its bookshelves and various small compartments. Strewn on the floor at the foot of the secretary was a heterogeneous assortment of items—stationery, books, pamphlets, and other ephemera.

Stooping to secure an envelope from among this hodgepodge, I placed the little fragment inside it—folded the envelope in half—and stuck it inside the hip pocket of my coat. I was about to turn back to Carson when my gaze lighted on a periodical lying directly beside my left foot. Picking it up, I saw that it was an issue of Mr. William Lloyd Garrison's abolitionist publication, *The Liberator.* That Wyatt would have been interested—if not actively involved—in this cause came as no surprise to me, given the remarks he had made, during his visit to my home, on the subject of bigotry and humanity's deplorable tendency to persecute those of different skin color.

"What's that you're looking at?" Carson asked from across the room.

I had just opened my mouth to reply when I froze.

The front door had creaked open. Someone had unlocked it and was now inside the house!

Carson—who had heard the noise, too—quickly raised a finger to his lips to enjoin me to silence. He then swiftly crossed the room and positioned himself beside the doorway. Flattening himself against the wall, he reached inside his jacket and withdrew the pistol I had given him, which he held at shoulder level, the barrel pointing upward.

The following moments were more replete with tension than any I had theretofore experienced in my life. As I stood facing the doorway—awaiting the imminent appearance of the unknown intruder—my heart beat so violently in my bosom that I felt sure its pounding *must* be audible to my companion's preternaturally sensitive ears. With each approaching footstep, I grew more firmly convinced that the newcomer was none other than Johnson himself, who had returned, for whatever nefarious reason, to the scene of his most recent atrocity. The agony of suspense caused the blood to congeal in my veins and the moisture to drain from my mouth. In another moment, I would be face-to-face with the awesome—the dire—the unimaginably vicious person of the Liver-Eater.

Seconds later, a tall, exceedingly lanky figure appeared in the doorway and stepped into the room. I saw at once that he was not the fearsome giant I had been expecting, but rather a hollow-chested young man, perhaps eighteen or nineteen years of age, who seemed startled to the point of paralysis by my own unanticipated presence in the room. As he stood there gawking at me—his pale eyes bulging, his mouth hanging open—Carson came up behind him and raised the pistol to the back of his head.

"Hands up, friend," commanded the scout, cocking the weapon.

The young man's reaction was as instantaneous as it was surprising. A startled yelp burst from his lips—his body was shaken with a violent tremor—and he collapsed to the floor in a dead faint!

"Skittish, ain't he?" said Carson, thrusting the pistol back into his belt after carefully lowering the hammer.

By this point, my wildly accelerated heartbeat had subsided to its normal speed, and the moisture had returned to my mouth. "Indeed," I observed, "he appears to be an inordinately timorous specimen of manhood."

Reaching down, Carson gently tapped the unconscious young man on one cheek. "Wake up, son," he said.

The young man gave a tremulous moan. His eyelids fluttered open. All at once, he sat bolt upright and threw his hands above his head. "Don't shoot!" he cried. "I'm not a thief!"

Seated on the floor, his elevated hands trembling with anxiety, the young man presented a most singular appearance. He was unusually thin, with long, spindly limbs. His head—which was somewhat undersized for his stature—sat atop an inordinately scrawny neck. An enormous Adam's apple bobbed up and down in a most disconcerting fashion with every word he spoke. He had a weak, recessive chin. As if to compensate for this deficiency, Nature had endowed him with great jug-shaped ears and an exceedingly conspicuous nose, somewhat resembling the beak of a common *Larus argentatus*, or herring gull. His pale eyes were large—round—and protuberant. His hat had become dislodged when he fell, revealing a headful of wildly unruly, frizzy brown hair. Altogether, he was one of the least prepossessing individuals I had ever encountered.

"On your feet, son," said Carson. "We won't harm you."

After gazing back and forth at us for a moment with a look of uncertainty, the young man scrambled awkwardly to his feet.

"You're not the police?" he said in a quivering, high-pitched voice.

"No," I replied. "We are here in the capacity of private investigators."

All at once, the young man's gaping eyes seemed to grow even larger. "I know who you are! You're Mr. Poe! And *you're* Kit Carson!"

"And who might you be?" said the scout.

"Pratt, Harry Pratt," said the young man, whose countenance had assumed an expression of the greatest conceivable excitement. "I can't believe it! Mr. Poe and Mr. Carson—in the flesh! By golly—this is really something! I was just reading about you in the *Mirror* this morning! Guess you're here to track down the killer, hey?—that Liver-Eating fellow?"

"That, indeed, is the mission that has brought us to these premises," I said. "But what, pray tell, is *your* business here?"

"Me? Oh, I helped out Mr. Wyatt. He couldn't see very well, you know, so he hired me to come to his house and read to him."

I now recalled that, during his visit to my residence, Wyatt had referred to a youth named Harrison who performed that function for him.

"That's me," declared the young man when I related this fact. "Harrison Pratt. Everyone calls me Harry, though. Except Mr. Wyatt. He had very formal manners—not stiff or anything, just very refined. A real gentleman—nice as they come. Why anyone would want to hurt him I'll never know."

Up until this point, young Pratt's attention had been so thoroughly focused upon Carson and myself that he had taken little note of his surroundings. Now—as he looked about the room—his gaze fell upon the gouts of dried blood that were visible all around the spot where Wyatt had met his dreadful end.

"Oh my," he gasped.

Fearful that the grisly sight might cause him to relapse into insensibility, I quickly sought to distract him. "Perhaps you are not aware of this fact, Harry," I said, addressing him in this friendly fashion to set him at ease, "but in a very real sense, I owe my involvement in this case to you; for had you not brought my essay to Mr. Wyatt's attention, that unfortunate gentleman would never have sought me out in the first place."

"What—?" Pratt said somewhat dazedly, his eyes still fixed on the sanguinary evidence of the slaughter. "Oh—you mean that article in the *Broadway Journal.* Yes. Mr. Wyatt was real taken with it—I'm not sure why. I don't mean it wasn't interesting. It *was.* Tremendously. That's why I read it to him to begin with. But I was surprised at how excited he became when he heard it."

"The reason," I replied, "is readily explained. Your employer believed that—in view of my expertise in the area of handwriting analysis—I would be able to authenticate the document to which he attached so much importance."

At this statement, a look of the deepest perplexity suffused Pratt's visage. "I don't quite follow you, Mr. Poe."

"Mr. Wyatt was in possession of a mysterious document which, if *genuine,* was evidently of enormous value—perhaps even priceless," I explained. "Tell me, Harry—were you at all aware of this circumstance?"

"No, sir," the young man exclaimed with a vigorous shake of the head. "Priceless document? Sorry. Wish I could help you, but . . ." He concluded the statement with a shrug of his narrow shoulders.

"When's the last time you was here, son?" Carson suddenly interjected.

"A few days before—before *this,*" the gangly youth replied, gesturing toward the blood-stained armchair to which the victim had been strapped by his fiendish killer, and which now lay on its side on the carpet.

"Judging from your mode of entry, Harry, am I correct in assuming that you possess a key to the front door?" I asked.

"That's right. Mr. Wyatt gave me one last winter. He didn't want me waiting outside in the cold in case he wasn't home when I arrived."

"Mighty thoughtful of him," said Carson.

Pratt swallowed hard, causing his Adam's apple to slide up and down the length of his throat. "That's the kind of gentleman he was," he said with emotion. "Real caring. I know he wouldn't have wanted anything to happen to my Butler."

"I beg your pardon," I said.

"My copy of Butler. Wait, I'll show you."

Taking care to circumvent that portion of the room where the butchery had occurred, the young man quickly crossed the floor to the secretary-bookcase. Kneeling at its base, he began to search through the volumes that had been tossed so heedlessly onto the carpet.

"Just what I was afraid of," I heard him mutter to himself. A moment later, he emitted a cry of relief—rose to his feet—and came striding back in our direction, a slender volume clutched in his hands.

"Here," he said, extending the book toward me.

Taking it from his hands, I opened to its title page and saw that it was an old, albeit well-preserved, edition of Samuel Butler's justly celebrated burlesque, *Hudibras*—a work whose many remarkable merits were marred only slightly by its gross deficiencies of style, tone, and versification.

"It's one of my treasures," remarked the young man, as I passed the volume back to him. "I brought it here last week to read to Mr. Wyatt. I got only halfway through it. Mr. Wyatt suggested that I leave it here, so I wouldn't have to keep carrying it back and forth. When I heard what happened to him, I thought I'd better come get it before something happened to it. It's pretty rare."

As he spoke, he caressed the fine Morocco cover of the book, as tenderly as the lover of a beautiful maiden might sit at her bedside and stroke her pale, fever-moistened brow as she languished in the grip of a virulent wasting disease.

"Well, Harry," I said, "I am pleased to see that you have successfully accomplished your mission. And now, if you will excuse us, Mr. Carson and I must attend to ours."

"Maybe I should stick around," the young man volunteered. "I could help look for that document."

"Much obliged, son," said Carson. "But we'll manage on our own."

"All right," Pratt said somewhat reluctantly. "But if you ever need my help, just let me know. You can find me down at Mr. Lowe's law office on Maiden Lane. I'm his junior clerk."

Giving each of us a hearty farewell handshake, the young man turned to leave. All at once, a thought occurred to me.

"Before you go, Harry," I said, halting him in his tracks, "tell me this. Did your employer ever receive any visitors while you were present?"

Arranging his features into a pensive expression, the young man reflected on this question for several moments before answering thusly: "Now that you mention it, yes. A couple of months ago. Someone showed up two weeks in a row while I was here. A very fine-looking gentleman."

"That exceedingly general description might apply to any number of individuals," I remarked. "Can you be more precise in your delineation of his appearance?"

"Let's see," said young Pratt. "He was short but very powerful-looking. Carried himself real proudly—head high, shoulders thrown back. *Regal*, you might say. Wore a black cape with red lining. Handsome, too—dark wavy hair, light blue eyes. He had a big, jagged scar down one side of his face, but it didn't hurt his looks any. That's about all I remember."

"That is very helpful," I said. "Have you any idea of the reason for his visits?"

The young man shook his head. "Mr. Wyatt took him into another room to talk. He didn't stay long—maybe ten or fifteen minutes, tops. After he was gone, Mr. Wyatt would come back into the parlor, and we'd pick up the reading where I'd left off. He never said a word about the man, and it wasn't my place to ask."

After absorbing this intelligence for a moment, I thanked Pratt for his help and assured him that, should we need his further assistance, we would not hesitate to seek him out at his place of employment. He then swiveled on his heel and strode from the room, his clothes hanging so loosely on his tall, spindly frame that his trouser-legs flapped and fluttered with every step he took.

"Stick that boy on a pole," Carson remarked as we heard the front door slam shut behind the departing young man, "and he'd make a first-class scarecrow." Then, glancing at me, he added: "You all right, Eddie?"

"Yes, yes," I assured him.

In truth, however, I was filled, at that moment, with a sense of the keenest frustration. Few experiences in life are more irksome than the inability to recall a fact that remains tantalizingly close to—but stubbornly beyond the reach of—our conscious awareness. It was in just such a state of acute exasperation that I now found myself. Pratt's description of Mr. Wyatt's mysterious visitor had struck a chord within my memory. I was convinced that I myself had, at some time in the past, seen the same dark-haired, imposing-looking gentleman.

For the life of me, however, I could not recall where.

CHAPTER FOURTEEN

N O SOONER HAD HARRY PRATT made his exit than Carson and I resumed our work. The examination occupied us until dark. We
searched every part of the house, not excepting Wyatt's bedroom,
along with its two spacious closets. Our investigation, however, turned up
nothing that might assist in locating the killer's whereabouts. Nor—though
we scrutinized every paper we came across—did we discover any written
document of apparent significance, leading me to believe that the small heap
of ashes Carson had found in the fireplace might well have represented the incinerated vestiges of Wyatt's mysterious treasure.

Our search being completed, we took our leave, departing—as we had
entered—through the rear of the house, so as not to excite the notice of any
policeman who might be patrolling the neighborhood.

As we rounded the corner of the building and emerged onto Fifth Avenue,
Carson said: "I could do with some food. Know any good eating houses
around these parts, Eddie?"

As I had not partaken of any sustenance since breakfast time, my own
hunger was intense. Equally acute, however, was my embarrassed awareness
that—having so recently treated myself to a dinner at Sweeney's—I could ill
afford the indulgence of another meal, however inexpensive, at a downtown
restaurant. Feeling somewhat nonplussed, I did not respond immediately.

Carson—with that finely attuned sensitivity which coexisted so incongruously with his warrior's temperament—seemed to intuit the source of my hesitation and immediately declared: "I'm buying."

"No, no," I protested. "I cannot permit you to pay my way. After all, it is *you* who are the guest here in my city."

"Reckon I'm of a different opinion," said the scout. "Way I see it, you're doing me a service. Least I can do is keep you fed."

I was forced to concede that there was a certain validity to his point of view.

"Since you put the matter in those terms," I graciously replied, "I can hardly refuse your generous offer. Permit me to make a suggestion. New York abounds in oyster saloons. As you have evinced a keen interest in the social customs of our city, perhaps you would care to try one of these establishments."

Never, by his own admission, having dined on oysters, Carson was intrigued by the novelty of my proposal and readily agreed. Accordingly, we proceeded downtown and arrived, in short order, at the popular eatery called Ludlow's, from whose entrance—located below street level—there issued both a continuous din and a distinctly *fishy* aroma. Descending a short flight of stairs, we pushed our way through the swinging doors and found ourselves inside the crammed—cacophonous—and exceedingly pungent oyster cellar.

Glancing over at my companion, I saw, in the murky light of the cavernous hall, that he was grimacing slightly, perhaps at the intense (if by no means unsavory) aroma suffusing the place—perhaps at its unremitting clamor. Between the chatter of the diners—the clink of the dishes—the shouts of the waiters—the cries of the cooks—the restaurant fairly reverberated with noise. To a man like Carson—whose ears were accustomed to the sublime stillness of the forest, where the sound of a snapping twig was sufficiently jarring to be a possible source of alarm—the racket must have seemed little short of deafening.

We had been waiting only a minute or two when a stout, middle-aged fellow with a coarse, ruddy complexion—cornflower eyes—and rust-colored hair as tightly curled as the wool of a merino sheep—appeared before us and greeted us with an extravagant display of courtesy. I took him at once for the proprietor, Mr. Ludlow.

"Follow me, gents," he declared, then ushered us past the long, crowded bar and across the smoke-filled hall to a little stall in the rear. Hanging our hats on the brass wall-hooks, we slid into our seats, while Ludlow handed each of us a well-worn bill of fare. He then enjoined us to "eat hearty" and hurried away to attend to a party of new arrivals.

Studying the menu, I saw that its offerings consisted of a dizzying variety of oysters—Cape Cods, Chesapeakes, Blue Points, Lynn Havens, Mattitucks, Peconics, and more—served either raw, broiled, fried, creamed, or scalloped. For those desiring more elaborate preparations, there were also oyster stew, oyster pie, fish with oyster sauce, and a dish denominated as *poulet à la Ludlow's*, which consisted of a poached chicken with oyster stuffing.

No sooner had I finished perusing the menu than a burly waiter in a badly stained apron materialized at our table to take our order.

"What's your pleasure, Eddie?" asked Carson.

"Though tempted by several of the choices," I replied, "I am unable to resist the oyster stew, which is universally regarded as the *specialité de la maison.*"

"Same for me," said Carson to the waiter.

"Anything to drink?" inquired the latter as he scratched our order onto his pad.

"Beer," said Carson.

Faced with a choice of beverage, I felt momentarily at a loss. Owing to a nervous constitution of more than usual sensitivity, I have, throughout my adult life, been inordinately susceptible to the stimulating effects of alcohol. I have therefore maintained the most abstemious habits in relation to drink. Despite the foul calumnies of my detractors—men whose meagerness of talent was surpassed only by their pettiness of character—I have never been guilty of intemperance.

At the same time—as a well-bred Southern gentleman—I have permitted myself to partake of modest amounts of liquor in certain social situations when to do otherwise would have seemed grossly inconsistent with the prevailing spirit of conviviality. The present was just such an occasion. Carson's offer to pay for my dinner had made him, in a very real sense, my host. To permit him to drink by himself would have seemed extremely unsociable, if not positively *rude.*

Accordingly, I ordered a large glass of rum punch.

"Be back in a jiff," said the waiter before disappearing into the smoky depths of the teeming dining hall.

During our examination of Wyatt's abode, Carson—displaying the same intensity of concentration he had shown in St. John's Park—had spoken very little. Now—as we awaited the arrival of our meal—I took the opportunity to ask what he had managed to learn from his search.

"Mighty little," he replied. "You seen the place, Eddie. Looked like a herd of buffalo stampeded through it."

"Were you at least able to pick up Johnson's scent?" I inquired.

Carson shook his head. "Too many people been traipsing through there. From the smell of it, I'd say Dunnegan and his boys ain't used to regular bathing. Didn't help matters that the windows was shut up so tight."

I responded with an understanding nod. Even I—whose olfactory senses were far less acute than those of the scout—had noted the thick, unpleasant odor that pervaded Wyatt's parlor and that appeared to be compounded of blood, sweat, and the stale aroma of the enormous Havana cigar James Gordon Bennett had lit up shortly after his arrival.

"Your allusion to the close, exceedingly airless atmosphere of the parlor raises an intriguing point," I said to the scout. "As you undoubtedly observed during our search of the house, all of the windows upstairs, including those in Wyatt's bedroom, were opened to their widest extent. In view of the inordinately oppressive weather that has afflicted the city in recent days, this circumstance is hardly to be wondered at.

"Now, if Wyatt sought relief from the heat by keeping the second floor of his abode thoroughly ventilated, it hardly makes sense that he would not do the same *downstairs*. It must therefore be assumed that the windows in the parlor were fastened not by Wyatt himself, but by his assailant.

"But why? Only one chilling answer suggests itself—to prevent Wyatt's screams from being heard on the street.

"Let us now consider several other factors in the case," I continued. "We know that Wyatt was secured to an armchair. We know, too, that—in contrast to little Annie Dobbs and Rosalie Edmonds—he was *not* dispatched with a savage wound to the throat. Indeed, he was still clinging to life, however tenuously, when I found him. Taken together, these facts—along with Johnson's precaution in closing the parlor windows—lead to an inescapable conclusion. The killer entered the house with the deliberate intention not merely of slaying the victim, but of subjecting him to *torture*.

"Again, we must ask—why? To say that Johnson was merely indulging in his unholy lust for cruelty is only part of the answer. After all, he has previously been able to satisfy his barbaric appetites without resorting to such elaborate steps as sneaking into a house, overpowering a victim, tying him to a chair, closing all the windows, et cetera.

"No. We must assume that, in subjecting poor Wyatt to this horror, Johnson was attempting not merely to inflict suffering for its own sake, but to force Wyatt into revealing something—no doubt the location of the mysterious document.

"This, I submit, explains the exceptionally tidy, undisturbed condition of the house at the time of the murder. There was no need for Johnson to ransack the place in his search for the document. Extracting the information from Wyatt by this unspeakable means was a far more efficient way of discovering what he wanted to know."

"Why'd he cut out Wyatt's tongue?" asked Carson. "Seems like a mighty foolish thing to do if you're trying to get a man to talk."

"The most likely explanation," I replied, "is that Johnson committed that particular atrocity *after* Wyatt had already revealed the secret location of the document. After all, it would appear—from the evidence you yourself discovered inside the fireplace—that Johnson was successful in his mission."

"You figure he burned up the paper after he found it?" Carson asked.

"So it would appear."

Carson reflected on this theory for a moment before saying: "One thing. You said something a minute ago about Johnson 'sneaking into' the house."

"That is correct," I said. "I have been proceeding under the assumption that he entered—as did I—through the partially opened window at the rear."

Carson gave a dissenting shake of the head. "It's likely that Johnson slipped out that way. But it ain't how he got in. There was only one set of tracks leading up to that window—*yours*."

"Then how," I wondered, "*did* he gain entrance to the house? Is it conceivable that Wyatt opened the front door to him?"

"Maybe so," said the scout.

"But why would he invite such a fiercesome-looking stranger inside his abode. Unless—" I said, with a sudden sense of dawning realization.

"Unless they wasn't strangers," Carson remarked, completing my thought.

At that moment, our waiter reappeared, bearing a tray with our dinners. "Here you are, gents," he said as he set an enormous, steaming bowl before each of us, along with our respective drinks. He then placed a basket of crackers in the center of the table and took his leave.

For a moment, Carson merely stared down at his meal with a look of uncertainty on his handsome visage. And indeed, the bowl of stew must have offered a somewhat daunting prospect to one unused to such a concoction. To begin with, there was the inherent unsightliness of the main ingredient—the oyster being a delicacy whose succulent flavor is notoriously at variance with its unappetizing appearance. Moreover—in keeping with the gargantuan portions for which Ludlow's was renowned—each of our bowls was heaped to the point of superabundance with dozens of the fat, glistening, milk-boiled mollusks.

Whatever qualms might have been induced in my companion by the *look* of the stew, however, were quickly overridden by its irresistibly luscious aroma. Tucking our napkins into our shirt collars, we snatched up our spoons and began—to employ a singularly apt colloquialism—to "dig in."

In view of what I knew about the hunters and trappers of the Far West— whose coarse and uncouth habits were consistent with the savagery of their environment—I was surprised to see that, in regard to etiquette, Carson comported himself with a finesse that would have done credit to a member of the English gentry. His fine table manners were all the more notable insofar as the stew was exceedingly awkward to eat—some of the oysters being of such inordinate size that a knife was required to slice them into three or four pieces before they could be consumed. Nevertheless, he managed to dine without spilling so much as a drop of liquid on his napkin.

At first—as we applied ourselves to our meals—we spoke very little, our conversation being limited to a brief exchange about the quality of the food, which Carson conceded was "right tasty." Gradually, however, a warm, exceedingly companionable sensation began to suffuse my bosom—the effect, no doubt, of both the rich, intensely satisfying stew and the unusually potent rum punch. I grew expansive. In response to the scout's query about the precise nature of my work, I began to regale him with a detailed description of several of the stories that—however bitterly disappointing in regard to their *pecuniary* success—had brought me broad recognition as an unrivaled master of the loftiest of all fictional forms, the short prose narrative.

As I proceeded to summarize the plots of these tales—"William Wilson," "Ligeia," "The Pit and the Pendulum," and one or two more—I could not help but notice that, while unfailingly polite, Carson's responses were of a somewhat perfunctory nature. It soon became clear—from certain terse, though pointed, comments of his—that he did not hold a high opinion of those who made their living by composing works of imaginative fiction.

At first, he refused to expatiate upon this prejudice. Eventually, however, I managed to discover its source. It derived from a singularly tragic incident that had occurred several years earlier.

In the fall of 1842 (so he related in his characteristically laconic manner), a couple named White were traveling by wagon along the Santa Fe Trail when they were set upon by a party of Jicarilla Apache Indians. White was slain, his wife taken prisoner. When news of the attack reached Taos, a rescue expedition was immediately organized, with Carson enlisted as a guide.

"We hightailed it out to where it happened," the scout explained. "Wasn't much left of Mr. White. The Indians had tied him to a wagon wheel and had their fun with him. The buzzards had took care of the rest.

"We buried what there was, then set out after the Indians. Hardest trail I ever followed. Took a week to catch up with them. We come upon their camp late one afternoon. Killed the whole dern crew. Too late for Mrs. White, though. She'd been stabbed through the heart not more than ten minutes before. Probably a mercy. From the looks of it, she suffered awful bad before being put out of her misery."

"Suffered in what way?" I tremulously asked, unable to contain my morbid curiosity, even while dreading what I might hear. Carson, however—with his usual reticence—refused to specify the nature of her torments, explaining that there would be no point in doing so, other than to spoil my appetite.

This answer only had the effect of causing my imagination to run riot. A powerful shudder coursed through my frame as I pictured the horrors to which the poor woman might have been subjected. At length—thrusting these hideous fantasies from my mind—I addressed the scout thusly:

"Though Mrs. White's ordeal is almost too painful to contemplate, I fail to see its relevance to your acknowledged contempt for the creators of narrative fiction."

Having just speared a large oyster on the tines of his fork and inserted it into his mouth, Carson—in keeping with his well-developed sense of social propriety—took a moment to masticate it thoroughly before replying.

"When we was gathering up her belongings," he said, "I come across a little book. First time I ever seen one like it. *Kit Carson, King of the Mountains,* it was called. After we dug a hole for her, I gave it a look.

"Never read such a load of hogwash," he continued, a distinct note of bitterness creeping into his voice. "Made me out to be a great hero, fighting a whole army of outlaws single-handed, and slaying Indians by the hundreds. I quickly seen how it was with poor Mrs. White. Knowing I lived nearby, she'd been clinging to that book like it was the Holy Bible. Praying that I'd show up in time and save her."

Here, the scout's handsome countenance darkened visibly. "It's a mighty hard thing to swallow, Eddie. Knowing how that poor woman's mind was filled with false hope by all the lies in that damned book."

For a moment, I made no reply. That Carson had no wish to be viewed as a

kind of buckskinned demigod—a more-than-human being capable of miraculous feats of heroism—was understandable. His resentment of those
writers of cheap "blood-and-thunder" fiction—who played on the gullibility
of an all-too-credulous public by portraying him in this wildly exaggerated
light—was justified. To condemn *all* literary men for the sins of a few talent-
less *hacks*, however, seemed excessively severe.

I opened my mouth to voice this opinion. Before I could speak, however, I
became aware that Carson and I were no longer alone. Someone had appeared
beside our table. Glancing up, I was startled to see a female of most striking
mien. She could not have been younger than thirty. In the prime of her womanhood, she must have been a person of exceptional loveliness. Even now, when
age and dissipation had coarsened her features, she possessed an arrestingly
handsome countenance: eyes large and of an emerald hue—lips of a voluptuous fullness—nose tending slightly toward the aquiline—thick red tresses
piled high atop her head and held in place by a pair of cheaply ornamented
hairpins.

Her natural endowments of beauty, however, had been subjected to the sadly
corrosive effects of a wayward, if not depraved, existence. Her handsome face
was heavily rouged; her full lips painted crimson. She was bedecked in a scarlet
gown that left her arms and bosom exposed to a shameful—to a *shocking*—
degree. In the unblushing freedom of her manner—no less than in the tawdry
style of her dress—there was ample indication that she belonged to that infamous class of womanhood who infest the shadowy byways and iniquitous
dens of the vice-laden metropolis.

Directly to her rear stood a sharp-featured youth, perhaps ten years her junior, whose "flash" appearance—well-oiled hair, green velvet waistcoat with
filigreed buttons, fancy neckerchief adorned with a paste stickpin, tight-fitting
plaid pantaloons—marked him as a member of the city's all-too-numerous
tribe of criminal "swells"—pickpockets, panders, and thimblerigs. It was clear
that he was in an advanced stage of inebriation. He seemed decidedly unsteady on his feet, and his face wore a stuporous expression. His bleary gaze
was fixed upon his female companion, who was now regarding the scout with
an appraising look that was—particularly for a female—brazen in the extreme.

"Did I hear right?" she said. Her slurred enunciation indicated that she, too,
had imbibed a considerable quantity of alcohol. "You really Kit Carson?" Evidently, she and her escort had been passing by our table on their way out of
the restaurant and had overheard our conversation.

"Yes, ma'am," the scout softly replied without looking up at the woman.

"Huh!" she exclaimed. "You ain't what I pictured. I pictured—I don't know—someone *bigger*. Didn't you picture someone bigger, Jimmy?" she continued, turning to her companion, who appeared to be experiencing a certain degree of difficulty in keeping his vision focused.

"I dunno," mumbled the latter in a sullen tone. "C'mon, Nell. Let's get the hell outta this joint."

"You're awful pretty, though, I'll say that for you," the woman continued, turning back to the scout. Leaning down, she placed one extravagantly braceleted hand flat on the table—reached out with the other—and softly tickled Carson under the chin with her index finger.

"Your friend's kind of cute, too," she added, turning to look at me in the most flagrant manner imaginable.

This shameless display of sheer—of unmitigated—*coquetry* brought a blush of indignation to my cheeks. My reaction, however, was mild compared to that of her companion, the inebriated young man called Jimmy.

"Hey, quit that stuff, Nell," he cried, grabbing her by the arm and yanking her into an upright position. "You're with me!"

"All right, all right," she growled back at him, pulling herself free of his grasp. "Don't bite my head off!"

"I'll do a helluva lot worse than *that* if you don't behave yourself. Anyways," he said, looking down at the scout with an exaggerated sneer, "I don't see what's so goddamned great about *him*. Big hero—hah! All he's done is get them two little girls killed."

"Ah, you stupid lunkhead—you don't know what you're talking about," Nell retorted derisively. "Don't you read the papers? *He* didn't do it. It was that other mug—Johnson!"

"You're the lunkhead, not me," the young lout snarled in reply. "Johnson'd never left the mountains if your friend here hadn't chased him east. He'd still be out there killing Indians. Doing us all a big favor, too. Fewer of them damned redskins around, the better. Why, there ain't one of them savages that's worth spit. I wish they'd all—"

Whatever odious thought the young reprobate intended to express was left unspoken; for at that moment, Carson swiftly reached out a hand—grabbed him by his gaudy neckerchief—and, with a single savage motion, jerked the fellow so close to the table that his face ended up only inches away from the scout's half-consumed bowl of oyster stew.

"We've heard just about enough from you, friend," Carson said, the very quietness of his voice conveying a quality of extreme—of overpowering—menace. "Understand?"

As the scout's knuckles were tightly pressed against the larynx of the vile young blowhard—whose formerly pasty complexion was rapidly assuming an alarmingly scarlet hue—it was impossible for the latter to respond with anything other than a rapid nod of the head and a vaguely affirmative gurgle.

Carson released his hold on the young man's neckerchief, while giving him a disdainful little shove. The wretch staggered backward a few steps, coughing and choking. Stifling a laugh at his discomfiture, his red-haired companion immediately took him by the arm and hurried him away from the table—though not before casting a glance over her shoulder and winking at Carson in a manner so suggestive that merely to witness it caused my own face to redden.

No sooner had this hopelessly degraded pair vanished from our sight than I reached for my tumbler and raised it to my lips. Somewhat to my surprise, only a tiny quantity of liquid remained, which I quaffed in a single sip.

"I regret your having been subjected to such vulgar attention by that scandalous specimen of womanhood, Kit," I declared, replacing the empty glass upon the table.

"Oh, she wasn't as bad as all that," he replied. "Right sociable, in fact. It was her gentleman friend I didn't much cotton to."

He then plucked the napkin from his collar. "Reckon I've had enough. How about you, Eddie?"

In truth, though my bowl was still more than half-full, my appetite had long since been slaked by the exceedingly rich preparation.

"To consume even one additional morsel of this delectable concoction would, I fear, place an intolerable strain upon my already overburdened organs of alimentation," I jocularly replied. "Shall we go?"

Carson summoned the waiter and settled the bill. We then rose to leave. As I got to my feet, I was overcome with a sudden sensation of vertigo—the result, no doubt, of the highly fortified punch, to whose inebriating influences I was particularly susceptible, no alcoholic beverage of any sort having passed my lips in many months.

Once outside on the street, however, my head began to clear somewhat. The temperature had moderated to a marked degree with the setting of the sun, and the evening air felt inordinately refreshing, especially in contrast to the smoke-filled confines of the overcrowded oyster saloon.

As we directed our steps toward home, I found myself brooding over our encounter with the redheaded Cyprian and her dissolute escort. Beyond the obvious matter of their inordinately offensive comportment, something about the pair continued to trouble—to *gnaw at*—me. I could not, however, identify the source of my uneasiness—the normal acuity of my cognitive processes remaining somewhat blunted by the aftereffects of the punch.

My companion, in the meantime, maintained his usual silence. Glancing over at him as we sauntered along the streets, I saw by the light of a gas lamp that his features were arranged into a singularly pensive expression. He, too, was obviously buried in thought.

The instant we came in sight of our destination, all thought of the two degraded wretches vanished from my mind. Merely to glimpse the warm glow of the upper-story windows behind which my darling Sissy and Muddy were safely ensconced drove all sense of care from my bosom. I was burning with eagerness to hear how they had spent their day, and how they had contrived to provide diversion for Carson's young son, Jeremiah. I stepped off the curb and began to cross the cobblestoned thoroughfare, which—owing to the lateness of the hour—was devoid of all vehicular traffic.

I was halfway to the opposite side when I suddenly grew cognizant that Carson was no longer at my side. Pausing, I turned to look behind me. The scout, I perceived, was still standing on the sidewalk, gazing upward at the narrow strip of sky exposed between the rooftops of the surrounding buildings.

"Is everything all right, Kit?" I called to him.

"Don't see a whole lot of stars in these parts, do you?" he replied, his voice tinged with a note of sadness I had not heard in it before.

"No," I answered. "Not, at any rate, in comparison to that wild domain from which you hail, where a man may stand upon a mountain peak at night and enjoy an unobstructed view of the heavens in all their vast and scintillant glory."

"You reckon there *is* a heaven, Eddie?" the scout unexpectedly asked.

"Most assuredly so," I said. "For do we not, in the soul-stirring music of the highest poetry, hear an echo of that supreme—that *supernal*—beauty that exists in the realm of the angels?"

"Some folks don't believe in angels," said Carson, rousing himself from his sky-gazing reverie and approaching the curb. "Nor heaven, neither. Indians don't. Take my wife's people. Far as they're concerned, the dead go off to a world just like ours. The Other Side Camp, they call it. Same mountains, same animals, same stars, same—"

All at once, the scout ceased to speak and drew to an abrupt halt. By the light of a nearby street lamp, I perceived that his features were wrought into an expression of extreme attentiveness, as though he had suddenly detected the presence of an impending danger.

An instant later, an alarming noise smote my ears—the sound, rapidly growing in volume, of an approaching vehicle—of pounding hooves and clattering wheels. Instinctively, I twisted my head toward the source of the clamor and immediately felt the blood congeal within my veins.

A fire-wagon led by a pair of wildly galloping steeds was swiftly bearing down on me!

So startling was this sight—and so dulled by drink were my normally quick and catlike reflexes—that I felt rooted in place. I was paralyzed by terror—not unlike a member of the species *Herpestes edwardsi*, or Indian mongoose, when confronted by the deadly, hypnotic stare of a cobra. In another instant, I would be crushed into a hideous mass of oozing blood—mangled flesh—and splintered bone. And yet, the only movement I could manage was to shut my eyes and mouth a silent prayer.

All at once, I felt a terrific force slam into my body, driving the wind from my lungs and sending me crashing to the ground. At nearly the same instant, my ears were filled with a thunderous din, as the charging fire-wagon went roaring past, mere inches from where I lay beneath the full weight of my companion. With little thought of his own safety, Carson had evidently launched himself from the curb and knocked me out of the way of the oncoming juggernaut just in the nick of time.

As the deafening clamor began to recede, Carson rolled from my body, stood up, and stared after the wagon as it disappeared down the street. Then, turning back in my direction, he extended a hand and helped me to my feet.

"You all right, Eddie?" he asked.

For a moment, I was too breathless to speak. At length, after gratefully drawing in several deep drafts of air, I replied thusly: "Thanks to your own swift and selfless action in throwing yourself directly into the path of the madly onrushing vehicle, I am perfectly fine. Indeed, the only injury I appear to have sustained is some minor bruising to my right arm, which bore the brunt of my fall."

"Can't figure why that driver didn't slow down when he seen you," Carson said. "You was lit up mighty clear by these street lamps."

"The answer to that question is readily given," I said. "It is a deplorable feature of our city that its volunteer fire companies are largely manned by denizens of the poorest and most degraded slum neighborhoods. For many of these brutes, membership in such an organization is little more than a license to drive their trucks in the most reckless manner imaginable. I myself once witnessed such a vehicle crash into an omnibus full of people, reducing it to splinters and sending its occupants flying through the street. Indeed, it is not at all uncommon for a fire-wagon on the way to a blaze to cause more damage to life, limb, and property than the conflagration itself!"

"That's just the thing," said Carson. "There *ain't* no fire, leastways not as far as I can tell. Look there," he said, pointing in the direction followed by the wagon. "See anything?"

Squinting into the darkness of the streets, I perceived that the sky above the rooftops was untinged by anything resembling the tell-tale glow of a burning building.

"No," I replied.

Tilting his head, Carson then inhaled deeply through his nostrils. "Don't smell nothing, neither."

"Perhaps the fire is occurring in a remote area of the city, beyond the range even of your singularly acute senses," I suggested.

"Maybe," said the scout, sounding distinctly unconvinced.

"In any event, Kit," I said, "I owe you my very existence. Come, let us proceed without further delay. I am more eager than ever to be reunited with my loved ones, and to tell them how you snatched me from the very jaws of death."

No sooner had the final words of this remark issued from my lips than a sudden realization flashed upon my mind, causing me to gasp aloud.

"What's wrong?" asked the scout.

"I have it!" I cried. "The solution to the puzzle that has been troubling me since we departed from Ludlow's restaurant. It relates to a remark made by the female named Nell. At one point, she admonished her companion to stop 'biting her head off.' Do you recall that comment, Kit?"

"Can't say as I do," the scout replied.

"Well, no matter," I said. "The point is this: I now realize that it was that particular turn-of-phrase which stirred, within my mind, some half-buried association that has now—with my own use of the expression 'jaws of death'— emerged into full awareness!"

Reaching out a hand, I clutched Carson's upper arm and gave it an excited shake. "It was *Mazeppa!*" I cried.

"I don't rightly follow you, Eddie," said Carson, his countenance wearing a look of the deepest perplexity.

"During our questioning of young Harry Pratt earlier today," I declared, "I asked whether his employer, Mr. Wyatt, had ever received a caller. As you will remember, Pratt answered in the affirmative, explaining that, on at least one occasion, Wyatt had been visited by a gentleman of most distinctive appearance. According to Pratt, this individual was a short but exceedingly powerful-looking fellow, with a regal bearing, unusually handsome features, luxuriant black hair, and a jagged scar along one side of his visage.

"Upon hearing this description," I continued, "I was convinced that I had seen this very personage somewhere before, though I could not recall under what circumstances. Now the memory has come rushing back to me. It was Mazeppa!"

"Who?" asked Carson.

"The Great Mazeppa," I exclaimed. "P. T. Barnum's world-renowned lion-tamer who recently suffered a terrible death. His skull was crushed by the savage bite of a jungle beast named Ajax when—while performing his trademark feat—he thrust his head into the creature's gaping jaws!"

Chapter Fifteen

Y EXCITEMENT AT HAVING identified Wyatt's mysterious caller was somewhat dampened by Carson, who was quick to point out that—in a city as populous as New York—there might conceivably be more than one individual who conformed to Pratt's description. I was forced to admit that this was a possibility. Still, I regarded it as an unlikely one—the features enumerated by Pratt having been *exactly* those which distinguished Mazeppa's appearance.

In the end, the scout and I agreed that there was only one way to confirm my belief. On the morrow, we would pay a visit to Barnum's museum and interview Mazeppa's closest acquaintances, in the hope that one of them might be able to shed light on the lion-tamer's presumed link to William Wyatt.

Having thus settled the matter, Carson and I quickly made our way across the street to Mrs. Whitaker's dwelling and, in another moment, had climbed the stairs to the second floor.

Entering my apartment, we proceeded directly to the parlor. The scene that presented itself to our view as we paused at the threshold was nothing less than enchanting. Bathed in the warm glow of the argand lamps, our loved ones formed a picture of perfect domestic contentment. Muddy—garbed in her widow weeds and white lace cap—was seated in the armchair, applying herself to the project that occupied most of her spare moments. This was the creation of a needlepoint sampler consisting of the legend "God Bless Our

Happy Home" surrounded by a border of colorfully stitched birds, butterflies, flowers, and fruit trees.

Across from her on the brocaded sofa sat my darling wife. A book lay open on her lap. She had just touched the tip of her right index finger to her exquisitely delicate tongue, and was in the act of turning the page. Her opposite arm was draped around the shoulders of Carson's son, Jeremiah, who leaned—with closed eyes and heavy head—against my beloved wife. From their respective attitudes, it seemed clear that the lad had dozed off while listening to Sissy read aloud to him.

Adding to the idyllic nature of the scene were Carson's mongrel yellow dog and our own beloved feline, Cattarina, who—remarkably—were curled up beside each other in the center of the carpet, as though they were two creatures who had sprung from the same litter and had passed their entire lives in each other's company.

As Carson and I crossed into the room, Muddy became aware of our presence and, laying her needlework down on the side table, sprang to her feet and, circumventing the two recumbent beasts, came bustling over to greet us. Sissy—evidently not wishing to disturb the dozing boy—merely looked up from her book and, smiling warmly, waggled the fingers of her free hand in a fond gesture of "hello."

"Eddie! Mr. Carson!" Muddy exclaimed. "We've been waiting for you to get back. How was your day?"

"Replete with incidents of a most interesting and even dramatic variety," I replied. "Indeed, only moments ago, I had an experience that—were it not for the remarkable reflexes of our good friend—might well have resulted in the most serious, if not fatal, consequences. I was nearly run over by a fire-wagon!"

"Good heavens!" she exclaimed, clasping both hands to her bosom.

"Are you all right, Eddie?" asked my wife from the couch. Though her tone was suffused with concern, she kept her voice at a subdued volume, so as not to waken her slumbering charge.

"Apart from some minor discomfort to my right arm—upon which I landed when Mr. Carson threw himself upon me with little or no concern for his own well-being—I am perfectly fine," I assured her.

"Oh, Mr. Carson!" Muddy exclaimed, grabbing the scout's right hand in both of her own and giving it an ardent squeeze. "Thank you so much for saving our dear boy!"

"No need to fuss, ma'am," said the scout, looking somewhat abashed at the good woman's effusion.

"Take off your jacket at once, Eddie," Muddy demanded, turning to face me, "and let me have a look at that arm."

"Now, now, Muddy dearest," I affectionately chided her. "There is no cause for alarm." Raising and lowering my injured limb several times, I continued thusly: "As you can see, my arm functions normally, having suffered nothing worse than a painful bruising whose most serious consequence is likely to be an unsightly *hematoma*, or, to use its common designation, black-and-blue mark."

"Well, at any rate, I insist that you come sit down," Muddy said, taking me by the hand. "You, too, Mr. Carson."

"Reckon I'd just as soon stand, ma'am," said the scout.

Allowing Muddy to lead me across the floor, I lowered myself onto the empty portion of the sofa cushion at the side of the slumbering boy, whose body was thus interposed between Sissy and myself.

"Are you sure you won't sit down, Mr. Carson?" Muddy asked, gesturing toward the armchair she had been occupying.

"I'm fine, ma'am," he replied. "You go ahead."

"All right, then," said Muddy, resuming her place.

"Please tell us without further delay how the three of you passed *your* day," I said, addressing my darling wife. "We are most eager to hear all about it."

"Oh, we had a lovely time," said Sissy. "We took Jeremiah for a walk along Broadway."

"I hope you did not overexert yourself, Sissy," I interjected, concerned, as always, about my dear wife's exceedingly fragile health.

"Not at all," she said. "It felt *wonderful* to be outside. It's been forever since I've had such a nice stroll. And being with Jeremiah made it even more fun. We held hands the whole time, while I explained what everything was. He was so excited by all the new sights. You should have seen the look on his face when we passed Mr. Judson's sundries store and saw the whirligigs and other toys in the window! Then we returned home and had a bite to eat. Afterward, we came in here to wait for you. I've been reading to him from Mr. Irving's *Sketch Book*."

"It is no wonder that he sank into so profound a slumber," I drolly remarked. "However estimable a stylist Mr. Irving may be, his tales are often bland to the point of *insipidity*. I am surprised, dear Sissy, that you did not choose more compelling reading matter. One of my *own* stories, for example."

"Now, why didn't *I* think of that?" my wife declared in a gently chaffing tone. "Let's see, which one would I have chosen? The story about the young lunatic who chops up his landlord and buries the pieces under the floorboards? Or perhaps the one about the madman who lures his rival into the depths of the catacombs and walls him up alive? Or maybe—"

"I take your point, Sissy dear," I interposed with a soft chuckle. "I suppose they might not be *utterly* suitable for a child of such tender years."

Favoring me with an affectionate smile—as though to let me know that her teasing was offered in the most loving spirit—Sissy then turned to the scout and said: "He's such a darling boy, Mr. Carson. And guess what? He's started to teach me some Indian sign language. Look."

With her free hand, Sissy performed a series of graceful gestures, first pointing to her eyes—next tracing a small circle on the left side of her bosom with her index finger—then extending her hand, loosely closed, and rapidly opening it outward so that its fingers were fully splayed.

"That's real fine," said Carson with a smile. "You're a mighty quick study, Mrs. Poe."

"I confess," I declared, "that—while possessing a smattering of knowledge on the subject of sign language—I am unable to fully comprehend the sense of your communication, dear Sissy."

"It is the Indian way of greeting a friend," she replied.

"It means she's plumb glad to see you," Carson elaborated. "The clouds disappear and sunlight shines into her heart when she sets eyes on you."

"How lovely!" exclaimed Muddy, whose broad, benevolent countenance fairly glowed with pride at this display of her daughter's dexterity.

"Yes, ma'am," said Carson. "Most Indians have a right poetic way of putting things."

"By the way, Mr. Carson," Muddy said. "We spoke to Mrs. Whitaker, and she has happily consented to board you and Jeremiah. And your dog, too, of course."

"Much obliged, ma'am," said Carson. Then, casting his gaze downward in the direction of the two dozing creatures, he shook his head slowly and added: "Never seen that hound cozy up to a cat like that."

"It's strange, isn't it?" said Sissy. "They took to each other right away."

"It is, indeed, a most curious phenomenon," I said. "It reminds me of nothing

so much as Mr. Barnum's inordinately popular attraction The Happy Family."
At a questioning look from Carson, I explained that the exhibit in question
consisted of a large cage filled with a collection of natural enemies—owls and
mice, foxes and rabbits, and a dozen other species of predators and prey—that
had been taught to coexist in a state of perfect harmony within the confines of
their shared receptacle.

"It's truly a splendid exhibit," Sissy declared. "Just like Mr. Hicks's famous
painting of *The Peaceable Kingdom*. You really ought to take Jeremiah to see it
while you're here, Mr. Carson. I'm sure he'd love it."

"I expect he would," said the scout. "Right now, though, I reckon I'll take
him downstairs and put him to bed."

"Will you join us for breakfast, Mr. Carson?" Muddy politely inquired.

"Be happy to, ma'am," said Carson.

Bidding us good-night, the scout stepped to the sofa and scooped up his
slumbering son. Then, turning to the dog, he somewhat unceremoniously
nudged the creature in the ribs with the toe of his boot. The canine made a
low protesting noise deep in its throat before rising to its feet and following its
master from the apartment.

For a half-hour or so following Carson's departure, Muddy, Sissy, and I remained in the parlor, while I regaled them with a more complete account of
the day's events. At length, the mantel clock striking ten, Sissy raised both
arms over her head and emitted a protracted yawn.

"It is no wonder that you are so tired, Sissy dear," I said. "In view of your de-
bilitated physical condition, your perambulations with Jeremiah must have
been exceedingly strenuous."

Muddy rose to her feet. "Come, dear," she said to her daughter. "It's time
for bed."

Bidding me a fond good-night, my loved ones retired to their bedroom. Before proceeding to my own sleeping quarters, I briefly repaired to my study,
where—after lighting the desk lamp—I removed from my coat pocket the
folded envelope containing the tiny fragment of charred paper discovered by
Carson in Wyatt's fireplace. I then carefully placed this envelope in the center
drawer of my desk—extinguished the lamp—and retreated to my bedchamber.

Upon divesting myself of my garments, I discovered that the upper portion
of my right arm was not merely bruised but badly abraded. Standing at the
washbasin, I thoroughly cleansed the injured area with water and soap. I then
donned my nightshirt and—with a grateful moan—flung myself onto my bed.

Such was my state of sheer physical exhaustion that I was asleep within minutes. My mind, however, had been so excessively stimulated by the events of the day that I derived little refreshment from my slumbers. My dreams were agitated by incidents of the most unsettling description.

Every species of calamity befell me. Among other miseries, I was assaulted by demons of the most ghastly and ferocious aspect, who tore at my flesh with their slavering jaws. At one point, I found myself naked and alone amid the burning sand-plains of the Sahara. At my feet lay crouched a fierce lion of the tropics. All at once, his wild eyes opened and, with a dreadful roar, he leapt to his feet and sprang at me, snapping at my head with his horrible fangs. At that instant, the scene changed. I was standing knee-deep in a brackish, foul-smelling swamp. Immensely tall trunks of trees, gray and leafless, rose up in endless succession as far as the eye could reach. Their roots were concealed in wide-spreading morasses, whose dreary waters lay intensely black, still, and altogether terrible.

Suddenly, one of the thick, serpentine roots came to life—slithered over my feet—and, like a member of the reptilian family *Pythoninae*, tightened itself around my ankles, causing them to burn and chafe in the most agonizing way. Frantically, I kicked my legs in an effort to free myself from the intensely painful grip of the animate root—but in vain. My struggles only served to cause it to redouble its hold upon me, and to intensify the discomfort to my ankles.

Mercifully, I awoke at that very moment. Sitting up in bed, I saw—by the bright morning sunlight streaming through my window—that my legs had become thoroughly entangled in my bedclothes. To free myself was the work of a minute. As I swung my feet off the mattress, however, I realized that the burning sensation which had so distressed me in my sleep was no mere phantasm. Examining my ankles, I was startled to see that they were covered with a score or more of small, raised, angry-looking marks, somewhat resembling the characteristic rash produced by leaves of the swamp shrub *Rhus vernix*, or, as it is more commonly known, poison sumac. Puzzled as to the precise nature of these inordinately irritating little bumps, I scratched at them furiously—an act which served rather to exacerbate than alleviate their maddening *itchiness*.

At that moment, the muffled sound of voices, conversing from a distant room, came wafting through my chamber door. Rising from my bed, I quickly performed my ablutions, threw on my clothing, and followed the noise into the dining room.

A delicious aroma—compounded of the mingled smells of coffee, bacon, freshly baked buttermilk muffins, and Muddy's special green rhubarb jam—

suffused the room. Carson and Jeremiah were already there, the former occu-pying the chair at the head of the table, the latter seated beside Sissy. At my en-trance, Muddy—who was in the process of setting a bowl of hard-boiled eggs on the table—looked up at me and exclaimed:

"Oh, Eddie, I was just about to knock on your door and tell you that break-fast was ready. How are you feeling, dear boy?"

"Less well than I might wish," I somewhat glumly replied.

"Oh no!" cried Muddy. "What's wrong? Is it your arm?"

In point of fact, I had been so distracted by the intensely unpleasant sensa-tion in my lower limbs that I had all but forgotten about the injury to my upper one. Now, flexing the latter several times, I declared: "Though some-what stiff and sore, my arm is not the source of my present discomfort. Rather, it stems from a peculiar collection of small but singularly irritating *welts* that mysteriously appeared on both of my ankles overnight."

"Welts?" exclaimed Muddy. "What kind of welts?"

"Here," I said. "I will show you."

Pulling one of the chairs away from the table, I seated myself upon it—crossed my left leg over my right knee—turned up the cuff of my trousers—rolled down my stocking—and displayed the badly inflamed ankle.

"Oh dear," said Sissy. "That really *does* look nasty. What in the world could it be?"

"From where I'm sitting," said Carson, taking a sip from his mug, "I'd say you was bit up pretty fair by chiggers, Eddie."

"Chiggers!" I exclaimed with a grimace.

Few members of the family *Trombidiidae* were, I knew, more noxious than the larvae of the so-called chigger mite. These minuscule creatures lurk on grass stems, weeds, shrubbery, and other vegetation during the spring and summer months. After attaching themselves to the exposed flesh of a passing host, they inject the latter with a powerful salivary secretion that causes the skin-cells to break down, permitting the chigger to ingest the liquefied tissue through its feeding tube. The effect of this process on the human host is an itching sensa-tion of maddening intensity that typically persists for a week or more.

"But how could I have come into contact with chiggers?" I cried.

"As I recollect," said Carson, "we was traipsing through some pretty tall weeds in that park yesterday."

I realized at once that the scout was undoubtedly correct. The badly overgrown lawns of St. John's Park provided an ideal environment for these parasites.

"But what about *you*, Kit?" I asked. "You were equally exposed to the nefarious actions of these intensely virulent creatures. And yet, you do not appear to have been afflicted by them in the least."

"No, I can't say as they bothered me none," said the scout. "I expect my boots kept them off."

No one who has not personally been beset by chigger mites can possibly conceive of the sheer—the *unmitigated*—discomfort of the experience. The urge to scratch my ankles was almost overwhelming. And yet, I knew that to do so would only aggravate my condition, and perhaps lead to even more extreme suffering in the form of an infection. Only by a nearly superhuman exertion of willpower, however, could I refrain from tearing at the tormenting irritation with my fingernails.

"Oh, what is to be done?" I exclaimed in a paroxysm of distress. "The itching sensation in both of my ankles is nothing short of unbearable!"

"Wait!" cried Muddy. "Do you remember that wonderful salve you bought for Sissy last summer, Eddie dear? When she was being driven nearly crazy by mosquitoes?"

"Why, yes," I replied after a momentary pause. "Dr. Kittredge's Celebrated Itch Remedy."

I had acquired this nostrum the previous year. We had been residing at the time in the countryside north of Eighty-sixth Street. The summer having been a singularly damp one, Sissy had been greatly tormented by mosquitoes. During one of my periodic trips downtown, I had paid a visit to Duychink's Pharmacy on Barrow Street. At the recommendation of the proprietor, who hailed it as a miracle cure for every form of skin irritation known to man, from eczema to ringworm to scrofulous ulcers, I had purchased a bottle for the somewhat exorbitant sum of fifty cents. The investment, however, proved to be worthwhile. Though causing a certain amount of unsightly peeling when applied to the skin, Dr. Kittredge's remedy had, in fact, proven highly efficacious in alleviating Sissy's itch.

"Do you still have any of the ointment left, Muddy dear? If so, I implore you to fetch it without delay!"

Hurrying from the dining room, the good woman returned several moments later, carrying two strips of white cotton cloth and a pint bottle nearly half-full of the somewhat repulsive-looking emollient. I quickly smeared a dollop of the latter onto each of my ankles and wrapped them in the cotton strips.

"What's in that stuff?" asked Carson, his expression registering a certain degree of distaste.

"According to the information on the label," I replied, "its principal ingredients are nitric acid and quicksilver, combined with a substance the precise nature of which is not specified by the manufacturer."

"Smells like bear fat," said the scout.

The aroma of the compound was, in fact, somewhat rank. Its soothing effect, however, was nearly instantaneous. Within moments, the tormenting itch had been reduced to a mere, barely noticeable *tingle*.

Relieved of my distress, I applied myself heartily to my breakfast, pausing only once to attend to Carson's dog, who—poking his head up from beneath the table and laying it upon my lap—stared at me with beseeching eyes until I fed him a piece of bacon.

At length, having finished the meal, we decided on our plans for the day. Jeremiah would once again remain with Muddy and Sissy, an arrangement that appeared to be intensely agreeable to all three of them. In the meantime, Carson and I would proceed to the museum and make our inquiries concerning the late Mazeppa.

No sooner had we settled this matter than a sharp rapping noise was heard at the door of our apartment. Casting me a quizzical look—as if to say, "I wonder who that could possibly be at such an early hour?"—Muddy rose from the table and went off to investigate. After the lapse of several moments—during which we could hear the muffled sounds of a brief exchange between my aunt and the unknown caller—the good woman returned to the dining room, bearing a wicker basket laden with foodstuffs. Setting this container down upon the table, she declared:

"It was Mrs. Whitaker. This basket just arrived. It's for you, Eddie."

"Really?" I said in surprise. "But who brought it?"

"A deliveryman, I suppose," Muddy said. "Mrs. Whitaker didn't say."

"I can't *wait* to see what's in it," Sissy exclaimed, as she eagerly leaned forward and began to empty the basket of its contents. When laid upon the table, these turned out to consist of a bunch of exceedingly lucious-looking grapes— a dozen Seville oranges—several varieties of cheese—a jar of pickled cauliflower relish—a second jar containing a glutinous substance that appeared to be stewed okra and tomatoes—and a honey cake wrapped in white paper.

"Whoever sent it didn't include a card," Sissy said in a somewhat puzzled tone, tipping the now-vacant basket toward herself so that she could peer inside it.

"It *must* have been our good friend Mr. Barnum," I said. "When I called on him the other day, I told him how grateful we were for the delicacies we received from him after his return from Europe. Now—perhaps as a token of gratitude for the assistance I rendered him during the riot—he has evidently decided to send us a similar gift."

"What a dear, dear man," exclaimed Muddy. "And to think of all the terrible things people are always saying about him! You must thank him for us, Eddie."

"I will be certain to do so the moment I see him," I said, as both Carson and I rose to make ready for our departure.

"I will put all this away for later," said Muddy as she began to replace the various items in the basket. "Perhaps we'll try some of this interesting-looking relish at dinner.

"And please, Eddie," she continued, looking at me with worried eyes, "do be careful when you go about the streets. I could barely fall asleep last night, thinking of how you were almost run over by that fire-wagon. This city is dangerous enough—even without that dreadful Johnson creature skulking about!"

CHAPTER SIXTEEN

⌒

I N THE AFTERMATH OF THE RIOT—as the scout had informed us—Barnum had temporarily closed his establishment to the public in order to repair the damage wrought by the rampaging mob. I therefore expected to find the sidewalk in front of the building free of the usual crowds that lined up each morning awaiting admission. As Carson and I approached our destination, however, I was greatly surprised to perceive a large group of people congregated outside the museum.

At my first glimpse of this assemblage, I was seized with a sharp pang of apprehension. Had the horde of lawless ruffians reassembled for a fresh assault on the premises? This worry, however, was quickly dispelled; for as Carson and I drew closer to Broadway, I saw that the gathering was composed of perfectly respectable-looking individuals, including a considerable number of children.

"What do you figure is going on over yonder?" Carson asked as we made our way across the teeming thoroughfare.

"I cannot say with certainty," I replied. "Knowing Barnum as I do, however, I can only surmise that he has contrived some means to draw attention to his showplace, even while its operations are suspended."

My assumption proved correct. Stepping onto the sidewalk and insinuating ourselves through the crowd, Carson and I soon found ourselves confronted with a sight that was guaranteed to attract the notice of any passerby. Situated before the main entrance of the museum was a squat, somewhat heavyset fellow with a thick head of coarse black hair and a lavish growth of whiskers. He was garbed, from the waist down, in the sort of loose-fitting pantaloons customarily worn by sailors. From the waist up he was entirely unclothed. The sight of a portly, half-naked man in the middle of Broadway would, in itself, have been sufficient to create a sensation. What rendered this individual truly noteworthy, however, was the dizzying collection of exotic tattoos that covered every inch of his exposed flesh, not excluding his face, neck, arms, and even the palms of his hands.

This singular personage, I recognized at once, was the popular human anomaly, Captain Aristedes Constentenus, Barnum's so-called "Miracle of Mortal Marvels." According to the information contained in the illustrated souvenir booklet sold at his performances, Constentenus had been captured in his youth by Barbary pirates, who had tortured him for many months by pricking hundreds of elaborate designs into his flesh with long, searing needles. Like so many of the stories promulgated by Barnum, however, this one was sheer "humbug." In actuality (as the showman had once confided to me) Constentenus was a highly eccentric, if perfectly amiable, Brooklyn workingman named Oscar Schmidt who—aspiring to the life of a popular entertainer but lacking in any particular talent—had voluntarily subjected himself to years of tattooing in order to transform himself into a sideshow attraction.

At the moment, he was striding back and forth before the crowd, distributing circulars from a fat sheaf clutched in one beefy hand. Glancing over the shoulder of the young woman beside me, who was perusing one of these sheets, I saw that it was a printed announcement composed in Barnum's inimitable style. Its upper portion was adorned with an engraved portrait of the showman himself, surrounded by a radiant halo and accompanied by the legend THE SUN OF THE AMUSEMENT WORLD FROM WHICH ALL LESSER LUMINARIES BORROW LIGHT! The text itself read as follows:

COME ONE! COME ALL!

THE MOST STUPENDOUS EVENT
IN THE HISTORY OF THE CIVILIZED WORLD!!

GRAND REOPENING OF
P. T. BARNUM'S AMERICAN MUSEUM—

THE GREATEST SHOWPLACE
IN EXISTENCE !!

SATURDAY, JUNE 7, 1845

GALA CELEBRATION!

STAGGERING SPECTACLES!

ASTOUNDING ATTRACTIONS!

MARVELOUS EXHIBITIONS!

 **SEE**

**The Living Hippopotamus! The Behemoth of Scripture!
The First and Only One of These Colossal Animals
Ever Exhibited in America!**

 **SEE**

**The Incredible Carolina Twins!
Inseparably Joined at Birth, Yet Capable of
the Most Graceful Individual Movements!
The Strangest Curiosity Ever Seen!**

 **SEE**

**The World Premiere Presentation of
"The Great Riot, or, New York in Flames!"
The Most Amazing Theatrical Spectacle Ever Staged!
Starring General Tom Thumb, the World's Smallest Dwarf!**

Over 100,000 Curiosities to be Viewed at All Hours!
The Splendid Cosmoramic and Stereopticon Hall!
The Great Aquaria!
Geological, Conchological, and Numismatic Collections!
Specimens of Natural History, Wax Statuary, Historical Relics!
Woodroffe's Bohemian Glass Blowers!
Phrenological Examinations and Charts by Prof. Livingston!

**Admittance to the Whole . . . Only 25 Cents!
Children Under 10 Years . . . Half-Price, All Times
Except Weekends and Holidays!**

Separating ourselves from the crowd, Carson and I approached Costentenus, who had paused to converse with a small group of juvenile admirers, one of whom—a plump, freckle-faced girl of perhaps eleven years of age—was pointing to a spot in the middle of his imposing belly.

"That one?" said Costentenus, peering down at the image indicated by the little girl—a large, striped serpent coiled around the center of his paunch. "Why, that there's the great poison Mambo snake of the African tropics. The fiendish Khan of Kashgar himself give me that tattoo. I was bound hand and foot for a week. Required over one thousand separate punctures, and every one of 'em burned like a red-hot poker."

"C-can I touch it?" the girl asked in a half-fearful, half-desirous tone.

For a moment, Costentenus merely looked down at her with a dubious expression. "Well, all right," he said at length. "I ain't in the habit of letting folks touch 'em. Not for free, anyway. But you look like a nice enough little girl. Go ahead."

Slowly extending her arm, the child placed the very tip of her trembling index finger against Costentenus's skin. At that instant, he rapidly rolled the muscles of his belly, causing the tattooed snake to wiggle in a most unsettling manner. Jerking back her hand, the little girl emitted a high-pitched shriek that elicited a great burst of hilarity from the bystanders.

Chuckling softly, Constentenus turned away from the squealing child (who, in truth, seemed more delighted than affrighted by his prank). As he did, his eyes—which, along with his fingernails, were the only visible parts of his person undefaced with tattoos—fell upon Carson and myself.

"Well, hello there, Mr. Poe," he exclaimed, extending his right hand, which gave the appearance of being sheathed in an elaborately embroidered glove. "Nice to see you, sir, very nice indeed. And what brings you here this fine morning?"

However irrational the feeling, I could not help but experience a small shiver of dread whenever I was required to shake hands with one of Barnum's human curiosities, as though the mere touch of such anomalous flesh might have a contaminating effect on my own. Even a self-created prodigy like Constentenus had the power to evoke this intensely disquieting sensation within me. Now, subduing my uneasiness, I reached out—firmly grasped him by the hand—and explained that we had come to speak to Mr. Barnum.

Tilting his heavily bearded chin in the direction of the main entranceway, the tattooed marvel said: "He was upstairs on the second floor last I saw him.

Checking on what got stole or broke the other night. Go right on in, Mr. Poe. Door's open."

I bid him thanks, and—with Carson beside me—turned and proceeded into the museum, whose vast, gaslit foyer possessed an unwonted air of desolation. Never before had I visited Barnum's establishment when it was not filled to capacity with hordes of excited patrons. Now it seemed as lifeless as the great mausoleum of Halicarnassus. As Carson and I mounted to the second floor, the silence was so pronounced that our footsteps echoed loudly on the grand marble staircase.

We found the showman, as expected, on the second floor, inside the Hall of American History. Hunched over a small display cabinet that rested on a waist-high wooden pedestal, he was writing in a notepad, as though taking inventory of his plundered collection. At the opposite end of the cavernous hall, I could perceive the figure of Barnum's custodian-cum-sign-painter, Oswald. Wielding a large broom, he was busily sweeping the floor, which was strewn with shards of broken glass, fragments of splintered wood, and other vestiges of the riot.

As Carson and I made our way across the hall, I saw that most, if not all, of the larger items on exhibit had escaped serious damage. No apparent harm had been inflicted on the (supposedly) actual skiff in which Washington crossed the Delaware River on Christmas Day, 1776—nor on the (ostensibly) genuine cannon employed by John Paul Jones during the battle between the *Bonhomme Richard* and the *Serapis*—nor on the (purportedly) original scaffold from which Nathan Hale had made his immortal declaration of patriotism. Many of the glass-fronted display cabinets, however, had been broken into and looted—the rioters having made off with whatever smaller items of value they could easily carry.

So engrossed was the showman in his examination of the pedestal-mounted case that he did not become aware of our presence until Carson and I came to a halt directly beside him. Only then did he look up suddenly and exclaim:

"Poe, m'boy! Bless my soul, but you're a welcome sight! And is that you, Kit? Heavens, your own mother wouldn't know you in those togs! Why, you look like a regular city slicker."

"Just blending in with the natives," said the scout, with a smile. "Eddie's idea."

"In view of Kit's great renown," I explained, "and the degree of attention he would surely attract were he to go about the streets in his distinctive Western garb, I felt that our investigation would proceed with fewer distractions if he was clothed in a less conspicuous manner."

"Really?" said Barnum doubtfully. That a person might deliberately seek to *avoid* publicity was clearly a strange, if not utterly foreign, notion to the showman, who never tired of devising new and outlandish ways of drawing attention to himself and his museum.

"Well, yes, I suppose that makes some sense under the circumstances," Barnum said at length. "At any rate, I'm glad to see you boys. Cheers me up no end. And, believe me, I could stand a little cheering up right now. Spent the last two days on a mighty dreary task—tallying up the damage done by those damned vandals. Here, have a look at this," he continued, indicating the display case.

Peering down at the case—a shallow box lined with black velvet and measuring approximately two square feet—I saw that its glass lid had been pulverized and its contents removed. All that remained was a hand-lettered descriptive label which read: ORIGINAL COPY OF THE DECLARATION OF INDEPENDENCE ON ACTUAL PARCHMENT!

"Good heavens," I cried. "It is no wonder that you are so distressed by the loss of this object. Its value must be beyond calculation. Was this truly the original document?"

"Why, certainly," Barnum exclaimed. "Depending on what you mean by 'original,' that is. It's not the original *original*, of course. Tried to get hold of that a few years back, but the government wouldn't sell it to me. National treasure and all that. Still, mine's the best original *copy* money can buy—absolutely first-rate. Created just for me by a German gent named Anbinder. Finest calligraphist in the civilized world. Done on real parchment, too—just like the label says. Paid a small fortune for it."

"I see," I dryly remarked, feeling somewhat chagrined at my failure to recognize, in the wording of the label, an all-too-characteristic bit of Barnumesque chicanery. "The pilfering of this facsimile, then, is not quite as catastrophic an event as I'd feared. Still, it is a great pity that your museum suffered so much damage."

"Yes, there's a right smart bit of cleaning up to do," said Carson, glancing over at the custodian, who had put aside his broom and was now in the act of restoring the head to a life-sized waxwork figure of Andrew Jackson that had been decapitated by the rioters.

"Oh, well," said Barnum. "No point dwelling on our losses. 'Look on the bright side'—that's P. T. Barnum's motto. At least those scoundrels didn't get their mitts on any of my *authentic* historical papers. I've got quite a little collection of them, you know. Keep 'em locked away in a special storage closet down in the basement. All sorts of treasures. Washington's handwritten copy of his first inaugural speech. Dr. Franklin's notes on his famous kite-flying experiment. The original Mayflower Compact. John Jacob Astor has been trying to buy that one from me for years. Why, every time I'm at his house for dinner, he says, 'Come, now, Phineas, name your price—I *must* have that Mayflower Compact!' But my goodness, I'd as soon think of selling my wife!"

In view of the showman's propensity for rhetorical excess, this latter statement might have been taken for mere hyperbole. Having once been introduced to Mrs. Barnum, however, I had little cause to doubt his sincerity in this particular instance.

"But tell me, my boys, how's the investigation going?" Barnum continued. "Any closer to tracking down that man-eating fiend, Johnson?"

"As of yet," I replied, "his whereabouts remain unknown to us. We are, however, assiduously following every conceivable clue. Indeed, it is in the pursuance of just such a lead that we have come here this morning. It concerns your celebrated performer, the late Mazeppa Vivaldi."

"The Great Mazeppa?" exclaimed Barnum. "Good Lord! How in heaven's name is *he* connected to this dreadful business?"

"We ain't exactly sure he *was*," said Carson.

"That is true," I added. "Our interest in the poor, doomed fellow derives from a bit of information that—while highly suggestive—can hardly be regarded as definitive. It would be exceedingly helpful if you could tell us all you know about him, commencing with the basic facts of his life."

"Can't be of much help, I'm afraid," Barnum observed, looking somewhat troubled. "Hardly knew the fellow. Not personally, I mean. Don't often socialize with the help, you know. 'Never mix business with pleasure'—that's P. T. Barnum's motto. He seemed like a nice enough gent, though. Descended from an old Boston family, as I understand."

According to the official story promulgated by Barnum, the Great Mazeppa had been the scapegrace son of Italian royalty who had run off to sea as a youth and ended up shipwrecked on the shores of darkest Africa, where he had joined a troupe of Arabian circus-performers, one of whom had taught him the ancient art of animal-taming. That this tale was a complete and brazen fabrication hardly came as a surprise to me. Like Oscar Schmidt—

the prosaic personality who had refashioned himself into Captain Aristedes Constentenus—nearly all of Barnum's performers adopted wildly exotic identities, designed to imbue them with an air of mystery and romance and to excite the fascinated interest of the public.

"Are you familiar with his true appellation?" I inquired.

"Dudley," said Barnum. "Thomas Dudley. That's just about all I know about him, too." Here he shook his head slowly and emitted a heartfelt sigh. "Tremendous talent, absolutely one-of-a-kind. Lord bless me, you wouldn't believe how many people showed up just to see his act. Especially the ladies. Couldn't get enough of him. He was a handsome devil, you know—a regular Apollo. And those long wavy locks of his! Good heavens—drove the women wild! Terrible loss—perfectly devastating. Still don't understand what made Ajax close his jaws on the poor fellow's head that way. Why, that old lion was as gentle as a kitten. Of course, the poor beast had to be destroyed after that. Can't let those big cats live once they've tasted human blood, you know—they develop a yen for it."

"There's men like that, too," Carson said grimly.

"Yes," I remarked. "The one we are seeking is just such a creature. And unless we succeed in stopping him, his unholy appetite is sure to demand further satisfaction before very long. Tell me," I said to Barnum. "Is there anyone among your employees who was more intimately acquainted with Mazeppa than yourself?"

Barnum made a thoughtful sound deep in his throat. "Hmmmmmm. Let me think. Hold on a minute." Turning toward his custodian, he then called out: "Oswald, my good man! Come here a moment, will you?"

Having just finished reattaching the manikin's head to its shoulders, the portly custodian came ambling toward us. As he approached, Barnum looked at us and said: "If anyone can help us, it's Oswald here. Spends his days going all around the building, fixing this, cleaning that. Doesn't speak much, but keeps his eyes and ears wide open. Not much around here that's a secret from Oswald. Everyone confides in him, too. Heaven knows why. Must be something about his face."

Precisely what it was about the custodian's visage that inspired others to reveal themselves to him was by no means apparent, his countenance being distinguished primarily by its unvarying expression of mild bewilderment. Nevertheless—after exchanging greetings with the fellow—I questioned him about Mazeppa's acquaintances.

Frowning deeply while pinching the flaccid flesh of his pendulous under-chin, Oswald thought for a moment before replying thusly: "I guess him and Monsieur Vox was pretty good friends."

"Monsieur Vox?" I said.

"My world-famous ventriloquist," said Barnum. "Don't you remember? I mentioned him to you just the other day."

"Ah, yes," I recalled. "The gentleman who performs scenes from *Othello* with dummies."

"That's the fellow," exclaimed Barnum. "Astounding act—simply extraordinary."

"And where is he to be found?" I inquired.

"Saw him not more than twenty minutes ago," said Oswald. "Upstairs in the theater. He was checking out his equipment backstage, making sure everything's in good order."

"Then you will excuse us while we go seek him out," I said to the showman.

"Of course, m'boy, of course," said Barnum. "I've been wanting you to meet him anyway. He's a great fan of your work, you know. He'll be thrilled to make your acquaintance—absolutely tickled pink."

As we bid Oswald and the showman farewell, I was gripped by a sense that I had forgotten to tell the latter something significant. Still, there was no time to be lost in standing there while I attempted to jog my memory. Proceeding out to the main hallway, Carson and I began to climb the stairs to the top floor of the building, which housed the spacious theater in which Barnum staged a wide variety of events, from his famous Fat Baby Contests, to his productions of popular melodramas, to his well-attended temperance lectures.

We had just reached the fifth-story landing when Carson turned to me and said: "You need for me to be there while you talk to this Vox feller, Eddie?"

"Why, no," I said. "I am certain that I can manage the interview without your presence. Why?"

"Figured I'd go find Chief Wolf Bear and say howdy," replied the scout.

"Very well," I said.

As we did not know precisely how much time our respective errands would require, we arranged to rendezvous by the reconstructed Mastodon skeleton in the main lobby in forty-five minutes. Carson then went off in search of the Indian, while I directed my steps toward the theater—still troubled by the gnawing sense that there was a matter of some importance which I had forgotten to mention to Barnum.

Chapter Seventeen

PON ENTERING THE THEATER, I paused for a moment to survey the scene. The vacant auditorium, with its row upon row of velvet-upholstered seats, was shrouded in gloom. The sole visible illumination was a faint yellow glow emanating from the left side of the backstage area. I waited at the rear of the hall until my eyes grew accustomed to the darkness, then proceeded down the center aisle.

As I approached the front of the auditorium, I thought I could discern the muffled sound of voices issuing from the same direction as the lamplight. Mounting the steps onto the immense, empty stage, I made my way behind the heavy front curtain and soon found myself in an area crowded with the many *accoutrements* of the theatrical trade—costume racks, painted scenery, and a heterogeneous assortment of props, including several full-sized Egyptian chariots employed by Barnum in his exceedingly popular biblical pageant, *Joseph and His Brethren.*

By this point, I had drawn sufficiently close to the source of the sound to distinguish two individual speakers. Both were evidently male, though one of them—to judge from his shrill, somewhat impudent manner of speech—appeared to be much younger than the other, perhaps an adolescent. Though their words remained indistinct, I deduced from the *tone* of their remarks that they were engaged in a lively dispute.

In another moment, I rounded the end of a large painted "flat" depicting an expanse of Saharan desert complete with date trees and a glowering sphinx, and came upon a sight that would have seemed peculiar in the extreme had I encountered it anywhere else. Here within the bizarre precincts of Barnum's establishment, however, it seemed like nothing out of the ordinary.

Perched atop a slat-back chair was a well-fed gentleman whose smooth, pink complexion and youthful demeanor contrasted sharply with the absolute—and apparently premature—whiteness of his hair. The latter—which he wore parted down the middle—was wavy and of the texture of silk. Though his age was impossible to ascertain with precision, I judged him to be no older than forty-five or -six. His visage was not unhandsome, though somewhat marred by the disagreeable fleshiness of his cheeks and the unfortunate shape of his nose, whose tip was excessively "snubbed." He was garbed in gray pantaloons, a checkered vest, and shirtsleeves, having divested himself of his jacket, which hung from the back of the chair.

Though I had never set eyes on this personage before, I recognized him at once as Monsieur Vox—a conclusion easily arrived at, as he was busily conversing with a child-sized manikin seated on his lap. This figure—whose wooden head had been carved with inordinate skill—bore a striking, not to say uncanny, resemblance to the ventriloquist himself. Its head was topped with a thatch of glossy white hair—a layer of pink-tinged pigment had been applied to its countenance—and its unblinking glass eyes were of the same light gray hue as Vox's. What differentiated its appearance most dramatically from that of its owner was the distinct cast of impish, if not diabolical, mischief that suffused its visage.

So absorbed was Vox in his business that, at first, he remained completely unaware of my presence, allowing me to observe him closely for several minutes. His skill was indeed extraordinary. Apart from some barely discernible movement in his laryngeal area, he produced his effects with no apparent use of his vocal organs. Despite the obvious artificiality of his dummy—whose mouth opened and closed in a highly mechanical way—the illusion that the little wooden figure was a living, fully articulate being was complete.

I had come upon the pair while they were embroiled in a discussion of the recent classroom behavior—or rather *mis*behavior—of the leering humunculous, whose appellation, I quickly discovered, was Archibald.

"What's the matter with you, Archie?" Vox was saying in the chiding tone of a parent who has discovered that his child has been routinely playing "hooky." "Don't you like going to school?"

"Oh, I don't mind going there," the dummy replied in its high, nasal voice. "It's *staying* there that bothers me."

"But what's so bad about school?"

"It's my teacher," said the dummy. "She looks like a saint."

"A saint?"

"Yeah. A Saint Bernard. She's got real unusual teeth, too. They're like stars."

"Stars?" Vox said. "Why—because they're bright and shiny?"

"No," sneered the dummy. "Because they come out at night."

"Oh, she can't be that bad."

"No," said the dummy. "I guess she ain't."

"You know, you really ought to watch your grammar," said Vox.

"Where is she?"

"Where's who?"

"My grandma."

"I didn't say grandma," Vox exclaimed. "I'm talking about your grammar. It's incorrect to say 'I *ain't* going.' It's 'I am not going.' 'You are not going.' 'He is not going.' "

"Well, ain't nobody going?" said the dummy.

"Let me explain," said Vox in the tone of a man struggling mightily to maintain his patience. "You see, 'I' is a pronoun."

"You is a *what*?" said the dummy.

Closing his eyes tightly, Vox remained silent for a moment, as though inwardly counting to ten. "Let me try one more time," he resumed at length in a somewhat strangled voice. "Now, why is it incorrect to say 'I ain't going'?"

"Because you ain't gone yet?" replied the dummy.

Up until this point, I had been standing by the edge of the painted scene of the Egyptian desert, watching Vox and his dummy unobserved. So sheerly hilarious, however, was their dialogue that—try as I might—I could not stifle a wild eruption of laughter. At the sound of my outburst, the ventriloquist swiveled his head in my direction and—arching his eyebrows—exclaimed: "Well, well—an audience. Small but appreciative. And who, pray tell, are you, my good man?"

Taking a moment to subdue my mirth and assume a suitably somber mien, I at length replied: "Forgive me for surprising you, but I did not wish to interrupt you in the midst of your rehearsal. My name is Poe—Edgar Poe. I was told by Mr. Barnum's custodian that I might find you here."

Vox's reaction to this statement was wholly unexpected. At the mention of my name, his eyes grew wide, his mouth fell open, and a soft exclamation of astonishment escaped his lips. Springing to his feet, he extracted his right arm from inside the rear of the dummy's torso, placed the little wooden figure in an upright position on the chair, and came hurrying toward me.

"Good Lord," he cried, coming to a halt before me and gazing at me with a wondering expression. "Poe the poet? Poe the author of that sublime masterpiece 'The Raven'?"

"The same," I replied with a small, gracious bow of the head.

"For once in my life I'm speechless, totally speechless," said Vox. "I simply can't tell you what a thrill this is. I've been begging Mr. Barnum to introduce us ever since I learned that the two of you are friends. He must have told you about my idea."

"Why, no," I replied in a tone of perplexity. "He said nothing about it. He merely mentioned that you were an admirer of my work."

"Is that what he said? Well, for the first time in his life, P. T. Barnum has actually been guilty of an understatement! Admirer? *Worshiper* is more like it. Why, I regard 'The Raven' as the greatest composition to flow from the human brain since the days of Homer!"

This encomium could hardly fail to fill me with a sense of the deepest gratification. "You are altogether too kind," I modestly replied. "Both Shakespeare and Milton, after all, produced several works which—while not necessarily *surpassing* my poem in sheer originality of conception—may certainly be considered its near equal."

"Nonsense!" cried Vox. "Nothing holds a candle to it. But tell me, Mr. Poe, is it true that Mr. Barnum didn't explain my idea?"

"He mentioned nothing about it at all," I replied to the ventriloquist, who had already succeeded in impressing me as a singularly discerning individual. "I am, of course, most eager to hear it."

"Well, it actually concerns you and your masterpiece. Let me explain. You see Archie over there," Vox said, gesturing at his dummy, who was seated limply in the chair. "I was just checking to make sure he's in good working order. The little fellow got banged up a bit during the hubbub the other night. Can't afford to let any harm come to him, you know. He's the real star of my show. Audiences can't get enough of him."

"I am by no means surprised to hear you say so," I remarked. "To judge from my brief observation of your act, the *repartee* between you and Master Archibald is nothing short of *rib-tickling*."

"It's a crowd-pleaser, all right," said Vox. "But that's just one part of my act. There's a lot more to it, you know. It's not all belly laughs. I try to work in some poetry, too. Give the public a little taste of the loftier arts."

"Yes," I said. "Mr. Barnum alluded to your remarkable enactment of Desdemona's death scene."

Vox nodded vigorously. "I've got a whole cast of Shakespearean dummies. Hamlet, Macbeth, King Lear. And Othello, of course. Fearsome-looking thing, black as night. You should see the way audiences respond when that big, maddened Negro smothers the life out of his poor innocent wife. Why, the gasps of horror fill the whole auditorium."

In view of his obvious acumen in regard to literary matters, I was somewhat surprised to hear Vox refer to the noble, if overly impulsive, Moor as "a big, maddened Negro"—a characterization that might have issued from the lips of Iago himself. Nevertheless, I merely replied: "It is indeed one of the most shattering moments in all of dramatic literature."

"That's exactly why it plays so well with audiences," said Vox. "People love that dark, tragic stuff. That's where you come into the picture."

"Me?" I exclaimed.

"Yes," Vox remarked with a triumphant smile. "I want to introduce 'The Raven' into my act."

So unexpected was this announcement that, for a moment, I merely stared wordlessly at the pink-cheeked, white-maned fellow. "Do you mean," I finally said in an incredulous tone, "that you wish to perform my poem with the aid of ventriloquial dummies?"

"Even better," answered Vox. "With a real bird!" Then—his words spilling out in a rush of enthusiasm—he proceeded to expound on his conception.

In brief, Vox wished—with my permission—to conclude each of his thrice-daily performances with a dramatic recitation of my famed ballad, *while a trained, living raven stood perched upon his shoulder!* At those moments in the poem when the grim, ungainly fowl uttered the melancholy refrain "Nevermore," Vox would employ his remarkable ventriloquial technique to project his voice into the mouth of the raven, making it appear as if the bird itself were croaking the word, and thus bringing the poem to startlingly vivid life.

"Just picture it," Vox exclaimed. He raised his right hand and—in the manner of a child playing at "shadow puppets"—formed it into the shape of a creature's head, arranging the thumb and fingers so as to suggest a mouth or beak. Then, in a sonorous voice, he declaimed:

> " 'Prophet!' said I, 'thing of evil!—prophet still, if bird or devil!—
> Whether tempter sent, or whether tempest tossed thee here ashore,
> Desolate yet all undaunted, on this desert land enchanted—
> On this home by horror haunted—tell me truly, I implore—

Is there—is there balm in Gilead?—tell me—tell me, I implore!'
Quoth the Raven—"

At this point, Vox paused dramatically. Moving the fingers and thumb of his elevated right hand, he mimicked the opening and closing of a beak. At that instant—apparently from the throat of the hand-creature—there came the harsh, *cawing* utterance: "Nevermore!"

So sheerly uncanny was Vox's skill that even this crude, manual approximation of a speaking bird caused a thrill of amazement to pass through my frame. It was easy to imagine that—if done with an actual raven—the performance would be nothing short of electrifying.

Even so, I felt deeply divided about his proposal. On the one hand, I could not help but endorse his desire to expose the public to works of high poetic genius. Indeed, in my *rôle* as a literary critic—whose chief duty, as I conceived it, was to elevate the deplorable taste of the masses—I myself had long been engaged in a similar enterprise.

At the same time, however, I could not entirely reconcile myself to the notion of having my poem—whose intended effect was to produce an intense exaltation of the listener's soul—performed under such frivolous, if not tawdry, circumstances. For all of Vox's superior intelligence and undeniable virtuosity, his act remained hopelessly entrenched within the realm of vulgar entertainment.

Before I could arrive at a decision concerning his suggestion, Vox—who had been regarding me narrowly—hastily declared:

"Naturally, you'd receive a fair share of the proceeds. Let's say half the take from the sale of souvenirs. How does that sound?"

"Souvenirs?" I said.

"Little hand-painted ravens perched atop the bust of Pallas. A special commemorative edition of your poem, complete with woodcut illustrations. Engraved likenesses of the celebrated author—that sort of thing. All available for purchase at the end of the show. Why, you'd be amazed at what I earn in any given week from my pamphlet, 'Vox on Ventriloquism.' Fifty, sixty dollars—sometimes more. I understand, of course, that you poets are above such crass concerns. Still, there's no harm in fattening up your pockets a bit while promoting the cause of great art, eh?"

"You are correct in asserting that no mere pecuniary considerations can play a part in my calculations," I replied. "My decision must be based solely on the *aesthetic* merits of your proposal."

"Of course, of course," said Vox.

"Fifty or sixty dollars?" I said.

"At least," said Vox.

Frowning deeply, I took another moment to reflect on the proposition before stating: "I confess that I am intrigued by your notion. Having weighed the matter carefully, I find that I am inclined to accept."

This announcement caused a look of pure, unmitigated delight to suffuse the ventriloquist's countenance. "Wonderful!" he exclaimed.

Then—in the hale and hearty fashion in which men are wont to demonstrate their feelings—he reached out a hand and delivered an exuberant slap to my upper right arm.

It is a peculiarity of our physiological makeup that, oftentimes, the least serious bodily afflictions are the source of the greatest distress. A cancerous growth that is slowly spreading through our vital organs and leading us inexorably to death may initially manifest itself as little more than a mild ache; whereas a paper cut on our little finger may be so tormenting as to prevent us from falling asleep at night.

The abrasion I had sustained when thrown to the cobblestones by Carson was typical of the latter variety of injury—i.e., essentially superficial, yet painful in the extreme. The reader may easily imagine my reaction, therefore, when Vox smacked me so enthusiastically on my arm. Though I managed not to cry out, I could not keep myself from wincing in agony and reflexively clutching at my poor, wounded limb.

"Good heavens!" Vox cried in alarm. "What's wrong, Mr. Poe?"

For several moments, I remained deprived of the power of speech. At length—the pain having so far subsided as to allow me to unclench my teeth—I proceeded to inform him of the circumstances that had resulted in my injury.

"Thank God for Kit Carson," Vox exclaimed when I had concluded my account. "I tell you, it's an absolute scandal that a great city like New York lacks a professional fire department. Those damned volunteer companies are a bigger hazard to public safety than the fires they're supposed to be fighting."

"I share your sentiments entirely," I said. "Indeed, I made much the same observation to Carson immediately following the incident. Still, I do not regret that it happened, for it proved to be a singular exemplification of the proverbial saying that there is a silver lining in every cloud."

"How do you mean?" said Vox, regarding me with a quizzical expression.

"As an immediate result of the accident," I explained, "I recalled something that may bear directly on the investigation in which I am currently involved. Indeed, it was with the hope of confirming my supposition that I came here this morning."

"I've been wondering about that," Vox said. "I was so excited to see you that I forgot to ask what brought you here. Sorry. Please go on."

"You are no doubt aware that Kit Carson and I are on the trail of the criminal known as 'Liver-Eating' Johnson, who has been responsible for the recent series of unspeakable murders that have terrorized our city."

"Of course. It's been all over the papers," said Vox. Then, knitting his brow so deeply that his bushy white eyebrows met above his nose, he added: "You don't mean to say that this Johnson character has some connection to the museum, do you?"

"That remains to be seen," I answered. "My immediate concern involves your late colleague, Mazeppa Vivaldi, with whom—according to the information supplied to me by Mr. Oswald—you were on exceedingly friendly terms."

At my invocation of the lion-tamer's name, Vox's countenance assumed an expression of extreme surprise. "I don't know if I'd use the word 'exceedingly,' " he remarked after a momentary pause. "But, yes, we were certainly friends. What on earth does poor Mazeppa have to do with all this?"

Ignoring this query, I responded with one of my own. "Tell me," I said, "did your late friend ever have cause to mention an acquaintance named Wyatt?"

Frowning thoughtfully, Vox silently reflected on this question. As he did, he dug his right thumb and index finger into the pocket of his vest and extracted a small silver box, oblong in shape. Opening the elaborately engraved lid, he then extended the little receptacle toward me and said: "Snuff?"

I refused the offer with a wave of the hand. "My sole experience with that exceedingly pungent substance occurred many years ago during my student days at the University of Virginia," I explained. "It had no other effect on me than to precipitate a violent paroxysm of sneezing."

"Yes," said Vox, "it'll do that, all right, especially if you're not accustomed to it. As for me, I've been using it for years. Keeps my nasal cavity clear. Breath control is half the trick for a ventriloquist, you know."

Employing his left thumb and forefinger as a sort of tweezers, he removed a small quantity of the pulverized tobacco from the box—inserted a pinch into each nostril—inhaled deeply—then wiped his nose with his pocket handkerchief. He then snapped the lid shut, returned the box to his vest pocket, and resumed his silent ruminations.

"Now that I think about it," he said at length, "I believe that Mazeppa *did* mention a Mr. Wyatt. Yes, I'm sure of it. There was one time, right before he died, when I ran into him as he was leaving the museum. He seemed to be in quite a hurry. When I asked him where he was rushing off to, he told me he had to see a gentleman by that name."

At this pronouncement, a thrilling sense of vindication coursed through my frame. I had been right after all! The Great Mazeppa was indeed the mysterious, wavy-haired visitor witnessed by young Harry Pratt!

"Did your friend offer any explanation as to the nature of his errand?" I inquired.

"Not that I recall," said Vox. "But what—if you don't mind my asking—has all this got to do with your investigation?"

"The personage whom Mazeppa intended to visit on that occasion was none other than William Wyatt—the very same individual who, two days ago, was horribly murdered by the depraved killer Carson and I are seeking."

"Good Lord!" cried Vox. "You mean the albino gentleman? I read his name in the papers, of course, but I never made the connection." Shaking his head slowly, he added in a musing tone: "Strange that the two of them were acquainted. But how could Mazeppa be involved? After all, the poor man was killed months ago in that horrible accident."

"I cannot yet answer that question," I remarked, "or, indeed, even state with assurance that such an involvement exists. My present purpose is merely to uncover as much information as possible, in an effort to determine what motive lay behind Mr. Wyatt's death. Can you tell me anything about Mazeppa that might shed light on his relationship to the victim?"

"Wish I could," said Vox. "We were on friendly terms but hardly intimates. What he did outside the museum I really can't say. I know he hailed from Boston. And that his real name was Thomas Dudley. Other than that . . ." And here, he ended his remarks with a shrug.

Having already garnered these few meager facts from Barnum, I was exceedingly disappointed by this reply. The excitement that had gripped me only moments earlier now drained from me in an instant, and was replaced with a sense of the keenest frustration.

I opened my mouth, intent on urging the ventriloquist to cudgel his brain for any further information regarding his friend. Before I could speak, however, I heard someone call my name from the auditorium. Muffled by the intervening curtain, the voice was too indistinct for me to recognize, though it

clearly was that of an adult male. Thinking that it might be Carson—or perhaps Barnum—I cupped my hands around my mouth and called out: "I am
here backstage, with Mr. Vox!"

My guess as to the person's identity proved incorrect on both counts; for, a
minute later, I was startled to see the figure of George Townsend making his
way around the various appurtenances cluttering the backstage area. Striding
up to us, he greeted me with a firm handshake.

"I confess that I am greatly surprised to see you here," I said after introducing the sharp-featured young fellow to Vox. "How did you find me?"

"Why, it was easy enough to do," he replied. "I went to your home and spoke
to your aunt, who told me where you and Mr. Carson had gone. So I came
directly to the museum and found Mr. Barnum, who sent me up here."

"But what has led you here?" I asked, feeling a sudden twinge of apprehension. "However little effort it has cost you to discover my whereabouts, I presume that you would not have exerted yourself even to that modest extent
unless you had some urgent reason to do so."

Townsend nodded, then glanced pointedly at Vox.

Interpreting this look as a signal for privacy, Vox graciously excused himself,
explaining that he had matters to attend to in another part of the museum.
"Can't tell you how thrilled I am about 'The Raven,' Mr. Poe," he said. "I plan
to start performing it as soon as the museum reopens. In the meantime, if
anything more about Mazeppa comes to mind, I'll let you know at once."

Stepping over to his dummy, Vox slipped his right hand into the rear of the
figure—raised it from the chair—and seated it upon his open left hand. All at
once, the little wooden figure seemed to spring miraculously to life. Swiveling
its head toward Vox, it opened its mouth and—in its shrill, nasal voice—
declared: "Well, it's about time! I thought you'd never stop gabbing!"

"Now, now, Archibald," said Vox. "I was talking to Mr. Poe about a very serious matter. He is attempting to solve a deep, dark mystery."

"Oh, I'm sure he'll figure it out," replied the manikin. "He ain't no dummy.
Unlike some people I know. And I don't mean *me*."

"I'm getting pretty tired of your insults, you know," Vox admonished. "It's
about time you started watching your mouth."

"Just be glad no one's watching *yours*," sneered the dummy. "They'd see
what a lousy ventriloquist you are!"

"That's enough out of you," said Vox. "Say good-bye, Archie."

"Good-bye, Archie!" said the dummy.

Then, with a little bow toward Townsend and myself, Vox and his wooden *alter ego* vanished around the end of the large painted backdrop whose anterior side depicted the vast expanse of Egyptian desert.

No sooner had he disappeared from sight than I addressed Townsend thusly: "Please inform me without further delay of the circumstances that have caused you to seek me out."

Without a word, the young man reached inside his jacket, extracted a folded sheet of paper, and handed it to me.

Opening it, I saw that it was a piece of stationery upon which the following message was inscribed:

Poe—

You were warned. Now you'll pay.

C. A. C.

"Cartwright," I muttered.

"It was delivered this morning, care of the newspaper office," said Townsend. "Mr. Morris received one, too, just as nasty. Evidently Cartwright wasn't too pleased to see your satire published in the *Mirror*."

"And does your employer regard these missives as a serious threat?"

"Serious enough to notify the police," said Townsend. "From what I hear, this Cartwright doesn't take kindly to personal insults. That's why Mr. Morris sent me to find you right away. He thinks you might be in real danger."

"Perhaps," I mused aloud, "Kit was correct about last night's occurrence after all."

"What occurrence?" asked Townsend.

"I was almost hit by a speeding fire-wagon while crossing the street before my home," I explained. "In view of the notoriously reckless habits of the city's volunteer firemen—many of whom, as you know, are denizens of the city's most noisome and degraded slums—I assumed that my near-collision with the vehicle had been an accident. Carson, however—thanks to whose lightning-quick reflexes I owe my very existence—suspected otherwise, especially since he could detect no evidence of a conflagration anywhere in the vicinity."

"Carson was right," said Townsend. "There *wasn't* any big fire in the city last night. I cover those stories for the *Mirror*."

"Could it be possible, then," I said, "that the driver of the wagon was deliberately attempting to run me down?"

"I'm afraid so," said Townsend. "Those firemen aren't exactly choirboys. Lots of them belong to gangs—the Plug Uglies, the Dead Rabbits, the Roach

Guards. There are some mighty nasty customers among them. Ever hear of Piker McGlynn?"

"The appellation is unfamiliar to me."

"Former president of the Hide-Binders," said Townsend. "Met him a few years back when I was reporting on crime in the Bowery. Charming gent. Used to hand out printed circulars, spelling out the cost of his services. Teeth knocked out, five dollars. Broken nose, ten. Ear chewed off, fifteen. Everything up to and including 'the big job.' That cost a hundred dollars and up, depending on the method—shooting, stabbing, strangling, or poison."

"Do you mean to suggest," I said, "that Cartwright might have hired one of these reprobates to murder me?"

"Mr. Morris certainly thinks so. That's why I'm here. To warn you."

The knowledge imparted by Townsend—i.e., that I might be the target of a hired assassin—had a twofold effect upon me. It filled me with a very natural sense of alarm, while confirming my contemptuous opinion of Cartwright's odious character. It was not that I disparaged the latter's desire to strike back at me. On the contrary. To respond to a perceived affront with direct physical action was, I felt, a perfectly justifiable impulse. I myself had never permitted an attack upon my name to go unpunished, my motto being *Nemo me impune lacessit*—"No one may insult me with impunity."

Having been reared in Virginia, however—where the prevailing code of chivalry governs *les affaires d'honneur* among gentlemen—I was used to meeting such injuries in the time-honored way of the well-bred Southerner: to wit, by openly challenging an adversary to a violent bout of bloody personal combat. To hire a lowborn brute to commit a surreptitious act of vengeance—as Cartwright seemed to have done—was a type of behavior deserving of the deepest scorn.

"I suppose I had better inform Kit of this development," I remarked, consulting my pocket watch. "It is almost time for me to meet him at our appointed rendezvous."

Making our way out of the theater, Townsend and I proceeded along the hallway, toward the main staircase. Our route led us past the museum's Grand Taxidermical Salon, housing Barnum's vast collection of stuffed zoological specimens—antelopes and black bears, cougars and dromedaries, elephants, foxes, mountain goats, hippopotami, ibexes, jaguars, and hundreds more—along with a staggering assortment of miscellaneous natural artifacts, from shark's teeth to gazelle horns to the shell of a giant Galapagos tortoise. As we strode past the taxidermical hall, my eye was caught by a large display just inside the entranceway. Pausing, I stepped inside the salon, Townsend at my heels.

"Why are we going in here?" he inquired in a puzzled tone.

The big hall was exceedingly gloomy, only a few of the many gas jets mounted along the walls being turned on. The light spilling in from the main hallway, however, offered sufficient illumination for me to see the display clearly.

It was mounted upon a circular platform, perhaps two feet high and ten feet in diameter, surrounded by a low wooden railing designed to discourage spectators from touching the objects on exhibit. These consisted of a kneeling, life-sized wax figure of a man, garbed in a colorful, though badly stained, costume. Its head, topped with a shiny black wig, was inserted into the gaping mouth of an enormous, stuffed, black-maned lion that was seated upon its haunches. A large wooden case standing behind this tableau held various items, including a whip, a three-legged stool, and—upon a separate shelf—a jar labeled "Major Meecham's Excelsior Hair Cream."

"Why, it's the Great Mazeppa," Townsend said.

"Yes," I said, closely scrutinizing the figure of the kneeling man, whose sculpted face was streaked with crimson paint, meant to simulate the blood streaming down from the terrible wound where the lion's teeth had penetrated his skull.

"What's your interest in *him*?" asked Townsend.

"Though I do not yet know to what, if any, extent this fact may bear upon our investigation, I have just ascertained that Mazeppa and Mr. Wyatt were acquaintances," I replied.

"Really?" Townsend said in a tone of extreme surprise. "That's odd. I was here, you know, when he was killed."

It was now my turn to evince amazement. "Do you mean to say that you witnessed the event?" I exclaimed, turning to stare at the young reporter.

"That's right," Townsend said. "My little niece, Mary Beth, was visiting from Philadelphia. She couldn't wait to see Barnum's museum. It was all she could talk about. We were in the audience when it happened. One thing's for sure, this setup doesn't begin to capture the real horror of the thing."

"I can easily imagine that the actual spectacle must have been inexpressibly ghastly," I said.

"It was beyond anything," said Townsend gravely. "Believe me, I've covered all kinds of accidents. Seen bodies mangled in more ways than I care to remember. But nothing like this. If I live to be a hundred, I don't believe I'll ever forget that god-awful sight. Or those terrible *sounds*."

"Sounds?"

"Yes. Just before its jaws snapped shut, the lion made this strange coughing noise. Then—*crunch!*"

A shiver coursed through my frame as I pictured Mazeppa's skull giving way beneath the crushing force of the great beast's jaws.

"Hell of a way to die," Townsend continued, slowly shaking his head. "Ending up as a midday snack for a lion."

This latter remark caused a sudden realization to flash upon my mind. "Huh!" I exclaimed.

"What is it?" asked Townsend, looking at me curiously.

"I have just remembered something that I meant to convey to Mr. Barnum when I spoke to him earlier. Come. I will tell him on our way out."

We found the showman on the second floor, where he was in the process of examining a display case containing the actual riding boots—complete with false heels for concealing secret military documents—worn by the arch-traitor Major General Benedict Arnold. As Townsend and I approached, he glanced up at us and—addressing the young reporter—exclaimed: "Tracked him down, eh, Mr. Townsend?"

"Yes," replied the latter. "I found him just where you said he'd be."

"Well, Poe," said the showman, turning his attention to me, "what did you think of Monsieur Vox?"

"Your assessment of his skill in the ancient art of biloquism was by no means exaggerated," I replied.

"What did I tell you?" said Barnum with a chuckle. "Why, the man's a colossus, an absolute titan! Towers over every other ventriloquist in the world! Believe me, I've seen them all. Signor Blitz. Alexander Vettermare. Christopher Sugg—the so-called 'Master of Internal Elocution.' *Ha!* Rank amateurs, each and every one. Why, it's like comparing Cicero to a pack of stammering schoolboys! Bless me, you wouldn't believe the feats that man is capable of! Why, that Archibald dummy of his can whistle the entire 'Casta Diva' aria from Bellini's *Norma* while Vox imbibes a full glass of buttermilk! I suppose he told you how much he admires your own poetry?"

"Indeed," I replied, "his comments regarding 'The Raven' were of such an exceedingly flattering nature that I have agreed to allow him to perform my poem as a special feature of his act."

"Splendid!" cried Barnum. "The public will go wild for it, absolutely wild! Have to add extra performances just to accommodate the crowds! I assume you and Vox worked out the financial details."

"Yes," I replied. "I am quite satisfied with the nature of our agreement."

"Fine, fine," said Barnum. "Happy to hear you'll be earning a few extra shekels. Be able to afford some special treats for those dear ladies of yours, eh, m'boy?"

"It is in reference to my loved ones," I said, "that I have sought you out. Both my Aunt Maria and my dear wife Virginia were exceedingly grateful to receive your latest gift—as, of course, was I. We wish to proffer our deepest thanks."

"Why, you're welcome, m'boy, heartily welcome," said Barnum, his countenance assuming a strange expression of uncertainty. "I'm not exactly sure, however, what gift you mean."

"Why, the foodstuffs that were delivered to our home this morning," I exclaimed.

"Foodstuffs?" said Barnum, frowning deeply. "There was that basket of goodies I sent after returning from Europe, of course. Ordered it from Park and Tilford—finest purveyors of delicacies in the city. Oh yes, it cost a good deal—more than you'd believe. But P. T. Barnum's not one to stint. 'Always give the best'—that's P. T. Barnum's motto! Still, that was several months ago."

"Do you mean to say," I exclaimed with a sudden foreboding at heart, "that you sent no such present to my home this morning?"

"Believe me, m'boy, I'd tell you if I had," the showman replied. "Must've been some other admirer. Great Scot, Poe, what's wrong? You've gone white as a ghost!"

Such was my state of agitation that I could make no coherent reply. With a wild cry of alarm, I spun on my heel and bolted for the staircase.

CHAPTER EIGHTEEN

C ARSON—AS WE HAD ARRANGED—was waiting for me in the lobby, idly examining the towering Mastodon skeleton that had been uncovered on a farm outside Schenectady, New York—purchased by Barnum for the unprecedented sum of three thousand dollars—and installed with much fanfare in his establishment the previous winter. At our approach, Carson acknowledged Townsend's presence with a cordial "Howdy." He then turned his gaze upon me and—perceiving the look of distress upon my countenance—demanded to know what was wrong.

"We must return home without delay," I said. "I fear that our loved ones may be in danger. Come. I will explain as we proceed."

Hurrying from the museum, the three of us bent our steps in the direction of my abode, while—speaking at a volume sufficiently loud to be heard over the environing racket of the streets—I shared my anxieties with the scout.

"I have come to believe," I said, after describing the note sent by Cartwright, "that last night's incident involving the runaway fire-wagon was—as you yourself suspected—no mere accident. Indeed, I am now persuaded that it was the work of a hired assassin. Having failed in his first attempt, it is only natural to assume that this wretch—whose fee is undoubtedly contingent upon my death—would promptly make another.

"While discussing this matter with Mr. Townsend," I continued, gesturing toward the young reporter who was keeping pace beside me, "he cited the example of a Bowery ruffian whose criminal services—listed on a printed card—ranged from simple assault to various forms of homicide, including murder by poison. Recalling this fact, I became thoroughly alarmed when I learned that the anonymous gift delivered to our door earlier this morning did not come from Barnum."

"You mean that basket of grub?" Carson asked. "You reckon it's been poisoned?"

"That is indeed my concern," I grimly retorted. "Let us pray that I am wrong. Or that—if my assumption is correct—the food has remained untouched in our absence."

Making our way as swiftly as possible along the teeming streets, Carson, Townsend, and I soon came in sight of our destination. It was a cloudless day, and in the bright morning sunlight, the little house presented a cheerful appearance utterly at odds with my own mood of dark apprehension. As we passed through the swinging gate of the picket fence surrounding the yard, we saw Mrs. Whitaker bent over a flower bed with a watering can in hand. Under normal circumstances, I would have paused to exchange pleasantries with the plump, gray-haired landlady. On this occasion, however, I merely gave a small wave of greeting, and—followed by my companions—rushed inside the house and up the stairs.

Pounding on the door to our apartment, I waited in an agony of impatience for a response. After the lapse of a moment (which, in my overwrought state, felt like an eternity), approaching footsteps could be heard from within. An instant later—to my inexpressible relief—the door was flung open by Muddy, who, after taking one look at my face, cried out: "Eddie! What is the matter?"

Stepping over the threshold, I clutched the good woman by the shoulders and exclaimed: "Is everyone all right, Muddy dearest?"

"Why, yes," she answered, her visage suffused with a look of confusion. "We're all perfectly fine."

At that moment, as if to demonstrate the validity of this assertion, Sissy and Jeremiah emerged from the direction of the parlor.

"What's wrong, Eddie?" asked my darling wife, while the boy regarded us intently.

"Nothing at all, now that I have assured myself that the three of you are apparently unharmed," I replied.

Stepping over to his son, Carson laid a hand atop the boy's head and fondly tousled the raven-black hair. "You been behaving yourself, Jeremiah?" he fondly inquired.

Smiling back at his father, the boy answered with an emphatic nod.

"You have already met Mr. Townsend," I said to Muddy and Sissy, indicating the young man beside me, who had politely doffed his hat. "We owe him a great debt of thanks for having alerted me to a grave potential danger."

A soft gasp escaped from my Aunt Maria's lips at this pronouncement.

"Tell me, Muddy dearest," I continued, "where is the basket of foodstuffs that was delivered this morning?"

"Why, I put it in the kitchen," she replied. "On the table."

"I take it that none of you has sampled its contents?"

Sissy shook her head. "Jeremiah and I certainly haven't. We've been in the parlor since you left, drawing pictures."

"I haven't touched a thing," said Muddy. "It's just exactly as it came."

"Thank heavens," I said, exhaling a sigh of gratitude. Without another word, I then turned and made for the kitchen, intent on examining the basket of food to see if I could discover any evidence of treachery.

No sooner had I stepped over the threshold than I came to a sudden, startled halt.

Lying at the foot of the table was the overturned basket, which appeared to have been violently knocked from its perch. Its contents—the grapes and oranges, relish jars and confectioneries—were strewn about the floor. My gaze was riveted by one item in particular: a block of Cheddar from which a large bite had evidently been taken. The sight of the partially devoured cheese, surrounded by a scattering of yellow crumbs, produced a sharp pang of dread within my bosom; for I already knew precisely what I was about to find.

An instant later, my fears were confirmed when—rapidly surveying the room—I saw, sprawled in the far corner, the inert form of Carson's faithful dog.

With a shout of dismay, I hurried across the floor and knelt beside the stricken beast. The dog was still alive, though barely. Its eyes were closed. Greenish froth bubbled at the corners of its gaping mouth, from which its long tongue lolled. Its chest rose and fell spasmodically, while a dreadful, tortured wheeze issued from the depths of its throat.

I saw at once that the poor creature was beyond any hope of salvation. At that moment, I heard a tumult behind me, as—responding to my shout—the others came crowding into the kitchen. I discerned Muddy's cry of horror—Sissy's gasp of dismay—Townsend's shocked exclamation. Even the unspeaking boy emitted a tremulous whimper of fright. Only Carson remained silent.

An instant later, he was crouching by my side. Glancing over at him, I saw that his countenance was taut with emotion. After grimly examining the animal, he swiveled his head to look at Sissy and said: "I'd be obliged, ma'am, if you took the boy into another room."

"Come, Jeremiah," my wife said in a tearful voice, then ushered the heart-broken child from the kitchen.

"Oh, Eddie," said Muddy, coming up to stand behind me. "What on earth has happened here?"

"It is as I feared," I replied, addressing her over my shoulder. "The basket delivered to us this morning was sent not—as we had assumed—by our friend Mr. Barnum, but by a mortal enemy bent on my utter destruction. Its contents have been infused with a virulent poison. Having innocently partaken of the deadly fare, Kit's loyal canine has fallen victim to the fate intended for myself."

At that instant—as Muddy wrung her hands in dismay—a thought struck me with the shock of a Galvanic battery.

"Where is Cattarina?" I exclaimed. Knowing our tabby's fondness for all manner of dairy products, I was suddenly terrified that she, too, might have succumbed to the irresistible enticement of the poisoned cheese.

"She is fine," said Muddy. "She has been curled up asleep on my bed all morning. But I will check to make sure." And so saying, she turned and left the kitchen.

"Anything I can do?" asked Townsend, who had joined Carson and myself at the side of the unfortunate creature.

"Ain't nothing anyone can do," said the scout.

This observation merely confirmed the conclusion at which I had already arrived. Crouched beside the dying brute, Carson, Townsend, and I could only look on helplessly as its labored respiration grew fainter by the moment. To those who have cherished an affection for a loyal and sagacious pet, the sheer *dreadfulness* of watching such a creature endure a slow and painful death need hardly be described. When at length the canine exhaled its last, tormented breath, my heart felt so weighted with pity that I could barely keep my emotions in check.

Looking over at the scout, I saw that his own expression had undergone no material alteration. Only the fiery gleam in his eyes—the inordinately tight compression of his lips—and the angry clenching of his jaw muscles hinted at his true feelings: his sorrow, rage, and sense of fierce resolution.

"I'll need to have a word with the boy," he declared. He then stood erect and strode from the kitchen.

Elevating myself to an upright position, I found that I was somewhat unsteady on my feet.

"You all right, Mr. Poe?" asked Townsend, who had also risen from his crouch.

"Yes, though deeply affected by the spectacle to which we have just been witness," I replied. "We must see to it that this surpassingly devoted creature receives a proper burial. To dispose of it in any less ceremonious way would be a grave injustice. I will go find Mrs. Whitaker and seek her permission to inter it in her backyard."

"That's a fine idea," Townsend said. "In the meantime," he continued, gesturing toward the items littering the floor, "I'll pick up this mess."

"Be careful that you do not touch any of the tainted comestibles with your bare hands," I cautioned.

"Right," the young man replied, extracting a handkerchief from the pocket of his trousers.

Leaving him to his task, I hurried from the apartment and—descending to the front yard—found Mrs. Whitaker still engaged in her gardening. In order not to alarm her with the truth, I told her that Carson's dog had suddenly expired after choking on the bone of a boiled chicken that had been cooling on a platter in the kitchen. I then asked if we might lay the animal to rest in her backyard. Merely to throw its carcass away with the trash, I explained, would render the loss of the beloved pet even more painful to the scout's young son.

Registering intense dismay at my news, the tender-hearted landlady readily agreed. Thanking her profusely, I then proceeded to the rear of the house, where—after taking a shovel from the little gardening shed—I stripped off my jacket, rolled up my sleeves, and dug a hole in a corner of the fenced-in backyard as far as possible from the privy. I then thrust the blade of the implement into the little pile of earth I had created and returned to my apartment.

Except for Carson—who was nowhere to be seen—everyone was gathered in the parlor. I was struck at once by the calm demeanor of Jeremiah, who was seated on the sofa between Muddy and Sissy. That the boy had been horribly upset by the death of the canine I had no doubt. The consternation he had exhibited upon seeing the stricken brute gave ample proof of his feelings. In contrast to my loved ones, however (both of whose faces wore expressions of intense sorrow), the lad now showed little, if any, emotion. In view of the famously stoic character of the race to which his mother belonged—as well as the equally cool and self-possessed deportment of his father—such composure was, perhaps, not to be wondered at, even in a child so young.

Approaching Townsend—who was standing silently beside the rosewood *étagère* belonging to the former tenant, Mr. Devereaux—I inquired as to Carson's whereabouts.

"He left a few minutes ago," Townsend replied. "Didn't say where he was going."

Hardly had he spoken these words than Carson reappeared from belowstairs with a small Indian blanket adorned with a handsome geometrical design. Carrying it into the kitchen, he emerged several moments later, cradling the dead animal, whose form was now completely wrapped within the blanket.

"Let's go bury him," Carson said simply, standing at the threshold of the parlor.

Following the scout downstairs, we proceeded into the backyard, where we were joined by Mrs. Whitaker. After gently laying the enshrouded dog into the hole I had dug, Carson removed his hat and, looking down at the grave, said: "He was a good dog. Fine tracker. Helped get me out of many a bad scrape. I'll be hard-pressed to find another like him."

Then, turning his gaze on his boy, he said: "Anything you want to add, Jeremiah?"

By this point, the boy's impassive bearing had begun to falter. Fighting back tears, he performed a series of swift gestures, making a motion as though cutting his hair—then running his hands down his face—and finally interlocking his two index fingers.

"What does he say?" Muddy whispered to Sissy in a tremulous voice.

Dabbing at her eyes with an embroidered handkerchief, my dear wife hoarsely replied: "That he grieves for the loss of his friend."

Carson reached down and squeezed his son's shoulder. Then—replacing his hat on his head—he grabbed the handle of the shovel, swiftly filled in the hole, and tamped down the dirt atop the little mound. When the job was completed, Mrs. Whitaker—who had been clutching a rose she had plucked from her garden—placed it at the head of the grave. She then turned to the rest of us and said:

"Please come inside and let me make you all some tea. There's a nice honey cake, too. I fixed it just this morning."

"That's very kind of you, Mrs. Whitaker," Muddy said. "Are you sure it's no trouble?"

"Not in the least," said the landlady.

"Come, Jeremiah," said Sissy, extending her hand toward the boy, who reached out and grasped it in his own.

"You all go on ahead," said the scout.

"Aren't you going to join us, Mr. Carson?" Mrs. Whitaker asked.

"No, ma'am," he replied. "I got something to do."

"What about you and your friend, Mr. Poe?" the landlady inquired.

"We will remain here with Kit," I announced. "Please proceed without us."

"Now, don't you boys do anything foolish," Muddy declared, her countenance wrought into an expression of excessive concern.

"Don't you worry none, ma'am," said Carson.

The three of us stood silently at the grave site while the women and boy departed from the backyard and entered the house through the rear door, leading directly into Mrs. Whitaker's kitchen. As soon as they were gone, Carson turned to me and said:

"You know where this Cartwright lives, Eddie?"

Reaching a hand into the breast pocket of my coat, I removed the envelope containing the threatening note that Townsend had conveyed to me.

"Forty-six Cortlandt Street," I said, consulting the sender's address inscribed on the envelope.

Carson nodded grimly.

"Let's go," he said.

Chapter Nineteen

~~~

T HE ITCHING SENSATION caused by the chigger bites having returned with renewed intensity, I hurried upstairs before departing and quickly applied a fresh coating of Dr. Kittredge's ointment to my badly inflamed ankles. I then rejoined my companions, who were waiting for me in front of the house.

During our previous travels through the city, Carson had insisted on walking. Such was his sense of urgency, however, that he now insisted on going by carriage, Cartwright's residence being located at a considerable distance from my own. Accordingly, we secured a hack and instructed the driver to take us to Cortlandt Street as speedily as the traffic would allow.

Throughout the ride, the scout said nothing, though his exceedingly grim expression spoke eloquently of his determination to exact full retribution for the murder of his dog. That Cartwright deserved to be dealt with in the harshest possible way I fervently believed. He had not merely destroyed the life of a loving and innocent beast, but—even more unforgivably—had endangered the well-being of the two angelic creatures I cherished most ardently in the world. Only great good fortune had prevented one or both of them (to say nothing of Carson's son) from partaking of the poisoned food and suffering the same fate as the doomed canine.

For such behavior no punishment was too severe. My only regret was that I myself would not be the one to inflict it. To judge from his implacable expression, Carson intended to reserve that satisfaction for himself.

Slightly less than twenty minutes later, we came in sight of our destination. Cartwright's neighborhood had, at an earlier epoch of the city's history, been among the most fashionable quarters in Manhattan. Now immense lofty warehouses had largely supplanted its aristocratic mansions. Several of these dwellings, however, were still to be seen, incongruously wedged among the vast commercial structures. It was in one of these dilapidated, though still-imposing, houses that Cartwright evidently resided.

As our vehicle drew to a halt before Number Forty-six, Carson, who was seated by the window closest to the curb, emitted a soft grunt of surprise. Tilting my head so as to obtain an unobstructed view through the window, I immediately saw what had elicited this reaction.

A small crowd of people was congregated on the sidewalk, talking excitedly among themselves as they gestured toward the residence. At my first glimpse of this assemblage, I experienced a tremor of alarm. Like a circling flock of vultures, such gatherings could only be interpreted as an ominous sign.

An instant later, my eyes fell on another, even more disconcerting sight. A short distance from the crowd, at the very edge of the curb, stood a stocky young police officer. Hands on his thighs, he was bent nearly double, violently disgorging the contents of his stomach into the gutter.

"What the hell?" muttered Townsend, who had leaned forward to peer through the window.

Dismounting from the carriage, Carson removed a coin from his small leather pouch and handed it to the driver. The three of us then strode toward the young policeman, who had straightened up and was now wiping his mouth with the back of his hand, while making soft, moaning sounds.

As we approached the squatly built fellow, his countenance—which was suffused with a sickly greenish hue—suddenly assumed a startled expression. My own reaction was no less surprised; for I recognized him at once as Officer Boyle—the very same person who had responded to my frantic cries for help two nights earlier, when I made my appalling discovery at the home of William Wyatt.

"Mr. Poe!" he exclaimed. "How did you get here so quick?"

"Why, whatever do you mean?" I replied to this exceedingly puzzling query.

"Captain Dunnegan just sent a man to find you not more than five minutes ago," answered Boyle in a shaky voice.

"Dunnegan's here?" said Carson.

Boyle nodded, then pointed a tremulous finger in the direction of Cartwright's residence. "In there."

"But we did not come at your captain's behest," I explained. "We are here to see Mr. C. A. Cartwright over a matter of utmost importance."

Boyle opened his mouth as if to reply. All at once, he was convulsed by a renewed fit of sickness. He pressed his hand over his mouth—his cheeks ballooned outward—nauseous sounds issued from his throat. Hurriedly turning away from us, he doubled over and—for a second time—loudly regurgitated into the gutter.

"Come on," said Carson, his handsome visage wrought into a look of extreme distaste.

Pushing our way through the crowd, we mounted the stoop and—ignoring the tarnished brass knocker—threw open the front door and stepped over the threshold.

"I've got a bad feeling about this," said Townsend. "A mighty bad feeling."

No sooner had we entered the premises than my olfactory organs were assaulted by an odor so offensive that I briefly wondered if Boyle's illness had not been induced by this stench.

"Whew!" exclaimed Townsend, wrinkling his nose.

"Stinks of cat in here," said Carson.

Indeed, the house was suffused with the pungency of feline micturition. As the reader is aware, my feelings for this species of domestic pet were of the warmest variety. Even to a cat-fancier such as myself, however, the smell pervading Cartwright's abode was of a barely tolerable intensity.

As we stood in the foyer, the muffled sound of voices reached us from above. Climbing the broad, winding staircase, we proceeded along a hallway whose walls were hung with an unusually large number of very spirited modern paintings in frames of rich golden arabesque. A moment later, we found ourselves at the entrance of a spacious private library, illumined by a single globe lamp which—hanging from the ceiling—shed but a soft and mysterious light throughout the chamber.

The predominating color of the room—shared by the curtains, carpet, and wallpaper—was a faint crimson. Aside from the bookshelves, the principal furnishings consisted of a morocco armchair, an octagonal table with a green baize surface, and a small couch or settee upholstered in a fabric that harmonized in hue with the other appointments. There was also a desk. From our vantage point at the threshold of the library, however, only a small corner of this object was visible to us, the rest being obscured by a group of brawny police officers, who were engaged in a lively consultation, their backs to the doorway.

The source of the unpleasant odor was immediately evident, for disposed about the room—prowling about the floor, curled on the cushion of the settee, draped over the back of the chair, settled on the tabletop—were no less than a dozen cats of every imaginable variety. Evidently, Cartwright belonged to that species of eccentric who—lacking the capacity to form intimate human attachments—strive to slake their desperate isolation by surrounding themselves with an inordinate number of domestic animals.

As we crossed the threshold of the room, one of these creatures—a small tortoiseshell—darted in front of me, causing me to step on its tail. The unearthly yowl of the beast not only made my own heart cease to beat but caused the police officers to turn around as one. Recognizing me at once, Captain Dunnegan—who was in the center of the group, and whose visage wore its usual glower—exclaimed:

"Poe! How the hell—?"

Pausing until my heartbeat resumed its normal rhythm, I cleared my throat and addressed the captain thusly: "From your expression of amazement, Captain Dunnegan, I perceive that—like your subordinate, Officer Boyle—you are at a loss to explain my arrival only minutes after your messenger set out for my home. In truth, your summons never reached me. My companions and I were already on our way to this address before your runner was dispatched."

"That right?" said Dunnegan, shifting his gaze to include Townsend and the scout. "And just what brings you here?"

It was Carson who responded. "We was figuring on having a little talk with Cartwright."

At this remark, Dunnegan emitted a bitter snort. "Be my guest," he said. Then, shoving aside the men who flanked him, he stepped away from the desk, affording us an unobstructed view.

There are occasions in life when we are confronted with sights so unnatural—so freakish—so sheerly *grotesque*—that we cannot, at first, comprehend the meaning of what we are looking at. Our eyes take in the spectacle, assuring us of its reality. Our minds, however—as though putting up the sternest possible resistance to the monstrous truth—refuse to make sense of what we are seeing.

Such was the case with the sight that now lay before me. A stout, well-dressed gentleman was seated behind the desk. That this personage had been the victim of a ferocious assault was plain. His scalped and bloody head was tilted backward at a violent angle. His throat had been slashed so savagely that his head seemed in imminent danger of becoming detached from his body. Great gouts of blood covered the entire front of his shirt and lay puddled on the top of the desk.

That much I understood. What I could not—or rather *would* not—comprehend was an apparent anomaly of his dress. He seemed to be wearing an exceedingly odd cravat, of a shape, thickness, and texture that were puzzling in the extreme. Depending from the base of his butchered throat, this singular necktie was heavily coated with blood, making its specific characteristics even harder to ascertain.

How long I remained staring at this bewildering sight I cannot say for a certainty. I was dimly aware of the reactions of my companions, who stood on either side of me. As though from a great distance, I could hear Carson's sharp exhalation of breath, like a prolonged hiss, and Townsend's tremulous, "Oh, my sweet Lord."

When at length I could no longer fend off the truth, I was overcome with a terrible sense of vertigo. My brain reeled—my vision swam—and it was only by a violent effort of will that I kept myself from swooning. Staggering backward, I collapsed into the morocco armchair, barely avoiding the calico cat that was settled on the cushion, and that managed to leap to the floor just in time to save itself from being crushed beneath my weight.

Lowering my head into my hands, I remained utterly motionless for several moments, waiting to recover from the dizziness induced by my awful—my *appalling*—realization.

The thing hanging from Cartwright's neck was not a blood-soaked cravat. It was his tongue. After gashing the victim's throat, the assailant had evidently reached inside the gaping wound, drawn out the entire length of the organ, from root to tip, and let it drape down the shirtfront.

By slow degrees, the spinning sensation subsided. Raising my head, I saw that Carson was now standing beside the desk, studying Cartwright's unspeakable wound with a cool detachment, while Dunnegan hovered nearby. Townsend, in the meantime, had removed himself to a corner of the room, where he was intently observing the scene while taking notes in his writing pad.

"I'd say Mr. Cartwright received a little visit from your friend Johnson," said Dunnegan.

"Looks that way," said Carson. "Reckon the Liver-Eater learned a few things from the Apaches."

"How do you mean?" asked Dunnegan.

"This here's an old Mescalero trick," said Carson. "Something they do to their captives for fun."

"Fun!" Dunnegan exclaimed. "Why, those filthy redskinned savages."

Turning to face the burly captain, Carson calmly remarked: "I was passing through St. Louis once. Seen a lynch mob torture a young Negro, no more than thirteen, fourteen years old, for talking sassy to a white whore. What they did to that poor boy makes this look downright civilized. That mob was having a whole lot of fun, too—whooping and laughing like it was a regular fiesta. And they were white to a man—not a red face amongst them. Savages ain't limited to just one color, Captain."

To this observation Dunnegan merely grunted in reply. Then, swiveling to face me, he said:

"What I can't figure out is how *you* fit into all this, Poe."

"Why, whatever do you mean?" I stammeringly replied.

"First Wyatt, now Cartwright. Far as I can see, they had only two things in common. Both of them were slaughtered like goddamned cattle by this crazy bastard Johnson. And they both had some business with *you*."

"No one can be more puzzled by that fact than I," I replied, feeling my face flush with indignation at Dunnegan's exceedingly coarse language. "Certainly, you do not mean to suggest that I am in any way implicated in these atrocities?"

"I ain't suggesting nothing," said Dunnegan. "It's just funny, is all."

Speaking up from his location across the room, Townsend inquired: "Mind if I ask how you came to be here, Captain?"

"Got a message from your boss, Mr. Morris, that's how," Dunnegan gruffly replied to the young reporter. "Cartwright was making some threats. I sent a couple of my men around to have a word with him. They found him like this."

"I see," Townsend said, scribbling in his pad. "But why was Mr. Poe sent for?"

"There was something on Cartwright's desk. He must've just finished it when Johnson snuck in."

Stepping to my chair, Dunnegan shoved his hand into his coat pocket, extracted a small square of paper, and thrust it at me.

As I reached out to take it, I saw that it was a sheet of stationery, folded in quarters and badly mottled with fresh blood. Holding it gingerly by the edges, I opened it up and began to peruse it.

"What does it say?" asked Townsend, crossing the room to stand beside my chair.

I made no reply until I had reached the end of the missive. "It is a letter from Cartwright to his attorney," I answered in a bemused tone, "instructing the latter to prepare a libel suit against me."

Snatching the letter from my hand, Dunnegan returned it to his pocket. "Just what exactly went on between you and Cartwright, Poe?" he demanded.

"In my professional capacity as the editor of a leading literary quarterly," I explained, "I had occasion to offer a balanced and highly judicious criticism of Cartwright's most recent novel. Objecting to the tenor of my review, Mr. Cartwright sent me a letter of such insufferable rudeness as to prompt me to compose a devastating parody of his work. The publication of this satire in the pages of the *Daily Mirror* inspired Cartwright to issue dark, if indefinite, warnings, to both Mr. Morris and myself. That he meant to exact some form of revenge was clear, though his precise intentions were left unspecified."

"Well, now we know," said Dunnegan. "He was planning to sue the shit out of you."

"So it seems," I replied to this unutterably vulgar—if seemingly valid—observation.

Dunnegan was on the verge of addressing another comment to me, when—glancing over the top of my chair—he suddenly said: "Coates! About time you showed up."

I turned and peered around the back of my seat so as to gain a view of the doorway. There, on the threshold, stood the tall—gaunt—inordinately pallid—coroner I had previously seen in William Wyatt's parlor.

"Great God," he said. "What's happened here?"

"More butchery," said Dunnegan. Then, glancing at me, Townsend, and Carson in turn, he added: "Time for you boys to clear out. We got work to do."

"Sure you don't want no help, Captain?" said the scout.

"All I want from you, Carson, is to mind your own affairs and leave us professionals to handle this," Dunnegan disdainfully replied.

For a moment, the scout merely stared levelly at the captain. Then, with a barely perceptible shrug, he said: "Have it your way. Come on, Eddie. Let's hit the trail."

Having already displayed a staggering lack of competence in their search of Wyatt's premises, Dunnegan and his men would—I felt sure—prove equally inept in the present case. Still, there was no point in protesting his rejection of our help.

I was, moreover, only too eager to depart from the premises. The sickening odor of the cats, combined with the dizzying sight of Cartwright's mutilation, had left me feeling nearly as unwell as Officer Boyle. Rising from the chair, I marched quickly from the room, made my way down the stairs, and hurried out the front door, pausing on the stoop to imbibe great, gulping mouthfuls of the outside air.

In another instant, I was joined by my companions, who appeared equally grateful to have escaped the noxious atmosphere of Cartwright's chamber.

Replacing his notebook in the side pocket of his coat, Townsend said: "I'd better head back to the office. This place'll be crawling with reporters soon. I've got to tell Mr. Morris what happened and get my story written up."

Bidding us good-bye, he then descended the steps and, in another moment, had vanished down the block.

Ignoring the calls of several bystanders, who were eager to learn precisely what had occurred within Cartwright's abode, Carson and I made our way down the stoop and strode west on Cortlandt Street, not pausing until we had rounded the corner of Greenwich.

We came to a halt beside the entrance of a stable, from whose murky interior there could be heard the stamping and snuffling of its equine occupants.

"What do you think, Eddie?" asked Carson.

"I confess that this development has thrown me into an even greater state of confusion than before," I said. "Our assumption that Cartwright was behind the two consecutive attempts on my life has now been called into serious question, if not thoroughly discredited. It now appears certain that he intended to seek redress for his perceived humiliation not by arranging for my death, but by taking me to court. We are therefore faced with a deeply perplexing mystery: If Cartwright was not the instigator of these assassination attempts, then who *was*?

"In addition," I continued, "there is a second, no less pressing, riddle—one which even the plodding intellect of Captain Dunnegan has managed to identify. Why did Johnson select, as his two most recent victims, individuals with whom I myself have lately become involved?"

"There ain't but one man who can answer that," said Carson. "The Liver-Eater himself. And it may be that we just got us a chance to ask him."

"Why, whatever can you possibly mean?" I exclaimed at this startling statement.

"From what I hear about Johnson, killing gets him all fired up," said Carson. "There was plenty of times he'd ride into a settlement with a half-dozen fresh Indian scalps dangling from his gun belt, get him a whore and a jug of whiskey, and hole up for a couple of days."

"Do you mean to suggest," I said, my face wrought into a grimace of disgust, "that the act of murder arouses his carnal appetites?"

"That's about the way of it," answered the scout.

A shudder coursed through my frame as I absorbed this appalling intelligence. It was true that I had read of such beings before—creatures like the infamous French madman Gilles de Rais, or the depraved Hungarian countess Elizabeth Bathory, whose fleshly lusts were inflamed by unspeakable acts of cruelty and bloodshed. I had always thought, however, that such monsters were a product of the long-ago past. That a fiend of this stripe might still exist in the modern-day world was a notion almost too terrible to contemplate.

"Way I figure it," Carson continued, "Cartwright's murder is a prime opportunity. Johnson just got done with his butchery. He'll be hankering for a woman. Knowing him, he won't be visiting any fancy bawdy houses, neither, but the most low-down place he can find. Maybe we can track him there."

"I suppose it is worth a try," I said.

"Got any ideas?" asked the scout.

"New York City is, sadly, replete with houses of ill repute, ranging in quality from the most luxurious bordellos to dens of more than infamy. If, as you suggest, however, Johnson is likely to seek out the most squalid—the most sordid—the most vile hellholes in the entire metropolis, there is only one area for us to search within."

"Where's that?" asked Carson.

"We must go to Five Points," I said.

PART FOUR

Bullet for a Badman

CHAPTER TWENTY

~

ITUATED AT THE CONVERGENCE of five tortuous streets in lower Manhattan, the district called Five Points had long been known as a realm of unparalleled misery and unspeakable vice. Indeed, its reputation was such that, during his celebrated tour of the United States several years earlier, Charles Dickens himself had insisted on exploring this surpassingly squalid neighborhood in order to compare its conditions to those of the notorious slums of London. Dickens's subsequent description of the area (in his sharply observed, if rather mean-spirited, travel book, *American Notes*) had made Five Points infamous throughout the civilized world—a place whose very name was a universal byword for the most deplorable suffering and irremediable sin.

During my own residence in Manhattan, I had never so much as set foot within this horrid precinct. For any respectable person to do so was foolhardy in the extreme, if not positively suicidal. Even the typical police officer was loath to find himself alone in Five Points, particularly after nightfall. Were it not for my own highly developed sense of civic responsibility—and the reassuring presence of my exceedingly able companion, Kit Carson—nothing could have induced me to venture within this infernal region of debauchery and crime.

Though located within a pistol shot of each other, a vast gulf separated the bustling business center of Broadway—with its vaunting palaces of trade— from the foul hovels and filthy stews of Five Points. The moment we crossed the border of Bayard Street, the scout and I found ourselves within a bleak, a *blighted* landscape of wretchedness, poverty, and gloom. Surrounding us on every side were tottering wooden tenements, so closely crammed together that no semblance of a passage was discernible between them. The paving stones lay at random, displaced from their beds by the rankly growing grass. Horrible filth festered in the dammed-up gutters. The very air seemed to reek of degradation—debauchery—and disease.

As Carson and I made our way through the narrow, winding streets—drawing exceedingly hostile looks from the ragged and sullen inhabitants—we soon became aware of a dilemma that we had not anticipated. Though houses of ill repute could be found in many areas of Manhattan, these vile establishments did not, as a rule, openly advertise their presence. On the contrary, as they were often located in close proximity to (if not actually *within*) perfectly respectable neighborhoods, they generally concealed the true nature of their business behind anonymous façades. Unless one knew of their existence, they were difficult to find.

In Five Points, the opposite situation prevailed. So openly—so profusely— did prostitution flourish within its boundaries that we were at a loss as to how to locate our quarry. Every ramshackle building on every foetid block appeared to function as a brothel. Women of all ages, nationalities, and physical types—their arms bare, their bosoms shamelessly exposed—stood in the doorways, beckoning to male passersby in the crudest conceivable terms. As Carson and I proceeded down Mulberry Street, we were assaulted with invitations of such a shocking—such a *scandalous*—nature as to scorch my very ears.

After enduring this ordeal for ten or fifteen minutes, Carson and I came to a halt on the corner of Cross and Pearl streets. Several yards away, a trio of hogs rooted in a pile of kitchen slops that had spilled from an overturned refuse barrel; while, seated on an old wooden crate nearby, a withered crone with a tuft of chin whiskers eyed us quizzically as she puffed lazily on a clay pipe.

Gazing into the handsome, rugged countenance of my companion, I saw by the dull glow of the street lamp that he was filled with a profound moral disgust at the sordid sights around us. For a being like Carson—whose entire life had been passed in the unsullied precincts of the Western frontier—Five Points must have confirmed every prejudice about the evils of city life to which the average country-dweller is prone. However much of violence—

ignorance—even outright brutality might be found in the wilderness, it was blessedly free of that hideously oppressive atmosphere of decay and corruption that pervaded every square inch of this foul—this *abominable*—slum.

"You weren't fooling about this place, Eddie," said the scout. "Never seen such a hellhole in my life. Hard to know where to look."

"Indeed, it would aid our search immeasurably if we knew something about Johnson's predilections in regard to his vile and illicit pleasures."

"How do you mean?"

"As you have no doubt observed from the sheer variety of females stationed at the entranceways, the teeming brothels of this infernal district offer something for every polluted taste. There are houses that appear to specialize in girls of a barely nubile age. Others are occupied by women of variegated color, from pure-blooded Negresses to light-skinned mulattos. Still others seem to cater to men who prefer women of a singularly corpulent stature. The great diversity of these dissolute creatures is, if nothing else, a testimony to the almost limitless range of human carnal desire. Knowing which of these types was most appealing to Johnson would, at the very least, permit us to focus our search more narrowly."

"Can't say as I know," Carson replied. "Out where Johnson's from, a man can't be too particular when it comes to women. I *can* tell you one thing, though. From what I've heard about the Liver-Eater, it ain't just whores he's after when he goes on a spree. He's mighty partial to drinking and gambling, too."

"I see," I replied. "That is indeed a helpful piece of knowledge. Needless to say, Five Points is rife with groggeries and gambling dens. I have heard, however, of one place in particular that has achieved an unparalleled level of notoriety: One-Eyed Donaho's Saloon on Orange Street."

"Lead the way," said Carson.

As the establishment in question was situated only a short distance from where we stood, it took us no more than two or three minutes to arrive there. At my first glimpse of Donaho's Saloon, I felt an iciness—a sinking—a sickening of the soul. Every feature of the building—from its worm-eaten façade, to its patched and grimy windows, to the Stygian darkness of its doorway—filled my heart with dread. Though the sun had barely set, a stream of exceedingly coarse-looking ruffians—some laughing raucously, others spewing vile oaths—was already pouring into this loathsome temple of sin.

Glancing over at Carson, I saw that his visage was arranged into its usual cool and unruffled look. I noticed, however, that, as we paused on the corner directly opposite to the saloon, he reached inside the front of his jacket and placed his hand on the butt of his pistol, as if to reassure himself that the weapon was within easy reach.

Making our way across the street with great care—so as to avoid the reeking mounds of offal and piles of unswept horse droppings that lay everywhere—we mounted the curb and stepped through the swinging doors of Donaho's establishment. Instantly my sensory organs were assaulted by the most disagreeable *stimuli* imaginable. The dismal, low-ceilinged room was suffused with a foul miasma, compounded of cheap cigar smoke—stale body odors—and the fumes of villainous "rotgut" alcohol. From a far corner came the infernal screechings of an inebriated fiddler, sawing away so tunelessly on his instrument that he made the egregious musicians at Barnum's museum seem like virtuosos by comparison. Strident peals of laughter issued from the lips of the painted Jezebels who sat perched on the knees of drunken patrons; while the shabby brutes hunched around the gaming tables emitted a torrent of blasphemous obscenities as they gambled away their money at faro.

Pausing at the entranceway, Carson let his eyes sweep around the room, taking in the scene. The two of us then strode across the floor and found a place at the long, crowded bar.

While we waited to be noticed by the saloonkeeper—who was busily dispensing his poison at the far end of the counter—my attention was riveted by a large oil painting hanging on the wall directly opposite from where I stood. Surrounded by a cracked and peeling gilt frame, the picture was of a voluptuous female reclining on a velvet couch. Apart from the edge of a fur-trimmed coverlet coyly disposed about her loins, her nakedness was entirely exposed. It was not her shameless state of undress, however, that rendered this image so indecent, but rather the singularly lewd expression with which she regarded the viewer. The excessively begrimed surface of the painting—a result of long years of exposure to the reeking, smoke-filled atmosphere of the saloon—seemed entirely in keeping with the foul—the *unclean*—nature of its subject.

My shocked inspection of this brazenly pornographic work was interrupted at length by the appearance of the saloonkeeper—a sallow, sunken-cheeked fellow with a leather eye patch and a jagged white scar that ran down one side of his face from temple to chin. Regarding us narrowly with his visible orb, he gruffly demanded our order.

"Beer," said Carson.

"The same," I said.

A moment later, Donaho set before us two chipped and soiled mugs containing a yellow-green fluid topped with a sulfurous head of foam. Taking a tentative sip of this vile-looking brew, I was immediately overcome with a reflexive urge to expel it from my mouth. Its taste brought to mind the urinary reek of Cartwright's cat-infested home. Subduing my revulsion, I forced myself to swallow the noxious liquid.

Carson, too, managed to imbibe only a single mouthful before setting his mug back down on the bar with a grimace.

"I swear," he muttered, wiping his mouth with his hand.

"Something wrong with the beer?" asked Donaho.

"That what you call it?" replied the scout.

"Sorry it ain't to your delicate taste," said the saloonkeeper. "What brings you fucking dandies around here anyway? Looking for a little tail?"

"We're looking for a man," said Carson.

Donaho curled his thin-lipped mouth into a sneer. "You come to the wrong place, my friend. There's houses for mollies like you, but this ain't one of them."

Ignoring this surpassingly odious remark, Carson said: "Got that picture of the Liver-Eater on you, Eddie?"

Before embarking on our manhunt the previous day, I had removed Horace Oswald's crude illustration from the front page of the *Mirror*. Though a mere approximation of Johnson's appearance, the portrait might, I felt, help jog the recognition of anyone who had caught a glimpse of our quarry. Removing it now from my pocket, I handed it to the scout, who unfolded it and laid it on the counter.

"Ever see a fellow like this?" Carson asked Donaho. "He's big, maybe six foot two or three. Red hair. Real thick, bushy eyebrows."

With barely a glance at the picture, Donaho shook his head.

"Didn't look very hard," Carson said in a voice grown suddenly cold.

"I seen all I need to," said Donaho. "Now why don't you and your little chum clear the hell out of here?"

Glancing sideways at my companion, I perceived that his eyes were ablaze, and that his lean jaw muscles had gone taut. Having witnessed the same expression on two prior occasions—just before he had pummeled the horse-beater outside St. John's Park, and again when he was on his way to Cartwright's house to exact vengeance for the killing of his faithful dog—I knew what it signified. In another instant, I fully expected to see him lash out at the churlish saloonkeeper and administer a well-deserved chastisement to the insufferable lout.

Before anything of this nature could occur, however, we were distracted by a violent commotion behind us. Turning, I saw that an altercation had erupted at one of the half-dozen card-tables disposed about the floor. A lanky young man had just leapt to his feet and was shaking a fist menacingly at the player seated across from him. This latter individual—a hulking, shabbily dressed fellow, whose massive back was toward us—remained absolutely motionless. The other players, in the meanwhile, had pushed their chairs away from the table, as though to place a safe distance between themselves and the two antagonists.

"Why, you dirty goddamned cheat!" shouted the young man, his face florid with rage. "I saw you palm that card!" His voice rent the air of the saloon, a deathlike hush having fallen over the room. Even the fiddle player had ceased his dreadful scraping.

"Now you hand back every damned cent you stole from me, you son of a bitch!" the young man screamed. "I don't give a shit how big you are. I ain't scared of you." He then lunged across the table, both arms outstretched, as if to scoop up the winnings gathered in front of the alleged card-cheat.

So far, the latter had not budged. All at once, however—with a speed that was positively shocking—his right arm shot straight out. In the dim light cast by the camphene lanterns hanging on the walls, I saw something flash in his hand. The young man gasped—straightened up with a jerk—and staggered backward a few steps, blood spraying from the side of his neck. He clamped his right hand to the wound, but to little avail, the dark arterial fluid continuing to spurt from the cracks between his fingers.

"Shit," muttered Donaho as he watched this awful scene. "That asshole's gonna bleed all over my saloon."

Hurrying along the length of the bar, Donaho emerged around the far end and strode across the floor toward the desperately wounded youth, whose complexion had turned a ghastly white. Just as the saloonkeeper reached him, the young man's legs gave way and his body crumpled. He collapsed backward, Donaho catching him under the arms before he hit the floor.

Legs outstretched—boot heels dragging on the boards—arms hanging limply at his sides—the victim was then hauled by the cursing saloonkeeper toward the doorway and outside onto the street. A moment later, Donaho reappeared through the swinging doors, his apron badly spattered with fresh blood.

"Bennie!" he yelled.

At this summons, a stoop-shouldered, exceedingly wizened old man—whose sunken lips and hollow cheeks denoted a mouth devoid of teeth—materialized from a far corner of the saloon.

"Yessir, Mr. Donaho?" he croaked in a servile tone.

"Get your bony ass over here and clean up this mess," said the saloonkeeper, pointing to the trail of blood that led from the table to the door. "What the hell am I paying you for?"

"Yessir, Mr. Donaho," said the old man as he turned and shuffled away, evidently to fetch his bucket and mop.

By then, the room had returned to its former level of activity, the cardplayers taking up their games—the prostitutes resuming their dreadful coquetries—the fiddle player launching into an execrable rendition of the popular favorite "Coal Black Rose."

Turning back to the bar, I found that my hands were trembling badly. The scene I had just witnessed had left me so severely shaken that I was actually tempted to imbibe another mouthful of the unspeakable brew in an effort to quiet my agitated nerves. Only the inordinately foul, lingering taste of my previous draught prevented me from doing so.

"I fear," I said to my companion, "that our expedition to this foul hole has been in vain."

Carson—who, apart from the grim set of his mouth, showed no sign of having been at all discomposed by the frightful act of violence that had just transpired—nodded in agreement. "I don't see no sign of Johnson. And we're not apt to learn much from the scamps in this place."

"Perhaps it is time to pursue our hunt elsewhere," I suggested.

"Maybe so," said the scout.

This response produced a powerful sense of relief within my bosom. Dante himself could not have been more eager to ascend from the dread abyss of the Inferno than I to escape from the awful confines of Donaho's hellish den.

All at once, however, I was possessed by a peculiar sensation. Someone standing outside the range of my vision was, I felt sure, regarding me intently. Looking to my left, I found myself face-to-face with one of the many dissolute specimens of womanhood plying their disgraceful trade at Donaho's. Evidently, she had come up beside me while I was conversing with Carson. She was standing sideways to the bar, one garishly bejeweled hand holding on to the edge of the counter, the other resting on her provocatively outthrust hip. Her scarlet gown revealed a scandalous expanse of her plump, milky-white bosom. As I turned to face her, the expression on her coarse (if not wholly unattractive) countenance suddenly changed from one of curious speculation to a look of lewd delight.

For my part—though her visage was, in fact, strangely familiar—I could not conceive of where I might have seen her before.

"I *thought* it was you two," she said, her words slurred, her breath redolent of cheap whiskey. "How sweet. You boys come all the way here to find little me?"

The moment she spoke, I realized with a start where we had met. This wanton creature was none other than the hussy denominated as "Nell"—the very same female Carson and I had encountered the previous night at Ludlow's oyster cellar, when the scout had found it necessary to silence her loudmouthed companion.

Leaning forward on the bar and peering around me, Carson—who had evidently recognized her at once—smiled politely and said: "Sorry, ma'am. That ain't why we came."

Arranging her painted mouth into an exaggerated pout, Nell replied: "That's awful cruel. You won't find no one nicer than me."

"We're not looking for someone nice," said Carson, sliding the newspaper portrait of Johnson along the bar in her direction.

Raising the illustration to the level of her somewhat bleary eyes, Nell squinted, frowned deeply, and began to move her hand forward and back— nearer to and farther from her face—until the picture came into focus.

"I've seen some ugly mugs in my time, but nothing like this," she said at length. "Wish I could help."

Returning the picture to the scout, she then leeringly added: "Maybe there's something else I can do for you."

"Much obliged," said Carson, folding up the piece of newspaper and placing it in the side pocket of his jacket. "But I believe I'll pass."

"Aw, don't be like that," Nell complained, thrusting out her lower lip in the manner of a petulant child. "You ain't afraid of little me, are you? Not the great Kit Carson. They say you're one hell of a horseman. Come on upstairs. I'll give you a ride you won't ever forget. Your friend, too. He's almost as cute as you."

My reaction to these words may be readily imagined. I was not merely sickened and appalled by the sheer—the overwhelming—indecency of the trollop's proposal, I was also greatly alarmed by her open declaration of my companion's identity. It seemed entirely possible, if not likely, that among the wretches gathered in Donaho's groggery there might be more than one individual who had participated in the riot at Barnum's museum several nights earlier. Such reprobates would bear little love for Carson, who, almost singlehandedly, had been responsible for subduing the mob.

Even before Nell blurted out the scout's name, I had felt exceedingly unwelcome in the inhospitable surroundings. Now my sense of uneasiness was magnified a hundredfold.

It did not take long for my apprehensions to be fully realized. Hardly had Nell finished speaking than I became aware that a renewed silence had descended upon the saloon.

Looking around, I saw to my dismay that Carson and I were now the object of the most intense scrutiny. All eyes appeared to be upon us. Some of the ruffians seated at the tables had laid down their cards. Others had displaced the women from their laps and had risen to their feet. The men at the bar were all staring in our direction.

"That really him?" I heard one of them say.

"He was wearing different clothes when I seen him," the man next to him muttered. "But yeah, now that I look at him, that's him, all right."

At least a dozen of the brutes began to converge upon us. In another moment, we were completely surrounded. They seemed to share a common physiognomy, characteristic of that debased urban type known as the "rough": flattened noses—massive jaws—low, receding foreheads—thick, thewy necks. Their red-rimmed eyes burned with hatred. The air was thick with menace.

Turning lazily around, Carson rested his elbows on the bar and, with utmost nonchalance, said: "Can I help you gentlemen?"

By this point, my mouth had gone completely dry. I could feel the violent thudding of my heart against my breastbone.

At that instant, several of the men standing in front of us were rudely shoved to either side, and an enormous figure interposed himself between them. I saw at once—from both his gargantuan stature and the excessive shabbiness of his clothing—that he was the same individual who had so savagely stabbed the young cardplayer moments before. His singularly repulsive visage was wrought into an expression unlike any I had ever seen before—one compounded equally of malice, bloodthirstiness, fiendish triumph, and dia-bolical merriment.

"I'll be damned," he growled. "It *is* you!"

At these words, my legs grew weak, and I felt the blood congeal within my veins.

The comment had not been addressed to Carson.

It was directed at *me*!

CHAPTER TWENTY-ONE

"M UST BE MY LUCKY DAY," said the fiercesome-looking brute. "You showing up here this way."

The intensity of my shock at being addressed in this manner may be easily conceived. My initial thought was that some error had been made, and that the fellow had mistaken me for someone else. I was therefore thrown into an even greater state of confusion when he drew back his lips in a snarl of sheer malevolence and declared:

"I'll say one thing for you, Poe. You're a hard little son of a bitch to kill."

It was the sight of his repulsively discolored teeth—devoid of the upper front incisors—that brought a cry of horrified recognition to my lips. My breast heaved—my knees tottered—my whole spirit became possessed with an intolerable feeling of dread.

"I know who you are!" I exclaimed with a gasp.

This ferocious individual, I now perceived, was none other than the loathsome cutthroat I had encountered during the riot at Barnum's museum—the very wretch who had attempted to enlist me in his plan to kill the showman! As the reader will recall, I had managed—in spite of the great disparity in our respective physiques—to overpower the bloodthirsty reprobate and render him unconscious. I had then relieved him of his formidable, double-barreled pistol—the same weapon that was now in Carson's possession.

Now, as I stared up at his surpassingly ugly countenance, a sudden realization—born of his remark that I was "a hard little son of a bitch to kill"—suddenly flashed upon my mind.

"Am I to understand," I stammeringly inquired, "that you have been responsible for the recent attempts upon my life? That it was *you* who tried to run me down last night?"

By way of response, the villainous fellow—whose fat, heavily stubbled cheek bulged with a quid of tobacco—spat a thick brown gob at my feet and said: "Goddamn right."

"And the delivery of the deadly food basket," I said. "That was also your doing?"

Arranging his features into a look of grotesque self-satisfaction—as though he took particular pride in having devised such a treacherous scheme—he nodded slowly several times.

In view of the excessive shabbiness of the wretch's appearance—which spoke vividly of his penniless state—I could only surmise that he had stolen the delicacies from the shop of a respectable grocer, then treated them with a cheap, readily available compound of arsenic—most probably a variety of rat poison.

"Yeah, that grub was a little gift from me, all right," the hulking brute growled. "What I want to know is—how come you ain't dead?"

Thinking that the longer I could engage him in conversation, the better chance Carson and I might have to extricate ourselves from our intensely perilous position, I responded thusly: "Mere chance saved me from partaking of the tainted fare. For my part, I am at a loss to comprehend how you discovered my name and home address."

The lout gave a snort of amusement. Digging inside the pocket of his threadbare trousers, he extracted a small object, which he held up and waved in the air.

"Look familiar?" he asked.

A soft ejaculation of surprise escaped my lips. I did indeed recognize it. It was my missing wallet!

A sudden recollection rushed to my mind. I remembered that—upon first encountering each other in Barnum's museum—the deplorable fellow had reached out and run his fingers over the front of my jacket, while remarking on the superior cut of my garment. This ostensible display of admiration, I now realized, was a mere ploy. In reality, he had been attempting—successfully, as it happened—to pick my pocket! As my wallet contained several calling cards imprinted with my name and address, there was little mystery as to how he had ascertained these facts.

"You got more lives than a frigging cat, Poe," the vicious brute now remarked. "But you know what they say about skinning cats."

He slipped my wallet back into the pocket of his execrable coat. When he showed his hand again, it was clutching a villainous-looking dagger—evidently the same weapon he had used to stab the young cardplayer in the neck.

"I'd shoot you down like the goddamned dog you are, if you hadn't a stole my pistol," he said, displaying a blatant disregard for the consistency of his zoological analogies. "But this'll do."

He then began to move toward me with a heavy—lumbering—gait, exuding an aura of sheer, overpowering menace that drove the blood in torrents upon my heart and produced a fearful ringing in my brain.

During the foregoing exchange between the two of us, no one else had said a word. All eyes had been riveted upon us. Carson, too, had observed the scene in silence.

Now, however, as the towering brute came to a halt directly before me, a sound could be heard in the room. It was the voice of the scout. Though softly uttered, his words echoed loudly in the highly fraught stillness of the saloon, penetrating the fear-induced tintinnabulation in my ears.

"If you want your pistol back," he said, "it's right here."

With a grunt of surprise, the massive brute swung his head around and stared at Carson. I, too, turned to look at him.

He was no longer leaning casually against the bar, but was standing erect, his hands hanging loosely at his sides. His jacket was unbuttoned, the front fully open, revealing the double-barreled pistol thrust through the belt of his trousers.

The beady eyes of the ruffian widened slightly at the sight of the weapon.

"That's mine," he said. "Give it to me."

"Why don't you come get it?" said the scout.

"Why, you lousy Injun-loving bastard," said the other. "I'll rip your frigging guts out."

In spite of the vehemence with which this threat was uttered, the deplorable wretch gave no sign of making good on it. Instead, he merely stood there and glowered at Carson. From the look in his eyes, he appeared to be engaged in a furious mental calculation, measuring the distance that separated him from his foe, as though debating his chances of reaching the scout before the latter could draw and discharge his weapon.

All at once, as I studied the brute's visage, he shifted his gaze slightly, registering something behind Carson. The corners of his mouth gave a quick, almost imperceptible, twitch, as though they had begun to curl into an involuntary smile which he had quickly stifled.

In the next instant, the silence was broken by a disconcerting noise: the harsh, metallic *cocking* of a firearm.

Glancing over my shoulder, I was startled to see the saloonkeeper standing behind the bar with a rifle in hand, its barrel directed at the back of Carson's head. Evidently—as was generally the case in "dives" like Donaho's, whose patrons routinely carried arms—the proprietor himself kept a weapon readily accessible for his own use.

"Don't move, Carson," said Donaho, "or I'll blow your goddamned head—"

What happened next occurred so swiftly that no mere description can convey the sheer, blinding speed of the action. Even before Donaho had finished uttering his threat, Carson—with a smooth, flowing motion as graceful as the undulations of Barnum's Royal Bengal tiger—ducked to the right—pulled the gun from his belt—spun fully around—and discharged one of the barrels into the saloonkeeper's shoulder.

With a shriek of pain, Donaho clutched at his wound, letting his rifle fall with a clatter onto the top of the bar.

Seeing this, the massive brute who stood before me emitted a furious roar and, raising his dagger high above his head, launched himself at Carson.

In that instant, a second explosion erupted as the scout whirled back around and fired the contents of the second barrel into the body of his attacker, who immediately dropped his knife—grabbed his chest—staggered backward several steps—and went crashing to the floor.

No more than five seconds had elapsed since Donaho uttered his threat. That the scout had managed to render both men utterly *hors de combat* within that fleeting moment of time seemed beyond the bounds of human possibility. Even I, who witnessed the feat with my own eyes, could scarcely credit the evidence of my senses.

While the others in the room looked on in stunned silence, Carson straightened up from his crouch, his spent pistol at his side, smoke curling from its barrels. All at once, a voice rose from the crowd.

"Come on, boys! He ain't armed no more! Let's get him!"

With that, a dozen of the ruffians came rushing at Carson. The first man to reach him was felled by a blow to the temple from the barrel of the scout's pistol. Another went down with a choking *gurgle* as Carson unleashed a driving punch that caught the miscreant in the center of the throat. The scout then hurled the empty pistol at another attacker, striking the brute in the forehead and knocking him unconscious.

As furiously as my companion fought, however, it was clear that he would inevitably be overpowered. One of his assailants grabbed an empty liquor bottle—smashed off its bottom against the edge of the bar—and swung it at Carson. Raising his right arm defensively, the scout was badly slashed on the hand. As he winced in pain, the ruffian drew back his arm for a second thrust, aiming the jagged end directly at Carson's face.

Perceiving the deadly peril of the situation, I leapt into action. Reaching behind me, I snatched Donaho's rifle from the countertop, leveled it at the bottle-wielding miscreant, and—in a loud, commanding voice—spoke thusly:

"Desist at once from your cowardly onslaught! I shall not scruple to discharge this weapon at the next man to make even the smallest movement!"

The sheer ferocity of this warning produced the desired effect. The ruffians suspended their attack, fixing me with baleful looks as I held them at bay with the rifle.

"Are you badly injured, Kit?" I inquired of my companion.

"Just a mite scratched," he replied. Reaching out with his good hand, he took the rifle from me and, holding it as one would a pistol, aimed it at the brute wielding the broken bottle.

"Drop it," said Carson.

The man obeyed without hesitation, the bottle shattering on the floorboards at his feet.

"Come on, Eddie," said Carson.

The two of us then backed our way toward the swinging doors, Carson keeping the rifle trained on the roomful of toughs, who stared at us sullenly, though they made no further move to attack.

Pausing at the threshold, Carson faced the villainous crowd and declared:

"First man that comes through these doors gets a bellyful of lead."

In the next moment, we were out on the street. As we stepped off the curb, I stumbled over something sprawled in the gutter. Looking down, I saw to my horror that it was the lifeless body of the young man who had been stabbed in the neck. He had evidently been dumped like so much refuse into the foetid— filth-clogged—street and left there to bleed to death.

We proceeded to make our way briskly up Orange Street. Casting a glance over my shoulder, I was relieved to see that the rogues had taken Carson's threat seriously. No one appeared to be following us.

We did not slacken our pace until we had emerged from the odious neighborhood. By then, Carson had disposed of the rifle, dropping it into a watering trough outside a junk dealer's shop at the corner of Bayard Street.

Having reached the relative safety of Walker Street, we paused briefly while Carson pulled his handkerchief from his trousers pocket and wrapped it around his bloody hand.

"I fear, Kit," I said in a solicitous tone, "that your innately stoic nature has led you to underestimate the severity of your wound, which appears far more serious than you have indicated."

"I've had a sight worse," he replied in a matter-of-fact tone.

"Perhaps so. Nevertheless, I suggest that we return home without further delay and allow my dear Muddy, whose nursing skills are of the highest order, to tend to your injury."

Agreeing to my suggestion, Carson soon secured a hack. Seated across from each other as the jouncing carriage made its way up Broadway, the scout and I conversed briefly about the exceedingly dramatic events of the past several hours. However dangerous and distasteful, our experiences at Donaho's had, at least, led to the resolution of one mystery: the identity of the culprit whose nefarious designs upon my own life had eventuated in the death of Carson's faithful dog.

"I am still somewhat amazed at the lengths to which the ruffian went in his efforts to seek revenge against me," I remarked. "After all, the actions I took against him were relatively minor: a blow to the back of the head to prevent him from committing cold-blooded murder upon Mr. Barnum, and the theft of the weapon with which he planned to perpetrate that foul deed."

"A rascal like that don't need much of an excuse for plotting mischief," said Carson.

"I suppose that is true," I said. "Do you think that he is dead?"

"If he ain't, he's lucky," said the scout. "Don't reckon he'll bother us no more, one way or the other."

Owing to the lateness of the hour, there was little in the way of vehicular traffic. Before long, we had arrived at our destination.

Entering the little house, we proceeded upstairs to my apartment. All was quiet inside. The only illumination was a soft light emanating from the kitchen. Following this, we found Muddy enjoying a cup of tea at the table, while perusing a newspaper which lay open before her. As we stepped into the room, she glanced up from her reading. Her mouth began to form itself into a welcoming smile. All at once, as her glance fell upon Carson's bandaged hand, her expression changed into one of extreme concern. Rising from her chair, she came hurrying toward us, clucking her tongue in dismay.

"Oh, Eddie! Mr. Carson!" she exclaimed. "Are you all right?"

"I am fine, Muddy dear," I declared in a soothing tone. "Kit, however, is in need of your ministrations, for he has sustained a wound that is, I fear, more serious than he is willing to admit."

"Oh, it ain't as bad as all that," said the scout.

"You come right over here, Mr. Carson, and let me have a look at you," she said.

"Where's your daughter and Jeremiah?" asked Carson as he followed Muddy to the table and lowered himself into a chair.

"He's downstairs with Mrs. Whitaker," answered Muddy, taking the seat beside him. "Sissy was not feeling very well after what happened earlier today and took to her bed not long after you boys left."

"Is she all right?" I anxiously inquired as I took the seat across from the scout and my aunt.

"She'll be fine," Muddy said, mustering a smile that did not entirely reassure me.

Turning to face the scout, the good-hearted woman then reached over, gently lifted his injured hand, and placed it on her lap. As she did, I saw that the spotless white handkerchief he had employed as a makeshift bandage was now badly stained with blood. She carefully unwrapped the cloth and removed it from his hand.

"Oh my!" she gasped.

Although I had assumed that Carson had suffered a severe laceration, I was unprepared for the sheer—sickening—appearance of the wound. A large, exceedingly jagged flap of skin had been peeled back from the top of the hand, exposing the throbbing, bloody tissue beneath.

"That's a very nasty cut," said Muddy. "I think you'd better have a doctor look at it."

"I don't set much store by doctors," said Carson, studying the gaping wound with an expression of mild curiosity.

"But I'm afraid it needs stitches," said Muddy.

"Yes, I expect you're right," said the scout. "I'd be obliged if you'd fetch a needle and some stout thread from your sewing kit, ma'am."

"Oh, I can't possibly perform such an operation myself, Mr. Carson," Muddy said.

"Don't mean for you to," he replied.

For a moment, Muddy and I merely stared wordlessly at him, reduced to a state of incredulous silence by the unavoidable implication of his statement.

"Surely you don't mean to do it yourself," Muddy said at length.

"Yes, ma'am."

That my friend was experienced in the performance of impromptu surgery I knew from my perusal of Samuel Parker's volume, which recounted an exceedingly dramatic episode from the scout's past. This had occurred when Carson—as a mere boy of sixteen—had undertaken his first journey along the Santa Fe Trail with a party of fellow adventurers. One of these, a man named Broadus, suffered a severe injury when the accidental discharge of his rifle shattered his right arm, which quickly became gangrenous. To save the poor man's life, an emergency operation was performed, in which young Carson was required to assist. While Broadus bit down on a piece of leather, his mortified limb was removed with an old carpenter's saw. The arteries were then cauterized with a heated wagon bolt, and the stump plastered over with axle tar. Remarkably, Broadus made a full recovery before the caravan reached its destination.

Still—even knowing how accustomed he was to the exceedingly primitive medical conditions of the frontier—I found it difficult to believe that the scout would think nothing of sewing up his own mangled flesh.

"Do you seriously intend to conduct this procedure on yourself?" I inquired, echoing Muddy.

"Ain't nothing to it, Eddie," he answered.

Perceiving that he was serious in his intent, my dear aunt rose from the table.

"If you don't mind, ma'am," he said as she made for the doorway, "I'll require a bowl of warm water, too."

Moments later, Muddy returned to the table with the requested items. After briefly rummaging through her sewing basket, she removed a spool and a needle, and proceeded to thread the latter. While she did so, the scout dipped his handkerchief into the water bowl and rinsed the blood from his wound. Taking the prepared needle from Muddy, he then placed his injured hand flat on the table and requested her to hold the ragged edges of his lacerated skin together. She obeyed, her fingers trembling slightly as she did so.

After heating the point of the needle over the chimney of the lamp for a moment, Carson then set to work.

The instant I saw him place the needle to his flesh, I raised one hand to my eyes. However paradoxical it may seem—in view of the intensely gruesome nature of my most celebrated tales—I had never been able to stomach the sight of even the most minor form of surgery. I therefore kept my eyes shielded until I heard the scout say:

"That'll do."

As I uncovered my eyes, I saw him raise his injured hand to his mouth and bite off the end of the makeshift suture with his bared front teeth.

"Wait," said Muddy, whose complexion looked uncharacteristically pale.

Rising again from the table, she hurried from the kitchen. After the lapse of less than a minute, she returned with a fresh strip of bandage and a bottle I recognized at once as Dr. Kittredge's remedy, whose properties as a healing elixir—not merely for insect bites but for all forms of burns, cuts, and infections—were much touted on its label.

Though its somewhat fulsome aroma caused him to wrinkle his nose in distaste, Carson made no objection as Muddy smeared a dollop of the ointment onto his repaired wound and bound his hand with the bandage.

"Good as new," he said, flexing his fingers several times. "Appreciate it, ma'am."

"Well," he added, getting to his feet. "Reckon it's time to head downstairs and get some shut-eye."

I walked with him to the front door of the apartment, where we paused on the threshold. Bidding Carson good-night, I expressed my regret that our visit to the Five Points had not, in the end, brought us any nearer to discovering the whereabouts of Johnson.

"At least we took care of that other son of a bitch," Carson said.

"There is indeed some satisfaction to be derived from that fact," I said. "Still, I confess to feeling somewhat at a loss as to how to proceed at this point."

"It ain't easy to think straight when you're all tuckered out," said the scout. "We'll put our heads together come morning."

Administering a companionable slap to my arm, he then turned and proceeded down the stairs to Mrs. Whitaker's apartment.

Returning to the kitchen, I found my aunt seated stiffly in her chair, her hands tightly folded on her lap, a grim expression on her countenance.

"What is the matter, Muddy dear?" I earnestly inquired.

"The matter?" she repeated in a tone of extreme dismay. "I am worried sick about you—*that's* what's the matter. What in heaven's name happened to you boys?"

As my loved ones and I abided within a sacred atmosphere of absolute honesty and trust, I was reluctant to prevaricate in any way with the dear-hearted woman. I knew, moreover, that she would discover the gruesome facts about Cartwright's brutal murder when she perused the newspaper on the morrow.

At the same time, I had no wish to alarm her unnecessarily. I therefore offered a somewhat bowdlerized version of the events that had transpired since Carson, Townsend, and I had departed following the backyard funeral of the murdered pet. I concluded by assuring her that—while the scout's nemesis, Johnson, remained at large—we had nothing more to fear from the personage who had sent the poisoned fare.

Muddy regarded me narrowly until I had finished speaking, then addressed me thusly:

"I may not be smart enough to understand half the things you write, Eddie dear, but you can't pull the wool over your Muddy's eyes when it comes to your safety. I can see that you are not telling me the whole truth. I can only assume that you were in terrible danger. Why, even Mr. Carson, who is a famous warrior, got badly hurt!

"Oh, Eddie," she continued, wringing her hands in distress. "You must promise me that you will stop right now and leave this dreadful business to others. What would become of Sissy and me if something happened to you?"

"There, there, Muddy dearest," I said in a comforting tone as I reached out and patted her hands. "You are underestimating your Eddie's ability to take care of himself. Indeed, were it not for my unusual prowess and exceptional reflexes, Mr. Carson might have suffered even greater—"

Before I could conclude this statement, I was distracted by a startling noise. Someone was rapidly pounding up the staircase from below. An instant later, I heard the door to our apartment burst open. Glancing behind me, I was astonished to see Carson framed in the entrance of the kitchen.

He wore an anguished expression I had never seen upon his countenance before. Beneath his weathered complexion, his skin had assumed a ghastly hue.

All at once, I became aware of the redness coating his hands. My first confused thought was that his wound had somehow reopened and bled afresh. I saw at once, however, that this could not be the explanation. The quantity of blood was far too copious, extending all the way to the wrists. And *both* hands were thoroughly ensanguined, not merely the one that had sustained the wound.

"Kit!" I cried, starting from my seat. "What's wrong?"

"He's got him!" the scout said hoarsely.

I shook my head in incomprehension at this bewildering remark.

"The Liver-Eater," Carson exclaimed. "He's taken Jeremiah!"

.

CHAPTER TWENTY-TWO

"TAKEN HIM?" I exclaimed, so thunderstricken by Carson's announcement that I was barely capable of articulate speech. "What?—How?—"

"Snuck in and snatched the boy," said the scout, his eyes ablaze. "Back door's been jimmied open."

The irony of the situation was almost too awful to contemplate. At the very time that Carson and I were out hunting for Johnson, our quarry was to be found right *here*—invading the sanctuary of our abode!

With trembling voice, Muddy urgently inquired: "What about Mrs. Whitaker?"

In reply, Carson shook his head grimly—a gesture that could admit only one, exceedingly dire interpretation.

Tears immediately sprang to Muddy's eyes. "Oh, the poor dear woman," she groaned, pressing both hands to her bosom.

"You'd best have a look, Eddie," said the scout.

Instructing Muddy to lock the door behind us, I quickly followed Carson downstairs.

The first thing to smite my vision upon entering Mrs. Whitaker's apartment was the sight of the landlady's mangled body, sprawled upon its back on the floor of the parlor. A single glimpse of the corpse told me that she had been subjected to the unspeakable outrage that had earned Johnson his notorious sobriquet. Her throat had been slit—the front of her housedress ripped open—and a hideous wound made under her rib cage, plainly indicating that her killer had excised the organ for which he had developed so depraved—so *unnatural*—a taste.

In addition to these other butcheries, Johnson had scalped the poor woman, taking her full head of wavy gray hair as a trophy. The exposed dome of her horribly mutilated skull glistened redly in the lamplight.

A large pool of blood lay to one side of the victim's body. I inferred from this fact that the landlady must have been lying face down when the scout entered the room and discovered her. He had then rolled her body over to examine her wounds. This would explain not only the present position of the corpse, but also the badly besmirched state of Carson's hands, which had evidently become imbrued with gore when he had moved her.

"Blood's pretty near fresh," said Carson. "He wasn't here too long ago."

"Let us be grateful for that fact, at least," I said. "Based on our knowledge of Johnson's two previous abductions—i.e., those of little Rosalie Edmonds and Annie Dobbs—it seems clear that he has spirited Jeremiah off to his secret lair, where his evil may be accomplished at leisure. The less time your son has been in Johnson's clutches, the greater our chances of finding him alive."

"I expect he'll keep the boy in one piece for a spell," Carson agreed, pointing his chin at the ghastly incision in the landlady's torso. "He's eaten his fill for tonight."

A shudder coursed through my frame at the thought of the unspeakable meal in which Johnson had indulged. Following the trail of bloody bootprints that led away from poor Mrs. Whitaker's body, the scout then ushered me to the small bedchamber used by his son.

Moonlight entering through the wide-flung, uncurtained window suffused the room with a spectral glow. Stepping to the dresser, Carson removed a phosphorous match from a small receptacle and ignited the oil lamp, affording us a better view of the scene.

From the extreme disarray of the bedclothes, it was clear that a violent struggle had taken place. The entrance of the intruder into his room must have awakened the slumbering boy, who had evidently fought with all his strength to free himself from the grasp of his abductor. That Muddy and Sissy had been unaware of the crisis occurring directly belowstairs was undoubtedly due to the fact that Jeremiah had not cried out for help. Either Johnson had clamped a hand over his mouth to prevent him from screaming or the boy's voice had become somewhat atrophied from disuse.

As I scrutinized the scene, I perceived several thick strands of jet-black hair lying on the badly disheveled bedsheets. My first assumption was that these had somehow been pulled from Jeremiah's head during his struggle. When I picked them up and examined them by the lamplight, however, I was startled to discover that the inky hue was, in fact, a dye which easily came off on my fingers.

"Lampblack," I muttered, deducing the nature of the substance from its distinctive texture.

"How's that?" inquired Carson, coming up beside me.

Extending my hand to reveal the coal-black smudges on the pads of my thumb and forefinger, I said: "We were correct in believing that Johnson might attempt to disguise his appearance by altering the tell-tale color of his hair. These strands—which I initially took for Jeremiah's—clearly came from his abductor.

"Look," I continued, holding them up to the lamp for Carson's inspection. "It is possible to discern the natural red hue beneath the coating of black. Your son must have torn them from Johnson's head while putting up a furious, if futile, resistance."

"He's a fighter," said the scout, a distinct note of pride audible in his emotion-fraught voice.

From the pattern of the bloody bootprints, it was evident that—after entering the room and grabbing the child from the bed—Johnson had made his exit through the open window. Climbing over the sill, Carson now dropped into the moonlit backyard and—kneeling—began to inspect the ground. I followed the scout, standing behind him while he bent close to the grass.

A moment later, he stood upright. Leaving the yard through the little swinging gate in the surrounding fence, he strode around the side of the house and emerged onto the street, his eyes surveying the ground. All at once, he swiftly crouched again. When he arose, I saw by the illumination of a nearby street lamp that something was dangling from his hand. Standing closer, I peered at the object and realized at once that it was the Indian pendant which had belonged to Carson's wife, Waa-nibe, and which Jeremiah wore in remembrance of his slain mother. The leather thong was unknotted. Either it had accidentally come undone, or (as seemed more likely) the resourceful lad had surreptitiously untied it and dropped it to the ground as a signal to his father.

Without a word, Carson pocketed the amulet and continued along the street, pausing at length before a small house situated a block away from Mrs. Whitaker's abode. A hitching post stood at the edge of the curb.

"Johnson must've tied his horse up here," said Carson after making a brief examination of the ground. "They headed off that way," he added, gesturing in an easterly direction.

Even in broad daylight, the possibility of tracing Johnson's route through the cobblestoned labyrinth of the city's heavily trafficked streets would have been exceedingly slight. In the darkness, it was all but nonexistent.

"There ain't no way to track him," said the scout, echoing my ruminations. "If you got any ideas, Eddie, I'm plumb eager to hear them."

Focusing my thoughts upon the seemingly insurmountable difficulty that confronted us—i.e., how to locate Johnson's lair in time to rescue Carson's child—I furiously cudgeled my brain. All at once, an inspiration came rushing to my mind. While there can be little doubt that our ratiocinative faculties, when highly developed, can solve problems of inordinate complexity, it is equally the case that there are depths within our souls from which sudden, unlooked-for insights can arise, as if from a level far below that of mere *consciousness.*

"What is it, Eddie?" asked the scout, who had been studying my face.

"Something has occurred to me," I said excitedly. "You will recall that earlier this evening, prior to our journey to Five Points, I questioned you about Johnson's carnal predilections. At the time, you could shed no light on the matter. It appears, however, that we can draw at least one conclusion concerning that exceedingly unsavory subject. In the past several weeks, no fewer than three young children have been carried off by this monster, your son being the most recent victim. Along with his other evil propensities, it is very evident that Johnson is inclined to prey upon juveniles of both sexes.

"Tell me, Kit," I continued, "during your sojourns in the mountains, were there any instances of child abduction of which you were aware?"

Carson nodded. "You'd hear about it from time to time. Some little girl or boy would go missing from their cabins. The Indians generally got the blame."

"Perhaps the guilty party was a white man," I said.

"Johnson," Carson said.

"In light of what we know about his *modus operandi*, that is a reasonable assumption," I replied.

"But how's that going to help us now?" Carson asked.

"During our very first conversation about Johnson in Mr. Barnum's office," I replied, "you speculated that he had come to New York City because he had formerly been a resident here. His obvious familiarity with the layout of the metropolis—through which he moves with such confident stealth—adds further support to that hypothesis. Let us suppose, therefore, that—prior to his departure for the Rockies—he was a denizen of Manhattan. Let us further suppose that his depraved taste for children did not commence with his arrival out West but predated it."

"Go on," said Carson.

"During the discussion to which I just alluded, you were asked why Johnson had gone to live in the mountains in the first place. Is it possible that he went there to escape justice—that he was fleeing the law after committing some heinous crime?"

"Could be," said Carson.

"To the best of your knowledge," I asked, "when did Johnson first arrive in the mountains?"

"Nine, maybe ten years back," said the scout.

"Here, then, we arrive at some basis for hope," I said. "Let us proceed under the assumption that nine or ten years ago, a series of crimes occurred in Manhattan involving the disappearances of children. Let us also assume that before an arrest could be made, the perpetrator absconded from the city and vanished into the trackless wilderness of the Far West, where he took on a new identity: John Johnson, soon to become known as the infamous Liver-Eater. If we can discover any information concerning his true identity—his actual family name, the neighborhood in which he resided—we will, I believe, be close to locating his present whereabouts."

"How do you aim to do that?" Carson said. I could hear in his tone the growing desperation of a father whose child is in dire peril, and who is agonizingly aware that every passing moment brings his loved one another step closer to death.

"I have an idea," I said. "Proceed at once to Broadway and secure us a hack, then drive back here and pick me up."

Without a word, Carson strode off in the direction of Broadway, while I hurried to the front stoop of the little house before which we had been standing. Its inhabitants, I knew, were a family named Russell, whose members included a strapping son of eighteen years of age. Pounding on the door, I waited in an agony of impatience for a response from within. At length, the door opened a crack, and I found myself looking into the visage of the gray-haired *paterfamilias*, who—from his appearance—had just been awakened from a deep slumber.

His bleary eyes widened in shock as I hastily explained that his neighbor,

Mrs. Whitaker, had been savagely murdered in her home. I then urged him to waste no time in sending his son for the police.

I had just received his assurance that he would act without delay when I heard the sound of a carriage drawing up on the street behind me. I spun on my heels, sprinted for the curb, and climbed into the hack, instructing the driver to take us as speedily as possible to the offices of the *Daily Mirror*, on Nassau Street.

CHAPTER TWENTY-THREE

F ROM MY LONG FAMILIARITY with their habits, I knew that members of the so-called "fourth estate" frequently toiled late into the night, preparing their stories for publication on the morrow. I had good reason to believe, therefore, that George Townsend would still be hard at work, even at that unreasonable hour.

In this expectation I was not disappointed. Arrived at the newspaper building, Carson and I hurried upstairs to the second floor. As we crossed the threshold of the editorial room, my gaze immediately lit upon the young reporter, who was furiously scribbling away at his desk by the warm glow of an oil lamp. A plate containing the remnants of what appeared to be a ham sandwich was situated beside his elbow, along with a water pitcher and a half-empty glass. I deduced from these objects that he had been working without respite throughout the evening. Rather than interrupt his labors to take his dinner at a restaurant, he had evidently consumed a hasty meal while continuing to write.

His employer, Mr. Morris, was there, too. Standing beside the young man's chair, he was perusing a sheet of paper clutched in one hand. From his look of intense concentration, I gathered that he was reviewing Townsend's article as it came from the latter's pen, preparatory to having it set in print.

Upon our entrance, both men immediately looked up from their respective occupations, their faces wrought into identical expressions of wonder. In view of the lateness of the hour—the sense of extreme urgency the scout and I un-doubtedly conveyed—and the dark coating of dried blood on my compan-ion's hands—their startled reaction was only to be expected.

"Great Scot!" exclaimed Morris. "What in the name of—?"

Dropping his quill, Townsend pushed back his chair, rose to his feet, and came hurrying over to meet us.

"Mr. Poe! Mr. Carson! What's happened?" he cried.

Under less exigent circumstances, I would have been happy to satisfy my friend's curiosity with a detailed account of all that had transpired since we parted earlier in the day. Time being of the essence, however, I was able to of-fer only the scantiest summation of events. Briefly, I told of the expedition that Carson and I had made to the Five Points—of our startling encounter with the murderous brute in Donaho's Saloon—and of the violent *dénoue-ment* of the affair. I then described the appalling discovery my companion had made after our return to Mrs. Whitaker's home.

The news that Carson's son had been kidnapped by the monster elicited si-multaneous gasps of horror from Townsend and his employer.

"My dear fellow," said the good-natured old gentleman, clutching Carson by the shoulder. "You have my greatest sympathy. Tell me, please, how I can be of assistance. I will do everything in my power to help get your little boy back alive."

"As will I," pledged Townsend.

Thanking both men warmly, Carson said: "Eddie reckons there's a fair to middling chance that Johnson lived in New York City maybe ten years ago or thereabouts. He figures the Liver-Eater might have stole a child or two back then."

"That is correct," I affirmed. "If my hypothesis is correct, then there may well be a record of such a crime in one of the back issues of your newspaper. Such an article might conceivably contain important clues as to the where-abouts of our quarry, since it seems likely that—upon returning to the city—Johnson would have sought refuge in his former neighborhood, where he felt most at home."

Even before I reached the end of my explanation, a deep shadow of gloom had settled over Morris's kindly visage. "It pains me to tell you this," he sadly remarked, "but the entire archives of the *Mirror* were reduced to mulch when the basement closet in which they were stored was flooded during a torrential rainstorm last summer. The issues you refer to no longer exist."

My heart sank at this exceedingly disappointing news, while Carson's lips drew so tight that they disappeared altogether.

All at once, Morris seemed to be struck with a thought. He furrowed his brow—lowered his eyes—and began to pull at his protruding nether lip in a gesture of intense contemplation.

"Wait a minute," he softly exclaimed after a moment. "I just remembered something. There *was* a missing child case about ten years ago. I was still doing some reporting myself back then—the *Mirror* was only a few months old, and I was putting out every issue almost single-handedly. I visited the child's home in the Bowery and spoke to her mother. Poor woman—driven half-insane by her daughter's disappearance. The name escapes me. All I can remember is her grief. She kept showing me a piece of pink hair ribbon. It was lying on the little girl's pillow when the mother discovered she was miss—"

"Pink ribbon?" I suddenly cried, cutting off Morris's recitation.

"Why, yes," said the elderly fellow, regarding me with a puzzled expression.

Turning to Carson, I excitedly said: "Kit—the wretched beggar-lady we encountered in St. John's Park—the one upon whom you so generously bestowed a silver dollar—do you recall her?"

For a moment, the scout appeared to have not the slightest recollection of the personage to whom I was referring. All at once, a look of recognition spread across his handsome countenance.

Turning back to the elderly publisher, I said: "Thank you, Mr. Morris. You have been exceedingly helpful after all. Now we must be on our way at once."

"I'm going with you," Townsend announced. He then glanced at his employer as though soliciting his approval.

"All right," said Morris. "If you'd like, you are welcome to the use of my coach. It's downstairs in front of the building. The driver's probably dozing. Just give him a poke in the ribs and tell him where you want to go."

Thanking him profusely, we turned to leave.

"Hold on a second," Morris said, staying our departure.

Extracting a pristine pocket handkerchief from his trousers, he saturated it with water from the pitcher on Townsend's desk, then gave it to Carson.

"Much obliged," said the scout.

The three of us then hurried from the office, Carson using the dripping cloth to cleanse the viscid coating of Mrs. Whitaker's gore from his hands as he strode beside me.

*   *   *

Fifteen minutes later, we arrived at our destination. Directing the driver to wait for us at the entrance, we hurried into the park and immediately began our search.

Had it not been a night of unusual brightness and clarity, we may well have failed in our attempt. It was Carson who, with his extraordinarily keen senses, spotted the old woman. We had been engaged in our hunt for several minutes when—pointing to a place a dozen yards away—he said:

"There!"

Squinting at the spot, I dimly perceived something that, to my own eyes, resembled a bundle of rags that had been dumped beneath some bushes by one of the miserable vagrants who made the park their home.

I opened my mouth to question Carson as to the nature of the object he was indicating.

By then, however, he was already striding swiftly across the lawn. I hurried to follow him, with Townsend at my side. As we drew closer, I perceived that the shapeless pile of apparent refuse was, in fact, a human being, huddled asleep beneath the shrubbery.

Bending low, Carson gently shook the inert figure, who awakened with a gasp—quickly struggled onto its hands and knees—and scurried away to a safe distance before rising to its feet. By the radiant light of the full moon, I saw that the wretchedly clad individual was the very personage of whom we were in search. Tightly clutching her tattered shawl to her frail, stooped body, she gazed at us wildly and, in a quivering voice, cried:

"Go away! Don't hurt me!"

"We don't aim to," the scout said gently. "My name's Carson. Remember me?"

Narrowing her eyes until they were little more than slits, the crone peered at us suspiciously for several moments before saying: "You're the nice young man that gave me that money."

"That's right," said the scout.

Thrusting out a bony hand, palm upward, the crone piteously said: "Do you have any more?"

"Sure do," said Carson. Removing his leather pouch from his pocket, he extracted a silver dollar, which he then held up for display.

Immediately, the old lady scurried toward us and—with surprising alacrity for one so decrepit—reached out and tried to snatch the coin from Carson's grasp. Before her gnarled fingers could close around it, however, Carson quickly withdrew his hand.

"Got to answer some questions first," he said.

"Questions?" she said in an uncertain tone.

"Yes," I interjected. "Yesterday, you showed us a scrap of badly faded pink ribbon. To whom did that article belong?"

"Why, to *her*," said the crone in a quavering voice.

"Her?" I said.

"My little girl. My baby."

"And what became of your child?" I inquired, fully anticipating what the answer would be.

"Gone," cried the old woman, confirming my expectation. "Taken away in the night."

At this statement, Carson and I quickly exchanged a look, while Townsend uttered a soft exclamation beside me. My assumption had been correct— the old lady standing before us was the same unfortunate mother whom Mr. Morris had interviewed ten years earlier in her home on the Bowery!

Suppressing my excitement, I turned back to the old woman and asked: "Taken by whom?"

For a long moment—during which I could do nothing but stand there in an agony of suspense—the old woman made no reply. The muscles of her sunken, deeply wrinkled countenance twitched spasmodically, as though she were in the grip of several violently conflicting emotions. When, at length, she finally spoke, her expression had resolved itself into one of overwhelming bitterness.

"It was *him*," she hissed, bubbles of spittle forming at the corners of her mouth. "I *know* it was. No one would listen to us. But we knew. We knew it was Albert Brown."

A thrill of excitement passed through my frame. Was "Albert Brown" the true cognomen of the villain we were seeking—the being who had gone west and metamorphosed into the notorious Liver-Eating Johnson? My instincts told me that the two were, in fact, one and the same. Still, we could not be certain without further confirmation.

"I am afraid," I said, "that I am unfamiliar with anyone by that name. Can you tell us more about this fellow—this Albert Brown?"

"Oh, he was a nasty one. Mean as they come. Lived in the house next door. When the child went missing, I knew right off who done it. So did Davey."

"Davey?" I asked.

"My husband," the old woman said impatiently, as if irritated that I would be ignorant of so obvious a fact. "He would have killed that Albert Brown with his bare hands. But the bastard disappeared."

That Brown had absconded from his neighborhood shortly after the kidnapping of the woman's child was certainly consistent with my hypothesis concerning Johnson. Still, it was hardly the definitive proof I was hoping for.

"What become of your husband?" Carson inquired.

"Died," said the old woman, blinking back the tears that had instantly sprung to her eyes. "They say he was killed in an accident where he worked in Mr. Doane's tannery. But I know what really killed him. Grief. His heart broke. That child was his shining joy."

At that instant, the old woman's own inveterate grief—which the passage of years had done nothing to mitigate—overwhelmed her, and she burst into clamorous tears. So piteous was the sight that—had the repellent state of her filthy, bedraggled garments not deterred me—I would have placed an arm about her shoulders to comfort her.

Carson, however—who appeared to have no such scruple—stepped to her side and patted her tenderly on the upper back while saying, "There, there." His compassionate gesture made me feel somewhat abashed, particularly since he himself was under the greatest imaginable strain at that moment. His son's life hung in the balance—and we *still* had not obtained the key piece of intelligence that might lead us to the boy.

At length, her weeping subsided. Reaching for her bony hand, Carson pressed the dollar into her palm and said:

"Here's your money, ma'am. You've been real helpful. We've got just another question or two. Can you tell us anything more about this Brown?"

"Who?" she asked, dabbing her eyes with a corner of her threadbare shawl.

"Why, the fellow that stole your little girl," exclaimed Carson.

"Little girl?" she repeated in a peculiar—intensely dreamy—singsong voice. "I've never had a little girl. I've always lived alone, right here in the park. It's a very nice place. A little cold in the winter. But I manage—I manage."

At this astounding declaration, I felt the blood drain from my countenance. From the strange lilt in her voice—no less than the bizarre content of her remarks—I could only draw one conclusion. The pain of recalling her past tragedies had been too much for her to endure. Her tenuous hold on reality had slipped, and she had retreated into a realm of delusion!

The timing of this occurrence could not have been more unfortunate. To conclude that Johnson and Brown were the same man—and that our quarry was therefore likely to be found in his familiar habitat on the Bowery—we needed to know more. To have come so close to obtaining the required information, only to be deprived of it at the last minute, was almost too maddening to bear.

For a moment, I was seized with the urge to grab the old woman by the shoulders and attempt to shake an answer out of her. Glancing over at Carson, I saw by his expression that his sympathy for her had likewise vanished. His countenance was suffused with despair.

All at once, the old woman shook her head rapidly from side to side, like a person emerging from a trance.

"Wait," she said in a tremulous voice. "Did you just ask me about Albert Brown?"

"Yes!" the scout and I exclaimed simultaneously.

As we stared at the woman, her expression underwent a remarkable transformation, twisting itself into a grimace of pure hatred such as I had never before witnessed on a human countenance.

"He looked like the Evil One himself," she snarled. "A great ugly devil, with glowing dark eyes, and hair as red as hellfire."

Chapter Twenty-Four

W E OBTAINED NO FURTHER information from the old woman. Immediately after spewing out her long pent-up hatred for the man who had robbed her of her daughter, she relapsed into her former state of confusion. We left her in the park, muttering incoherently under her breath, while she clutched the silver dollar with the fierce possessiveness of a child holding tight to a beloved bauble. Nothing more could be done to relieve the plight of the piteous creature. We might give alms to her body, but her body did not pain her. It was her soul that suffered, and her soul we could not reach.

Our interview with the old woman had produced one important result. We had narrowed the probable location of Johnson's lair to a single neighborhood of the city. Even so, we faced a considerable challenge in attempting to uncover the monster's hiding place, the area of the Bowery comprising not only the tawdry, mile-long thoroughfare of that name but all of the surrounding streets. Had we been able to learn the precise address of the old woman's former abode, our task would have been infinitely simpler. Unfortunately, she had slipped back into dementia before we could discover that key piece of information.

As it happened, however, she had inadvertently supplied us with a vital clue. In speaking of her deceased husband, she had alluded to his place of employment—Doane's tannery, one of many enterprises relating to the processing of cattle to be found in the Bowery (which, from early in its history, had been a center of the meat business). As we climbed back into the waiting coach, George Townsend revealed that he was familiar with Doane's, having written a story, several years earlier, about a dreadful accident that had occurred on the premises when a worker sliced off his hand and bled to death. The tannery was located on Pike Street, close to the river.

Proceeding under the assumption that the old woman and her family had resided in the vicinity of her husband's workplace, we now directed our driver to take us to that locale with all possible dispatch.

In spite of the lateness of the hour, the gaudy avenue of the Bowery itself was still aswarm with humanity, seeking amusement in the countless dance cellars—concert saloons—beer gardens—minstrel halls—dime museums— and raucous playhouses that lined the sidewalks. As our coach proceeded eastward, however, the streets became progressively deserted, until, by the time we reached our destination, barely a soul was to be seen.

Dismounting from our vehicle at the intersection of Pike and Monroe, we paused to take our bearings. The buildings here were less tightly crowded together than in other parts of that inordinately congested quarter. In addition to various humble-looking dwellings, there appeared to be a number of somewhat ramshackle warehouses and (to judge by the distinctive reek pervading the street) at least one abattoir. There were also several stores.

Though infused with the greatest imaginable sense of urgency, we remained rooted to the spot for several moments, somewhat at a loss as to how to proceed. Other than making our way to the Bowery as speedily as possible, we had formulated no real plan. Luck, however (whose critical *rôle* in human affairs has been insufficiently investigated by metaphysicians) intervened on our behalf; for—as we stood on the corner, looking about us—my gaze fell on the window of a nearby shop specializing in the sale of paint, cutlery, mechanics' tools, and miscellaneous housekeeping hardware.

Emitting an excited cry, I hurried over to the store. Affixed to the interior of the display window were printed advertisements for a wide assortment of products: Miller's Harness Dressing—Rising Sun Stove Polish—Talbot's Miracle Asbestos Furnace Lining—Pearltop Lamp Chimneys—Payson's Sanding Apparatus—the Triumph Self-Wringing Mop—Chase's Asphaltum Varnish— and more.

Among the most prominent of these signs, occupying a place in the center of the window, was one that read:

ALDINE'S PEERLESS LAMPBLACK—THE WORLD'S PUREST PIGMENT—UNSURPASSED FOR STAINS, PAINTS, INKS, AND DYES—NONE FINER!

"Look here!" I exclaimed, pointing to this sign.

Townsend was greatly perplexed by my interest in this advertisement. Quickly I described the strands of artificially blackened hair I had found on Jeremiah's bed.

I then turned to Carson and said: "While lampblack is, of course, readily available throughout the city, it is reasonable to assume that Johnson made his purchase in his own neighborhood. I suggest, therefore, that we speak to the proprietor of this store at once."

"Where do you figure on finding him?" asked Carson.

Pointing to the second-floor windows, whose drawn curtains were clearly visible in the moonlight, I said: "There. Apparently—like most shop owners in the poorer districts of the city—he resides above his store."

Without another word, Carson strode to the front door and began to pound upon it with his uninjured left fist.

At first, there was no reply. All at once, the casements flew open—a head protruded from the window—and a gruff voice called out: "What's that god-damned racket?"

"You the fellow that owns this place?" Carson asked, stepping back from the doorway and looking up at the shopkeeper.

"Who wants to know?" the latter angrily replied.

"Name's Carson," answered the scout. "Kit Carson."

Until this point—at my own suggestion—the famed scout had done his best to conceal his identity from the public. Now, however, he had evidently sensed that the flaunting of his name might serve to facilitate, not hinder, our investigation.

His intuition proved correct. At the mention of his name, the shopkeeper's exceedingly hostile tone underwent an immediate change.

"Kit Carson?" he said wonderingly. "For real?"

"Yessir," said the scout. "Sorry to trouble you but it's mighty important. We'd like to have a word with you."

"Be down in a jiff," said the storekeeper.

Several moments later, the front door opened and we found ourselves face-to-face with a small—skinny—middle-aged fellow, clutching a tin candle-holder. From the rumpled state of his shirt and his carelessly buttoned trousers, it was clear that he had donned the garments hurriedly after being roused from his bed. His head was entirely bald. As if to compensate for this condition, he had cultivated a beard of such luxuriant growth that his lower face was entirely hidden beneath it. In the lambent glow of the candle, his dark eyes glittered as he studied Carson intently.

"Come in, come in," he said, waving us inside the store.

Crossing the threshold, we found ourselves in a narrow, musty-smelling room. Though the glow from the shopkeeper's taper was not sufficiently bright to illuminate every corner of the store, I could see that its walls were lined with long, sagging shelves stocked with every variety of hardware.

"Name's Mulligan," said the proprietor, coming to a halt in the center of the aisle. Surveying the scout from the tips of his boots to the crown of his Western-style hat, he then declared: "Kit Carson, I'll be damned. I pictured you different somehow—bigger and wearing one of them mountain man getups. Wait'll Maggie hears about this. That's the missus. She's snoring away upstairs. Nothing wakes that woman once she's asleep. Crack of doom itself wouldn't rouse her. Why, she'll be fit to be tied when I tell her Kit Carson was here. Oh, she's a big admirer of yours. Reads all them books about your exploits. Why, she was just reading one the other night—*Kit Carson, the Fighting Trapper*. No, wait, that ain't it. What *was* that thing called? *Kit Carson, Warrior of the Rockies*? Something like that. Anyways—"

How long the exceedingly hirsute shopkeeper might have continued in this vein can only be surmised. It was Carson who finally brought his prattle to a halt.

"We are plumb in a hurry, Mr. Mulligan," the scout interjected. "There's a man we're looking for."

"You mean that Liver-Eating Johnson?" said the shopkeeper. "Sure. Read all about him in the papers. Sounds like an ugly customer, all right." All at once, he raised his eyebrows in surprise. "Is *that* what brought you here?"

It was I who replied to this query. "We were drawn to your store," I said, "by the advertisement in your window for a well-known brand of lampblack. Can you tell us if you have recently sold any of that substance to a man of particularly imposing stature?"

"Matter of fact," said Mulligan after a brief pause, "I *did*. A few days ago. A big ugly bruiser came into the store and bought a package of Aldine's. You think that was *him*?" he added in an awestruck tone.

"Perhaps," I said. Though encouraged by the shopkeeper's testimony, I could not be certain that the customer was Johnson without additional evidence.

"Do you recall any other details of his physical appearance?" I said. "Johnson is easily recognizable by the color of his hair, which—until he disguised it with a dye made from lampblack—was of a vivid red hue. As you are undoubtedly aware from the newspapers, he also sports a full red beard even more abundant than your own."

"Couldn't see his hair," said Mulligan. "His hat was pulled down to his ears. Don't recall any whiskers on him."

Though somewhat disappointing, this information was far from unexpected. After all, I myself had speculated that Johnson would shave off his facial hair—such an expedient being the simplest way to effect a change in his appearance.

"Hold on a minute," said Mulligan, who had been tugging meditatively on the end of his own beard. "There *was* something else. His ankles. He kept bending down and scratching at them. Must have itched something terrible. You should've heard the way he swore. Why, it made my ears burn to hear it—and believe me, I've heard some cussing in my time."

At this statement, Carson and I exchanged a look of undisguised excitement.

"It is *him*!" I cried. "There can no longer be any doubt of it!"

"There's a mighty fair chance of it, all right," said the scout.

"But how can you be sure?" George Townsend asked in a deeply puzzled tone.

I hastily described the chigger bites that I had received during the initial trip Carson and I had made to St. John's Park. "Johnson must also have been exposed to these exceedingly noxious insects while disposing of young Rosalie Edmonds's body in the undergrowth," I explained.

"Any notion of where he lives?" Carson urgently inquired of Mulligan.

"Why, just a few blocks from here," said the latter. "I saw him the other day, coming out of a place between Water and South. Can't miss it. It's set back a ways from the curb. Run-down old place—used to be a junk-shop run by a Jew named Zerkow."

Thanking him for his help, we made for the door.

"Want me to go for the police?" he called after us. "I'd be happy—"

We did not hear the remainder of his offer. Before he finished speaking, we had bolted from the store and were hurrying in the direction of the river.

As we strode briskly through the deserted, moonlit streets, I glanced over at Carson and perceived the same steely expression to which I had grown so accustomed. His clenched jaw—flared nostrils—and glinting eyes spoke plainly of his fierce resolve. He was focused, with every fibre of his being, on the mission at hand.

While sharing his sense of determination, I myself felt somewhat apprehensive about our coming encounter with Johnson. Though my faith in Carson's martial prowess was complete—and though we outnumbered our opponent by a ratio of three to one—the prospect of facing so fearsome a foe could not fail to be daunting. Johnson's inordinate strength, his singular brutality, and the desperation he would undoubtedly feel at finding himself cornered made for an exceedingly dangerous combination. Added to my concern was the condition of Carson himself, who was both injured and unarmed.

Nevertheless, I did not allow these considerations to interfere with my stern sense of duty. Subduing my qualms, I marched boldly alongside my companions, silently praying that we were not too late to save the life of Carson's son.

The house described by Mulligan was readily found. It stood near the far end of Pike Street, sufficiently close to the piers that we could hear the water lap against the pilings and smell the brackish aroma of the river. The front yard was littered with a wild collection of refuse. In the moonlight, I could discern the twisted remnants of an iron bed frame—several broken carriage wheels—an overturned, ancient bathtub—and a myriad of other worthless items of the sort amassed by the typical Bowery junk-dealer.

The house itself was little more than an oversized shack: a large—single-story—wooden structure, badly dilapidated and devoid of the slightest ornamentation. No light was visible from within. The two windows that flanked the front doorway were as black and vacant as the hollow sockets of a death's head.

Standing in the shadow of a derelict warehouse that stood across the street, Carson whispered instructions to Townsend and myself.

"I'll go first," he said, keeping his voice so low that we were required to bend our ears close to his mouth in order to hear him. "You boys follow just where I step."

We nodded our understanding; whereupon the scout immediately lowered himself into a crouch and moved swiftly across the street. Keeping low, he then began to make his way with the uttermost stealth across the yard, avoiding any of the countless objects that lay scattered about the grass. Townsend and I followed directly behind him, making certain that we placed our feet precisely where his had gone before. However difficult, this method of navigating the yard was an absolute necessity. One misstep and we might accidentally tread upon some article of debris made of wood, tin, or pottery, producing a noise that would serve as an alarm to our enemy.

We had nearly reached the front of the house when Carson halted abruptly, gesturing down at something that lay several feet away. Squinting, I perceived an oblong object half hidden in the grass.

It was a steel beaver trap, its serrated jaws open and ready to snap shut on the leg of any unwary caller. Clearly, it had been deliberately placed on the lawn to guard against intruders. I could only assume that there were others like it scattered around the property. Whatever doubts I had that this ramshackle house belonged to our quarry were instantly dispelled by the sight of this treacherous "booby-trap."

Continuing on in this exceedingly careful manner, we soon made our way around to the north side of the house, where we squatted beneath a window that—like the others—was utterly black.

Exerting the utmost caution, Carson slowly raised himself until his eyes cleared the level of the sill. He then cupped his hands on either side of his face and peered inside the window. An instant later, he dropped back down.

"He's in there," he said in the merest whisper. "I can hear him moving around. And it ain't dark in there. The window's blacked out—painted over with tar."

Glancing around him, he reached for an object lying nearby in the grass and placed it in my hands. It was a stone of considerable heft.

"Count slow to ten," he said to me, "then chuck it through the window."

Without another word, he then swiftly made his way back toward the front of the house, keeping his lithe body bent low as he moved.

Obeying his directions, I silently began my count, as Townsend crouched tensely beside me. Having arrived at the designated number, I rose to my feet, raised the rock high above my head, and hurled it at the window.

The glass shattered, revealing a dull light from within. In the next instant, there came the deafening blast of a rifle from inside the house—the remnants of the window disintegrated in a spray of pulverized glass—and a bullet whistled by me, so close as to ruffle the hair atop my head. This was immediately followed by the noise of splintering wood emanating from the front of the house as Carson (to judge from the sound) battered down the door and burst into the shack.

Without a moment's hesitation, Townsend sprang to his feet and dove through the window, while I scrambled inside directly behind him.

My first impression, as I gazed wildly about, was of a realm of utter chaos. The dimly illuminated interior was damp—mouldy—and choked with a suffocating mixture of foul odors. On every side—piled against the walls—strewn about the floor—hanging from the rafters—was an indescribable profusion of dust-blackened, rust-corroded debris. Attached to the walls at irregular intervals were large iron hooks from which depended all manner of decayed bridles, old halters, and other outworn items of tackle.

A terrific commotion was taking place at the far end of the room, where the front door hung loosely from its frame, having been torn halfway off its hinges from the force of Carson's entrance. The scout was grappling ferociously with another man—a figure of such titanic stature as to make the hulking brute we had vanquished at Donaho's seem puny by comparison. This colossus, I saw, could be none other than the fearsome Liver-Eater.

His lower body was clad in crudely made breeches of dressed deerskin. Above the waist, however, he was entirely unclothed. Beneath the densely matted, auburn-colored hair that covered his upper torso like animal fur, I could discern enormous, bulging muscles that glistened with perspiration. His arms were of inordinate length, and his hands so enormously broad as scarcely to retain a human shape. The thick shock of hair that rose from his head was of an unnaturally shiny jet-black hue.

Clutching each other in a savage embrace, the two men wrestled fiercely. Though greatly overmatched in regard to size, Carson was holding his own against his opponent. Their struggle was of the most desperate sort, both men grunting loudly as each strove to gain an advantage over the other.

All at once, the two snarling combatants—still locked tightly together—went crashing to the floor and began to pummel each other with such extreme—such unbridled—fury that the very walls shuddered. Frantically, I cast my gaze about, searching for a weapon with which I could go to Carson's aid. George Townsend had already snatched up the empty rifle that Johnson had discarded after discharging its contents through the window. Wielding it like a club—its barrel clutched in both hands—its stock raised high above one shoulder—the young reporter positioned himself close to the spot where the two men were rolling wildly upon the trash-cluttered floor. So thoroughly intertwined were the combatants, however, that it was impossible for Townsend to strike a blow at Johnson without risking serious injury to the scout.

As I turned to look behind me in my search for a weapon, I caught sight of something that brought a gasp to my lips.

It was Jeremiah. He was suspended upside down from a rafter by means of a length of coarse rope, tightly affixed to his ankles. He was as naked as though he had just sprung from the womb, every stitch of his clothing having been stripped from his smooth, slender body. A filthy rag had been shoved into his mouth and secured with a leather thong that encircled his head—a needlessly cruel expedient in view of the boy's muteness.

Our arrival could not have occurred at a timelier moment; for I saw at a glance that Johnson had been preparing to butcher the lad. A tin washtub—

horribly caked with gouts of dried gore—had been placed directly beneath the dangling boy to collect the blood from his soon-to-be-severed throat.

My first impulse was to relieve the pressure on his legs. From the ghastly discoloration of his feet, I perceived that they were in imminent danger of becoming mortified from prolonged lack of circulation.

As I hurried to his side, my notice was attracted by a sinister object propped against the wall several feet away. It was a slender wooden pole from which there depended three human scalps. From the length, color, and texture of the hair, I deduced that two of these tresses had been taken from very young females—no doubt the monster's previous child victims, Annie Dobbs and Rosalie Edmonds. The third I recognized at once as the wavy, iron-gray hair of my butchered landlady, Mrs. Whitaker.

Averting my gaze from this hideous sight, I came up beside Jeremiah and quickly surveyed the floor for an implement with which I might free him. Almost at once, I spotted a jagged piece of rusted tin among the scraps of detritus scattered at my feet. Stooping, I quickly retrieved this object. Then—supporting Jeremiah with one arm—I proceeded to saw through the rope until it parted with a snap. I then carefully lowered him to the floor, stripped off my jacket, and wrapped it about the shivering lad, while assuring him in soothing tones that he was in no further danger of harm.

At that very instant, I heard a sound so alarming as to cause each separate hair on the back of my neck to bristle and stand erect: a yowl of demonic triumph such as might have issued from the lips of the arch-fiend himself. Swiveling my head, I saw to my uttermost horror that in the life-or-death battle between Carson and his foe, it was the latter who had apparently triumphed. His flushed, coarse-featured visage wrought into an expression of malevolent glee, Johnson was slowly rising to his feet, while Carson—his limp arms outflung, a stream of blood gushing from his head—lay motionlessly, perhaps even *lifelessly*, on his back.

Before Johnson could stand fully erect, Townsend—emitting a shout of fury—charged at the half-naked colossus, bringing the rifle butt down in a great sweeping arc. Had he struck his intended target, the monster's skull would undoubtedly have been riven in pieces. Johnson, however—moving with an astounding agility for a man of his size—sidestepped the blow. In the same motion, he drew back his enormous right fist and let fly a punch that landed with a sickening thud in the center of the young reporter's face, causing the latter to drop his rifle and stagger backward several steps, blood spurting from his crushed nose.

As the young man reeled, Johnson grabbed him by his shirtfront—lifted him off his feet as though he were no heavier than a child's rag doll—and slammed him back against the wall with terrific force. He then let go of Townsend and took a step backward, keeping his gaze riveted on the young reporter.

In light of the tremendous impact with which Townsend struck the wall, I fully expected to see him slide down to the floor in an unconscious heap. What happened instead seemed so unaccountable that, at first, I could make no sense of it. Much to my bewilderment, he remained suspended in the air— the soles of his boots perhaps three feet off the ground—as though kept aloft by a spell of levitation.

As Johnson emitted a guffaw of fiendish amusement, Townsend's body was shaken with violent paroxysms. His arms and legs twitched spasmodically. A ghastly gurgle issued from deep inside his throat. Then his mouth fell open, and he vomited forth a stream of crimson gore that splattered onto the floor and dribbled down his slack chin.

As the truth of what I had just observed forced itself upon my consciousness, I was seized with a feeling of such intense—such overpowering—horror and dismay that it was all I could do to keep from falling into a swoon. Nothing that I have experienced since that time has been able to efface in the slightest degree the memory of that indescribably hideous moment.

My young friend had been impaled on one of the large iron hooks interspersed along the walls. Its point had penetrated his back in the area between his shoulder blades and emerged in the center of his chest, where—I now perceived—a grotesque protrusion was visible in his shirtfront.

Throwing back his head, Johnson emitted a roar of uproarious laughter, as though the ghastly convulsions of the skewered young man were the most comical sight imaginable. He then turned in my direction and began to advance upon me, stooping along the way to retrieve an iron pump handle that leaned against one wall.

My doom was now approaching, and there was little or nothing I could do to avert it. The sheer horror of what I had just witnessed had so unstrung my nerves that I felt paralyzed in every limb. Huddled on the floor at my side, Jeremiah looked up at me with wide—panicked—eyes, as though silently imploring me to take action. But my situation, I knew, was utterly hopeless. Even had I been in full possession of my physical capabilities, what chance did I stand against the towering monster who had dispatched both of my companions so easily?

An instant later, Johnson halted before me. Looming there, he appeared to be one of the monstrous figures that populate the realm of children's wonder-tales, such as the club-wielding, cannibal giant encountered by the hero at the summit of the magical beanstalk.

With a vicious snarl, he raised the iron pump handle high into the air. In anticipation of the crushing blow that was certain to end my existence, I clamped my eyes tight.

No sooner had I done so than I heard a sharp cry of distress issue from Johnson's lips. This wholly unexpected sound was immediately followed by another—the heavy clang of the iron pump handle as it struck the floor.

I opened my eyes and peered up at my would-be assassin. The sight that greeted me was bewildering in the extreme.

Johnson's right hand, now devoid of its weapon, was raised to his face, which wore an expression of utter astonishment. A knife—appearing as if from nowhere—had completely transfixed his hand. Its long, bloody blade emerged from the center of his palm, while its hilt protruded from the back.

At the sight of the stag handle, a thrill of recognition coursed through my frame. I had seen the knife before! It was the very one that Carson kept concealed inside his boot, and that he had used to break open the back door of William Wyatt's residence. In the excitements of the past twenty-four hours, I had forgotten its existence.

Quickly, I cast my gaze across the room. My heart leapt with joy at the marvelous sight that greeted me. There stood Kit Carson, his right arm still extended from the motion of his remarkable throw. Though still bleeding copiously from the scalp, he had managed to hurl his blade with unerring accuracy directly into Johnson's hand, thus saving my life yet again.

As Johnson, with an agonized roar, gripped the hilt of the knife in his opposite hand and ripped it free, Carson—like a quadruped of the species *Oreamnos americanus*, or Rocky Mountain goat—lowered his head and charged his colossal foe, striking him directly in the solar plexus. The breath knocked completely out of him, Johnson fell to the floor with a tremendous crash.

Before Johnson could in any way recover, Carson dropped to his knees, straddling the chest of his foe. Snatching up the fallen pump handle, he raised it in both hands and brought it down with shattering force. Had Johnson not, at the very last second, turned his head to one side, he would have been killed instantly. As it was, the iron handle merely grazed his skull. Even so, the blow was sufficient to stun him. A fluttering groan escaped from his lips, and his eyes rolled back in their sockets.

Again Carson raised the heavy club, intending to deliver the *coup de grâce* to his detested adversary. There was in his countenance a look of such sheer— such implacable—hatred as to chill the very marrow in my bones. Once more, I shut my eyes. Though I possessed not the slightest whit of sympathy for Johnson, I had no wish to observe his gruesome—if well-deserved—execution.

Before the deathblow could descend, however, a terrific commotion could be heard at the front door, as though an army were bursting inside the shack. Booted feet trampled against the floorboards. Discordant cries went up. One harsh, familiar voice called out: "Don't move! Stay where you are!"

In another instant, we found ourselves surrounded by no fewer than a half-dozen men. Most were uniformed police officers, led by Captain Dunnegan himself, who had been the source of the shouted commands.

As I gazed around me, I spotted in their midst the person who had pointed our way to Johnson's lair: the hardware store owner, Mr. Mulligan. Evidently he had taken it upon himself to go for help—as he had offered to do as we were leaving his establishment. Immediately upon our departure—as I afterward discovered—he had hurried to the headquarters of the police, located only a short distance from his home, and informed them of our intent.

Fearing that we would be no match for the ferocious killer, Dunnegan and his men had hurried to our assistance. But it was Johnson himself who, in the end, had required their aid, and whose life had been saved by their sudden intervention.

Chapter Twenty-Five

⌒

A s may be readily supposed, the capture of the monster who had so terrorized Manhattan produced the most intense feelings among the inhabitants of the great metropolis. Excitement and relief were foremost among these emotions, followed closely by a ravenous curiosity to learn every fact concerning Johnson's discovery and arrest. So avid were New Yorkers for the smallest details of the case that—for several days following the dramatic events just described—every newsboy in the city found himself besieged by customers, who snatched up unprecedented numbers of the various daily gazettes. Indeed, it was the rare "newsy" who—positioning himself on a street corner and commencing his morning business—did not manage to sell out his entire stock of papers within minutes.

Though due credit was given to the police for their part in the arrest, it was, of course, Kit Carson who was the main object of the public's interest—gratitude—and even adulation. However much he disdained the *rôle* of hero—however devoutly he wished to be regarded as nothing more than an ordinary man—the unparalleled courage, fortitude, and prowess he had displayed in his pursuit and defeat of the notorious Liver-Eater could not fail to enhance his already legendary reputation. In the press, he was depicted as nothing less than an American demigod, a native-born counterpart to the fabled monster-slayers of the past: Perseus, Beowulf, Saint George.

My own contributions to the successful resolution of the affair were duly noted in the papers (except for the *Herald*, whose publisher, James Gordon

Bennett, still bore an evident grudge against me, stemming from my refusal to accommodate his wishes at the time of William Wyatt's murder). Though gratified by this recognition of my (admittedly vital) part in ferreting out Johnson's lair—without which the monster would still be at large—I had no wish to bask in the acclaim of the public. My most heartfelt desire was to return to the mundane routines of my existence, and to devote as much of my time as feasible to the care of my loved ones, especially my darling wife, Virginia.

Indeed, while the city as a whole rejoiced in the outcome of the affair, my own mood was distinctly more subdued, if not positively somber. Partly, this was due to my sorrow over the horrific murder of George Townsend (whose heroic death while assisting in the rescue of Carson's son received the acclamation it deserved in a moving tribute composed by his employer, Henry Morris, and published on the front page of the *Daily Mirror*). Though our acquaintance had been of only short duration, I had come to feel the most sincere respect and even affection for the young reporter. The memory of the hideous end he had met at the hands of the Liver-Eater would, I felt sure, never cease to haunt me for as long as I lived.

Added to this was my concern for the well-being of my darling Sissy. Her health—precarious even in the best of times—could not fail to be adversely affected by the shocking events that had occurred under our very roof within recent days: the poisoning of Carson's dog—the butchering of Mrs. Whitaker—the abduction of Jeremiah. Though she was, of course, overjoyed that the boy had been saved—the killer apprehended—and I myself unharmed—her inordinately frail constitution was bound to be shaken by the unprecedented series of calamities that had so severely disrupted the normal tranquility of our lives.

I was greatly relieved, therefore, when—less than twenty-four hours after Johnson's capture—Carson and his son materialized on our doorstep, appearing hardly the worse for wear. Both had spent the intervening time at New York Hospital, where they had received medical attention for their injuries. Happily, these proved to be relatively minor—a nasty-looking but superficial gash on Carson's forehead (sustained during his battle with Johnson) and a severe abrasion of the ankles, along with various contusions of the limbs and torso, in the case of Jeremiah.

The latter had also shown signs of extreme emotional distress, which had been treated with an injection of morphia. This had induced a profound slumber lasting nearly eighteen hours, from which the boy had awakened much refreshed.

I was, as I have said, delighted to see Carson and his son again. The mere presence of Jeremiah at our home would, I knew, serve as a revitalizing elixir for my wife, who had remained bedridden since the backyard funeral of the poisoned dog. In this expectation I was not disappointed. No sooner did Sissy set eyes on the lad than her spirits rose perceptibly—the color returned to her pallid cheeks—and she emerged from her sickbed for the first time in two days. He seemed equally thrilled to be reunited with her, throwing himself into her arms as though embracing his own lost mother.

As the downstairs portion of the house was so fraught with evil associations for the boy, it was decided that he and his father would move into our apartment. Jeremiah would sleep on the parlor sofa, while Carson (who was accustomed to slumbering on the ground) would unfurl his bedroll on the floor. This arrangement could not, of course, have been sustained for very long, our apartment being too small to comfortably accommodate so many people. It was intended to be merely temporary. Now that his mission had been accomplished and Johnson was in custody awaiting certain execution for his crimes, Carson was eager to return to the trackless wilds of his native habitat.

Sissy—seeking to delay the inevitable—urged the scout to remain in the city for at least another week, so that Jeremiah might fully recover from his ordeal before embarking on such an arduous journey. This appeal to Carson's paternal instincts could hardly be resisted, and—much to Sissy's delight—he agreed to postpone his departure.

It need hardly be said that while assisting in the hunt for Johnson, I had put aside all other pursuits, including my professional duties. Indeed, a full week had now passed since I had last been in the office of the *Broadway Journal*—a fact pointed out to me by its owner, Mr. Briggs, in a letter delivered to my home at approximately two o'clock on Thursday afternoon, the fifth of June. After praising my brilliant work on the murder case (which he had followed with keen interest in the papers), he let it be known that my skills were now desperately required at work, where production of the latest issue of the magazine had come to a virtual standstill. He further reminded me that—as a partial owner of the magazine—I owed it not only to him but to myself and my family to do everything in my power to ensure its success.

The implication of this note—i.e., that my prolonged absence might have dire financial consequences for our still-nascent undertaking—could hardly fail to inspire me with the greatest sense of urgency. Accordingly, I resolved to visit the office at once. Though the afternoon was already well advanced, there was still time for me to accomplish a certain amount of work, particularly if I remained at my desk until late in the evening (as I often had in the past). At the very least, my appearance upon the premises would serve to reassure Mr. Briggs that my energies and attention were now, once again, fully concentrated on our enterprise.

Before departing, I treated my ankles with another application of Dr. Kittredge's unguent. Though the itching sensation had, in large measure, subsided, it had not wholly disappeared. I then went to bid good-bye to my loved ones, who were cozily ensconced in the parlor—Muddy absorbed in her needlework, Sissy sketching a crayon portrait of Jeremiah, who posed cross-legged on the floor, his shoulders thrown back, his arms folded over his chest, his mother's polished bone amulet hanging once again from his neck. Only Carson, of all the members of our household, was missing. He had gone off several hours earlier on an unspecified errand from which he had yet to return.

No sooner had I emerged from our dwelling, however, than I saw him approaching from across the street, his arms laden with bundles. As he strode up the front walk, I greeted him warmly.

"Where you off to, Eddie?" he asked.

I briefly explained that—having just received a somewhat perturbing letter from my employer—I had decided to visit my workplace at once. Then, gesturing to the packages in his arms, I expressed my curiosity as to his purchases.

"Just a few things I picked up," he replied. "Gifts, mostly."

"Gifts?" I said.

"Bought a real fine jackknife for Jeremiah. He's been after me to get him one for a spell. And there's something for your auntie—a silver-handled mirror. And a pretty new parasol for Mrs. Poe."

"Why, Kit," I exclaimed. "That is exceedingly generous of you. I am certain that Muddy and Sissy will be absolutely delighted." That Carson had not merely taken it upon himself to purchase these tokens for my loved ones but had chosen such apt and feminine items was entirely consistent with what I had come to know of his character, in which manly virtue was combined with a singular delicacy of feeling.

"There's something for you, too," he continued, indicating the largest of the bundles. "New duds. Had them fitted out in a dry-goods store down on Orchard Street."

To say that I was touched by this gesture would be a gross understatement.

"There was no need for such an extravagance, my friend," I said in a voice husky with emotion.

"Oh, yes, there was," he replied with a smile.

In truth—having been subjected to an extraordinary degree of wear and tear in the course of the last, inordinately eventful week—the clothing I had loaned him had undergone a conspicuous deterioration.

The scout then went on to explain that—before embarking on his shopping expedition—he had paid a visit to the Tombs to check on the progress of the case against Johnson. Seeking out Captain Dunnegan, Carson had learned that the Liver-Eater appeared wholly indifferent to his present circumstances, adopting an attitude of defiant unconcern that Dunnegan attributed to mere bravado. Sneering at his captors, Johnson vowed that he would never be hanged and that the police would rue the day that they had arrested him. In contrast to most other accused murderers, who typically protested their innocence, Johnson appeared to revel in his guilt—freely, even gloatingly, admitting to his crimes.

"Is he, in fact, the individual named Albert Brown who, ten years ago, abducted the little daughter of the wretched woman we spoke to in St. John's Park?" I inquired.

Carson nodded. "He's the one. That poor girl was the first he ever killed. He hightailed it out of town right after. Always had a hankering to go out west. And he knew the woman's husband was on to him."

As for his more recent outrages—i.e., the slaying and cannibalization of little Annie Dobbs and Rosalie Edmonds, as well as Mrs. Whitaker—Johnson had not merely confessed to these atrocities but described them in terms so graphic as to cause even the most hardened of his interrogators to blanch.

"What about William Wyatt and C. A. Cartwright?" I asked. "I assume that he provided specific details of those murders as well."

"Matter of fact," Carson replied, "he claimed he didn't have nothing to do with those killings."

So surprising was this statement that, for a moment, I merely gaped at the scout in silent wonder. "Do you think he is telling the truth?" I asked at length.

"I doubt it," Carson said. "The truth ain't something he sets much store by. Anyways," he added with a shrug, "he'll hang one way or the other. That's the main thing, far as I'm concerned."

A moment later, the two of us parted, Carson proceeding inside the house, I making my way toward Broadway.

For reasons of both economy and daily exercise, it was my custom to walk to and from work. The hour being so late, however, I decided to travel by means of public transportation on this occasion. Boarding an omnibus at the corner of Broadway and Walker Street, I took a seat and, within seconds, was so deeply engrossed in thought that I barely noticed the violent jouncing of the vehicle as it lumbered down the busy thoroughfare.

I was deeply troubled by the information just conveyed to me by Carson. Why would Johnson deny his reponsibility for the murders of Wyatt and Cartwright? To be sure, the word of such a devious creature could hardly be trusted. Still—in view of the perverse pride he took in his evildoing—I could see no motive for such prevarication. Was it possible that he was telling the truth, and that he was innocent of those two unspeakably hideous crimes?

All at once, I recalled something anomalous I had noticed several nights earlier in the infernal squalor of Johnson's abode. The horrors of that evening— and especially the ghastly death of young George Townsend—had driven all thought of this peculiarity from my mind. Now the memory of it came rushing back with overwhelming force.

While hurrying to Jeremiah's aid, I had—as the reader will recall—observed a slender pole from which dangled the scalps of Johnson's recent victims. Even at the time, I had been struck by the fact that only *three* of these ghastly items were thus displayed—two belonging to the young females, one to Mrs. Whitaker. Where, I now wondered, were the scalps of William Wyatt and Cartwright? It seemed unlikely that Johnson would have chosen not to hang them alongside the others. It was a point of pride among the Indians (whose customs in this regard Johnson had clearly adopted) to collect and exhibit as many of these grisly trophies as possible. (Indeed, among the Creek, a brave whose war-pole held fewer than seven scalps was regarded with outright contempt.)

Could it be, then, that Wyatt and Cartwright had *not* been scalped by Johnson?

I now remembered something else. During our initial search of St. John's Park, Carson—by means of his extraordinary olfactory powers—had been able to *smell* the lingering evidence of Johnson's presence. This had not been the case, however, at either Wyatt's or Cartwright's abode. I had attributed this fact to the singularly oppressive atmospheres of these crime scenes, both of which had been thick with foul odors (cigar smoke, perspiration, blood, and—in the case of Cartwright's dwelling—feline micturition). But now another, far more unsettling, explanation suggested itself—perhaps Johnson had not been present at either place!

And what of the priceless document that I had been hired to authenticate? I was firmly convinced that Wyatt's killer had been in search of this mysterious paper. Was it likely that such a rarefied item would hold any interest for Liver-Eating Johnson—a brute who seemed driven solely by a lust for bloodshed and torture, and an unholy taste for human flesh?

Taken together, these considerations pointed to a startling conclusion. William Wyatt and C. A. Cartwright had not, in fact, been slain by Johnson. They had been murdered—as I now believed—by another, still-unknown killer, who had evidently carried out his crimes with inordinate savagery in order to deflect suspicion from himself and cast it upon the person of the Liver-Eater!

But who could this killer *be*?

It *must*, I reasoned, have been someone with whom Wyatt was on familiar, if not intimate, terms. For one thing, the killer had clearly known of the existence of the secret document. For another (as Carson had deduced), he had freely entered Wyatt's abode through the front door.

But how did C. A. Cartwright fit into the picture? As Captain Dunnegan had suggested, the only apparent connection between the two victims was their relationship to—*me*. If this was the case, then the killer had to be someone who was both closely acquainted with Wyatt and familiar enough with my own work to know of my feud with Cartwright.

Was there anyone I knew of who met these criteria?

When the answer hit me, I must have emitted an audible gasp; for I soon became aware that the other passengers were staring at me with curious expressions.

Quickly I turned my head and peered out the window. I had intended to ride the omnibus all the way down Broadway to my office. Perceiving, however, that we were close to Maiden Lane, I sprang to my feet and, urging the driver to stop, leapt from the omnibus and began to run.

Chapter Twenty-Six

I T HAS OFTEN BEEN NOTED that proverbial sayings are no less valid for being clichés. This was certainly the case with the age-old observation that "a book cannot be judged by its cover"—a truism I had blithely ignored in regard to Harry Pratt, the young law clerk who had served as William Wyatt's reader, and whom Carson and I had so badly affrighted during our search of the latter's abode.

It was not merely Pratt's spindly physique and fainthearted demeanor that had so misled me (as I now believed). I had also been deceived by his bookish inclinations and almost childlike enthusiasm for my own writings. How could a young man so physically unimposing—so timorous—so astute in his literary judgments—be capable of savage, unspeakable murder?

And yet—assuming that I was correct in inferring the existence of a second, still-unknown killer—who besides Pratt so perfectly matched the conception I had formed of this malefactor: i.e., someone with both ready access to Wyatt's residence and sufficient familiarity with my own work to be aware of the animosity between C. A. Cartwright and myself?

Still, I could not be absolutely certain of Pratt's guilt without further confirmation. My plan, therefore, was to seek him out at his place of employment and, by means of a subtle line of questioning, trap him into making some admission that would reveal his culpability for the crimes.

From comments made by both Wyatt and Pratt himself, I recalled that the young clerk worked for an attorney named Lowe whose offices were located on Maiden Lane. Making my way along this narrow, exceedingly crooked street, I soon spied a somewhat dingy, three-story, brick building whose front was adorned with a string of small wooden signs listing the occupations of the inhabitants. Along with shingles for George Bridges Brown, matrimonial agent—W. W. Young, boardinghouse broker—Henry Wisch, dentist—J. P. Ludlow, dealer in engravings—Myron Burt, watchmaker—and a half-dozen others was one that read ALEXANDER LOWE, ESQ., COUNSELOR AT LAW.

Hurrying up the staircase, I soon found myself in a cramped—musty—poorly lit office occupied by a stout, middle-aged fellow whom I took to be the proprietor. He was seated at a desk whose top was buried under a mountainous pile of papers. Hunched on a stool at a writing table nearby was an ancient copyist who—quill in hand—was laboring over a document, the steady scratching of his quill the only noise to be heard in the otherwise tomblike silence of the room.

No one else was present. Gazing around, I saw—in a far corner of the office—another, smaller desk littered with papers and books. The slat-back chair behind the desk was vacant.

Introducing myself to Lowe as an acquaintance of Pratt's, I inquired as to the whereabouts of his clerk.

"Wish I knew," said Lowe, his not unpleasing features wrought into an expression of mild concern. "He didn't show up for work this morning. To be frank, I'm a little worried about the lad. It's not like him to miss a day of work without getting word to me."

"Perhaps he has fallen ill," I suggested.

"Possible, entirely possible," said Lowe. "He hasn't been himself lately."

"How so?" I inquired.

"Hard to describe, exactly. Something's been weighing on his mind. Wouldn't you say so, Milbourne?" This latter query was addressed to the ancient scrivener, who had not paused in his copying since my entrance.

"Indeed I would, Mr. Lowe, sir," the latter responded in a voice as desiccated and whispery as the rustle of autumn leaves. "Weighing mighty heavily."

"Perhaps I shall go to his home and look in on him," I suggested.

"Capital idea," said Lowe. "Thought of sending Milbourne to check on the lad, but the old fellow's not much use for running errands these days. Lucky just to make it up the stairs in the morning, eh, Milbourne?"

"Yes, sir, Mr. Lowe," said the exceedingly wizened scrivener. "Very lucky indeed."

Having introduced myself as Pratt's acquaintance, I now found myself in an awkward position, for I had not the least idea as to where the young clerk lived.

"It has been so long since I have visited Harry at home that I have forgotten his precise address," I said in an embarrassed tone, hoping that the lawyer would not find this ostensible lapse of memory suspicious.

Lowe, however, merely replied that the young man rented an apartment at Number 48 Gold Street, within easy walking distance of the office.

"As long as you're on the way there, would you mind taking that book along?" he added, motioning to the unoccupied desk. Following his gesture, I saw that he was pointing to a slender volume bound in green morocco that rested atop a small pile of papers on the center of the desk.

"If the lad *is* sick, it's sure to perk him up," Lowe continued. "You should see him at lunchtime. Sits there nibbling away on a sandwich and chuckling madly over every line."

Crossing the room, I picked up the volume and, opening to its title page, saw that it was the edition of Samuel Butler's *Hudibras* that young Pratt had come to retrieve from Wyatt's home the previous week. I was about to close the book again when my gaze fell upon a small engraved plate pasted to the inside front cover. "*Ex libris* L. Harrison Pratt," it read.

"L. Harrison Pratt?" I wondered aloud.

"Why, yes. That's the lad's full name. The *L* stands for Lochinvar. Damned silly thing to call a child, if you ask me. I suppose Harry feels that way, too, which is why he doesn't use it."

"His father must have been an enthusiast of the work of Sir Walter Scott," I replied in a musing tone. "The name, as I assume you are aware, is that of the gallant young knight in the latter's stirring, if sadly outdated, poem *Marmion*."

"Yes, I expect you're right," said Lowe. "Amazing what some folks will christen their offspring. Why, I once had a client named Plotinus Plinlimmon. Would you believe it?"

"I once knew a chap named Ben Dover," the ancient scrivener interposed.

"No!" cried Lowe. "Ben Dover? Ha-ha!"

Politely excusing myself at this juncture, I hurried from the office and down onto the street.

As I bent my steps toward Pratt's dwelling-place, my thoughts were wholly occupied with the fact I had just learned. During our search of William Wyatt's residence—as the reader will recall—Carson had discovered a tiny scrap of paper among the ashes in the hearth. We had been able to discern the inscription "Lo" upon this badly charred fragment. Was it possible, I now wondered, that these letters were the beginning of Pratt's baptismal name? If so, only one deduction seemed logical: that the incinerated document contained incriminating information about the young clerk which he had sought to obliterate; and that Wyatt—who had presumably been aware of this information from perusing the document—had been killed for the same reason, i.e., to ensure that Pratt's secret was never exposed.

Less than five minutes later, I arrived at Pratt's address. This was a four-storied brick edifice that, to judge from its appearance, had at one time been the private residence of a wealthy owner. Now—like many of the buildings in that once-fashionable but now distinctly *passé* neighborhood—it had been subdivided into numerous apartments which were rented by tenants of limited means.

As I did not know which of the rooms was occupied by Pratt, I was under the necessity of knocking on several doors before I found an elderly woman who was able to direct me to the third floor, where "the dear sweet boy" (as she called him) resided in apartment number 15. Making my way up the stairwell (which was pervaded by the heavy aroma of cooking, the reek of boiled cabbage being predominant), I quickly located the young clerk's chambers and rapped sharply on the door.

When no one responded, I tried again, but with the same fruitless results. My disappointment was intense at finding that Pratt was, evidently, not at home after all. On impulse, I tried the doorknob. To my surprise, it proved to be unlocked.

Slowly opening the door, I leaned in my head and called out: "Hello. Is anyone here?"

No one replied.

Swiftly stepping inside, I closed the door behind me and cast my gaze about. The entire apartment consisted of a single, exceedingly meager room. There was no carpet on the floor; no picture on the wall; nothing to relieve the general impression of extreme—almost Spartan—austerity. The sole furnishings were a narrow, neatly made-up bed—a rudimentary bookcase fashioned from rough-hewn oak boards and bricks, and containing several dozen leather-bound volumes—an ancient mahogany chair—and a rickety writing table holding an inkstand, several quills, a penknife, and a slender journal bound in marbled paper. The chamber was unmistakably that of a young bachelor of ascetic habits and a literary bent, whose only indulgence was the acquisition of books for his burgeoning personal library.

That the apartment door was unfastened suggested one of two likely expla-
nations. Since Pratt owned nothing worth stealing apart from his books (and
even these were of value only to a fellow bibliophile), he saw no need to lock
his door. Alternatively, he had merely gone off on a brief errand and could be
expected to return momentarily.

Seizing the opportunity to investigate my suspicions concerning the young
clerk, I stepped to the writing table and—after laying down the copy of
Hudibras—picked up the journal and raised its front cover. Immediately, the
pages fell open of themselves to a place near the center of the volume. I was
startled to perceive dark, crimson smudges on the margins of the facing leaves,
as if someone with bloodied fingertips had been perusing this very portion.

Casting my gaze down the page, I quickly came upon the following passage,
dated the previous March 14th:

> Last night, Mr. Wyatt received another visit from his mysterious caller—
> the handsome, wavy-haired stranger with the jagged facial scar that some-
> how only enhances his dashing appearance. As soon as the latter showed up,
> Mr. Wyatt—to whom I was in the midst of reading the latest installment of
> Mr. Dickens's *Martin Chuzzlewit*—requested me to step outside the library.
> Naturally, I did as I was asked. Curiosity, however, drove me to place my ear
> to the keyhole and eavesdrop. I am ashamed to admit such *sneaking* behav-
> ior, even to the privacy of my journal, but honesty compels me to confess it.
>
> Though I could not make out *all* that was said, I did get the gist of their
> conversation. The stranger had brought Mr. Wyatt a letter, evidently written
> by the same hand that composed the precious document to which Mr. Wyatt
> has alluded to in my presence. Heaven knows what this document is! It ap-
> pears—to judge by the terms in which I have overheard Mr. Wyatt refer to
> it—to be absolutely priceless, less, perhaps, in regard to its monetary value
> than in relation to Mr. Wyatt's passionate political beliefs, especially con-
> cerning the great evil of slavery.
>
> I gathered that the dark-haired stranger had somehow contrived to get
> hold of the letter by illicit means. At all events, Mr. Wyatt was greatly excited
> to have it in his possession. All he now needed, he declared, was to find
> someone who could authenticate the document by comparing its script to
> the handwriting on the letter. Once the authorship of the document was
> proved beyond a doubt, he exclaimed, "our cause will be in possession of a
> powerful weapon to combat the barbaric prejudices of our foes!"

By the time I had reached the end of this entry, my heart was palpitating
with excitement. Though frustrating in its lack of specifics—particularly in

regard to the whereabouts of the mysterious document—the passage still shed light on several key points.

To begin with, I now knew something of the nature of the document—to wit, that it bore a vital relation to the issue of Negro slavery. That Wyatt had been a confirmed abolitionist was unsurprising. Even during our single, brief encounter, he had forcefully expressed his abhorrence of bigotry. I recalled, too, the copy of William Lloyd Garrison's abolitionist publication, *The Liberator*, that I had found while searching his residence. Judging by the remark recorded in Pratt's journal, it was clear that Wyatt strongly believed that the mysterious document would be an invaluable boon to that fiery cause.

Mazeppa's *rôle* in the affair had also been clarified by the young clerk's journal. Evidently, the lion-tamer had managed to obtain a handwriting specimen, in the form of a personal letter, that could be used to establish the authenticity of the document.

Where, I wondered, would he have found such an article? The most probable explanation—and one which conformed to Pratt's supposition that Mazeppa had employed "illicit means"—was that he had surreptitiously removed it from the collection of rare historical papers kept in the basement of Barnum's museum. As the reader will recall, the showman had referred to such an archive during our conversation several days before.

That Harry Pratt (contrary to his earlier disavowals) knew of the existence of the priceless document was indisputable. Even so, I no longer believed that he was the killer of Wyatt and Cartwright. Any youth of such punctilious conscience as to feel a qualm of guilt over a minor act of eavesdropping could not possibly have been the perpetrator of two unspeakably hideous murders.

For all the knowledge I had gleaned from the journal, however, the most urgent mysteries remained unresolved—what and where was the document? And who butchered Wyatt and Cartwright?

The answer to the first of these riddles, I felt, might help unlock the others. Accordingly, I resolved to proceed to Barnum's museum at once. My reasoning was thus: The letter purloined by Mazeppa was penned by the same illustrious individual who composed Wyatt's document. If, therefore, I could find out precisely which letter was missing from the showman's collection, the identity of this personage would be revealed. Armed with this vital clue, I might then be able to deduce the content of the mysterious document.

Replacing the journal on the writing table beside the copy of *Hudibras*, I turned to leave. As I did so, my gaze lit upon something I had not previously noted.

Directly across the room from the writing table was the door of what appeared to be a narrow closet. The floorboards beneath this door were stained with a reddish-brown substance that had evidently leaked from inside the closet, and that bore an unmistakable resemblance to dried blood.

Seized with a sudden premonitory chill, I stepped across the room—placed my trembling hand around the glass knob—and yanked the door open.

A shriek of delirious horror burst from my lips as a naked male body tumbled from inside the closet and collapsed onto the floor.

Violently quaking in every limb, I stared down at the unclothed figure sprawled lifelessly at my feet. It was young Harry Pratt, his hands tightly bound behind his back. He had been subjected to a species of torture so grisly—so vicious—so sheerly appalling that, for several moments, my reeling brain refused to accept the evidence of my senses.

His organs of generation had been utterly excised. The area between his legs was unnaturally smooth and heavily smeared with a coating of gore. Hideous as this mutilation was, however, an even more grotesque atrocity had been perpetrated upon him.

The severed parts had been stuffed into his mouth.

CHAPTER TWENTY-SEVEN

A WAVE OF SICKNESS threatened to engulf me. My breast heaved—my knees tottered. I felt the strength drain from my limbs.

Squeezing my eyelids tight so as to shut out the inconceivably hideous spectacle sprawled at my feet, I struggled to keep oblivion at bay. I could not permit myself to fall into a swoon.

Slowly, I reopened my eyes. Keeping my gaze averted from the young clerk's outraged corpse, I staggered from the room—down the staircase—and out onto the street. For a moment, I leaned heavily against the rough brick façade of the building, drawing in deep, hungry draughts of the bracing outside air.

At length, my dizziness subsided. I knew that the police ought to be notified of my discovery—but more urgent business was at hand. My worst suspicions had been confirmed. A second killer, no less barbaric than Liver-Eating Johnson himself, was at large in the city. Not a minute was to be lost in the effort to identify this inhuman fiend.

Turning, I hurried in the direction of Barnum's establishment, where, I felt sure, the answer to the mystery would be found.

A short time later, I came in sight of the museum. As I strode up to the front entrance, who should emerge but the showman himself, attired somewhat more formally than usual. He wore a new beaver hat, a frock coat of the finest black cloth, and striped kerseymeyer pantaloons. In one hand he held his highly polished ebony walking stick, topped with a brass head in the shape of a trumpeting elephant. Though he appeared to be in a great hurry, he came to an abrupt halt upon seeing me and exclaimed:

"Poe, m'boy! Lord bless you—is everything all right? Why, you look as if you've seen a ghost."

"I have, indeed, been exposed to a sight more appalling than the fearful apparition encountered by Prince Hamlet upon the ramparts of Elsinore castle," I replied.

"You don't say!" exclaimed the showman. "Heavens, that sounds ominous— mighty ominous, indeed. Tell you what, m'boy. I'm eager to hear all about it— immensely so. Trouble is, I'm dreadfully late for an appointment. Baron Poniatowski's in town. He's got a little business proposition on hand—wants me to put some capital into it—and I tell you, m'boy, I could do worse, I could do a deal worse. Perhaps you and I can rendezvous back here in, say, an hour or so?"

"Very well," I replied. "Before you rush off, however, permit me to ask one question. During our previous conversation in your Hall of American History, you alluded to a basement storage closet in which you house your archives of rare documents. To the best of your knowledge, is anything missing from this room?"

At this query, the showman's eyes grew wide.

"Great Scot, Poe, but you're a wonder—an absolute wonder! How in the world did you know? Why, it's as if you possess occult powers of the mind! Puts Madame Sosostris, my world-celebrated Rumanian clairvoyant, to shame!"

"Then one of the papers *has* been removed by an unauthorized person?"

"Discovered it just yesterday," said the showman. "First time in months I've been down there. Went looking for a replacement for my looted Declaration of Independence, when I realized something was missing. Couldn't believe it at first. Turned the place upside down. But it was gone—vanished—*poof!*—like a disappearing dove in the Amazing Presto's internationally acclaimed conjuring act! Horrible loss, simply devastating! This wasn't one of your phony imitations, either—not that you'll find anything the least bit fraudulent at P. T. Barnum's museum, mind you—but an actual bona fide letter written by President Thomas Jefferson himself! Acquired it a few years back from a collector in Philadelphia. Cost me next to nothing. Poor fellow was desperate for cash— wife ill, business failing, creditors hounding him night and day. Tragic situation, perfectly heart-wrenching. Worked out nicely for me, though. Got it for a song. Splendid item—absolutely choice! All about the Louisiana Purchase."

This statement brought a number of realizations thronging to my mind. I recalled my first and only meeting with Wyatt, at the conclusion of which he had queried me about my personal knowledge of Jefferson and my familiarity with the latter's *Notes on Virginia*. Given Wyatt's singular interest in our third president, it made perfect sense that the purloined letter should have been written by that illustrious figure.

It also seemed clear that it was this very letter whose residue was found in Wyatt's fireplace. I had been wrong to assume that this incinerated paper bore some relation to Pratt. In view of what Barnum had just revealed, I was now firmly convinced that the fragment of writing I had discerned on the charred scrap—"Lo"—referred not (as I had previously surmised) to the name Lochinvar but to the word "Louisiana."

Something else now occurred to me—something that struck me as exceedingly curious. All three men with knowledge of the stolen letter had come to inordinately violent ends. Wyatt and Pratt had been hideously butchered. Mazeppa had also been horribly killed. In his case, however, his death had been the result of a random accident.

Or had it?

"I have no wish to detain you any longer than is necessary," I remarked to the showman, who was anxiously consulting his pocket watch. "But there is one final question I must put to you before you depart. It concerns the death of your celebrated lion-tamer, Mazeppa. Are you aware of any peculiar circumstances surrounding his tragic demise?"

"Only that it happened at all," said the showman, snapping his timepiece shut and replacing it in his vest pocket. "It's just as I told you a few days ago. Old Ajax—the beast that did him in—was the most good-natured creature that ever lived. Why, I've known house cats with nastier dispositions! He *did* make a funny noise, from what I hear, just before chomping down on poor Mazeppa—a coughing sound or something of the sort."

"Strange," I said, frowning thoughtfully. "George Townsend, who witnessed the incident, mentioned something similar."

"You don't say?" Barnum remarked. "Well, I'm intrigued, immensely intrigued. At the moment, however, I really must be going. The baron's a military man, you know—military to the backbone! Doesn't stand for any sort of tardiness. And there's a tidy little sum riding on this deal. Whole oceans of money, gulfs and bays thrown in! Tell you what, m'boy. Let's you and I have a little powwow when I return."

"Very well," I said. "In the meantime, I trust that you will not object if I wait for you inside the museum."

"Not in the least!" said Barnum, hurrying off. "Make yourself at home!" An instant later, he had disappeared around the corner of Ann Street.

Passing into the museum—which still had not reopened for business—I mounted to the fifth floor, my footsteps echoing loudly as I ascended the marble staircase. My intention was to reexamine the exhibit devoted to the late Mazeppa, in the hope of finding some clue I had previously overlooked.

Arrived at the Grand Taxidermical Salon, I crossed the threshold of the vast, gloomy hall and proceeded directly to the circular wooden platform where, nearly a week earlier, I had stood with George Townsend.

Shaking off the sorrowful sensation that immediately descended upon my soul at the memory of that worthy young man, I concentrated my full attention upon the display. As I have previously described, its central feature was a singularly lifelike re-creation of the moment when—an instant after Mazeppa inserted his head into the gaping maw of Ajax—the great beast closed its jaws, utterly crushing the skull of its trainer. A wax replica of the latter, bearing an uncanny resemblance to the living man, was arranged in a kneeling position before the taxidermically mounted figure of the lion. The manikin was garbed in the actual costume worn by Mazeppa when the tragedy occurred. The copious bloodstains covering the shoulders and running down the back and chest of this garment vividly attested to the severity of the injury he had sustained.

Along with this tableau, the exhibit featured a number of Mazeppa's possessions displayed on shelves, including—very prominently—the unguent he had used on his famously beautiful locks: Major Meecham's Excelsior Hair Cream.

I had previously viewed this exhibit from the vantage point of any other spectator. Now I stepped over the low wooden railing and climbed onto the platform for a closer look.

By all accounts, Mazeppa had performed his thrilling feat countless times without incident. What, I wondered, had caused the lion to bite down on his trainer on this occasion? And what, if anything, was the significance of the strange noise reported by several observers, including George Townsend?

For many minutes, I stood staring at the tableau while meditatively pinching my lower lip between my right thumb and forefinger.

The artisan who sculpted the wax replica of Mazeppa had outfitted the figure with an exceedingly realistic-looking wig, clearly fashioned from actual human hair. A thick coating of Major Meecham's cream had evidently been applied to the lush—wavy—jet-black tresses, which—even in the dim illumination of the hall—possessed a distinct, a brilliant, *sheen*.

I shifted my gaze to the visage of the lion. As I studied the creature, I was struck by the way in which the taxidermist had arranged its features: nostrils flared—mouth agape—lips drawn back—eyes narrowed into slits. Though the intent had evidently been to endow it with an expression of extreme ferocity, the result had been nearly the opposite—for the beast bore a strong, almost comical, resemblance to a man about to let forth a thunderous *sneeze.*

At that instant, a strange—a *startling*—notion flashed upon my mind.

Stepping over the kneeling manikin, I reached up and removed the jar of hair cream from the display shelf, opened the lid, raised the glass container close to my face, and inhaled deeply.

Immediately, a powerful sneeze erupted from my nose!

I tried the experiment again—with the same convulsive result.

By this point, my heart was pounding wildly. Dipping a forefinger into the jar, I removed a small quantity of the concoction and rubbed it between my thumb and the tip of my first digit.

The cream had a peculiar, granular texture, wholly inconsistent with the normal consistency of such *pomades.* Holding my breath—so as not to inhale any of the sneeze-inducing substance—I held the jar close to my face and scrutinized it closely. The reader will readily imagine my reaction when I perceived—mixed into the white cream—a fine brownish powder the nature of which I recognized at once.

It was *snuff*!

A cry of amazement burst from my lips. My intuition had been proven correct! Mazeppa's death had not been an accident but a diabolically contrived murder! Someone had deliberately mixed a quantity of snuff into his hair cream prior to his act, knowing full well the effect it would produce when the performer placed his head directly beneath the nostrils of the great beast. The sound that George Townsend and other observers had noted was not a growl or a cough—but a sneeze!

But who had been responsible for this inexpressibly evil—this *fiendish*—deed? A vague recollection stirred within my mind. Someone to whom I had recently spoken had offered me snuff. Desperately, I cudgeled my brain in an effort to recall the identity of this personage.

When, at length, the answer struck me, I gasped and cried aloud: "Good Lord!"

At that instant, I was startled to hear a voice behind me—a shrill, nasal voice, speaking in an intensely sneering tone:

"I told you he wasn't no dummy."

I spun about. My sense of wonder was extreme when I saw, standing a short distance away, at the foot of the display, the very personage whose identity I had just deduced:

Monsieur Vox!

He was carrying his wooden alter-ego, Archibald, who was seated upon the ventriloquist's open left hand. Vox's opposite hand was hidden behind the back of the puppet. I was struck anew by the uncanny resemblance between the human being and the manikin, both of whom wore identical looks of devilish amusement.

"Bravo, Mr. Poe, bravo," said the ventriloquist. "Yes, it was a mere sneeze that did the Great Mazeppa in, poor fellow."

"I guess Shakespeare would say it was much achoo about nothing, eh Voxie?" sneered the dummy. Though the intensely grating voice of the manikin appeared to be emanating from inside its throat, its mouth, oddly enough, did not move at all—as though Vox's concealed hand was not working the mechanism that controlled the motions of its jaw.

Ignoring his dummy's somewhat *labored* pun, the ventriloquist addressed me thusly: "Of course, it comes as no surprise to me that you have figured out how Mazeppa met his sad end. I expect nothing less than brilliance from the mind that conceived of 'The Raven.' That's why I've gone to so much trouble to protect you."

"Protect me?" I said. "How so?"

"By killing Mr. C. A. Cartwright, for one thing," said Vox.

"But that gentleman meant me no physical harm," said I. "He merely intended to sue me."

"Really?" exclaimed Vox. "Well, how was *I* to know? You seemed quite certain that he had hired someone to run you down with a fire engine—at least that's what you told the young reporter who came looking for you the other day."

Casting my thoughts back to that occasion, I recalled that—immediately after Townsend's arrival—the ventriloquist had excused himself, presumably to attend to other business. Evidently, however, he had hidden himself behind one of the painted backdrops—eavesdropped on our conversation—then proceeded directly to Cartwright's abode and perpetrated his grisly crime.

"But why have you been so solicitous of my safety?" I inquired.

"Because I've been hoping that your stellar mind will lead me to the thing I covet most—Mr. Wyatt's oh-so-precious document. As you have no doubt surmised, my efforts to learn its whereabouts from either Wyatt or his little flunky, Pratt, have been notably unsuccessful."

"In spite of the unspeakable torture you inflicted on those unfortunate beings," I declared.

"Yes," Vox replied with a cruel smile. "The one refused to talk, the other did not know. Of course, my little torments served another purpose as well."

"To throw the police off your own track," I said, "by making it appear that these outrages were committed by Carson's brutish adversary, Johnson."

"Exactly so," said Vox. "When those two little girls were found butchered and scalped, it became clear that a madman was at large. I decided to copy his methods as a smokescreen. Of course, I couldn't resist adding a few flourishes of my own."

"I presume," said I, "that you are referring to the fact that—unlike Johnson's atrocities—each of your own murders involved the victim's organs of speech. Wyatt's tongue was excised—Cartwright's was yanked through the gaping wound in his throat and left there to dangle like a neckerchief—while Pratt's mouth was stuffed with his own severed genitalia."

"Very good, Mr. Poe," said Vox in a tone of keen self-satisfaction. "Yes, that was a little improvisation of my own. A bit of artistic embellishment from Monsieur Vox, the Master of Vocalization!"

Whatever doubts I may have harbored about the ventriloquist's sanity were, by this point, thoroughly dispelled. Though his sincere appreciation of my own poetic genius bespoke a sound aesthetic judgment, his *moral* faculties were hopelessly impaired. In spite of his apparently rational demeanor, it was now abundantly clear that Vox was a desperately deranged individual.

"I take it that mimicry is another of your vocal gifts," I said. "A neighbor of Wyatt's reported that—on the afternoon of the murder—he called on the latter and briefly conversed with him through the closed front door. Am I correct in assuming that the voice which he heard—and which he swore was identical to Wyatt's—was actually your own?"

"Indeed it was," chuckled Vox, appearing inordinately pleased with himself. "Few men can match the magnificent Monsieur Vox when it comes to the art of vocal simulation!"

"Oh, you ain't so hot as all that," scoffed Archibald. "Bet you can't imitate *my* voice!"

Once more, I was struck by the strange immobility of the dummy's mouth, which remained utterly stationary as he spoke.

"Quiet, Archie," scolded Vox. "Enough of your foolishness. And now, Mr. Poe, it's *your* turn to do a little vocalizing. I want you to tell me right now where I can find Wyatt's document."

"I fear you have overestimated my investigative abilities," I said. "I have no idea as to its whereabouts. Indeed, I am ignorant even as to its precise nature. From information just conveyed to me by Mr. Barnum, I assume that its author was Thomas Jefferson. Beyond that, I know nothing."

Narrowing his eyes, Vox studied me intently for a moment before addressing me thusly:

"Have you ever heard of Sally Hemings?"

"Why, yes," I replied. "She was the beauteous Negro slave with whom—according to the whispers of his political enemies—Thomas Jefferson was in love. Their purported relationship lasted nearly forty years and supposedly produced a number of illegitimate offspring."

All at once, the full implication of the ventriloquist's query struck me with overwhelming force. "Do you mean to suggest," I said, "that the document of which you have been in such dogged—and deadly—pursuit relates, in some way, to the scandalous rumors concerning Jefferson's illicit liaison with this female?"

"Unfortunately, they weren't mere rumors," said Vox, his voice suddenly taking on a tone of extreme bitterness. "Yes, Mr. Poe. That's exactly what I mean. The document is a page from Thomas Jefferson's personal diary that substantiates, beyond any shadow of a doubt, his disgusting entanglement with that black-skinned harlot."

The vituperative manner in which Vox spewed out these words brought to mind the equally disparaging way in which he had referred to Othello during our earlier conversation. Clearly, the ventriloquist bore no great love for the Negro race.

I now understood, moreover, why William Wyatt—whose sympathies *were* on the side of that oppressed people—would have regarded such a document as a powerful weapon in the abolitionist cause. To prove that the revered Jefferson—author of our nation's most cherished political document, the Declaration of Independence—had not merely been in love with a female slave but had sired several progeny by her would lend enormous moral weight to the arguments of those in favor of recognizing the full humanity of the Negro.

"Am I correct in assuming," I said, "that you wish to get hold of this exceedingly significant page in order to suppress its contents?"

"Suppress?" cried Vox. "Why, I mean to wipe all trace of it from the face of the earth! To destroy it utterly! And to destroy everyone with knowledge of its existence. I've already taken care of most of them. Beginning with someone you yourself have some connection to—the former tenant of your present rooms, Mr. Devereaux."

"Devereaux!" I exclaimed, recalling that it was this gentleman who had first provided Mr. Wyatt with the precious document. "I was under the impression that he had absconded overseas."

"Overseas?" Vox said with a snort. "No. He is beneath the water, not across it. In little pieces."

Shuddering at the sheer cold-bloodedness of this remark, I said: "But how did that gentleman first come into possession of the page?"

"No idea," replied Vox with a shrug. "Apparently, he got his hands on it while traveling through the South some years back. Devereaux was the worst sort of scoundrel—utterly unprincipled. Only cared about money. I don't know how much the albino paid for the page, but I'm sure it was a pretty penny. Of course, Wyatt couldn't reveal its contents until he had established its absolute authenticity. So he enlisted the help of his fellow abolitionist, Thomas Dudley—better known as the Great Mazeppa. Mazeppa 'borrowed' one of Jefferson's letters concerning the Louisiana Purchase from Barnum's collection. The idea was to have a handwriting expert—you, my dear Poe— compare the script on the two papers. I learned all this from Mazeppa himself. We were good friends, as you know. He assumed I shared his political views— a belief I encouraged in him until I had extracted the necessary information."

"And then you murdered him by mixing a quantity of your snuff into his hair cream right before one of his performances," I said.

"Yes," said Vox. "I'm particularly proud of that little stratagem. I knew what would happen when the big lion inhaled a snootful of my sneeze-powder. Worked like a charm, too."

"But why did you burn the letter about the Louisiana Purchase?"

"To torment Wyatt. I made him watch while I set a match to it and tossed it into his fireplace. I wanted him to see, before he died, what would become of his precious diary page when I finally got hold of it.

"Well, Mr. Poe," he continued, his countenance suddenly assuming an exceptionally menacing look. "I have obliged you by answering all of your questions. Now you will oblige me by answering mine. I ask you for the last time—where is the document?"

"But I do not know!" I cried.

"Too bad," said Vox, removing his concealed right hand from behind the dummy. I now saw why the manikin's mouth had not moved while speaking.

The ventriloquist's hand had not been operating the mechanism that operated the puppet's mouth.

Instead, it had been clutching a pistol, whose barrel was now pointed directly at my heart!

"You are absolutely certain that you don't know?" Vox asked, setting the manikin down on the wooden platform while keeping the weapon carefully aimed at my bosom.

"If I did, I would most certainly tell you," I said, my voice quavering slightly.

"Then you will go the way of Devereaux, Wyatt, and Mazeppa!" cried the maddened ventriloquist. "Those Benedict Arnolds—those traitors to their race!"

All at once, I was struck with a realization that hit me with the force of a physical blow.

"Wait!" I shouted. "Do not fire! A thought has just occurred to me! I may, in fact, have deduced the location of the page you seek!"

"Where is it?" demanded Vox, glaring at me with a crazed intensity.

"On Wyatt's person!" I exclaimed. "Buried with him in the graveyard!"

Chapter Twenty-Eight

I N ADDITION TO HIS OTHER, more obvious peculiarities—his snow-white skin and hair, rabbit-pink eyes, and other albino traits—Wyatt (as the reader may recall) had been sporting footwear that struck me as highly anomalous during his visit to my home. In spite of his inordinately tall and slender physique, his boots had been equipped with heels of an exaggerated—and seemingly superfluous—height.

It was Vox's invocation of Benedict Arnold that caused me to realize, for the first time, the true significance of those oddly proportioned shoes. Just several days earlier, while speaking to Barnum outside his Hall of American History, I had noted a display case containing the actual boots belonging to the arch-traitor. These had been outfitted with tall—deceptively designed—hollow heels in which Major Arnold had smuggled military secrets on behalf of the enemy. The appearance of these cunningly constructed boots, I now realized, precisely matched that of the footwear worn by Wyatt!

Without lowering his pistol, whose barrel was still pointed directly at my heart, Vox now exclaimed: "The graveyard? What the devil do you mean?"

Quickly, I explained to the ventriloquist the mental association I had just made between the singular construction of Wyatt's boots and the historic pair in Barnum's collection.

"When I arrived at Wyatt's abode on the evening of the murder," I continued, "the poor man was still clinging to life, albeit barely. As I held him in my arms, he managed to utter a noise that sounded like 'he'—though the ghastly mutilation inflicted on his mouth made the word difficult to hear. I assumed that he was employing the masculine pronoun in an effort to identify his killer. An instant later, his right foot began to shake convulsively, as though he had been seized with his death throes. I now believe, however, that he was attempting—through both his utterance and the violent motion of his foot— to direct my attention to the heel of his right boot!"

"So *that's* where it was," muttered Vox. "Safely tucked inside a phony heel. Sneaky bastard. But how do you know it's in the grave with him?"

"I have deduced as much from the published newspaper accounts of Wyatt's funeral, which clearly stated that the victim was interred in the clothes in which he was found murdered."

For a moment, Vox mulled over this intelligence.

"You may put down your gun now, Monsieur Vox," I continued, nervously eyeing the weapon which remained leveled at my bosom. "There is no need to worry any longer about the missing page. It is, for all intents and purposes, lost forever, and can no longer serve the cause to which you are so fanatically opposed."

"Forgive me for questioning your logic, Mr. Poe," replied the ventriloquist. "No one respects your brilliance more than I. But what if you're wrong? What if it *isn't* concealed in Wyatt's boot? I cannot take the chance that it might be floating around somewhere in the world."

"But what choice do you have?" I said. "After all, there is no way to prove absolutely that the page is where I believe it to be."

"Oh, but there is," said Vox with a smile so grim as to chill the very marrow of my bones. "There most certainly is."

Less than one hour later, I found myself passing on foot through the wrought-iron gate of a small, isolated cemetery situated in the rural hinterland of the city, north of Eighty-fourth Street.

We had traveled most of the way to this dreary—this *desolate*—spot by means of a hack. Keeping his gun tightly pressed against my back, Vox had marched me out of the museum, then secured a cab, instructing the driver to take us with all possible dispatch to the Bloomingdale Road. During our journey, the ventriloquist had—with no prodding on my part—volunteered further details about the content of the incendiary diary page. In it, Jefferson had confessed to having entered into an amorous relation with the beauteous young slave while living in Paris during his tenure as minister to France in

1789. The immediate result of this union was a child named Tom, who had perished shortly after birth. In succeeding years, following Jefferson's return to America, his Negro paramour had given birth to five additional offspring—all sired by the master of Monticello—four of whom had survived into adulthood.

As Vox recounted this tale, his voice grew increasingly bitter. From the sheer virulence of his tone, it was clear that he regarded miscegenation as a crime far more abominable than the atrocities he himself had committed and which he appeared to regard (in the manner of all inveterate villains) as justified by a higher necessity.

While Vox spewed forth his invective, my mind raced with thoughts of my own predicament. The freedom with which the ventriloquist had revealed the details of the diary page filled me with dread. By his own admission, he had already meted out ghastly deaths to everyone who knew of the content of the exceedingly controversial document, beginning with the former tenant of my abode, Mr. Devereaux. That he intended to deal with me in the same manner—once I had finished serving the grim purpose he had in store for me—could hardly be doubted.

And yet, I saw no means to effect my own deliverance. To leap from the carriage as it galloped north along Broadway would undoubtedly prove fatal. If Vox did not manage to fire off a shot as I lunged for the door, I would almost certainly suffer grave injuries from the fall. To attempt to alert the driver was out of the question. Any cries for help would be drowned out by the clatter of the hoofbeats and the rumble of the wheels. I might try to throw myself at Vox and grapple for the gun. But with the hammer cocked—his finger on the trigger—and the barrel pointed at my heart—such a desperate measure was almost sure to lead to my instant demise.

The best stratagem, I finally concluded, was to bide my time and await a better opportunity to overpower the ventriloquist and effect my escape.

To ensure that there would be no witnesses to our ghoulish undertaking, Vox had directed the driver to leave us at a spot in the vicinity of Seventieth Street. Once we dismounted and the carriage had turned and disappeared around a bend in the densely tree-lined road, we proceeded to hike the remaining distance to the cemetery.

It was a night of singular dreariness and gloom, the sky heavily laden with low-hanging clouds—the moon utterly obscured. As we traipsed through the silence of the countryside, my soul was filled with a sense of keen anticipatory dread—not merely for the repugnant task which loomed before me, but for the fate which awaited me once it was completed.

At length, we arrived at the little graveyard. It lay far from any human habitation at the end of a narrow lane that led through a woodlet of elm trees. The stir of the wind in the foliage—the distant bark of a farmer's dog—the occasional, mournful hoot of an owl—were the only sounds to disturb the utter silence of the surroundings.

Entering through the creaking gate in the waist-high iron fence that encompassed the cemetery, we quickly discovered the small wooden shed in which the caretaker stored his implements. Removing a lantern and a spade, Vox ignited the first with a phosphorous match and passed it to me. He then picked up the digging tool in one hand and—motioning with the pistol which he held in the other—led me in search of Wyatt's grave.

We located it in short order. Apart from the headstone that identified its inhabitant, the grave was easily recognizable by the mound of raw, freshly turned earth which covered the hole and which contrasted so starkly with the grassy appearance of its neighbors.

Thrusting the spade blade-first into the dirt, Vox took the lantern from my hand, rested it at the base of the tombstone, and said: "Time to get to work, Mr. Poe. May I take your jacket?"

"And what if I refuse to submit to your wishes?" I boldly declared.

"Then—with the greatest reluctance—I shall be obliged to splatter that splendid brain of yours all over this hallowed ground," he replied, raising the pistol so that its muzzle was pointed directly at my brain.

"But it is plain that you intend to do away with me whether I comply or not," I exclaimed. "By your own admission, you have brutally disposed of everyone with knowledge of the exceedingly inflammatory content of the missing diary page. Why should I not spare myself the acute physical strain and extreme mental anguish of the abhorrent task that you have brought me here to perform?"

"Why, Mr. Poe," Vox replied in a wounded tone, "you've completely misjudged my intent. Do you honestly believe that I would rob the world of its greatest living poet? Deprive future generations of the masterpieces that are certain to flow from your rhapsodic pen in the coming years? Heavens, no! Besides, I trust you implicitly in this matter. I know that your sympathies cannot possibly lie with Wyatt and his ilk. After all, you are not merely a Southerner but a Virginian. Surely you would do nothing to besmirch the memory of the great Jefferson—or to promote the desperately misguided cause of Negro emancipation."

For a moment I made no reply, while my mind raced furiously. His assurance that he intended to spare my life was not wholly implausible. Though his murderous acts bore ample proof of his extreme *moral* insanity, his appreciation of my literary genius appeared genuine. It was also true—as he had intimated— that I had never allied myself with any mere social or political crusade, my passions and energies being consecrated to a far higher calling—i.e., the pursuit and cultivation of Ideal Beauty.

In the end, I chose not to resist. At the very least, my execution would be postponed for an hour or more—the period of time, according to my estimate, necessary for the accomplishment of my task. A chance to extricate myself from my dire predicament—either by contriving an escape or by finding a way to overpower and disarm the ventriloquist—might well present itself during that span.

Stripping off my coat, I handed it to Vox, who carefully draped it atop the headstone. I then grabbed the spade by the handle and set to work.

Had the dirt been more tightly packed, my job would have been infinitely more difficult. Owing to the freshness of the grave, however—which had been dug less than a week earlier—the soil gave way easily beneath the blade of my implement.

Even so, I was soon perspiring freely. Before long, every muscle in my arms, shoulders, and back was on fire, every movement accompanied by a searing— an *agonizing*—pain.

The physical discomfort I suffered, however, was trifling in comparison to my emotional distress. The sour aroma of the overturned earth—the glimpses of the fat, slithering bodies of the Conqueror Worm—the thought of the hideous object that would soon be exposed to my view—filled me with a sense of the deepest revulsion.

By slow degrees, however, a merciful numbness stole over my spirit. I lapsed into a species of emotional lethargy. I grew oblivious even of the extreme muscular torment in my arms and upper body. My digging became a purely mechanical operation, not unlike the motions of the uncannily lifelike *automata* in Barnum's Hall of Engineering Marvels.

How long I persisted in this stuporous condition I cannot say. I know only that I was eventually roused from it by the sudden, startling scrape of my spade against wood, followed immediately by a sharp exclamation from Vox, who—looming several feet above me—cried out: "That's it! You've hit it!"

Gazing down dully, I saw that I was standing atop the dirt-covered lid of a simple pine coffin.

"Break it open," cried Vox. "Hurry!"

Having no wish to view a greater portion of the corpse than was absolutely necessary, I positioned myself at the head of the coffin—wedged the blade of my implement between two of the slats at the opposite end—and pried open a space at the foot of the box.

Immediately, an unspeakable stench wafted up from the interior. My brain spun—my gorge rose—my knees began to buckle. Tilting my head upward, I gulped in several large mouthfuls of the chill night air. Then—holding my breath—I bent to one knee and, with violently trembling hands, reached inside the coffin and lifted out the lower right leg of the cadaver, every fibre of my being rebelling at the mere touch of the dead thing. For several harrowing moments, I fumbled with the heel of the boot, attempting to twist it open—but to no avail.

"Just pull off the whole damn boot and toss it up here!" cried Vox, who was kneeling above me at the edge of the pit.

I did as he commanded. Then—letting the stiff, unshod, inexpressibly *foetid* extremity drop back into the coffin—I staggered to my feet and stumbled backward as far as the exceedingly cramped, narrow space would permit. Frantically extracting my handkerchief from my trousers pocket, I clamped it over my nose and mouth, fighting against the dizziness—nausea—and sheer delirious horror that threatened to overwhelm me.

"It's here!" Vox joyously shouted.

Gazing up, I saw that he had put down his gun and—having managed to undo the heel of the boot—was in the process of unfolding a small piece of paper he had just extracted from its hiding place. A gleeful expression suffused his countenance as he quickly cast his eyes over the sheet—the dull orange glow of the lamp endowing his features with the lurid appearance of a Hallowe'en jack-o'-lantern.

It might be supposed that the chance to effect my own deliverance had finally arrived. The heavy spade was still in my hands, while my captor had put aside his pistol and was concentrating his full attention upon his prize. Unfortunately, I was unable to take advantage of this opportunity. I was trapped in a hole nearly six feet beneath the level of the ground. I could not possibly hope to sneak out of the pit without attracting Vox's notice. I gave fleeting thought to employing the spade as a spear by hurling it at the ventriloquist's head and rendering him unconscious. But my arms were so weary that I could barely manage to move them (indeed, even the simple act of throwing the boot upward to Vox had cost me a nearly superhuman effort).

I was thus reduced to a state of utter impotence. My only hope was that the ventriloquist would prove as good as his word and—having finally gotten his hands on the treasure he had sought for so long—would allow me to go free.

Having completed his perusal of the page, Vox now took up his pistol once again and rose to his feet.

"Well, Mr. Poe," he declared in a hearty tone, "congratulations are in order all around. I've gotten what I came for—while you, once again, have demonstrated your incomparable brilliance. Not to mention," he added with a chuckle, "your unexpected skills as a grave-digger."

"I am grateful, of course, for your flattering appraisal," I said somewhat wryly. "The latter half of your compliment is, however, somewhat exaggerated, as I was merely reopening a grave, not digging one."

Slowly raising the pistol, Vox said: "Oh, but you were."

The appalling import of these words caused the blood to congeal in my veins.

"But you said that you intended to free me once I had done as you requested," I exclaimed.

"Did I?" said Vox. "So many things come out of my mouth—and in so many different voices. Even I don't always know when I'm telling the truth. Sorry, Mr. Poe. But you can take comfort from one thing, at least. Even while your carcass lies rotting in the ground, your poetry will certainly live on forever. And now, my dear Poe, '*Out—out are the lights!—out all!*' "

As the maddened ventriloquist declaimed this line from the thrilling threnody in my own vividly original tale "Ligeia," a sense of despair flooded through my bosom and drove the blood in torrents upon my heart. I squeezed my eyes tight, anticipating the deafening blast that would prove to be the last mortal sound I ever heard.

It never came.

At that very moment, something *twanged* in the night. An instant later, Vox emitted a sudden, startled grunt, followed by a peculiar *gurgle*. Unclosing my eyes, I was confronted with a sight so bewildering that, at first, I endeavored in vain to understand what I was seeing.

The ventriloquist was standing unsteadily on his feet, eyes wide with a mixture of shock and incomprehension. A pointed shaft, slick with blood, protruded from the center of his throat. As I watched, his grip loosened on his pistol—the weapon dropped from his hand—his legs gave way—and he collapsed onto the ground.

The combined shocks and strains of the evening—both physical and mental—finally overcame me. I felt the strength drain from my body. A swirling black cloud enveloped my vision. With a tremulous moan, I tottered and pitched forward.

All at once, outstretched hands reached down and caught me by the arms. I felt myself hauled from the hole and placed gently on the ground. Lying on my back in the damp grass, I looked up and found myself staring into the worried faces of Kit Carson and Chief Wolf Bear!

As I struggled to sit erect, the scout knelt beside me and placed a comforting hand on my shoulder. "You just rest easy for a spell, Eddie," he said.

"But how on earth," I hoarsely inquired, "did you find me here?"

"We got the chief to thank for that," said Carson, jerking a thumb toward the Indian, who was grasping the feather-adorned bow from which the lethal arrow had been launched. "He caught sight of you being led from the museum by this Vox fellow. There was something mighty fishy about it. The chief never did cotton to Vox. Said the man was always bad-mouthing Indians and Negroes and such. So the chief come and fetched me, and we followed your trail up here."

"I would scarcely believe that such a feat was possible," I said, "had I not previously witnessed your extraordinary skills as a tracker."

"Oh, they're fair to middling, I reckon. Nothing like the chief's, though. Why, he could track a ghost over the coals of hell. Of course, it wasn't so hard as all that. Not with that chigger-ointment smeared all over your ankles. Why, a dead man could sniff it a mile away."

Rising unsteadily to my feet with Carson's assistance, I extended my right hand to the chief, who—after studying it somewhat quizzically for a moment—reached out and clasped it in his own.

"Please accept my heartiest gratitude, Chief Wolf Bear," I said. "I owe you a debt which will be difficult, if not impossible, ever to fully repay."

Though ignorant of my language—as I was of his—the chief could hardly fail to grasp the import of my statement from the fervency of my tone, and acknowledged my pronouncement with a grunt of satisfaction.

"But what the devil's been going on, Eddie? Why did Vox haul you all the way up here?"

"I shall be happy to relate the entire story in due time," I replied. "Suffice it to say for the present that it was Vox who was responsible for the murders of both William Wyatt and C. A. Cartwright, as well as two other equally atrocious slayings, including that of poor Harry Pratt."

"Well, I'll be damned," said Carson.

At that instant, the faint scent of smoke rose to my nostrils. Carson and

Chief Wolf Bear became aware of it at the same instant. As a man, the three of us swiftly cast our eyes down toward the source of the odor.

It was emanating from the lantern. Vox lay beside it, his right arm outstretched, his hand poised over the open top of the glass chimney. It was apparent that the chief's arrow had not immediately killed him. With his final bit of strength, he had managed to crawl toward the light and shove the diary page inside.

Quickly, I bent to the lantern to see if the paper was in fact consumed; there was nothing left of it.

Reaching out my hand, I placed it atop the ventriloquist's chest. There was no sign of a heartbeat. He lay as lifeless as his wooden dummy, his blood-smeared mouth twisted into a smile of sheer—infernal—triumph.

Chapter Twenty-Nine

N THE DAY FOLLOWING the events just described, I found myself offering alternate versions of the truth to different audiences. To those closest to me—not only Muddy and Sissy, but Carson as well—I withheld no detail of the story, describing the precise nature of Vox's monomaniacal quest and the full content of the paper that had been the cause of so much suffering and death.

I also shared this information with Barnum, who was much aggrieved to learn of the destruction of the rare historical letter stolen from his collection. As for the exceedingly controversial page from Jefferson's diary, the news of its incineration left him positively stricken.

"Reduced to ashes!" he exclaimed when I told him of Vox's final, spiteful act. "Bless my soul, but it's the most shattering loss I've ever heard of! Catastrophic—absolutely catastrophic! Why, the destruction of the Great Library at Alexandria was paltry by comparison! Have you any idea—can you begin to *conceive*—of the fortune I could have made from that page? Why, I would have been obliged to open a second ticket booth just to accommodate all the customers! I tell you, m'boy, it grieves me—absolutely breaks my heart—to think of something that valuable gone to waste."

While my loved ones and friends were made privy to the full truth of the matter, the situation was very different as regards the world at large. In my interviews with the police and members of the city press following the conclusion of the affair, I adopted a pose of ignorance, pretending that I knew nothing specific about the document so rabidly sought by Vox, beyond the fact that it possessed immeasurable pecuniary value. I made no mention of the startling light it shed on Jefferson's long-rumored *amour* with Sally Hemings. With no tangible evidence to verify the truth as I knew it to be, any assertion I made on the subject would have had no other effect than to embroil me in controversy. My testimony would be embraced by some and savagely denounced by others.

Having no wish to be drawn into this violent and now irresolvable conflict, I chose to prevaricate. The question of the relationship between the Founding Father and his beauteous slave would thus remain a matter of heated dispute for all time to come.

Notwithstanding his chagrin over the destruction of the irreplaceable Jefferson papers, the showman's mood remained exceedingly buoyant, owing to the imminent reopening of his museum—an event trumpeted with typically *Barnumesque* fanfare in daily front-page newspaper advertisements—colorful fliers distributed by an army of juvenile hirelings—and gaudy placards posted everywhere throughout the metropolis. Even the death of Monsieur Vox— one of Barnum's leading attractions, whose thrice-daily performances generated considerable revenue for the museum—did nothing to dampen his spirits.

Indeed, with his peculiarly American gift for shameless exploitation, he quickly found a way to capitalize on the tragedy, announcing that, in addition to the other unparalleled wonders—astounding novelties—and amazing curiosities to be viewed at his newly refurbished showplace, visitors would now be able to see, at no additional cost, a thrilling exhibition devoted to the heinous crimes of the "Malevolent Monsieur Vox, the Greatest Monster of the Age!" In addition to the box of diabolically doctored snuff, by means of which he had contrived the death of the martyred Mazeppa, the display would feature his famously droll and quick-witted dummy, Archibald, as well as his full cast of Shakespearean villains, including Richard III, Macbeth, and Iago, whose bloodthirsty deeds (so the showman averred) paled beside those of the fiendish ventriloquist himself.

On the day prior to the big event an envelope arrived at our abode, hand-delivered by Barnum's celebrated living skeleton, Slim Jim McCormack—an exceedingly affable gentleman who, at a height of nearly five feet ten inches, weighed a mere sixty-three pounds fully clothed. From his somewhat breathless condition—as well as from the crowd of people (most, though by no means all, of them children) following in his wake—I deduced that he had traveled from the museum on foot: a mode of locomotion no doubt insisted on by his employer, who regularly sent one or another of his human oddities out into the world as a means of drumming up publicity for his museum.

After refreshing himself, at Muddy's insistence, with a glass of lemonade, Slim Jim took his leave. It was only then that I slit open the envelope. It was addressed to our entire household—myself, Muddy, and Sissy, as well as Kit and Master Jeremiah. Inside was an embossed invitation, requesting the pleasure of our company at the "Grand Ceremonial Reopening of Barnum's American Museum, the Greatest Amusement Establishment on the Face of the Globe!" Turning over the card, I discovered a handwritten note inscribed in the showman's somewhat florid script.

"Dear Friends," it read. "Consider yourselves my guests of honor! A coach will arrive for you at five! Special box reserved at the theater for your private use—best seats in the house! Prepare yourselves for an evening of unprecedented entertainment—the most glorious dramatic spectacle ever conceived by man! Your humble servant, P. T. Barnum."

As I read aloud this message, Sissy clapped her hands excitedly, while Muddy beamed with pleasure. Carson's reaction was considerably more subdued. His departure had been planned for the following morning, and he was loath to delay the start of his journey back home.

Sissy's heartfelt appeals, however—as well as the entreating looks cast by Jeremiah—could hardly be resisted. In the end, the scout consented to postpone his leave-taking for an additional twenty-four hours.

"Reckon it won't do no harm to stick around for another day," he said, blushing visibly when Sissy rewarded him for his decision by delightedly throwing her arms about his neck and placing a kiss on his cheek.

Owing, perhaps, to the intensity of her excitement, Sissy awoke the following day with a sick headache that threatened to keep her from attending the gala event. Muddy remained at her side throughout the morning, applying warm compresses to her forehead and spoon-feeding her frequent sips of hot green tea. Thanks to these ministrations, my dear wife made a rapid recovery and was able to rise from her bed by midday, cheerfully intent on proceeding with our plans, though looking somewhat wan.

While the rest of us made our preparations for the evening, Carson—who had dispensed with the clothing I had loaned him and was now attired in his original buckskin garb—announced that he had something important to do. As he and Jeremiah would be embarking on their journey early the next day, it was time for him to retrieve his confiscated Colt revolver from Captain Dunnegan. Unsure as to how much time would be required for this errand, he arranged to meet us at the museum in time for the commencement of the show. He then donned his broad-brimmed Western hat and set off for police headquarters.

By four-thirty, my loved ones were ready, Sissy having arrayed herself in her nicest blue-calico dress, while Muddy had selected a simple black frock, set off with a white widow's cap. As we sat in the parlor, awaiting the arrival of our conveyance, a touching scene took place. Sissy was perched on the sofa beside Jeremiah, relating the tale of "The Stolen Child," one of her favorite stories from Thomas Crofton Tyler's well-known collection of faerie legends. All at once, as he looked up at her raptly, Jeremiah reached behind his neck, undid the leather thong that held his mother's amulet, and extended it toward Sissy.

For a moment, she merely stared down at the object, as though perplexed by the meaning of the gesture.

"Oh, no, Jeremiah," she exclaimed at length. "I couldn't."

Nodding vigorously, the boy thrust the necklace into her hand, then proceeded to make a rapid series of gestures that caused moisture to well in Sissy's eyes.

"What does he say?" inquired Muddy, who—like me—had been observing the scene.

"He wants me to have it," my dear wife responded with a catch in her voice. "He says that it holds his mother's spirit, and that she will watch over me and see that no harm befalls me."

At these words, Muddy's lips began to tremble and a tear rolled down one ruddy cheek.

Though Sissy continued to protest, the boy was so insistent that she was finally forced to relent. Tying the thong about her slender neck, she peered down at the polished bone disk for a moment before turning to Jeremiah and, in a voice fraught with emotion, expressing her warmest gratitude.

At several minutes before the designated time, we descended to the street.

Promptly at five, a coach pulled up at the curb. As I had been expecting, the driver was another of Barnum's human prodigies, a young man I knew well from my earlier visits to the museum. This was Gunther the Alligator Boy, an unusually shy and sweet-tempered youth who suffered from a remarkable dermatological condition that endowed him with the scaly appearance of a member of the order *Crocodillia.*

Descending from his perch, Gunther opened the door for us as politely as a royal footman. He then climbed back onto his seat and urged the horses into motion. Less than twenty minutes later, we arrived at our destination.

Even before we dismounted from the vehicle, I saw that Barnum's efforts to excite public interest in the occasion had produced the desired effect. An enormous crowd of people, possessed of a noisy and inordinate vivacity, packed the sidewalk and spilled into the street. Indeed, I had not witnessed such a tumultuous scene since the evening of the riot that had caused the closing of the museum in the first place.

In contrast to that earlier, intensely ugly occasion, the mood this time was exceedingly jolly. Everyone present—from the bright-eyed urchin clutching his father's hand—to the dapper young swell proudly squiring his fair-haired sweetheart on his arm—to the elderly, long-married couple fitted out in formal evening attire—wore a look of delighted anticipation. Adding to the festive atmosphere was a small band of entertainers—a juggler, a clown, a sword-swallower, two acrobats, and a midget on stilts—who had been sent outside to provide some diversion while the crowd awaited admission. Laughter and applause greeted the antics of this singularly amusing *troupe.* Amidst these happy sounds, the only discordant notes were those produced by Barnum's egregious brass-band who—seated upon the wrought-iron balcony that overlooked Broadway—were sending forth a characteristically tin-eared rendition of the popular ditty "Fair Maggie o' Dumblane."

Pushing our way through the crowd, we entered the building and found Barnum stationed in the lobby, accepting the tributes of various well-wishers. At his first glimpse of us, he threw open his arms in an expansive gesture of welcome and cried: "Why, Poe—you didn't tell me that you were going to be escorting two of my most celebrated performers to this event! Wait! Can it be? Mrs. Poe? Mrs. Clemm? Is it really you? Heavens—I mistook you for the Amazing Meleke Sisters, my twin Circassian Beauties! And who is this strapping young lad? Jeremiah? No! Bless my soul, but you must have grown six inches since I last set eyes on you! But where is your father?"

Briefly, I explained the nature of Carson's errand, assuring Barnum that the scout had promised to be back in ample time for the commencement of the show.

"It's so nice to see your museum open again, Mr. Barnum," observed my darling wife. "Everything looks wonderful."

"Yes," concurred Muddy, gazing around the grand foyer. "I'd forgotten how splendid it is."

"Why, thank you, dear ladies, thank you, indeed," Barnum said, beaming with pleasure. "Yes, it's been completely renovated, top to bottom. Spared no expense. Brought in the world's greatest architect—Sir Rupert Smythe-Jarvis. Surely you've heard of him? Why, the man's a genius, an absolute genius. Crowned heads of Europe are always after him to do this or that—remodel their castles, spiff up their ancestral estates, that sort of thing. Spent a fortune to bring him over here. Bundles of money—whole trunkloads of it! Worth every penny, though. 'If you're going to do something, do it right'—that's P. T. Barnum's motto!"

In truth—apart from repairing the damage wrought by the rampaging mob—Barnum, so far as I could see, had made no alterations at all to his establishment, which appeared precisely the same as it always had. Moreover—in spite of my extensive knowledge of the leading architectural figures of the day—I had never heard the name Sir Rupert Smythe-Jarvis, who, I suspected, was a complete fabrication of the incorrigibly mythomaniacal showman.

Extracting his watch from the pocket of his checkered silk vest, Barnum consulted the time and exclaimed: "Good heavens! Curtain goes up in less than ten minutes! Best head upstairs and take your seats. I'll see you dear people after the show."

Ascending to the top floor, we were greeted by none other than Oswald the custodian, who had evidently been enlisted to serve as an usher. He was garbed in a tight-fitting royal-blue frock coat adorned with gold epaulets—a matching sash that engirdled his considerable paunch—cream-colored pantaloons—and highly polished boots that extended to his knees. Seeming very ill at ease in this elaborate (and, in truth, rather ludicrous-looking) uniform, he led us wordlessly to our box, then took his leave with a stiff little bow.

The gaslights had just begun to dim in the auditorium when Carson made his appearance in our box. Glancing over at him as he removed his hat and seated himself beside Jeremiah, I perceived that he had successfully accomplished his errand. Strapped about his slender waist was his hand-tooled gun belt, from the holster of which there protruded the walnut grip of his deadly Colt revolver.

Having previously attended one of Barnum's theatrical presentations, I knew very well what to expect: a two-hour extravaganza which—in lieu of the intensely elevating effects that may be achieved by the dramatic arts—offered nothing beyond garish spectacle, coarse amusement, and cheap sensationalism. My expectations in this regard were fully matched by the surpassingly vulgar production that ensued. The first half of the show offered a seemingly endless parade of frivolous and often bizarre novelty acts, from Herr Jacob Driesbach, "The Man with the Iron Jaw" (whose *specialité* consisted of lifting a forty-gallon, water-filled barrel with his teeth)—to the somewhat scandalously clad aerialist, Mademoiselle Victoria, "Queen of the Lofty Wire"—to a trained palomino named Newton the Wonder Horse, who could perform simple computations by tapping out sums with his left hoof. Confirming the showman's intuitive grasp of his countrymen's childish tastes, the audience responded to these excessively puerile entertainments with the greatest imaginable enthusiasm.

The grand climactic event, however, was yet to come. Following a brief intermission, the curtain rose upon a scene that elicited gasps of awe and admiration from the entire assemblage, not excluding my own dear wife and aunt. Even I was forced to concede that, in mounting this portion of the production, the showman had clearly gone to considerable trouble and expense.

By means of an elaborately rendered backdrop—supplemented by several painted "flats" and other props—the stage had been transformed into a very creditable replica of the corner of Broadway and Ann Street at night. The ensuing drama depicted the riotous actions of the mob, represented by several dozen of Barnum's performers, who were costumed in the shabby garb of Bowery ruffians, and armed with a variety of makeshift weapons. Their leader was portrayed by the "Arabian Giant," Colonel Routh Goshen, who—displaying a surprising histrionic flair—delivered a lengthy monologue, urging his cohorts to wreak utter destruction upon Barnum's establishment, which was described as a towering monument to art, culture, and civilization itself (and thus a hated symbol of all that was most offensive to the debased sensibilities of the city's lower classes).

The scene then shifted to the grand foyer of the museum. This change was ingeniously accomplished by rotating the entire set, which had been constructed upon an enormous revolving platform. Intent on lynching Chief

Wolf Bear, Goshen and his anarchic crew burst into the building, where they were confronted by none other than Barnum himself. Adopting the pose of a classical orator—one hand inserted into the front of his jacket, the other elevated high in the air—the showman proceeded to deliver a stirring paean to the great democratic principles upon which our nation rested.

This speech, however—which was interrupted by frequent and prolonged ovations from the audience—only seemed to incite the brutes to a greater pitch of fury. Pushing the showman aside, they made for the staircase, the lower portion of which had been reproduced onstage. An instant later, Chief Wolf Bear (who had somehow been persuaded—or, as seemed more likely, *coerced*—into portraying himself) was led down the steps by Goshen and several of his cohorts. A noose was produced by one member of the mob. All seemed hopeless.

Of a sudden, the main door flew open and in strode a minuscule figure, barely more than two feet in height, decked out in a Western outfit precisely resembling that of Carson, down to the fringes dangling from the sleeves of his tiny deerskin shirt. This was General Tom Thumb, the prodigiously talented dwarf whose comical impersonations of historical figures from Frederick the Great to the Emperor Napoleon had made him the most popular of all Barnum's performers, winning the admiration of Queen Victoria herself, with whom the showman had managed to wangle an audience during his recent European tour.

The entrance of the dwarf was greeted with a sustained and deafening ovation, much of the audience rising to its feet and cheering wildly at the mere sight of the little fellow. Walking to the front of the stage, he removed his black Western hat—made a sweeping bow—then signaled to the orchestra, which immediately struck up a jaunty tune. Then—in a high, piping, though by no means unmelodious voice—he launched into a ditty, the first verse of which went as follows:

> *"My name is Kit Carson,*
> *The Man of the West.*
> *At tracking and scouting,*
> *Why, I am the best!*
> *I may be no giant*
> *Who blocks out the sun,*
> *But I'm tall in the saddle*
> *And quick with a gun.*

I'm fierce in a battle.
My nerves never rattle.
When my enemies see me,
They turn tail and run!
Now I've come to New York
On a dangerous quest.
My name is Kit Carson,
The Man of the West!"

This performance elicited another burst of thunderous applause from the audience. Even Carson—who might well have objected to seeing himself portrayed by a twenty-five-inch dwarf—seemed vastly amused by the little fellow's song.

Turning back to confront Chief Wolf Bear's captors, the diminutive hero demanded the immediate release of the Indian. When Goshen refused with a disdainful laugh, the dwarf leapt into action. First, he danced a Highland fling that left the mob gaping in wonder. Then he executed a series of somersaults and handstands, bedazzling his enemies with his skillful acrobatics. Before they could recover from their stupefaction, the little man whipped out a miniature pistol and fired off a succession of shots that caused their weapons to fly from their hands. Finally—though small enough to stand upright on the outstretched palm of the giant—he made a headlong dash at Goshen himself and wrestled the latter into submission.

For the climax of the show, the entire cast assembled onstage and joined voices in a rousing rendition of "Columbia, God Preserve Thee Free!"—all except for Chief Wolf Bear, who stood somewhat apart from the crowd, arms folded over his chest, his visage arranged into its usual, utterly impassive expression.

The stamping and clapping—the whistles and cheers—the shouts of "Hurrah!" and "Bravo!"—that followed this performance were nothing less than deafening. Stepping forward, Barnum gestured for silence. By slow degrees, the clamor subsided. It resumed at an even greater volume, however, when—pointing to our box—the showman introduced "the Nestor of the Prairies—the Galahad of the Rockies—the greatest, most courageous specimen of American manhood ever to spring from the vast, untamed territories of the Wild West—the one—the only—Christopher 'Kit' Carson!"

Looking deeply abashed, the scout was finally prevailed upon to rise to his feet and acknowledge the vociferous acclamation of the crowd before hastily resuming his seat.

Once the audience—still abuzz with excitement—had filed from the auditorium, we sought out the showman to congratulate him on the success of the evening.

"Yes, it was a triumph, all right," declared Barnum. "Grandest evening of entertainment since the time of Scheherazade! And the general! Great Scot—did you ever witness a more splendid performance in your life? Well, that's only to be expected, of course. The little fellow's a perfect wonder—nineteen pounds of sheer unmitigated talent! I trust that his magnificent impersonation of your own esteemed self met with your approval, Kit?"

"Yes, it was a right enjoyable show, take it all around," replied the scout. "Of course, I don't exactly recollect dancing a jig in front of them rascals when I first came to town."

"Well, you can't expect absolute, one hundred percent historical accuracy in a production like this," Barnum breezily replied. "It's the *essence* that counts. That's where the general excels. Goes right to the heart and soul of things. Bless my life, but you should see him do Washington at Valley Forge, rallying his men with a stirring rendition of 'My Country 'Tis of Thee.' Why, you'd think you were right there with the Continental Army, listening to old George himself singing his heart out! Sure you won't change your mind and remain with us a bit longer, Kit m'boy?" added the showman, who had been apprised of the scout's planned departure. "You could come to work for me. Do one or two performances a day, twirl your gun a bit, regale the audience with a few colorful anecdotes about your Indian-fighting days. Maybe put on a mock battle with Chief Wolf Bear. Why, you'd be my biggest star in no time."

"Much obliged," said Carson, "but it's time for me and the boy to be moving along."

"Sorry to hear it," Barnum said with a sigh. "Well, if you ever decide to give up the strenuous outdoors life—hunting buffalo, chasing outlaws, blazing trails to California, that sort of thing—there'll always be a place for you here. And as for you, Master Jeremiah," the showman continued, extracting a small square of paper from the inside pocket of his coat and handing it to the boy, "here's something to remember me by."

I recognized this item as one of the coupons Barnum habitually passed out to potential customers, offering a free bag of peanuts with every fully paid weekday admission to his establishment. Being unable either to read or to write, Carson's son did not understand its intended purpose. The small engraved image of the museum that appeared at the top of the coupon seemed to please him greatly, however. Folding the little paper in quarters, he carefully inserted it into the deerskin pouch that hung from his belt and that served as a sort of wallet.

Shortly thereafter, we bade good-night to Barnum and made our way outside to the curb, where a coach was waiting to drive us home. Twenty minutes later, it discharged us in front of our abode. Bidding good-night to Gunther, we turned and walked toward the dark and vacant dwelling.

It was an evening of singular clarity and brilliance. In the refulgent glow of the moon, the walkway leading up to the house seemed paved in silver. Sissy, holding the hand of her juvenile companion, was at the head of our little procession. Next came Muddy; while Carson and I brought up the rear.

My emotions at that moment were of the most melancholy sort. Though my acquaintance with the scout had been of relatively brief duration, the sheer intensity of our adventures had forged a powerful bond of manly camaraderie between us. I felt that with his departure early the following day, I would be bidding farewell to one of the finest individuals I had ever known. My heart was also heavily laden on behalf of my darling wife, who, I felt sure, must be suffering acutely at the prospect of separating from the young boy to whom she had formed an attachment that was nothing less than maternal.

Gazing ahead, I saw that Sissy had arrived at the wooden stoop that led up to the front door. Letting go of Jeremiah's hand, she began to mount the steps.

A dark form rose up from behind the bushes at the side of the house.

It raised a hand. I saw a knife.

"Look out!" cried a voice I did not recognize.

The warning came too late. The blade came slashing down at Sissy's throat.

As she fell to the ground, another shriek rent the air, this one issuing from Muddy.

I, too, attempted to scream, but my powers of vocalization had been rendered useless by shock. I stood rooted in place, paralyzed by horror.

At my side, there was a sudden movement, then a succession of deafening blasts, each accompanied by a bright orange flash—*blam! blam! blam! blam! blam!*—so rapid as to blend into a single explosion.

With an agonized roar, the great hulking shadow let go of its weapon—clutched at its face—and collapsed backward onto the lawn.

The fall of the monster broke the spell that had enchained me. With a cry of dismay, I threw myself forward and dropped to Sissy's side, where Muddy and Jeremiah were already kneeling.

"Sissy!" I cried, gently raising her head onto my lap.

To my inexpressible joy, her eyes fluttered open.

"Wh-what happened?" she asked.

"It was Johnson," I exclaimed. Though I could not conceive, at that moment, how the brute had gotten free, I had no doubt that it was he; for—even in my thunderstricken state—I had recognized, by the light of the moon, both his gigantic stature and the general cast of his features.

"He attempted to kill you," I continued. "I cannot say why he did not succeed."

"It was this," said Sissy, fingering something at her throat.

Gazing down, I saw that she was touching the amulet that had been given to her by Jeremiah. Johnson's blade had struck the center of the polished bone disk, which now bore a deep gouge.

"It saved my life," said Sissy.

"It was supposed to." To the astonishment of Muddy, Sissy, and myself, these words were spoken by Carson's son.

"Jeremiah!" cried Sissy. "You—you can speak!"

"Yes," he said. "My voice returned to try to warn you."

As Sissy hugged the lad, Muddy asked: "Can you stand, Sissy dear?"

"Oh yes," my dear wife replied. "I'm fine."

Rising, I helped her to her feet. In spite of her reassuring statement, she appeared somewhat unsteady—a circumstance only to be expected, in view of the terrific shock she had suffered, as well as her fragile physical condition.

"Please take her inside," I said to Muddy. "I will join you momentarily."

As my loved ones disappeared into the house, I went in search of the scout.

By then, the street was filling up with people, as the neighbors, roused by the noise of Carson's gunfire, began to pour out of their houses. All at once, we heard the pounding of approaching horses. An instant later, a troop of police officers materialized at our side.

The story was soon told. Johnson—who had been complaining of an agonizing pain in his stomach—had made his escape while being escorted to the infirmary by Captain Dunnegan, who—whether out of carelessness or bravado, it is impossible to say—had undertaken to transfer the prisoner with no assistance. He had paid for his rash act with a broken neck.

"Looks like the chief was right," muttered Carson.

For a moment, I was deeply puzzled by this statement. All at once, I recalled the sign I had seen Chief Wolf Bear make in Barnum's office on the evening of the riot—a gesture which seemed to predict that Dunnegan was certain to meet his doom at the hands of "Red Death" (as the Crow had denominated Johnson).

"Come on, Eddie," said Carson. "Let's head inside."

"Is—is he really dead?" I inquired of the scout, indicating the body that lay sprawled in the grass.

"He'll never be any deader," said the scout.

Before passing into the house, I cast my gaze downward for one final look at the monster. The impact of Carson's bullets, however, had rendered his features unrecognizable, concealing his visage beneath a coating of gore that glistened darkly in the moonlight like a loathesome black veil.

EPILOGUE

WE FOUND MUDDY, Sissy, and Jeremiah in the parlor. In spite of her exhaustion and the urgings of her mother, my wife had refused to go to bed, knowing that this was to be her last opportunity to spend time with the boy of whom she had grown so fond. As if to exercise his newly recovered powers of speech—and to repay Sissy for the many hours she had spent reading to him from her favorite storybooks—Jeremiah, seated beside her, regaled her with legends and tales that had been passed down to him by his departed mother.

One of these fables has remained alive in my memory ever since. I was the more forcibly impressed with it as it revealed a poignant awareness of human mortality unusual in a child so young. The narrative, which was entitled "Spider, Hare, and Moon," ran very nearly, if not entirely accurately, thus:

"Moon was sad. She had spent many years looking down upon the Earth, and she saw that its people were afraid. They were afraid of dying. So she called on her friend, Spider, to carry a message to them.

" 'Spider,' she said. 'The people of Earth are afraid of dying, and that makes me very sad. Please tell them that, though everyone must die sooner or later, it is nothing to be scared of.'

"So Spider slowly made his way down to Earth, carefully picking his way on moonbeams. He had only traveled a short distance, however, when he chanced to meet Hare.

" 'Where are you going, Spider?' asked Hare.

" 'I am going to give the people of Earth a message from Moon,' said Spider.

" 'Oh, but you move so slowly,' said Hare. 'It will take you forever to get there. Why don't you tell me the message, and I will deliver it for you?'

" 'Very well,' said Spider. 'Moon wants the people of Earth to know that they are bound to die sooner or later—'

" 'Right!' cried the ever-impatient Hare, cutting off Spider. 'Tell the people of Earth that they will all die.' And before Spider could say another word, Hare turned and disappeared off to Earth.

"Spider gloomily made his way back to Moon and told her what had happened. Moon was very cross, and when Hare returned to say that he had delivered the message, she hit him on the nose. And that is why, to this day, Hare has a split lip.

" 'You had better do as I say and take the message yourself,' Moon said sternly to Spider.

"And to this day, Spider is still carrying Moon's message. It is written in the web he spins in the corners of our rooms, for those who are able to read it."

When Jeremiah had finished this story, Sissy squeezed his hand. "Thank you," she said softly. "I'm ready to sleep now."

Bidding one another good-night, we retired to our respective places of repose—Muddy and Sissy to their bedchamber; I to mine; Carson and his son to their bedrolls spread out upon the parlor floor. My intention was to awaken at daybreak, so that I could see my friends off. Owing, perhaps, to the extreme emotional fatigue induced in me by the shocking events of the evening, however, I sank into a profound slumber, from which I did not awaken until the morning was well advanced.

Quickly performing my ablutions and throwing on my clothing, I hurried into the parlor. But there was no sign of our guests, apart from a folded sheet of paper resting on the cushion of the settee. Opening it, I found a characteristically laconic message inscribed in a laborious hand—the last communication I would ever have from Kit Carson:

"Adios" was all it said.

ABOUT THE AUTHOR

HAROLD SCHECHTER is a professor of American literature and culture at Queens College, the City University of New York. Renowned for his true-crime writing, he is the author of the nonfiction books *Fiend, Bestial, Deviant, Deranged, Depraved*, and, with David Everitt, *The A to Z Encyclopedia of Serial Killers*. He previously featured Edgar Allan Poe in his acclaimed novels *The Hum Bug* and *Nevermore*. He lives in New York State.